The Loch Linnhe Murders

Dankworth Mysteries, Volume 1

Victor de Almeida

Published by Seal Street Books, 2024.

This is a work of fiction. Similarities to real people, places, or events are entirely coincidental.

THE LOCH LINNHE MURDERS

First edition. March 13, 2024.

ISBN: 979-8224857869

Written by Victor de Almeida.

To Xeli:

For seeing the burning flame and making sure it remained ignited.

Thank you.

To Rojito:

For being an alpha, beta, and delta reader, listener, and everything in between.

Thank you.

URSULA

July 27th, 1949

Ursula Doyle stood in relentless anticipation of her imminent encounter with a killer. Shrouded in the thick London fog, she felt a shiver travel down her spine as its icy tendrils coiled around her like malevolent fingers. On nights like tonight, the City of London felt alive, as if eager to divulge the secrets of hundreds and thousands of souls. Living or dead.

A sudden gust of cold air swept through the night like the eerie breath of a dormant monster. Ursula cinched her trench coat tightly around her and turned to the street sign on the wall. It read: *Durward Street.* As the city's mist continued to wrap around her, Ursula wondered whether the winds had been trying to deliver a foreboding message of some sort. Ursula, however, was not easily deterred and ignoring the directive to stay within sight, ventured deeper into the misty street.

At this point in their marriage, Robert had grown accustomed to her spontaneous nature. Ursula had never conformed to the conventional role of a wife and that was precisely how she preferred it. Unlike her school friends, who'd settled into mundane lives, Ursula harboured dreams beyond being a mere trophy wife. She refused to let her aspirations take a backseat to her husband's or be relegated to the role of a human breeder, forever confined to her home. She could only assume that it was precisely this determination to be recognised as an equal that had drawn Robert to her.

Ursula had first met Robert at her friend Leah's engagement party. While she had never given much credence to the notion of love at first sight she could not deny feeling an instant fascination with him, especially when he openly expressed his sympathy for the Communist movement. Ursula's brother, Rodrigo had vanished after joining to fight in the Spanish Civil War. Before then, she had spent numerous nights engrossed in Rodrigo's impassioned discussions about social equality and the importance of saving Spain from the clutches of the Fascist regime. Robert filled that void. His conversations and intellect were greater than any man she had ever met and his behaviour towards her was just as gentlemanly. What began as a thoughtful conversation swiftly evolved into a deep friendship, eventually blossoming into a romantic relationship—all while she simultaneously took on the role of his assistant in his detective agency.

Ursula found a fulfilment and passion in sleuthing that she could never have anticipated and the bonus of having Robert, the love of her life, by her side to guide her only enriched the experience. Together, they embarked on a journey of mystery and intrigue and garnered such a reputation, that it was not long until the Metropolitan Police came calling.

Robert and Ursula had grown accustomed to investigating various murders—crimes of passion or greed, typically. However, their experiences were but a prelude to the grisly case that now confronted them. Ursula, who had only ever read about other infamous cases like that of Jack the Ripper, H.H. Holmes, and the seldom-mentioned Thames Torso Murders, found that everything they had previously unravelled seemed meek compared to this new challenge.

The victims, all women of similar ages and backgrounds, had suffered a gruesome fate—dismembered bodies, meticulously washed limbs, and faces devoid of any trace of makeup. Panic rippled through East London, fuelled by sensationalist newspapers dubbing the murders a 'new ripper,' an eerie echo of a dark history six decades old. Despite the Metropolitan Police's attempts to quell the frenzy, the voracious tabloids, driven by both bloodlust and greed, persisted in perpetuating the chilling narrative

In the stifling heat of a London summer, Ursula found herself seated in the corner of a spacious office adorned with the finest polished mahogany furniture. The considerable windows stood open, a futile attempt to invite a breeze that the oppressive heat had unapologetically stifled. It was within this sweltering atmosphere that Ursula vividly recalled their first encounter with Harold Scott, the Metropolitan Police Commissioner. Harold Scott was a man with short snowy white hair and beady eyes hidden behind large round spectacles. Ursula thought he had the appearance of a rather disagreeable man and unfortunately, his conduct throughout the meeting confirmed her suspicions.

"Those ruddy journalists aren't happy unless they're weeding fear into every household in London," the Metropolitan Police Commissioner had said. "We therefore need to make sure that we aren't seen to be investigating this any more."

"How would you propose we do that?" Robert asked him.

"We tell them that a suspect has been arrested," he replied. "Hopefully, you find him before he commits another murder."

Ursula's eyes shot up from her notebook, a profound sense of disbelief settling in as she processed the magnitude of what she was hearing. The Police commissioner's intention to mislead the public, completely disregarding the potential jeopardy to women's safety, left Ursula intensely disturbed. She had read enough about the Commissioner to grasp that he was not a man worthy of trust. There were numerous accounts of him doing everything in his power to protect his position, with rumours still circulating that he had blackmailed the previous incumbent into resigning. Some even speculated that he was merely biding his time before turning his attention to Whitehall, eyeing a political career. Ursula looked from Robert to the Commissioner with bated breath, hoping to hear a response that would rebuff the suggestion.

"I am not convinced that's the best approach," Robert said politely.

The Police Commissioner didn't reply immediately. Instead, he leaned back in his chair, nodding his head slowly, as if considering Robert's refusal.

"Luckily, I run this town and say otherwise," the Police Commissioner said after a while.

Robert summoned a smile, a well-practised mask that betrayed none of the mild irritation simmering beneath the surface. Ursula, having shared her life with him for long enough, possessed an acute awareness of his shifting moods. These nuances manifested in subtle gestures—a gentle caress of the nose, a fleeting scratch of the head, or the telltale clearing of his throat. On this particular occasion, it was the tautness in his back and the rhythmic scratch of his beard that signalled the unspoken tension coursing through him.

"I hope you didn't write any of that down, girl." Harold Scott said, looking at Ursula.

Ursula felt the heat rising within her, her blood beginning to boil. However, Robert, as adept at deciphering her moods as she was at discerning his, swiftly extinguished any potential for a testy response with a prompt and deft rebuttal.

"Can you give us more information on all the victims up until now?"

The Police Commissioner glanced at his table, where four folders lay, and opened them one by one.

"Mary Lou Pearce, 38, our first victim was found in Durward Street at about 5 am by a member of the public on his way to work, a man named James Kelly. He follows the same route every morning, towards Billingsgate Market."

"All of this information was verified?" Robert asked.

"Yes. His wife vouched for his alibi; Lisa Kelly confirms she went to bed after him, at eleven in the evening and woke up before him four in the morning the next day. According to her, James Kelly didn't get out of bed until half past four," the Commissioner replied. "It takes him about fifteen minutes to walk from his house to Durward Street."

"So, our first victim, Mary Lou Pierce, was discovered on the 4th of June at around 5 a.m., correct?" Ursula asked, jotting down the details.

"That is correct," the Police commissioner affirmed. "The second victim, Kelly McDonald, aged 34, was found on the 18th of June by a young police officer. It was his first night on the beat, poor lad."

"What time was that?" Robert inquired.

Harold Scott flicked through the folder. "As soon as the officer arrived for his patrol, so ten p.m."

"Which means the murder could have happened between—" Robert began.

"Nine and ten in the evening? Seems like a rather short time frame, unless the officer arrived later than ten," Ursula interjected.

"No," the Commissioner replied defensively, "I was assured they were on-site precisely at ten."

"Sunset in June doesn't occur until after nine in the evening," Robert pointed out. "That would give our suspect less than forty minutes to locate the victim, kill, dismember the body, clean it and return it to Durward Street. It's improbable."

"But not impossible," Harold Scott argued stubbornly.

"Stating that something is 'not impossible' doesn't make it possible, Commissioner," Robert replied, his tone unwavering.

"I could contact the Met Office and consult with Julian Endersby. They will have recorded the exact time of sunset in London on that day," Ursula suggested.

"Yes, that's a great idea," Robert agreed.

"Fine, let's assume that it's improbable to complete all those actions in forty minutes—" the Police Commissioner argued.

"Let us not assume anything, Commissioner," Robert asserted firmly. "It isn't enough time."

"For the love of god, they are prostitutes, how long would it take to convince them? A shilling would have one on their knees within a second!" the Police Commissioner spat.

"And you know this from experience, do you?" Ursula blurted before she could stop herself.

"Watch who you're talking to, *girl*!" he bristled.

"I'll need you to watch how you address my wife, Commissioner," Robert retorted. "Now, do I have leave to continue presenting my argument, or would you prefer to seek alternative assistance in this case?"

Commissioner Scott was flustered. Robert typically saved his stern tone for challenging individuals, opting to sway situations through gentle persuasion. Commissioner Harold Scott, however, was not one to be delicately handled. His nature demanded a firm approach; any failure to meet him with resolve would result in him effortlessly circumventing Robert.

"You may proceed," the Commissioner said tensely.

"Forty minutes *isn't* sufficient time. There is something we're missing," Robert said thoughtfully.

The Police Commissioner stood up, moving towards the window in search of a nonexistent breeze. This gave him time to ponder what Robert had been explaining and allowed Ursula to propose an alternative theory.

"Perhaps he is killing them elsewhere and *then* taking their bodies back to Durward Street," Ursula concluded.

"Yes, that's a possibility," Robert said, considering her words. "But why would he go through the effort of going back?"

"All of the victims lived within one or two miles of the location," the Commissioner said. "Not to state the obvious significance of that street. I wouldn't be surprised if our killer knew that would generate more attention. "

Durward Street was, of course, formerly known as Buck's Row, made infamous by Jack the Ripper. That was the location where the body of his first victim had been found.

"But," Ursula started. "If he wants to generate attention, it would also mean he wants to be found?"

"Not necessarily," the Commissioner replied. "Dear Old Jack never wanted to be found. He just wanted to be remembered."

"That's a rather interesting interpretation," Robert said, frowning.

"If you don't mind me saying, Commissioner. Given that you intend to lie to the press about the Metropolitan Police's success in capturing the killer—" Ursula said.

"Lie is a rather strong word, girl. We're obscuring facts," the Police Commissioner interrupted.

Ursula continued, ignoring the comment. "Since there have been no further killings in about a month, perhaps, you should stop sending officers to Durward Street, day and night."

"That would be likely to invite him back onto our streets." Commissioner Scott said, shaking his head.

"Patrolling that street will only deter him from leaving their remains there, but *not* from killing," Robert said. "Not to mention that heightened security will only serve to continue to create panic. I think you *should* remove officers from the streets—"

Robert raised a hand to stop the Police Commissioner from protesting and continued.

"It'll give him a false sense of security and you know what else? If he is fond of the limelight, telling the press and the public you've arrested the culprit—"

"Will anger him," Ursula muttered.

"And he'll be out looking for his next victim, at which point, we pounce," Robert finished, nodding.

"I can keep watch for a few nights," Ursula offered.

"Absolutely not!" Robert exclaimed. "We can get officers to do that out of uniform."

"Random men loitering about will raise his suspicion," Ursula argued. "It makes sense if I do it. Your time is better spent—"

"—visiting local brothels. You're right." Robert said, offering a small smile.

"Sounds like a plan," Ursula retorted, turning to look at the bewildered Commissioner.

That's how she ended up standing on the corner of the notorious *Bucks Row*, now known as Durward Street. Ursula shivered, watching her breath hang in the frigid air. She couldn't recall a colder summer night or one more endless. Time seemed to have slowed as the world around her shrunk into an eerie silence. Perhaps amplified by the thick mist.

Woosh.

Ursula turned to the sound. Through the dense haze, a subtle but unmistakable movement caught her attention, and another shift confirmed her suspicion. She instinctively slipped her hand inside the folds of her trench coat and gripped the firearm Robert had provided for protection. As she squinted into the murky unknown, her heart quickened its pace, each beat resonating like a warning in her ears. Blood pulsed viciously in her throat, and she felt the throb of her veins echo the tension in the air. She took a step back, weighing her options. Should she run and escape the veiled danger lurking in the mist? *No.* This was their opportunity to catch the killer. Ursula tightened her grasp on the cold handle of the gun, a silent vow to herself. The silhouette continued moving towards her, intensifying the unsettling anticipation. And then, it revealed itself. It was a fox.

For a few moments, they eyed each other, both uncertain of the other, but then with a sudden burst of energy, the fox bolted away, disappearing into the mist as quickly as it had appeared. Relief flooded her senses, yet she couldn't fully dispel the tremors coursing through her. The encounter lingered. Those few moments of uncertainty, where the veil of mist concealed a potential face-to-face with the elusive killer had left an indelible mark etched in the recesses of her mind.

As the echoes of the adrenaline-fuelled fear subsided, Ursula's consciousness grappled with the aftermath. The abruptness of the encounter served as a potent lesson – she couldn't afford to let her guard down as she had in that fleeting moment of terror. Every step through the mist-laden night should be taken with the acute awareness that danger might lurk just beyond the next turn, like a hunter of the night, waiting to pounce.

Ursula stood still as a statue for the next few moments. Placing her two fingers beneath her jaw, she felt her pulse slowly decline. Once she regained composure from the scare, Ursula released her grip on the gun and retrieved folded photographs from her pocket. Her eyes were fixated on the chilling, lifeless ones in the image. The first victim was Mary Lou Pearce. Her dark auburn hair had been meticulously pulled back into a ponytail. The killer's signature - a perfectly etched anchor - marked her neck.

In the second photograph, the second victim, Kelly McDonald, who had met her demise two weeks later. They had been unable to recover her head, so the image only displayed her decapitated torso. She was similarly naked, similarly marked. The third picture depicted Elizabeth Eddowes. Her hands were bound in a distinctive hitch knot. Ursula recognised the unique pattern of the knots, a skill learned from her sailor uncle, who had taught her various rope-tying techniques. Returning her attention to the symbols etched on their bodies, she couldn't help but wonder how the killer had achieved such impeccable precision—perhaps with a knife, maybe a scalpel, or could it be a Swiss blade?

"Is he a sailor?" she whispered to herself.

It would make sense. The anchor, the sailor's knot...the killer had to have been connected to the sea somehow. London was not a port city but the city was abundant with people from all over the country, and all over the world. One thing was certain, the perpetrator had taken his time judging by how clean the anchors were on the victims.

Ursula swivelled her head, alarmed. This time it wasn't a fox, she was sure of it. They were the unmistakable sound of footsteps. Ursula drew her firearm and aimed it into the darkness.

"Who's there?" she demanded.

A calloused, rough hand clamped onto the back of her neck, yanking her to the ground. A musky, nausea-inducing scent of vanilla hung in the air. Ursula shrieked with desperation as her assailant grabbed her by the hair and started dragging her down the street. She heard the echoes of her desperation get lost in the misty night as she thrashed violently, fighting tooth and nail to break free from their assailant's grasp. The panic caused an instant deprivation of oxygen that sent a shockwave through her.

In that harrowing moment, she felt with chilling certainty that her life was at its end. Destined to die alone in the clutches of her ominous assailant. His menacing countenance, hidden from view by the thick fog until this point, drew perilously near. Before she could see anything beyond his malevolent stare, consciousness slipped away.

URSULA

July 29th, 1949

Consciousness tiptoed tentatively back to Ursula, yet her eyes felt heavy, like lead, resisting to participate in the waking world. Each fluttering attempt was a battle against an overwhelming fog of dizziness, succeeded by a searing ache that enveloped every fibre of her being, pulsating like a merciless storm of agony. Slowly, the room materialised around her - it was a sterile expanse of pristine white so stark it stung her eyes. A sharp contrast from the moody darkness etched in her mind from the night of the attack.

"Ursula," Robert said.

His voice was a balm to her fractured consciousness.

"It's me. Robert."

Amidst the bustling crowd, Ursula could have recognized Robert's distinctive timbre. Even now, through the haze and echoes of pain, the outline of his comely face stood clear, drawing her back to the world.

"You're in hospital," he added, sensing her confusion.

Ursula forced a smile, meeting her husband's bright hazel eyes. In that fragile moment, fragmented flashbacks of the attack flickered in her mind. A menacing figure skulking towards her through the mist. The hand that grabbed her throat. The sound of her desperate cries...the cold, daunting eyes. Her pain intensified once more and was only calmed by Robert's embrace. His warmth felt like a beacon of hope, an escape from the dark labyrinthine corridors of her mind. Ursula sat wrapped in Robert's cocoon of safety for what appeared to be an eternity. As the dark chains that held her mind hostage began to loosen, she summoned the strength to pull herself away.

"How long have I been—" she began.

"Two days," Robert gently caressed her face, his emotions overwhelming him. "I thought I'd lost you."

The relief in Robert's voice carried the weight of fear as he pulled Ursula into another tight embrace, his strong frame trembling. The warmth of his tears drenched the collar of her hospital robes. Unable to find words, she held him just as tightly, allowing the vulnerability of the moment to seep in. In that embrace, amidst the sterile hospital scent, she wondered how she would have coped with the mere thought of losing Robert - would she have remained as resolute?

As Ursula pressed a gentle kiss on his forehead, a silent assurance that everything would be okay, she caught a waft of the sweet, musky scent of the oud he'd been gifted. Its potent aroma intertwined with the sickly sterile hospital smell, creating a peculiar blend that stirred conflicting emotions within her. Gratitude washed over her as she realised they had the opportunity to share this moment, to embrace each other after the brink of potential loss. Yet, a poignant reminder lingered—those women in the images, frozen in time, had not been granted the same fortune. The scent became a bittersweet reminder of the fragility of life and the resilience of love.

"But you didn't," Ursula managed a fragile smile.

"I should've never agreed to it," he paused, deep regret etched on his face. "The Commissioner was right."

"He'd rather see me in an apron, in the kitchen, obediently waiting at the dinner table, like a 'proper' woman," Ursula replied with a touch of anger.

"You should never have been there alone," Robert pushed past her frustration and held her hand tenderly. "There's something else..."

A blend of apprehension and excitement danced in his eyes, creating an intriguing mosaic of emotions. The silence between them hung in the air, pregnant with the weight of undisclosed thoughts. Ursula observed an unusual hesitation in Robert, feeling a subtle unease settle in. His atypical behaviour put her on edge, prompting an uncomfortable shift in her posture. She waited patiently, her curiosity tinged with a hint of anxiety, while Robert grappled with the challenge of articulating his thoughts.

"You're pregnant," Robert beamed, breaking the silence with the life-changing news.

A heavy silence enveloped them as Ursula deliberately looked away from him, unable to meet his eyes. She could not bear to see his excitement, too ashamed to show him the fear in hers. This wasn't a path she was ready to undertake, and he was well aware of that. They'd had numerous conversations about it. Ursula felt a slight pang of resentment towards Robert. This wasn't going to change his life in the same manner it would hers. The last thing she wanted to do was look at the face of someone whose feelings around the subject of parenthood didn't reflect her own.

"I can't be. I would have known," she replied.

"They confirmed you're twelve weeks pregnant."

Dread surged within her as silent tears strolled down her cheeks, making it increasingly challenging to conceal the truth. She pulled her hand away from his.

"Sweetheart," Robert's voice trembled, echoing like the breaking of a heart.

This time, it was Ursula who struggled to find the words to convey what she was feeling. She desperately wanted to tell him that she was content with things as they were, that the current moment was not the juncture for such changes and that she did not want to be a mother, not now. Perhaps not ever.

Her life was filled with boundless possibilities and motherhood would ruin all that. She wanted more time with Robert, not less. Ursula yearned to continue on her career path, not stall it. The thought of relinquishing her freedom to assume the role of a mother filled her with nothing but overwhelming anxiety.

Motherhood, a prison Ursula had spent part of her adulthood fighting to evade, now loomed like her own personal Alcatraz. She feared she'd never be able to break free and swim back to the shores of her former life.

Ursula would have loved nothing more than to embrace being a mother and acquiesce to the weight of societal pressures, but she found herself unable to. Did that make her unworthy of being a woman? The last couple of years instilled in her a passion for detective work that she did not want to let go of, and suddenly, she heard her mother's voice echoing in her mind: '*A woman's duty is to be a wife to her husband and a mother to her children. There should be no other devotion.*'

"Did you catch him?" Ursula said, breaking the silence.

As she turned to him again, she couldn't help but notice the distant gaze in his eyes. There was a stoicism etched on his face, a rigidity in his posture, and a clenching of the jaw—all signs of restrained anger. Though physically present, it was evident Robert's mind had ventured elsewhere, likely grappling with Ursula's unfavourable reaction to the news of impending parenthood.

"We tracked down an address for a brothel on Poland Street," he replied curtly, after a short time. "All the victims had been known to frequent it," his tone darkened. "There's been another murder. Ann Stride. She also had connections to the same brothel and had been missing for a couple of days. Her body was found in Mitre Square."

"Not too far from Durward Street," Ursula noted. "Any leads?"

"Yes, some of the girls at the brothel mentioned a young man, Yuri F. Milan. He worked there cleaning rooms after punters were done. They said he seemed harmless, but the girls always felt a little uneasy around him. I got a second address, to another brothel in east London, down by Gunthorpe Street. Ye Olde Pub. I spoke to the landlord and confirmed that he did have a young man by the name of Yuri

F. Milan working there, but he hadn't turned up in weeks. The landlord didn't seem to think he could have anything to do with the murders."

"Yuri F. Milan? Sounds like a foreign name," Ursula said.

"That's exactly what I thought."

"It might be Italian," Ursula suggested.

"Or Spanish," Robert added.

"Yuri doesn't sound Spanish," Ursula said thoughtfully. "Perhaps French? I'll reach out to the embassies to check for any individuals registered under that name."

"Sweetheart," Robert's tone shifted. "Can we talk about it?"

Ursula sat up, took a deep breath, and met her husband's gaze.

"We have four deceased women and a killer still at large. So, no, I don't want to discuss it today. I'm exhausted. Would you mind leaving me alone?"

Understanding that avoiding an argument was the wiser choice, Robert planted a gentle kiss on his wife's forehead and silently departed. Ursula watched her husband walk away, as an ache welling within her. A part of her wished he had chosen to stay, even if just to sit in silence. Little did she know that this yearning for his presence would become a recurring sentiment in the years to come.

URSULA

December 24th 1953, 7:49 AM

No matter how many times death beckoned, Ursula couldn't bring herself to let her in. The temptation was ever-present, often coaxed by her curiosity, and then, at the very last moment, her resolve crumbled. Not that it came as a surprise, running away was her custom. She'd left Somerset for London when her brother needed her the most, a decision that'd haunted her for years, especially since the news of his disappearance. Ursula was certain she could have convinced him to stay had she been present to address the issue head-on. Instead, she ignored his letters and calls, failing him as a sister and, more importantly, as a friend. They had been thick as thieves as children, often mistaken for twins. Ursula was in no doubt that her absence and quiet rejection of Rodrigo contributed to his decision to go fight in the Spanish Civil War. It was a burden she would carry for the rest of her life.

Ursula hadn't just faltered as a sister; she had also stumbled as a daughter. Unable to confront her father's sudden illness, which occurred only months after her mother's passing, she chose to stay in London, resisting Robert's persistent advice to return. Ursula allowed her work to consume her, using it as a shield against the inevitable. By the time she mustered the courage to journey back home, it was too late—death had already claimed him.

She wondered how long she could elude death's grasp. Anticipating its return, she feared the inevitable night when death would come knocking again, whispering her name in a sweet, dulcet tone. Ursula had come dangerously close to accepting death's embrace one night in her Notting Hill flat, shadows concealing her pallid face framed by long, raven-black hair cascading like a river of ink. Transfixed, she watched as her eyes, akin to pools of the darkest night, and lips resembling a rose kissed by morning dew, drew nearer. Robert intervened that night, saving her life, but she knew death would return—it always did, like a jilted lover. Ursula chuckled, envisioning death at her doorstep, crying out her name like Marlon Brando in *'A Streetcar Named Desire'*.

It had been six arduous and torturous months since that incident, a year since Lucía's passing and over four since the night of her attack. She felt a chill run through her as her mind lingered on all that had occurred. Ursula rose from the bed and approached the large window that overlooked the expansive hotel grounds. She watched as delicate snowflakes descended onto a bed of their brethren, only to disappear, leaving no trace of their existence. A gentle smile graced her lips as the image of her daughter, Lucía, materialised in her mind. She had loved the snow. Ursula turned around, half expecting to see Lucía tugging at her nightgown, but the laughter she had once cherished was nothing but the echoes of her loss. There was no one in that room except her and the man who had shared her bed the night before.

Settling into a delicately crafted wooden chair propped against the window, she lit a cigarette, inhaled the noxious fumes and surrendered to the tranquil ripples that coursed through her body as the nicotine worked its magic. Her eyes were drawn to the man sleeping in her bed, his chest wild with a carpet of thick hair, rising and falling with the deliberation of a hibernating bear. Ursula closed her eyes and, recalling the night they'd shared, felt his hands caressing her face and his tongue tracing a tantalising path from her breasts to her navel. Ursula's carnal dalliance with the stranger was the first time she'd felt desired since her divorce.

Unfortunately for Ursula, the memory of her ex-husband loomed like a haunting spectre, overshadowing the vestiges of pleasure she'd felt at the hands of the stranger. Annoyed, she opened her eyes once more, attempting to dispel the intrusive memory of Robert. In frustration, Ursula reached for the bottle of whiskey on the writing table, seeking solace within its contents, hoping that it would wash away the vivid image of Robert.

"A bit early for that, don't you think?" the man said.

Ursula mustered a smile and locked eyes with his. They were a warm golden brown, twinkling disarmingly under the room's light. She took a few more puffs of her cigarette, savouring the moment as she observed the man's striking appearance. A defined jawline, peppered with thick black stubble, framed a face that James Dean would be proud of. Silky, coal-black hair added to the allure. What intrigued her most was the air of nonchalance he exuded, a rare quality in a place like the Grand Loch Linnhe Hotel, which was often full of stuffy, holier-than-thou personalities.

"Last night was—" the man started, breaking the awkward silence.

"I'm tired." Ursula interrupted as politely as she could. There was a smidgen of severity in her tone. Enough so that he understood she did not wish to engage in small talk.

Men were not always equipped to understand the subtleties offered in a conversation. On this occasion, and perhaps in an attempt to protect his pride, the man rose from the bed and began dressing himself. Ursula watched him, appreciating his physique, especially the thick, veiny hands that had slid so gently across her skin. It was then that she noticed the shadow of a ring around his ring finger. She paused and allowed her mind to fill with speculation. Could he have been married and seeking an escape from the tribulations that often accompanied a separation?

"Are you going to be alright?" he asked, buttoning his shirt.

His voice carried a genuine note of concern that resonated with Ursula. It was a simple question but one that almost broke her. Ursula considered her response and wondered what he would do if she confessed that she *wasn't* alright. Would he cradle her in his arms and try his best to pull her out of her pit of sorrow? Would he wipe away each tear as they fell? Would he reassure her and ask that she keep faith?

"Yes," she said. "Thank you."

The slight twitch of the lips indicated to Ursula his disbelief. She could feel an unspoken question hanging in the air, reflected in the mesmerizing dance of his eyes across her face. His hesitation at taking her word was warranted; after all, only a few hours ago, he'd yanked a drunken Ursula off the cliff's edge. Deciding against pushing the subject, he continued getting dressed. When he was done, he stood awkwardly, shifting his weight from one foot to the other, clearly considering his next words.

"I guess I'll see you around?"

"Mhm," Ursula nodded with a thin smile.

As soon as the door closed behind him, Ursula reached for the whiskey, taking a gulp, followed by another drag from her cigarette. The exhale carried the weight of her emotions, but even in the confines of her solitude, Ursula struggled to release her tears. When was the last time she'd cried? Even on the day she laid Lucía to rest, Ursula had found herself incapable of shedding a tear, as if an impenetrable dam obstructed the torrent of her emotions, creating an internal ache that could only be snuffed with the aid of alcohol. It was the only thing that numbed the overwhelming pain.

Ursula savoured the final sip of her scotch, its liquid tendrils flowing down her throat when a piercing scream echoed from the hallway. Without a second thought, still in her nightwear, she rushed across the room towards the door. In the expansive hotel corridor, Ursula saw a distressed blonde woman in her silk pastel-pink nightgown, huddled against the wall as her anguished cries reverberated through the walls.

The same man who had shared Ursula's bed only moments ago now knelt beside the distraught woman. Their eyes met in an awkward exchange. Ursula felt her cheeks flush, and her stomach churned with disgust as her gaze instinctively darted towards his ring finger, now adorned with a wedding band. He looked away from Ursula, embarrassed, and turned his attention to the woman on the floor, continuing his efforts to soothe her pain.

"We'll find her," the man said softly.

The jangling of a sizable set of keys announced the arrival of Ophelia Clyde, the hotel manager. She was a petite and plump woman of advanced age with greying black hair framing an intense pair of small, black eyes. Her already small mouth appeared even tinier as she pursed her lips. Despite the early hour, Ophelia was attired in her black uniform—a simple, ankle-length dress. With an air resembling that of a headmistress, conveying a stern demeanour one dared not defy, her vigilant eyes scanned the surroundings with every step as if anticipating a potential threat at any moment.

Following close behind Ophelia, was the groundskeeper, Finlay Muir. His impressive physique, with broad shoulders and a muscular build, combined with his pale blonde hair and cold blue eyes, gave him an almost mythical Viking-like appearance. If he had introduced himself as Ragnar Lodbrok, it would have gone unquestioned. He was a figure shrouded in an enigma. Rarely seen and even less often heard. Ursula recalled their encounter from a few days prior at the station. He had been polite enough, but the manner in which he stared at her so intently, made her feel ill at ease. He'd treated her with the utmost courtesy and made her feel as welcome as his stoicism allowed, yet, the intensity of his gaze had left her feeling uncomfortable. To further his mystery, it seemed as if he was currently trying to conceal a limp that Ursula was certain the groundskeeper hadn't had when they met. Finlay noticed her eyes following him and abruptly came to a halt, shifting his weight to lean against the wall, and turning his attention to the unfolding scene.

"What's the matter, Mrs. Blakesley?" Ophelia asked the blonde woman.

"It's Blanchette, we don't know where she is," the man replied in her stead.

We? The man had said, the use of the plural form was the confirmation she needed. She'd been nothing more than a married man's temporary distraction.

"Finlay," Ophelia said, noticing the cluster of guests in the corridor. It was only then that Ursula turned to see that she hadn't been the only one drawn to the scream. "Could you escort Mr and Mrs Blakesley to their room?"

"Aye," mumbled the groundskeeper.

Mr Blakesley extended a hand to help his wife off the floor, still making a conscious effort to avoid Ursula's gaze.

"My sincere apologies for the disruption," Ophelia said to the remaining guests.

"Do let us know if you locate the girl," a man with a raspy voice remarked.

Ursula studied the man in luxurious burgundy robes, his raven-black hair streaked with hints of white framing a friendly face. His eyes, however, remained stern. Close behind was a tall and handsome man with dark olive skin and piercing green eyes, something about his features suggested North African origins. Two women completed the group. The first, with rich ebony skin and saucer-like brown eyes, absent-mindedly fingered a gold chain, concern etched on her otherwise pristine face. The second, a little older and exuding regal poise and a daring flair reminiscent of a young Katherine Hepburn, observed curiously with one hand tucked into her suit trouser pocket. All four, unmistakably part of the same group, entered a room together, leaving Ursula as the sole observer.

"Is there anything I can assist you with ma'am?" The hotel manager had encroached so closely that she had taken possession of Ursula's personal space.

"No..." Ursula replied but stopped before entering her room. "Ms Clyde, do keep me informed."

"Of course, Ms Dankworth. I'm sure we'll find her soon. Blanchette is a troublesome child, this would not be the first time she caused a ruckus."

The hotel manager turned to leave, prompting Ursula to return to her room. Sinking into her bed, she immediately reached for a cigarette, her eyes falling on the empty whiskey bottle resting on the bedside table. How would she have coped without that numbing elixir? It had extracted a high cost, yet paradoxically, it had also been a lifeline, warding off the beckoning call of death. Ursula delved into the bedside drawer, retrieving an unopened whiskey bottle. Closing her eyes, she summoned every ounce of inner strength to resist the urge to open it, when fragments of the night of the attack materialised in her mind, each memory a jagged knife to her consciousness. *A menacing figure skulking towards her through the mist. The hand that grabbed her throat. The sound of her desperate cries...the cold, daunting eyes.* This time, however, there was no Robert to cocoon her in warmth and love. She had nothing but her solitude and whiskey.

Inevitably, she took a drink.

URSULA

December 24th 1953, 9:23 AM

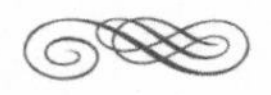

The warm melody of *'I Love You for Sentimental Reasons'* filled the dining hall as Ursula entered. On the stage stood an enchanting African-American man, singing every note of the song as if it were his last. His voice, like liquid honey to her ears, instantly transported her to a magical time when she was surrounded by the love of Robert and her daughter, Lucía. With the rhythm of bittersweet nostalgia pulsating in her ears, Ursula settled onto one of the vacant tables nearest to the stage, the singer's timbre evoking the spectre of Lucía's laughter.

To fend off the painful memories lurking at the edges of her consciousness, Ursula redirected her attention to the expansive dining room hall and its beautiful Christmas decorations. Tired and inebriated when she'd arrived the previous afternoon, Ursula hadn't fully grasped the grandeur of the Grand Loch Linnhe Hotel. The furnishings, reminiscent of a bygone era, stood frozen in time, exuding the timeless elegance of an extravagant 1920s palace. Hundreds of twinkling lights cast a celestial glow overhead, illuminating the hall like a star-studded sky. The roaring fireplace, large enough to accommodate a handful of people, beckoned with its warmth and dancing flames, offering solace from the winter chill. In one corner, towering majestically, stood the tallest Christmas tree Ursula had ever beheld, its branches adorned with a lavish display of red, silver, and gold baubles that glistened like precious jewels. As Ursula took in the breathtaking scene before her, she couldn't help but feel a pang of awe, finally understanding why families chose to spend their Christmas in this enchanting sanctuary—a haven where time seemed to stand still.

Tense whispers shattered Ursula's reverie, drawing her gaze to a nearby table where the four guests she'd seen earlier that morning were embroiled in a heated discussion. Their voices lowered to mere murmurs at the prompting of the olive-skinned man, who seemed to sense Ursula's scrutiny. Despite his attempt at a smile, the furrow creasing his brow betrayed the unresolved tension lingering among them. She offered a polite smile as the man with salt-and-pepper hair, glanced her way, his forced grin quickly fading as he returned to his breakfast.

"Good mornin', Ms Dankworth," said a young voice in a thick Scottish accent.

"Good morning," Ursula replied, still a little distracted.

She looked up to see a pock-marked, fair-skinned adolescent with fiery red hair standing at her side. He looked down at her with watery grey eyes that revealed his inner innocence and youth. He couldn't have been much older than sixteen or seventeen, certainly teetering at the cusp of manhood. Ursula noted a sullen demeanour, further accentuated by puffy, red eyes, as if he'd been crying. He extended the breakfast menu to Ursula, which she perused briefly before placing her order.

"I'll have the eggs florentine and the breakfast tea, please," she said with a polite nod of gratitude.

The young man acknowledged her order with a brisk nod before departing. Ursula continued to watch him, noting his unkempt appearance. The boy's oversized uniform— a thin white overcoat with a grandfather collar and black detailing around the chest pocket and front placket— hung loosely around his thin frame. The black trousers, stopped short at his ankles, two inches too short for him.

Her eyes tracked him as he walked past a young boy sitting at a table by himself, deeply engrossed in quiet conversation with a well-worn wolf stuffed toy. Sensing her gaze, the boy looked up from his plush companion, meeting Ursula's eyes briefly. His vacant eyes seemed to pierce *through* her, his expression illegible. The young boy offered a faint smile before swiftly returning his attention to the stuffed toy, leaning in as if anticipating a response to a comment he'd made.

It was peculiar, though not entirely unheard of, for children—especially those on the shy and introverted side—to form profound connections with their toys. It was, however, uncommon to witness such behaviour in a boy of his age, seemingly on the brink of adolescence. Ursula, too, had owned a doll that she'd treated as a real companion. Angela had been her bedtime confidante for years, witnessing countless tea parties with her and Rodrigo, much to his chagrin. A twinge of envy touched Ursula as she reminisced about that period in her life. She longed for the days of escaping into make-believe realms, a luxury often scarce in the adult world with its burdensome troubles.

"Can I join you, ma'am?" a voice asked, his unmistakable American accent cutting through the air.

The singer had descended the stage and walked over to Ursula. He had a wide, friendly smile, which revealed dimples likely to be the auteurs of many a broken heart.

"Of course," Ursula replied. "But only if you promise to drop the ma'am."

"My apologies ma—It's a force of habit, I'm James Wilson," the singer said introducing himself.

"I'm Ursula Doy—Dankworth," she stopped to correct herself. She was still having trouble adjusting to the idea of having to use her maiden name. "Pleasure to meet you."

"The pleasure is all mine, ma—I mean...Ms Dankworth."

Their conversation was interrupted by the waiter's return. His pale face turned an instant shade of red at the sight of James sitting at Ursula's table.

"Is he troubling you?" the waiter asked.

"Hamish, c'mon!" James said quietly, though ruffled by the waiter's attitude.

"You shouldn't be sitting with guests."

"Sorry, I didn't quite catch your name," Ursula said.

"Hamish, ma'am. Hamish Mackenzie," the waiter replied.

Ursula offered him a thin smile. "What gave you the impression that Mr Wilson was troubling me?"

"He's sat next to you, Ma'am."

"You assumed Mr Wilson was troubling me because he is sitting next to me?" Ursula said, serving herself some tea.

"Staff members aren't allowed to sit with guests, it's—"

"Do I look troubled?" Ursula interjected.

"No, ma'am but—"

"But nothing," Ursula cut in.

"I just thought...you know? He is...a...a..."

Hamish looked at the singer, his eyes almost apologetic.

"He is a...?" Ursula started coaxing the rest of the waiter's sentence.

"A negro. Is that what you're tryna to say, Hamish?" James asked, unable to hide the disappointment in his voice.

Hamish shifted uncomfortably and looked down towards his well-worn shoes to avoid eye contact. Seeing his face twist with discomfort and noticing that the hushed dining room had become a stage for their awkward exchange, Ursula decided to put the boy out of his misery.

"You have my leave," Ursula dismissed the waiter.

"My apologies, ma'am," Hamish murmured, as a blush of shame coloured his pallid cheeks. With a silent nod, he turned to leave.

Ursula and James sat in contemplative silence for several moments until the singer eventually broke the quiet.

"Do you know what the worst thing is? We play cards every night. But I guess, no matter where I go, I am a negro."

She didn't know how to respond, but the depth of emotion in his eyes revealed more than mere hurt. Ursula wished she could undo the exchange, erasing the fleeting but palpable pain on the singer's face.

"What brings you to Loch Linnhe?" Ursula asked, trying to brighten the mood. "It's quite a long way from—"

"Birmingham, Alabama, ma'am," James said, before adding quickly. "I mean Ms Dankworth."

"Quite a long way indeed. Have you enjoyed your stay?"

"Summer was beautiful. But as soon as Fall came," James shivered. "Damn, it was cold. Beautiful, but cold," James leaned towards Ursula and lowered his voice. "The beautiful British women make up for the cold."

Ursula let out a genuine laugh.

"Not as many as you'd hoped perhaps?" Ursula quipped, glancing around the empty dining hall.

"The right amount," James said, revealing those charming dimples again.

Ursula was not one for easy flattery, but she felt a subtle flutter within her as James looked into her eyes, a spark of something intriguing. His unwavering stare left her without any doubt of his intentions. Breaking eye contact, she served herself a fresh cup of tea, followed by a dash of milk.

"You hardly put any milk in," James observed.

"I put in the right amount," Ursula replied, with a smile, the echo of their earlier banter lingering in the air. "It's an art, you see. Mother always said that you truly love someone when you can make tea just the way they like it, without you even having to ask. It becomes second nature," shifting the conversation, she continued. "My ex-husband had his in a large mug, with two tea bags to make sure it was strong enough. He always complained I bought the wrong brand of tea. He was a Yorkshire tea man and I, more of a PG Tips kind of woman," Ursula was unable to hide the hint of nostalgia in her voice, nor the longing. "He liked just a drop of milk. No sugar."

"Ex-husband?" James enquired, with a note of curiosity.

"Indeed."

"Is that what brings you here?"

"Loneliness, you mean?"

"No, that's not what I meant-"

"And yet, that is *exactly* what brings me here," Ursula replied.

"You chose the end of the world to run away from loneliness?" James asked.

Ursula balanced delicately on the precipice of vulnerability in James' presence. His attentive eyes and genuine curiosity seemed to weave an ethereal refuge, coaxing her hesitant heart to contemplate unveiling its concealed depths. There was a quiet assurance within him that made Ursula feel as if whatever she revealed would be embraced without harsh judgement. But could she divulge her grim truth? Could she tell him that she didn't plan on leaving Loch Linnhe alive? Perhaps she should confide in him about the fleeting moment on the snowy cliff? Perhaps she should let him know that were it not for her trusted companions, Messrs Whiskey and Gin, who'd created enough doubt to grant Mr Blakesley the time to step in and save her from the precipice, they might not have been having this conversation.

"Yes," Ursula replied, sipping her tea and deciding not to burden the singer. "Why did *you* choose the end of the world?"

"I think the end of the world chose me," James replied with a smile.

"I see," her curiosity sparked, Ursula leant back in her chair, her cup of tea firmly in her grasp. "How so?"

"Well, I think I was drawn here," he whispered, leaning in.

"You were drawn here?"

"Mhm."

"Horse and carriage?" Ursula joked.

"Do you believe in the mutual attraction of energies?"

"No, I don't," Ursula replied.

"You should. We're livin' it now."

"We are?"

"Mhm," James nodded. "People are made up of energy. Positive and negative. Positive energies of the same nature, attract one another. We're drawn to them. To each other. The horse and carriage," he said, circling back to her comment with a smile. "Comes later."

"Is that a proposal?" Ursula retorted, unable to stifle a laugh.

A piercing scream tore through the tranquil hall, interrupting their conversation. Ursula and James sprang to their feet, their shared sense of urgency propelling them out of the dining room towards the source of the tumult. There, in the centre of the foyer, stood Ophelia Clyde, her countenance rattled and pallid as if she'd seen a ghost. Seated on the stairs in front of the hotel manager was Mrs Blakesley, her inconsolable state even more pronounced than earlier that morning. Beside her, Mr Blakesley enveloped her in a tight embrace, his eyes staring into the distance, and devoid of the emotion Ursula had seen in the privacy of her bedroom. The gesture, often employed by men to convey a semblance of protection, looked as vacant of emotion as his eyes. Meanwhile, Finlay Muir hovered near the entrance, cradling a red bundle in his arms. His eyes were low, not meeting those of Mr and Mrs Blakesley.

"Darling, look at me," Mr Blakesley said, trying to sound firm. His wife, whose face was buried into his shoulder, tilted her head towards him. "Everything is going to be fine."

"This definitely belongs to Blanchette?" Ophelia Clyde asked, grabbing the bundle from Finlay.

Mrs. Blakesley nodded, wiping away her tears as she stared at the red woollen coat, covered in flecks of snow and dirt.

"Can I see it?" she asked.

Ophelia passed the coat to Mrs Blakesley, who unfastened it, revealing the name tag inside: *'Blanche.'* Almost immediately, a heart-wrenching cry escaped her lips once more, breaking Ursula's heart in tandem. She knew all too well the anguish of witnessing a mother's worst fears unfolding before her eyes. The foyer soon filled with the arrival of the four quarrelling guests and the little boy, still clutching his stuffed wolf toy, his gaze vacant as ever. Shortly after, the waiter, Hamish Mackenzie, entered.

"I'm sure she'll be fine. Might be outside somewhere," Ophelia said reassuringly.

Ursula's attention was suddenly drawn to another presence in the foyer. One she hadn't previously noticed - the pianist. Amidst the captivating aura of James' charm, she had completely overlooked him during their performance.

The pianist stood in stark contrast to James. Short and stout, with a bald head and restless eyes that darted from left to right, he exuded a reserved demeanour, unlike James' extroverted nature. Her eyes lingered on Lyle, who appeared to sense her scrutiny and took a subtle step backwards.

"Where did you find it?" Theron asked the groundskeeper.

"O-o-over by the tree, past the gardens," he stuttered.

"Hamish," Ophelia said. "Could you get Julia and Silvia to help you look for her inside the hotel?"

The young waiter nodded stiffly, his eyes trembling with shock. "Yes, ma'am."

"She might've snuck into one of the empty rooms and fallen asleep," Ophelia continued.

She watched Hamish leave the foyer and could have sworn to have heard him sniffling. Ursula surveyed the faces of those present and took note of those who weren't, her thoughts drifting to her ex-husband, the infamous Robert Doyle. In situations like these, he would have sprung into action, taking charge with characteristic confidence and authority. Ursula felt a twinge of envy; she wished she could have felt the same self-assurance, but instead, found herself retreating inward. Her psyche was pummelled by a myriad of thoughts. Could it be that the trip Ursula had planned to end her life would result in her helping to investigate the disappearance of a child? Her hand shook with the thought...the last time she had done anything of the sort was before she'd found out about her pregnancy...it had been in that dark, misty London alley...and suddenly the flashbacks of that night came haunting:

A menacing figure skulking towards her through the mist. The hand that grabbed her throat. The sound of her desperate cries...the cold, daunting eyes.

"Mrs. Blakesley," the man with salt-and-pepper hair said. "Why don't you join us in the library for a cup of tea whilst the staff look for her? We can make it an Irish tea. Might help to calm the nerves."

"That might be a good idea," Mr Blakesley said, nodding but his wife shook her head and tethered herself ever more firmly to the bannister, refusing to move.

"Finlay," the hotel manager said. "Could you conduct a thorough search of the grounds, whilst Hamish and the girls check the rooms?"

The groundskeeper nodded and departed through the dining hall. Ursula stood still, trying to quell the sudden surge of nausea that gripped her throat. Despite the voices around her discussing the missing girl, she felt immobilised, as if her muscles were frozen, leaving her trapped in her mind while the world moved on without her.

If only she could reach for the whiskey...

"Ms Clyde, Lyle and I are happy to help search the grounds," James offered.

"Thank you, that would be very helpful. We need to be quick about it. Looks like the winds are picking up again," Ophelia noted looking through the large windows out into the front gardens.

"I'll go with you," Ursula said to James, finding her voice.

As the burden of doubt continued to weigh heavily on Ursula, she recognised the pressing need to overcome these uncertainties, especially when the safety of a child was at stake. Determined, Ursula ascended the stairs to her room to fetch her jacket. Upon entering, her gaze fell upon the glinting whiskey bottle on the desk, bathed in the cold winter sunlight. An involuntary twitch coursed through her hands as she stared at it, her mind's eye enveloped in fog, the ominous silhouette from the night of the attack looming within. With a determined breath, Ursula tightly shut her eyes, took three deep breaths, and upon reopening them, found the fog dissipating along with the menacing figure. Stepping forward, she reached out her trembling fingers towards the bottle, hesitating briefly before unscrewing the cap. The rich, seductive aroma enveloped her senses, beckoning irresistibly. Her parched throat pleaded for relief, and without further hesitation, she drank. Each sip felt like a step towards reclaiming her sense of self, until at last, she felt grounded once more.

BLANCHETTE

December 23rd 1953, 19:22

The grandeur of the hotel never failed to astound Blanchette. Having visited the Grand Loch Linnhe Hotel every Christmas, except for the year of her father's death, she found herself continually captivated by its opulent charm. No matter how often she strolled through its majestic corridors, the sight of the tall arched ceilings, diamond-like chandeliers, and the plush burgundy carpet, made her feel as if she were walking in a real-life fairytale. In this enchanted realm, she was a forlorn princess, seated in a tower, yearning for her prince to come to her rescue.

Blanchette paused to stare at one of the many portraits gracing the cream-coloured walls and found herself face-to-face with the one depicting King James I of Scotland. He sported a well-groomed beard which framed a strong jawline. His countenance displayed authority, yet his eyes were gentle and curious.

Resuming her stroll, Blanchette recalled with fondness how, in the company of her father, she used to rise at the crack of dawn to witness the first light dancing on the fields.

Surrounded by expansive snow-covered mountains and fields, it was a sight to behold, one she would cherish forever, particularly, as it was one of the last moments she had shared with her father. Now, she longed to one day be able to share that experience with her husband and children, hoping to create similar cherished memories with them.

Blanchette had always dreamed of finding a husband and starting a family of her own, aspirations that grew stronger after her father's passing. Her mother dismissed these dreams as fit for little girls. But at fifteen, Blanchette believed it was time to start thinking about marriage. After all, Mary, Queen of Scots, and Marie Antoinette were already married at her age. Even the new Queen Elizabeth, rumour had it, had started corresponding with Prince Philip when she was just thirteen. Her mother's scepticism only made Blanchette more determined to find her own prince charming. She needed a beacon of hope amidst the sorrow that had shrouded their home.

She couldn't understand her mother's negativity towards the idea of falling in love. After all, her mother had discovered happiness in the embrace of Mr. Blakesley, whose charm resonated deeply with Blanchette. Their marriage was proof of the beauty of love. It seemed unjust that she should discourage Blanchette from seeking the same happiness.

Her thoughts lingering on Mr. Blakesley, Blanchette remembered how reluctant she'd been to warm up to him, fearing it might somehow betray her father's memory. However, he proved to be a challenging man to dislike. The captivating tales of wartime experiences he had shared with her father, keeping his memory alive, helped to soften her resistance. He narrated them with such flair and gusto that one might have mistaken him for a poet, telling grandiose tales penned by a skilled hand.

Mr. Blakesley's arrival hadn't been altogether positive, for it introduced another presence—his son, Uriah Blakesley. He was everything his father wasn't and the furthest thing from endearing Blanchette could have imagined. Uriah was a spoiled, cadaverous, insufferable boy with strange reddish-brown eyes. He was as volatile as a volcano, often leaving Blanchette uncertain and unsettled and it was because of him, that she found herself meandering through the hotel's corridors. She could never understand why her mother and Mr. Blakesley insisted on rooming them together during Christmas. She wouldn't have minded but his immaturity and odious behaviour were too much for her to bear.

Uriah's conduct was *not* the sole reason Blanchette had decided to leave her room. The looming snowstorm had led to several guests cancelling their reservations, resulting in the unusual absence of the usual bustling crowd. Blanchette felt a pang of sadness upon learning that her dear friends, Lisa Wellesley and Samantha Rodgers, would not be joining her at Loch Linnhe this year. Over the years, their companionship had made her Christmases truly special, providing her with moments of joy amidst the holiday festivities. She fondly remembered their mischievous antics, like the time they conspired to lock Blanchette and the skinny, pockmarked, stuttering waiter together in a broom cupboard, resulting in her regrettable first kiss. Despite the embarrassment, they had laughed about it for days. Their absence this year meant she would miss their laughter and warmth dearly. Their company had always been a welcome reprieve from Uriah, whose presence she found less than agreeable.

The dearth of guests had forced her mother and Mr Blakesley to seek alternative dinner companions and invited a friendly young couple to their table one evening. There was Mr Oliver White, who possessed a tall, slender frame, coupled with a handsome face and raven-black hair peppered with strands of white. He had a warm and genuine smile that reminded Blanchette of Montgomery Clift in *'A Place in the Sun'*. Mr White had the same brooding intensity, casual elegance and mystery about him. His wife, Mrs Ariel White emanated an air of independence and had a mischievous twinkle in her eye. Blanchette found herself captivated by Ariel's sense of style, particularly her loose-fitting trousers and ivory-coloured blouse adorned with pearls.

Despite the enchanting presence of the Whites, Blanchette's attention had been elsewhere. Two tables away sat the most exotic of couples. One was a stunning dark-skinned woman with eyes that sparkled like black moonstone jewels. She was clad in a captivating green silk dress that accentuated her every curve. Seated opposite her was the most beautiful man Blanchette had ever seen. The man had flawless caramel skin and dark thick eyebrows above mesmerising jade-green eyes that darted towards her table every few seconds. She watched him between mouthfuls of her chocolate mousse as he ruffled his pillowy black hair. Feeling her cheeks blush, she thought she might have found her prince charming.

"Is this your first time in Loch Linnhe?" Blanchette's mother inquired.

"During Christmas, yes," Mr. White replied. "My business partner has been here a handful of times and has had nothing but good things to say, and I see why."

"Even the weather?" quipped Mr. Blakesley.

"Well, but who travels to Scotland for the weather?" Mrs White responded, prompting laughter from all.

"What's your business partner's name?" her mother asked. "If he's been here during Christmas before, we may have met him."

Blanchette rolled her eyes. She recognised this as her mother's subtle way of gauging whether they were 'new money' or not. Her mother had repeatedly cautioned Blanchette to steer clear of such circles.

"Benjamin Daniels, son of Lochlan Daniels—" Mr White started.

"The Commissioner of the Bank of England?" her mother asked in genuine surprise. "You wouldn't happen to be the son of Conran White?"

"Yes," Oliver replied meekly.

"Oh, why I never made the connection!" Maude said raising a glass, clearly relieved not to have wasted her evening with two upstarts. "So it's just the two of you?"

"Yes. This year we decided to spend the holidays without the pretence," Mr. White explained. "We love family, but quite often, we suffer through the Christmas holidays. So it's just us and our friends this year."

Mr White gestured towards the couple sitting two tables away.

"Your friends?" asked Mrs. Blakesley.

"Yes," Mrs. White affirmed.

"Oh, we didn't know... we would have invited them to join us," Mr. Blakesley mentioned.

Blanchette knew better. Her mother was not one to mingle with anyone she deemed 'other' and was certain she would not have extended the invitation.

"I did see you at breakfast and dinner with them yesterday," her mother added. "But I thought they might have been your servants."

It was a *blink-and-you'll-miss-it* moment but Blanchette was certain that Mrs White had flinched at the mention of the word 'servant'.

"Ndeshi and Hachem travel everywhere with us. They are the family we chose," Mrs. White replied stiffly.

The response was delivered with gravity, creating a momentary divide between the couples. Mr Blakesley, who was less pretentious than her mother, shifted uncomfortably, his eyes drifting to the table where an elegant woman sat alone.

"Ndeshi is from Namibia and Hachem is Moroccan," Mr. White added to break the silence.

"How incredibly exotic. I visited Egypt with my dearly departed ex-husband once. Couldn't wait to leave because of the mosquitoes," her mother remarked.

Hachem. Blanchette repeated the name in her head as she thought about his beautiful, thick lips and piercing eyes.

Hachem. She said once again, savouring the way it rolled effortlessly off her tongue.

The very next morning, Blanchette took care to wait for him in the dining hall and as soon as Hachem made his way towards the exit, she excused herself from the breakfast table and followed. Engaging him in conversation, she asked about his origins, and Hachem shared tales of Tangier and his friendship with Mr. and Mrs. White but oddly enough, he did not mention his wife. Upon reaching the second floor, Hachem bid her goodbye but instead of returning to her room, Blanchette sat on the stairs, lost in daydreams of him.

He was the reason Blanchette now found herself climbing the stairs to the second floor. She intended to knock on his door and propose a walk—an audacious idea, she admitted. There was little reason to do so, but what if he rejected her? Blanchette, though not the most attractive girl in school, had her fair share of snobby teenage suitors, including the irritating waiter from last year. Her family's wealth attracted attention, primarily from those eager to benefit from it, a fact she couldn't deny. Nevertheless, she enjoyed popularity. With her mother's inheritance secure, Blanchette would make for a more interesting prospect compared to Hachem's wife. While she might not rival her in beauty, wealth trumped all. There was little that someone from a mosquito-riddled country could offer that she could not.

Blanchette was on the verge of reaching the second floor when she heard someone calling out to her. As she turned to see who it was, her expression shifted to one of surprise and mild disappointment. It was Hamish.

"What do you want?" she asked, crossing her arms.

The unfriendly tone caused the smile that had decorated the waiter's bland face to fade.

"I wanted to talk is all. You didn't reply to *any* of my letters...I waited for you in Trafalgar Square like you'd said. Took a bus from Paisley to London..."

Blanchette sighed, feeling irritated. After their kiss in the broom cupboard, they'd shared a brief Christmas romance. However, she'd felt so embarrassed about it that she hadn't even confided in Lisa Wellesley and Samantha Rodgers. Hamish was far from what Blanchette was looking for, but she supposed every princess had to kiss a few frogs before finding her prince.

"Sorry about that, mother refused to let me leave the house that day," Blanchette lied. She had in fact, never had any intention of meeting with Hamish, besides, he should have known better than to think he ever stood a chance.

"I understand," he said pathetically. "But why didn't you reply to any of my letters? You could have let me know and I would have tried to come see you another time."

Blanchette felt a surge of frustration as she looked at Hamish in his oversized uniform and perpetual bed hair, resembling someone caught in a perpetual snowstorm. She took a moment to think about her next words. Blanchette could either let him down gently, which might entail enduring Hamish's attempts to talk to her for the rest of her stay, or she could make it unmistakably clear that it was over.

"Hamish," Blanchette started. "You're the help, I can't be with the help. Even if I wanted to, I am pretty sure mother would die of embarrassment, and quite frankly, so would I. Look at you."

She offered one final look of utter disdain and turned away before he could reply. She didn't want to spend any more time looking at his woeful face. Trying her hardest to forget the encounter, Blanchette made her way down the corridor, her heart racing the closer she got to number two hundred and twenty-two.

Upon reaching the door, she placed her ear against it, wanting to make sure that he was inside before gathering the courage to knock. She listened carefully. Sounds were coming from inside the room, she could hear someone...moaning. It was a very breathy kind of moan, almost like they were tired or...no, not tired...she couldn't quite place it. It sounded very much like the sounds she heard coming from her mother's room some nights.

A woman's laughter rang through the door, and Blanchette felt her heart sink. Hachem *was* inside and appeared to be enjoying the company of his wife. Disappointment seeping in, she turned with frustration, accidentally banging the door with her elbow. Blanchette froze in panic, the silence amplifying the approaching footsteps. Just as she snapped out of her momentary dread, the door swung open, revealing Mrs. White's face.

"Mrs White?" Blanchette gasped in shock.

"What are you doing here?!" Mrs White spat, her face now red as a tomato.

Blanchette took a step back, alarmed by the anger in the woman's eyes. She couldn't understand why Mrs White was in Hachem's room, especially dressed in nothing but the hotel's bedsheets and with her hair dishevelled as if she'd just woken up. It didn't make sense; Blanchette had seen her at dinner not long ago.

"I..." Blanchette started.

"Honey, is that Hachem?" came the voice of a second woman. "Tell him we're not finished—"

Blanchette's mouth fell agape as the naked, curvaceous body of Ndeshi, Hachem's wife, came into view. The smile on her face slowly faded as she laid eyes on Blanchette. Her mind raced, trying to make sense of the moment. Why were Mrs White and Ndeshi alone and naked? Before she could dwell further on these puzzling circumstances, Mrs White grabbed the collar of her dress, pulling her close until their noses were nearly touching. Fear coursed through Blanchette as the once warm and friendly eyes now bore down on her like those of a mortal enemy.

"If you speak of this to anyone, I promise you—"

"Ariel," Ndeshi said, trying to pull her lover away from Blanchette. "Leave it be."

A touch from Ndeshi had been all that Mrs White had needed to calm down. She released Blanchette, who fell to the floor with a mighty thud. The lock to the room opposite turned, and when it opened, it revealed Hachem in a bathrobe and behind him, Mr. White. She looked dumbfounded from one couple to the other.

"What is—" Mr White started, as Hachem walked back into the room muttering something in his native tongue. Noticing a distressed Blanchette on the floor, he kneeled and helped her up on her feet, offering a wide smile as he did so, his eyes, however, were stern. "Go back to your room, okay? Pretend this never happened."

No scenario allowed Blanchette to pretend she hadn't stumbled upon what appeared to be a secret love affair between the couples. If Lucy Wellesley and Samantha Rodgers had been present, she would have run straight to them to share what she'd seen. Blanchette couldn't wait to get back to London, so she could call them and share her scandalous discovery.

"Are you listening, girl," Mrs. White demanded, shaking Blanchette.

"Ariel!" Mr. White admonished before turning back to Blanchette. "We could get in a lot of trouble. We need you to promise not to say anything, okay?"

"I won't," Blanchette lied.

"Okay, go," Mr. White said.

Heart pounding, Blanchette ran down the hallway not looking back and only slowed down when she reached the stairs. Her mind was a whirl with thousands of questions. Her dream was completely shattered. All those plans she'd started to make with Hachem in mind, but it appeared his heart was already taken... by Mr. White!

Blanchette slowed her pace on the way down, taking a moment to glance out of the window and find solace in the stillness of the night. Beneath the mellow lights cast onto the hotel grounds, two figures emerged into view. As they drew closer to the light, Blanchette recognised them as her mother and Mr. Blakesley. Agitated gestures passed between them, and the lines on their faces revealed a depth of anger and disdain she had never seen before, instantly shattering the image of the happy couple they had portrayed. A gasp escaped her lips as Mr Blakesley's hand struck her mother, sending her sprawling to the ground. Blanchette watched in disbelief as he turned away, disappearing into the enveloping darkness of the night. Time seemed to stretch endlessly as Blanchette watched her mother cry beneath the falling snow.

Up until that very moment, Blanchette had clung to the belief that Mr. Blakesley was the knight in shining armour her mother longed for. Their relationship seemed to prove that true love existed. Now, confronted with this harsh reality, she had to grapple with the possibility that perhaps there were no prince charmings.

URSULA

DECEMBER 24th 1953, 10:02 AM

Ursula's breath escaped in visible puffs, dissipating into the frigid air as the unforgiving Highlands winter sunk its teeth into her, gnawing like a hungry beast, tearing through the flesh and clutching onto her bones. The scarf around her neck was the only barrier against the icy assault, even if it felt more like an itchy, constricting noose.

Her eyes swept across the motionless, frozen loch that lent the region its name. It seemed to emanate an unsettling glow as a sliver of light broke through the thick grey clouds, and danced across its surface. Behind her, stood the hotel, an imposing figure, a beautiful and elegant beast made of stone. In front of her, the entirety of the highlands, sprawled like an icy wilderness, waiting patiently, eagerly even for whomever dared stray alone. Ursula's eyes continued to scan the area, landing on the imposing silhouette of the mountains. Their rugged peaks cast long shadows in the soft morning light, creating an aura of mystery and grandeur. Like stoic sentinels, they loomed over the land, their presence commanding respect and reverence. Ursula felt a mixture of awe and trepidation as she absorbed their majestic beauty.

As the soft crunch of feet on snow echoed behind Ursula, diverting her attention, a shiver coursed through her body in response to the bitter cold. She turned to see James Wilson walking hastily, catching up to her. His smile was a radiant beacon of warmth in the frigid air. His cousin Lyle, trudged along further behind, his body trembling violently, unable to withstand the cold.

"You like a professional power walker or somethin'?" James grinned.

"I needed the fresh air," Ursula replied.

James searched her eyes for the truth, but she looked away before he could find it. He'd shown himself to be attentive, sensing her slight hesitation in the foyer and making small conversation on the way out to the grounds as they started their search for Blanchette—an obvious attempt to distract her. Ursula, however, simply smiled and ventured ahead of James and his cousin, cautious that he might catch a hint of the whiskey on her breath.

"Is everything alright?" the singer asked her.

"Mhm," Ursula nodded, looking out into the expanse of white. For a moment, she was reminded of the hospital room she'd woken up in after her attack, the sweet, musky scent of Robert's oud mingled with the sterile hospital smell, returning along with that memory.

"I'm sure the girl is fine," James said. "We'll find her."

Finally mustering the courage to look at him, she fell deep into those pools of honey he called eyes, and realised she was utterly smitten. That James was an attractive man was undeniable. However, for Ursula, beauty had never been the sole magnet. She was connecting with something far deeper than his appearance.

"God, it's cold," Lyle mumbled, through gritted teeth, catching up to them.

"Lyle doesn't like to stray too far from his room...or the piano for that matter," James quipped.

"I ain't for this kinda weather, Ms. Dankworth. Gimme a mild spring day any day of the week and you'll have me outdoors all day and night," Lyle said.

James had explained that he'd been travelling across Europe with his cousin Lyle for the past two years. They had performed in Lisbon, Paris, London, Zurich, and now Loch Linnhe, the latter sticking out like a sore thumb. It was a location lacking any of the glamour or notoriety of the other cities, an odd and curious choice of destination, particularly considering James's outgoing personality.

"Maybe we should head back to the hotel," Lyle suggested, wrapping his arms around himself ever more tightly in an attempt to generate more warmth. "If the wind picks up any more, we'll be the ones lost in the snowstorm."

"It is gettin' pretty bad," James agreed. "They might've found her by now. Besides, who'd survive in this weather, and without their coat on?"

It was a thought she'd been having ever since the start of their search and one she'd pushed aside. What if they turned back and the Blakesley girl was still nowhere to be found? The very idea tore at her consciousness, the last thing she would do was willingly add another name to the list. Another failure. Ursula smiled and nodded, acknowledging their concerns, however; it didn't feel right to abandon their search.

"We should keep going just a little longer," Ursula said.

"But—" Lyle started.

"You heard her," James interjected with a scowl.

"I suppose it doesn't snow in Alabama?" Ursula changed the subject and continued walking forth.

"Actually," the singer replied with a sad smile. "November twenty-fourth, nineteen fifty. I remember it clearly, because...it was the day we buried my little sister."

"I'm sorry," she said.

Ursula often thought about the use of the word 'sorry' when consoling someone for the loss of a loved one. It seemed to carry such an awkward weight in such circumstances. What, exactly, was the person 'sorry' for? Death, after all, was an inevitable part of life. There was nothing anyone could do to shield themselves from its inevitable touch. Unfortunately, Ursula had become all too familiar with that apologetic phrase. Uncertain of what else to say to James, but humbled by his willingness to share a moment of vulnerability, Ursula let silence settle between them, punctuated only by the howling winds and her contemplations on mortality.

Noticing something on the snow-covered ground, Ursula came to an abrupt halt and scanned the surrounding area.

"Footprints," James muttered, stopping beside her.

She knelt down and gently traced the footprints with her finger. In between each footprint, were ominous drag marks etched deeply into the soft snow, painting a rather sinister picture.

"Do you see this?" Ursula said, gesturing towards the marks.

James knelt beside her, his brow furrowed and eyes narrowed, joining Ursula in the intense scrutiny of their surroundings. Together, they surveyed the landscape, each movement deliberate and calculated, as they searched for any hidden clue amidst the snow-covered terrain.

"The drag marks stop here," the singer gestured, before turning back to face the direction the footprints came from. "They came from down there."

The Grand Loch Linnhe hotel sat at the centre of one hundred acres of land, its various exits opening to different parts of the expansive grounds. Judging by the footprints, it appeared that whoever had left them likely took a different route than theirs, for they hadn't seen any tracks before now.

"Let's follow them," Ursula suggested, striding forward before James or Lyle could object. She shivered slightly but loosened the scarf around her neck for added comfort as she trailed the footprints. Despite the increasingly violent winds, she could hear James and Lyle following closely behind her, their footsteps crunching through the snow.

The bitter wind and cold stung her eyes, but through the tears, she could just make out the silhouette of a solitary tree, a defiant sentinel amidst nature's onslaught. Like the legendary Spartans, standing firm against armies of thousands, it braved the tempest, its leaves clinging tenaciously to its branches.

"Didn't Finlay say he found the coat near the tree?" James asked, his tone sombre.

Several more footprints adorned the snowy landscape—four sets, to be precise. However, they overlapped for the most part, making it challenging to distinguish three of them from each other. Among them, one set, resembling the initial footprints they had identified, distinctly continued in the direction of their original location. Notably, they could see that the drag marks originated from here.

"What's clear is that there was more than just one person here, at some point within the last twelve hours," Ursula concluded. "The footprints here are very difficult to make out one from the other," Ursula said, kneeling and gesturing to an area where the prints seemed most hurried. "But just there we can see three distinct sets of footprints going back to the hotel."

James walked up to the footprints which continued towards the loch and hovered his foot above them to measure.

"Well, I wear a US size ten, and this footprint seems larger," He turned to his cousin. "Lyle, what size do you wear?"

"About the same," Lyle replied.

As Lyle stepped up to the footprint and lifted his foot to measure, he clumsily lost his footing, falling to the ground with a loud thud as his head bounced off the snow.

"Lyle!" shouted James with concern, rushing to his cousin's side. "Are you alright?"

"Yeah, I'll be fine," Lyle grunted, sitting up and refusing James' help, politely. "One thing I was thinkin'...how can we be sure the prints haven't been here for a while?"

"The snowfall would've covered it," James replied.

"It didn't snow last night," Ursula added.

"It did this mornin'," Lyle countered.

"Yes, but not quite enough. That tells us these tracks are from last night. Look at it, they've almost turned to ice. If they had been made this morning, it'd be softer," Ursula explained. "This gives us more of a timeframe, quite a wide one. I'd need to know when she was last seen to try and narrow it down."

"Still, it doesn't guarantee these belong to the girl," Lyle said.

He was right, of course. Even if the Blakesley girl had wandered out of the hotel at night, those footprints could have belonged to anyone. Ursula might have strolled through them herself, for all she could remember. There may not have been any foul play at all, and she hoped fervently that this was the case. She wanted it to be nothing more than a simple case of a momentarily missing girl.

"Let's walk back towards the Loch," Ursula replied. "Retrace our steps and make sure we didn't miss anything. We probably won't be able to stay out much longer anyway. We'll need to make our way back to the hotel soon."

"Have you done this before?" James Wilson shouted over the winds, as they made their way back to where they'd initially spotted the footprints. "You seem very sure of what you're doing."

Ursula offered a faint smile, her head tilted slightly as she pondered how to address the question. Would they believe her if she revealed her ex-husband was a detective, and that she had played a crucial role in solving numerous cases alongside him? She wondered how James would react, considering her timid and indecisive demeanour in the foyer earlier that morning, hardly what one would expect from a seasoned detective. Then again, she wasn't one. While Ursula had contributed significantly to resolving several cases, Robert would likely have closed them even without her help.

"Don't tell me you're a cop?" Lyle Wilson asked, reading into her silence.

"Not quite, but my ex-husband, Robert, was a detective. I was his assistant," she replied.

"A detective?" James said. "Like James Bond?"

"We didn't indulge in quite as many Martinis," Ursula retorted with a smile. *At least, not then.*

The singer paused, his eyes widening with realisation.

"Wait? Ursula? As in...Ursula Doyle? Your husband was Robert Doyle?" James Wilson asked, surprised.

"You've heard of him?" Ursula replied, unable to hide her surprise at James's familiarity with Robert. Then again, Robert was a prominent figure, having handled some of the biggest cases in the last decade. With numerous articles written about the son of a viscount turned detective, his reputation preceded him. The attention garnered was not solely due to his lineage; Robert's exceptional skills made him stand out in his field, possibly the best. With Ursula by his side, they had successfully solved every case that came their way. All except one.

"Did you ever catch The Anchor?" Lyle asked, his voice now brimming with enthusiasm. "We read about it in the papers back home. They were sayin' it was a Jack the Ripper copycat. Is it true the police pretended to arrest him?"

Ursula would have preferred not to discuss the case. It haunted her thoughts every day and plagued her dreams every night with the faces of the victims. Dubbed the Anchor Ripper, it marked the beginning of the end of her relationship with Robert. Her pregnancy and reluctant motherhood forced Robert to divide his attention between caring for little Lucía in Ursula's mental absence and investigating the case. Part of him held Ursula accountable for his inability to solve it, though he never explicitly said so. While Ursula could pinpoint several moments that led to the downfall of their marriage, the catalyst was the day the case was taken away from him. The tipping point came with an article in the Daily Herald.

"Look at this," Robert said one morning, tossing a newspaper onto the kitchen table.

'Uncovering the Truth: Doyles Role in the Daring Anchor Ripper Escape From Justice'.

Based on insider information from the Metropolitan Police, it appears that the investigation into the murders contained several deficiencies that ultimately enabled the killer to elude capture. Furthermore, the source claims that Robert Doyle and his spouse were never sought out for aid in the matter and that their unauthorised actions resulted in further casualties.

It was a scathing article, meticulously crafted to absolve the Metropolitan Police and the Police Commissioner of any culpability. With four additional murders, they needed a scapegoat, and the detective and his wife fit the bill. Since then, the love they once shared slowly disintegrated, replaced by bitterness and suspicion. It was here that Ursula learned the fragility of the heart, akin to fine china, but unlike the latter, rarely handled with care.

"We never solved it," Ursula said to Lyle, averting her gaze as memories of those years threatened to engulf her.

"I read that he carved an anchor in the bodies of his victims," Lyle persisted. "Is it true?"

"How about," the singer interrupted, sensing her unease. "We carry on without bringing any of that up? Gives me the heebie-jeebies."

Ursula acknowledged him with gratitude and made a conscious effort to push away thoughts of her failures in that case. Dwelling on them only invited a tidal wave of guilt, which was partly why she had turned to drink. Before that, each morning had been a haunting reminder, the faces of the victims forever etched in her mind: *Mary Lou Pearce, Kelly McDonald, Elizabeth Eddowes, Ann Stride, Jane Nichols, Catherine Chapman, Ada Millwood.* They had all been someone's mother, sister, or daughter... all lost and denied justice due to her inadequacies.

"Yes, let's," she said before taking the lead so that neither man could see her wipe a tear.

As they pressed on, Ursula felt her footsteps grow heavier, weighed down by an unexplainable sense of dread. Her throat tightened as if invisible hands were slowly closing around it, suffocating her. The air itself seemed to carry an ominous chill as if it were trying to deliver a message of foreboding. With James and Lyle flanking her on either side, mirroring her cautious vigil, Ursula meticulously scanned the vast grounds ahead. Each step felt like a battle against the relentless, biting winds, their attempts to shield themselves from the unforgiving cold, futile.

Her unease intensified, a nagging sensation gnawing at her insides. She halted abruptly. Before her lay a well-worn wooden spinning top. Picking it up, Ursula furrowed her brow, her disquiet deepening with each passing moment. Upon closer inspection, she noticed several scrapes and marks marring its surface, along with a small letter 'T' engraved on one side.

"What is that?" James said, diverting her attention from the spinning top, gesturing towards an odd mound of snow that seemed entirely out of place amidst the pristine landscape. Adjacent to this unusual heap of snow, a patch of earth displayed withered grass, creating a stark contrast—an aberration in the natural setting. An instinctive chill crept down her spine as they approached the mound, her trepidation growing with each step, uncertain of what she might uncover.

She looked around at James and Lyle, noting the identical expressions of concern and dread mirrored on their faces. Her heart raced, each beat resonating louder than the howling wind. As they reached the mound, she felt her pulse pounding in her ears. Kneeling beside it, Ursula could discern strands of blond hair peeking out from beneath the snow.

Ursula stretched out her hand, her fingers quivering with fear and sorrow. It was as if the very air around her was heavy with the weight of impending tragedy. James, sensing her distress, gently held her wrist, offering silent support amidst the desolation and she felt a sudden rush of warmth and reassurance from his touch. A brief respite in the face of tragedy.

Summoning all her strength, Ursula took a deep breath. With a shaking hand, she began to brush away the snow, each movement revealing more of the lifeless form hidden beneath. The dread intensified with every flake she cleared, the truth emerging from the cold, unforgiving grasp of winter. The sight Ursula uncovered was as harrowing as it was devastating. James, standing beside her, took a step back, and Lyle, behind them, found the scene so distressing that he covered his face with his hands and turned away.

Ursula, despite having seen several dead bodies in various states, couldn't help but shed a silent tear as she kneeled in front of Blanchette's lifeless body.

BLANCHETTE

December 23rd 1953, 19:54

Blanchette found herself engulfed in a whirlwind of stairs, portraits, and busts as she wandered aimlessly, attempting to process everything she'd seen. Her feet carried her forward, oblivious to their destination. When she finally focused on her surroundings, she realised she was standing in the deserted foyer. Uncertain of her next move, Blanchette sank onto the bottom step, seeking solace and a moment to gather her scattered thoughts.

She'd often heard her mother discussing the concept of people wearing masks in public, not in the literal sense, but figuratively. According to her, these metaphorical masks served as shields against the harsh and often unjustified judgements of others. However, her mother also elaborated that the masks had another purpose: to shield the world from witnessing the true nature of individuals who understood that their actions were better kept concealed. The disdain and vitriol Blanchette witnessed during the altercation between her mother and Mr Blakesley made it evident that her mother wore a mask not only in public but also in private. Prior to this incident, Blanchette had never perceived any imperfections in the way they treated each other; their disagreements seemed no different than those of any ordinary couple.

Mr and Mrs White certainly wore their masks with an eloquence akin to guests at a masquerade ball. Their connection felt so genuine to Blanchette that she could never have fathomed it was a mere act. Beneath the well-executed performance she had mistaken for love, lay a bed of lies. Under the covers, they concealed their extramarital affairs, which also happened to be homosexual liaisons.

How could she have been so stupid? Those fleeting glances from Hachem towards their table hadn't been meant for her; they were directed at Mr. White! Here she was, lost in a fantasy, while he was eyeing someone else. Blanchette couldn't have felt any more embarrassed if she tried. They were probably laughing at her expense! She felt anger colouring her cheeks as she wondered if her mother had been aware of Mr and Mrs White's abnormality. Knowing her mother's strong disapproval of such inclinations, Blanchette was convinced that she would not have shared a table with them if she'd suspected the truth.

"Awright, lassie," came a tender voice.

Raising her eyes from contemplation, Blanchette found Aonghus, the hotel cook, standing before her. She greeted him with a warm smile. Aonghus had been a fixture at the hotel for as long as she could remember, consistently showing kindness to Blanchette. He never hesitated to offer her generous portions of Christmas pudding, always accompanied by an extra serving of brandy sauce, knowing it was a particular favourite of hers.

Blanchette shrugged.

Taking a seat beside her, Aonghus stretched his stiff leg, a lingering reminder of his time as a soldier in the Great War. Despite his wartime experiences, he carried himself with an air of resilience, unlike the sombre demeanour often seen in other veterans Blanchette had encountered. Aonghus rarely spoke of his injuries, but his connection with her father, who'd been eighteen years old during the Great War, was undeniable. Against hotel policy, which was clear about fraternisation between guests and staff, they would stay up late, sharing stories over bottles of scotch until the early hours of the morning.

"What's got you all upset?" he asked, looking at her through kind blue eyes.

"I saw something..." she hesitated. "Only I promised not to say anything...but it upset me."

"Ah, I see," Aonghus said leaning back on the stairs. "If you promised to keep it a secret, then maybe you should."

"But it's a lie! Why can't people just be honest!"

"Are your reasons for wanting to tell someone about this secret honest?"

The flush in her cheeks deepened, although this time it was due to embarrassment. The cook had a way of making people think deeply about their actions without showing any judgement.

"If the secret could cause harm," Aonghus continued. "For example, if it has the potential of placing someone in danger, then by all means, tell someone about it. But if you want to tell people, because it upsets you, then perhaps you have some thinking to do. Namely, the consequences revealing it could have on those involved."

"Why do adults get to lie all the time?" came Blanchette's frustrated reply.

The cook paused for a few moments before speaking. "I've often thought that lies are like grapefruits. A lie, like the grapefruit, is bittersweet. Its outer appearance promises a sweet, refreshing taste, much like the façade of a lie. The person offering the grapefruit, that is the lie, hopes you focus on its outward appearance. However, the problem arises when you bite into it or stumble upon it, and it reveals itself for what it truly is: a sour grapefruit. I understand how you feel. Deceit is bitter, but quite often, knowing the truth can taste far more tart."

Aonghus rose to his feet, then turned back to her with a smile.

"Christmas Eve tomorrow and I'm up at the crack of dawn. Did I tell you I perfected my Christmas pudding recipe?"

Blanchette smiled in return and shook her head.

"Ah, you'll love it!"

"I'm already salivating just thinking about it," Blanchette remarked.

The cook whistled a merry Christmas tune as he exited the foyer, bringing a smile to her face. However, her happiness was fleeting as she remembered everything that had transpired, and realised she would soon have to return to her room. There, her curmudgeon of a step-brother would likely be engaged in one of his mysterious, in-depth conversations with his stuffed toy.

Blanchette had always found his attachment to the toy unsettling. He wasn't that much younger than her and while she was ready for marriage, Uriah was still hiding in his room, treating a stuffed animal as if it were a real person. He had even gone so far as to name it, though he only uttered the name 'Zeke' when he thought no one was around. Blanchette had caught glimpses of this peculiar behaviour on the several occasions she had taken to spying on him. Uriah rarely let it out of his sight, finding comfort in its presence and staunchly refused to let anyone clean it, despite it becoming dirty and smelly.

Weary of seeing Uriah with the toy in its dilapidated state, Blanchette's mother instructed the maids to wash and repair it as best they could. However, Uriah reacted with an unprecedented tantrum, unlike anything Blanchette had ever witnessed. His screams of rage were so intense that she feared he might strain his vocal cords. Perhaps, had he known that even Blanchette hadn't seen as much kindness from her mother before, he may have been appreciative of her actions. Instead, the only thing Uriah offered in return was several hundreds of pounds worth of broken china.

"It's very dear to him," Mr Blakesley explained, helping to pick up the broken china resulting from his son's outburst.

"I understand," her mother lied, the tautness of her face betraying her true feelings.

"No, I don't think you do," Mr. Blakesley remarked.

Her mother raised her eyebrows, affronted by his response.

"Everyone in this room has experienced loss—" she argued.

"Uriah has lost *a mother*," Mr Blakesley interrupted. "That's something that *no one* in this room can understand," Mr. Blakesley continued, without breaking eye contact. "The toy was her last birthday gift to him. He doesn't want it washed or mended; he wants it to remain as he remembers her."

That conversation raised a few questions that Blanchette hadn't considered before. Firstly, who was Uriah's mother, and secondly, how did she die? Mr. Blakesley had always been reticent to speak about her or anything relating to his life before entering theirs. The only detail Blanchette knew was that he had served in the same regiment as her father. Their bond had been so strong that he'd entrusted Mr Blakesley with delivering a farewell letter to his wife should anything happen to him. Beyond that, Mr. Blakesley's life before meeting them remained an enigma.

A chilly breeze bit at her cheeks, snapping Blanchette out of her thoughts. She had become so immersed in contemplation that she hadn't even realised she'd moved from the foyer. Taking a brief moment to orient herself, she looked around and was met by nothing but dark stone walls. Frowning, she tried to figure out where she'd walked to and suddenly realised she must be in the basement.

The stern hotel manager had always warned about the hazards of entering the basement, cautioning children about loose stones on the ceiling and walls. Despite this, Lucy Wellesley, who fancied herself as adventurous as D'Artagnan, disregarded the warnings and ventured into the depths below. When Blanchette later spoke to Lucy, she recounted an encounter with a ghost lurking in the shadows of the basement. While Blanchette dismissed such tales, she couldn't ignore the whispers of other guests who claimed to have heard eerie sounds emanating from the basement at night.

Her thoughts lingering on Lucy's experience, she felt a shiver cascade through her spine, urging her to head back upstairs, but as she turned to leave, she heard it—an unmistakable grunt echoing through the silent basement. Her heart racing with a mixture of fear and intrigue, Blanchette descended towards the noise. The stale scent of dust filled her nostrils, and each step seemed to amplify the silence, punctuated only by the faint echo of her footsteps. She placed a trembling hand on the cold, damp stone walls, feeling the slimy humidity cling to her skin. Dread coiled within her as she hesitated, torn between the urge to retreat and the curiosity pulling her deeper into the basement. The musty odour of decay filled the air, and the sound of dripping water reverberated in the dimly lit corridor, intensifying her unease. Despite her instincts urging her to turn back, Blanchette couldn't shake the feeling of curiosity that compelled her to press on.

Clonk!

Blanchette stifled a small squeak, quickly covering her mouth to prevent herself from screaming. That noise wasn't a grunt – someone was there, moving around in the darkness. Could it possibly be a ghost? The sound of her heart pounding in fast, rhythmic beats resonated so loudly that she feared she might faint from the adrenaline rush. Every instinct urged Blanchette to return upstairs, but her morbid curiosity subdued her fears, compelling her towards the end of the hallway. There, a door loomed, seemingly staring at her with unseen eyes. Approaching the door, she felt a fresh breeze, unsettling the large, cascading, old and unused chandeliers that hung loosely from the ceiling. They swayed in a grotesque dance, casting eerie, dancing shadows.

Summoning her courage, she outstretched her hand, hesitant but determined to confront what lay behind the door. She took a sharp breath, steeling herself for what awaited her.

"Hello?" she called, waiting for a response from something she wasn't even certain was there. With a trembling hand, Blanchette twisted the doorknob and held her breath.

It was locked.

Pressing her ear against the door, she heard the grunt once more – someone was undoubtedly on the other side. Her stomach churned into knots, fear refusing to be quelled. Blanchette attempted to turn the doorknob again.

Nothing. Locked.

"May I help you, Miss?"

Blanchette let out a shrill scream, her heart skipping a beat as she turned to find Ophelia, the cantankerous hotel manager, standing behind her. Despite her short stature, in the dim light and under these eerie circumstances, Ophelia seemed to tower over Blanchette. The hotel manager approached her with deliberate slowness, heightening the sense of intimidation.

"May I help you?" Ophelia repeated.

Though her face was shrouded in the basement's shadows, the severity of her tone made it clear that Blanchette was in trouble. The dozen keys hanging from her waist jingled ominously, their outlines resembling blades in the dim light. Instinctively, Blanchette retreated until her back was pressed against the door, the coldness of it sending another shiver down her spine. Ophelia's gaze seethed with anger, her eyes a tempest of fury. The hotel manager stopped inches from Blanchette, and their eyes locked in a silent yet palpable standoff.

"May I help you?" Ophelia said. Each word spoken seemed laced with a different threat.

"No...I....I got lost. Wasn't paying attention and..." she stammered.

"And?" Ophelia pressed.

"I thought I heard voices from behind that door."

"Impossible."

"I'm certain—"

"You cannot be certain of something that's impossible," Ophelia said, this time with far more venom. "If I were you, I'd return to your room. You seem to be stumbling into things you shouldn't tonight."

Blanchette's throat tightened as she swallowed hard, the weight of Ms. Clyde's words sinking in. She must have found out about her encounter with Mr. and Mrs. White. Panic gnawed at her insides. With a sinking feeling in her chest, Blanchette knew she was in for a world of trouble when her mother inevitably heard about this.

"Is there anything else I can do for you, Miss?" Ophelia asked.

"No," Blanchette replied, edging away from the door. "But I am certain I heard something—"

"You are a petulant child," Ophelia said. "Every year a new story. Trouble becomes you, Miss Darlow. You are the boy who cried wolf and you must be weary because at the end of the story, the wolf does come," Ophelia paused and took a step away from her. "You heard nothing. Do you know why you heard nothing? Because *I* am the only person with a key to that room, and that room has been locked for years. The only way someone could be behind that door is if I put them there. Are you insinuating that I locked someone against their will?"

"No, of course not..."

"Then it is settled. You heard *nothing*."

Blanchette nodded, shot past Ms Clyde and ran up the stairs. Upon reaching the ground floor landing, she could have sworn she heard the locks turning and faint sounds suggesting the presence of a guest no one knew existed.

THERON

December 24th 1953, 10:05 AM

"Blanchette!"

Theron Blakesley's call pierced the frozen atmosphere, only to be met with an unanswered echo. Beside him, his wife, Maude, kept her eyes fixed on the ground, her lower lip quivering. Whether from the cold or fear, Theron couldn't discern. Maude had always been exceptionally reserved, her displayed emotions carefully considered and sparing. It therefore surprised Theron to see her so visibly affected by her daughter's disappearance.

Neither of them shared a particularly close relationship with their children. While Theron understood the reasons behind his struggle to connect with Uriah, grasping Maude's emotional barrier towards her daughter was more challenging. Perhaps, the emotional distance was a common outcome for those who frequently delegated the upbringing of their children to maids and nannies. Theron, hailing from a modest background, adhered to the belief that it took a village to raise a child.

Maude's relationship with her own mother was notably cold; their conversations resembled those between two long-lost third cousins rather than a mother and daughter. How could one be a good mother if they hadn't experienced the love of one? On the contrary, Theron did not share the same excuse. Despite their lack of economic or social status, his parents provided an upbringing brimming with love and laughter. Theron should have known how to be a good parent because he had been raised by the epitome of good parenting.

Theron reached for his wife's hand, attempting to offer comfort, but she slipped away from him without uttering a word. Given his actions the previous night and the more pressing issue of Blanchette's disappearance, he refrained from taking offence. He felt a stirring within his loins as his mind wandered to Ms. Dankworth and the night they'd shared. Theron wished he could've mustered a modicum of guilt, but he'd never been faithful to Maude, a fact of which she was well aware.

This trip to Loch Linnhe had been envisioned as a chance to breathe life back into their marriage—a union teetering on the brink of collapse due to his numerous infidelities. Yet, even in the face of emotional calamity, Theron found himself unable to resist temptation. The anger and disappointment that brewed within him were palpable. He understood that a fleeting lapse in judgement could unravel everything he had painstakingly built. He'd spent so much time preventing Uriah from destabilising their home and had overlooked the damage his actions could inflict.

The realisation that he and Maude couldn't bridge their differences even in the face of dire circumstances saddened him. While most couples found solace and support in each other's arms during challenging times, Theron and Maude remained distant. Their absence of affection for each other had always cast a shadow over their relationship—a sombre reality, he was certain, they would be unable to escape. Their differing social class and perspectives on life was a persistent source of tension. Another divide that he knew could never be bridged. No matter how hard he tried, he couldn't summon the kind of love she needed and if she were honest, she would admit to also falling short in reaching the depths of emotion they both needed to connect. Their marriage was like a field of flowers lacking the vivid hues to bring it to life.

"Blanchette!" he heard Maude scream.

Maude's call snapped him back to the daunting task at hand. He'd lost track of how long they'd been searching for Blanchette; once they passed the hotel gardens, the world transformed into a vast, white canvas where time seemed inconsequential. Theron continued to call into the void, more out of obligation than the belief that Blanchette was out there. She'd always been a troublesome girl, and her propensity for disappearing acts had only grown with age, perhaps in another futile attempt to gain her mother's attention. Theron sighed and squinted through the fast-falling snow, spotting three figures in the distance beyond the sturdy solitary tree. It appeared to be Ms. Dankworth, the singer, and the pianist.

A faint smile touched his lips as his mind conjured memories of his night with Ms. Dankworth. He felt a tingling sensation at his fingertips, and the sweet scent of lavender from her perfume seemed to envelop his senses once more as if she were standing right before him. No one had ever stirred such feelings within him. Most of his past encounters had been mere transactions, driven by financial gain or the allure of wealth he could extract from his partners. He had hoped for something deeper with Maude and yearned to fall in love with her, but life seldom unfolds as planned.

He redirected his thoughts to the ongoing search, the weight of exhaustion burdening his feet like bricks. Each step Theron took seemed like an exercise in enduring torment. It forced him to contemplate the likelihood of someone surviving in such brutal weather overnight. Blanchette, despite her flaws, was an astute girl. Theron couldn't imagine her willingly discarding her coat. This wasn't her first time in Loch Linnhe, she knew how fierce the weather could get.

"Maybe we should go back," the groundskeeper said as the winds started to pick up.

"No!" Maude exclaimed. "I am not going back until I find my daughter."

His eyes shifted to the groundskeeper walking a few paces ahead. He hadn't uttered a single word since they began the search. Any attempt to speak with him had been met with monosyllabic responses. Theron couldn't shake the feeling that he wasn't even looking, as if he knew it was a fruitless exercise. He remained silent for a few moments glancing from Finlay to his wife, feigning contemplation on the matter, though the decision was quite clear. They had to continue. The winds were strengthening and visibility was deteriorating, but what if Blanchette was a stone's throw away? Still, there was the grim possibility that they might lose their way if they stayed out too long.

"We should carry on," Theron shouted over the wind.

"There's a storm coming! We might not make it back!" Finlay replied.

Theron gazed up at the roiling grey clouds, a lone snowflake landing on the tip of his nose. There was no way Theron would abandon the search. With their relationship already hanging by a thread, self-preservation outweighed common sense in this instance. If the liaison from the previous night hadn't already been the culminating incident spelling the end of their marriage, going against her wishes now would certainly seal that fate. Theron had accepted the impossibility of loving her; at the very least, he could feign support.

When he'd arrived at her doorstep with Uriah in tow, his initial Lokian plan was to woo her, even if it demanded considerable patience. Theron had always excelled at charming and persuading women, but Maude was different. Her marriage to Lieutenant Kenneth Darlow had left her emotionally drained, which meant he had to work twice as hard to break her defences. Her bitter perspective on love made sense. Kenneth had had no interest in Maude, he'd married her because his wealth allowed and because he'd been a close friend of her family. Maude had been no more than a commodity, wedded to the most advantageous suitor, irrespective of their hidden secrets. Once Theron understood this, unlocking the chains around her heart came easy.

Things seemed idyllic, at first. Maude was younger than the average widow he tended to go for and far more vibrant. Unfortunately, things did not take long to sour. Her family, in particular, were detestable. They embodied an elitist mindset and openly sympathised with the *'plight of the German people,'* effectively expressing support for the Nazis. Such conversations grated on Theron, whose great-grandfather was a Jewish immigrant. Inevitably, it caused countless arguments, every one of them augmenting his growing disdain for Maude and her family. He knew even then that the best thing to do was to try and find a way to bridge the chasm before it became too wide, but instead, he sought refuge in the beds of other women. One evening, after one of his escapades, Maude made it glaringly evident that she was well aware of his dalliances.

"Did I ever tell you about my aunt Grace?" she had asked him as they were getting ready for bed.

"No," Theron replied.

"Aunt Grace was one of the happiest people I ever met. But, you see, that joy I thought I saw was nothing but a porcelain mask, a smokescreen to hide her sadness. Her marriage was troubled, we had no idea. One day, out of the blue, her husband left and that porcelain mask of hers slipped and shattered. She was unable to hide that sadness any longer. Aunt Grace longed for nothing more than to be loved," Maude had turned to him, her stare intense. "That's all she ever wanted. Love. She sought it until she could bear the loneliness no more. They saw her as damaged goods. In her forties, with three children...suitors were scarce. No one wanted to be with a divorcee. Not in our circles, anyhow.

One day she woke up and decided she couldn't bear the agony of being alone. She was found washed up against the shores soon after," Maude explained.

"That's heartbreaking," Theron replied, perplexed about why she was telling him that story.

"When I married Kenneth, it didn't take me long to realise who and what he was. But I vowed never to be alone. Never to be an Aunt Grace. I see what happens to women of a certain age, and how people look at them as if they were rotten fruit. When a marriage ends it is the woman who was lacklustre, the woman who couldn't satisfy the husband, the woman who was unable to provide what he needed. It is never the man that's at fault, no matter how treacherous they are," Maude continued. "At least Kenneth was smart enough to keep his activities away from the mouths of rumour mongers."

"Maude, I–" Theron had tried to defend himself, more so out of habit than any real sense of hurt.

"I need you to be more like Kenneth, okay darling? People are starting to talk."

In the months preceding Christmas, their relationship had shown signs of improvement. The journey to Loch Linnhe was intended to solidify their newfound happiness, yet it only underscored the growing distance between them. Perhaps this realisation had subconsciously pushed him into Ms Dankworth's arms. The writing was on the wall, and he found himself in need of an escape plan in the form of yet another lonely, vulnerable and financially stable woman to seduce.

The snowfall intensified as they pressed on, shouting Blanchette's name into the swirling white, only to have it swallowed almost instantly by the storm. Theron raised his hands to shield his face from the relentless wind, which had now decided to unleash its fury, creating an eerie, haunting howl that reverberated off the nearby mountains.

In the distance, three figures clustered around something on the ground captured his attention. Was that still Ms. Dankworth? A nervous tinge overtook him. What were they standing over? Their fervent discussion suggested a significant discovery, and moments later, they abruptly turned and sprinted back towards the hotel. Perhaps, fearing the harsh weather, they had decided to end their search.

"We have to head back!" Finlay shouted over the winds.

Theron was thankful to the groundskeeper for this.

"Not without my daughter!" Maude replied and without warning ran away from them, screaming her daughter's name as she did so.

He frowned, and shook his head, frustrated. It was almost as if Maude didn't know her own daughter! This was typical Blanchette behaviour. Theron was certain she'd be waiting for them as soon as they arrived.

"Honey!" Theron said, screaming after her. "Come back! Oh, for Christ's sake!"

Theron rushed after Maude, battling the howling winds and the snow that threatened to engulf them. In a matter of seconds, the snowstorm's fury intensified and rendered the world around him a formless void. He called after Maude as the white tempest threatened to make him a victim of nature's wrath.

"Maude!" he screamed.

Theron raised his arms to protect himself from the flakes that struck his face. They were beginning to feel more like icy blades. Their sting was so harsh he struggled to keep his eyes open or discern his path forward. Eventually, he caught up with Maude, who stood lost and helpless against nature's merciless grip.

"Theron...I—" she said.

"We need to go back to the hotel, Maude!"

"I can't leave her here!"

The tone of her voice was not confrontational but rather pleading. Theron had little time to dwell on it before a muffled scream reached their ears. Through the white haze, the silhouettes of Finlay and another man emerged.

"Mr. Blakesley!" they called. "Mrs. Blakesley!"

"Here!" Theron replied, covering his face to keep away the spitting snow.

The singer emerged, snow-covered, his black curls topped with a blanket of white. His eyes conveyed an unspoken message to Theron before turning to Maude.

"Mrs. Blakesley," he began solemnly. "You need to come back to the hotel."

"Did you find her?" Maude's optimism was palpable for a fleeting moment until she caught the singer's sombre expression.

"Honey, let's go back before the storm gets worse!" Theron yelled above the roaring winds.

"Did you find her?" Maude repeated, ignoring Theron and moving closer to the singer.

James Wilson shifted uncomfortably, exchanging a look with Theron. He had seen that expression countless times during the war on the faces of those who had lost friends in the trenches.

"Maude—" Theron began, but she moved away from him before he could finish.

"Did you *find* her?"

"Ma'am—" James started.

Maude collapsed to her knees, her silence more crushing than any words Theron had ever heard. As he looked up to meet the singer's eyes, they conveyed the devastating truth: Blanchette was dead.

FINLAY

December 23rd 1953, 19:42

Finlay Muir sat perched on the hotel steps, peering into the darkness and mist that enshrouded the building. A chilly gust of wind extinguished the cigarette between his lips, eliciting a shudder. Annoyed, he ran his calloused hands through his hair, seeking to restore the order the wind had destroyed. Disorder had always irked him, a trait ingrained in him for as long as he could remember. His dad may have been a drunk, but he was an orderly drunk. Failure to keep things in their rightful place had resulted in one too many beatings, leaving scars as proof.

The war had provided a welcome reprieve from his father's tyranny. Instead of breaking him, as the Great War had done to his father, Finlay emerged stronger and more resolute in his ideas. Overall, the Second World War only served to amplify aspects of his personality that were already present, affording him a sense of structure and purpose while granting an escape route from the life he would have otherwise led in Orkney.

Though he loved the sea, the life of a fisherman held little appeal; it was all Orkney could offer him, that or the vinegar factory. Finlay wanted more for himself than to stink of salt water and fish or vinegar; his true ambition lay in painting. His first visit to the National Gallery in London had served as confirmation of this. He remembered standing rooted to the spot for hours, utterly entranced by Edvard Munch's *'The Scream.'* The chaotic whirl of colours within the frame seemed to come alive, each stroke undulating like a hypnotic dance, beckoning him into the vortex of reds, blues, and yellows. The anguished central figure mirrored the turmoil within Finlay. Much like the figure, he too had stifled silent screams and yearned to find a voice, to break free and echo through the halls of history.

Finlay's life had been a symphony of muted pain, finding only temporary release during the war. Memories of the trenches, muddy and infested with rats, flooded his mind. Amidst that maelstrom of thoughts, the blank stare of a young soldier he'd killed stood firm—the first of many. If circumstances had been different, it could have been him lying there motionless. Closing his eyes, Finlay recalled the sudden rush of adrenaline that coursed through him, standing over the dead soldier. That power was his opium, just as addictive and destructive as any drug, and equally perilous.

Then, as if in the throes of an out-of-body experience, Finlay witnessed two spectral figures materialise from the shroud of night's mist, contorted in a manner reminiscent of Edvard Munch's haunting painting. Among them stood his own likeness and that of the first soldier he'd killed. Finlay's muscles tensed involuntarily as he watched his spectral counterpart press the barrel of a rifle against the trembling form of the German soldier. Ignoring the pleas for mercy, Finlay's apparition pulled the trigger, the echo of the shot reverberating through the fog. The German soldier's ghostly form crumpled to the ground in an instant.

The contorted visage of Finlay turned to face him, its hands framing its ghostly countenance, mimicking the tormented figure in Munch's masterpiece. Slowly, it opened its gaping mouth, emitting a silent scream that seemed to pierce through the very fabric of reality. Finlay's gaze lingered on the spot where the apparitions had stood mere moments before, as he lifted the cigarette to his lips, the ember casting an eerie glow in the mist-laden darkness.

"Can I have a light?" said a soft voice.

He turned to see Ms Dankworth, the alluring guest he'd picked up from the station earlier that day, making her way gingerly down the stairs. The lingering scent of freshly picked lavender trailed after her, evoking a sense of familiarity he'd often encountered during his time in London.

"Aye," he responded, acknowledging her presence.

With a practised flick, Finlay ignited his Sheppard lighter and offered it to Ursula, a silent invitation in the dim room. The soft click of the lighter echoed, accompanied by the faint crackle of the igniting rope. His gaze lingered on Ursula as she savoured the first drag of her cigarette, her lips tracing delicate wisps of smoke. Entranced by her beauty and vulnerability, Finlay edged closer, drawn by an irresistible allure. Just then, he caught a whiff of alcohol mingling with the smoke, and a twinge of disappointment crept in. Few things turned him off more than a woman overindulging in drink, knowing it often complicated matters.

The hotel door swung open, revealing Ophelia, standing in the doorway, momentarily shrouded in darkness. Finlay's stomach tightened as he watched her take in the scene before her, noting that it may have appeared far more intimate than it was.

"Good evening, Ms Dankworth," Ophelia Clyde said stiffly.

Without uttering a word, Ms. Dankworth turned to Ophelia before stumbling into the enveloping darkness. Finlay Muir watched her struggle to maintain her balance, a fleeting impulse to follow tugging at him. Yet, he knew better than to act on it. Resisting the urge, he turned away, ascending the stairs in an attempt to avoid Ophelia's gaze. However, before he could evade her completely, she seized his wrist, halting him in his tracks.

"This is a place of work," she reprimanded.

"I know," he whispered in response.

"Do you? I took you in because I owed it to your mother. Don't make me have to think again," she continued.

"I wasn't doing anything," Finlay said defensively.

"You think I don't know what you get up to? Stay away from our guests! Have your way with the poor kitchen maids as you please. But keep your distance from our guests. Or I'll be forced to make a call, do you understand?"

Anger surged within Finlay as he grappled with his disdain for Ophelia and her holier-than-thou demeanour. Despite begrudgingly acknowledging her past acts of generosity—offering him shelter and employment as a favour to his mother—their relationship remained steeped in mutual animosity. Although technically his aunt, the familial bond between them was tenuous at best, marred by stark differences and a lack of genuine affection. Finlay had grown up with his mother's scathing descriptions of Ophelia, painting her as a woman consumed by her own self-importance. Over a year ago, after finding himself entangled in trouble in Edinburgh, Finlay sought refuge. Reluctantly, Ophelia agreed to take him in as a groundskeeper. Despite finding the hotel devoid of soul and the work monotonous, it was an ideal place to lay low.

"You should be more thankful," Ophelia continued.

Finlay had become accustomed to her snide remarks and veiled threats and often took the high road. On this occasion, given the insincerity in her tone, he decided to hit back.

"Don't pretend to be a saint. I'm only here to help ye with your monster."

Ophelia's slap landed without warning, but instead of recoiling, he smiled, a rush of satisfaction flooding him. The pained expression she tried to conceal betrayed the impact of his words, evident in the subtle contortion of her features. He relished the sight. A small victory in their ongoing battle.

The wide doors of the hotel swung open once more, framing the figure of Mr. Blakesley. He strode past without sparing them a glance, followed closely by Mrs. Blakesley, her expression contorted with fury. The intolerable woman chased after her husband, hurling expletives into the night.

Soon, their warring forms disappeared into the darkness, leaving behind only the fading echoes of their argument.

"I've been speaking to Mr and Mrs White," Ophelia said. "They complained about the Blakesley girl. It appears she was listening in behind their door. As you can imagine, they are very disturbed by her behaviour."

The girl, whom Finlay had met for the first time the previous Christmas, embodied the stereotype of those born into privilege—entitled and convinced that the world revolved around their desires. If trouble had a face, it would likely bear a striking resemblance to hers.

"I also found her lurking around in the basement. Please keep an eye on her. Her parents seem unable to," Ophelia requested, glancing out into the darkness.

"Of course," Finlay replied.

Ophelia shot him a final venomous glare before heading back into the hotel. Finlay bided his time, savouring the remnants of his cigarette before re-entering through the staff entrance, which granted direct access to the kitchen. In one secluded corner, trying to discreetly pour a shot of cognac, stood the very person he sought—Silvia McPherson, accompanied as always by the brutish Julia Majewski.

At eighteen, Silvia McPherson exuded the innocence typical of a sheltered small-town girl with a devoutly religious upbringing. Hailing from a family of sheep farmers in a nearby village near Loch Linnhe, Silvia's seasonal employment was vital for her parents to make ends meet. While she may not have been the most strikingly beautiful woman Finlay had ever encountered, she served a purpose and possessed a certain charm. Silvia's petite frame, plump face, and large brown eyes, reminiscent of Bambi, added to the overall aura of innocence that surrounded her.

"Psst!"

Silvia turned around and offered a smile, but her less-than-friendly friend, Julia Majewski, rolled her eyes at the sight of him. A summer misunderstanding between them had escalated more than necessary. Fortunately, Julia had the sense to keep quiet about it, but she had been a constant annoyance ever since, acting as a barrier between him and Silvia. With a significant age gap of a decade, Julia had taken on a quasi-maternal role in Silvia's life. As a result, Finlay found himself thwarted by Julia's constant presence, leaving him with fewer opportunities to be alone with Silvia.

"You busy?" he asked.

"Christmas Eve tomorrow," she replied, reading his intentions. "Need to be up early."

Hamish Mackenzie hurried into the kitchen, interrupting their conversation, his eyes puffy and red. He grabbed a bottle of wine from the table before turning to acknowledge their presence.

"Up for a game of cards tonight, Fin? Me and the yanks about to get started," he asked.

"Only if Silvia breaks my heart by rejecting my company," Finlay quipped.

"Ah, Silv! Don't do that to the poor lad," Hamish chimed in with a forced smile.

"Ms Clyde will be angry if we are not up early tomorrow," Julia interjected firmly.

Aonghus, the cook, came whistling into the kitchen, a perpetual smile etched on his face.

"You joining us for a game of cards, Aonghus?"

"Aren't you happy with all the money you won from me last time? I'm bankrupt," he joked. "As soon as I finish a few bits around the kitchen, I'll make my way."

"It is late," Julia emphasised, looking at Silvia. "Tomorrow is a busy day, we should get an early night."

"Busy? There's five guests," snarled Finlay, losing his charm for a fraction of a second before going down on one knee to try and recoup the moment. "Please, Silvia? Just ten minutes of yer time?"

Silvia's eyes shifted from Finlay to Julia, who stood with her arms crossed, fully aware of the decision her friend was about to make. Finlay wore a forlorn expression, resembling a sad puppy as if attempting to tug at her sympathy.

"Ah Julia," Aonghus said with a smile. "Young love, let them enjoy it while they can. I have a special vodka somewhere here we can drink while they go and do whatever it is young lovers do."

The cook winked mischievously at Finlay, hooked his arm around Julia's and pulled her away from Silvia.

"Only ten minutes," Silvia said, giving in.

Finlay smiled at Aonghus, offering a slight nod of gratitude. The cook radiated warmth and friendliness, effortlessly connecting with everyone around him. Aonghus possessed a keen understanding of timing and discernment, knowing precisely what to say and to whom. Since Finlay's arrival, Aonghus had often acted as a mediator in various conflicts, with even Ophelia occasionally seeking his counsel.

Leaving a concerned Julia behind, Finlay and Silvia exited the kitchens and ventured into the hotel grounds, their footsteps echoing against the frozen path. They passed the gardens, where the cherub fountain stood eerily still in the winter chill. In the warmer months, Finlay and Silvia had made a habit of slipping out of the hotel nearly every night, finding solace beneath the solitary tree in the fields as they gazed up at the stars. However, Finlay had grown bored with the routine and attempted to steer Silvia towards more adventurous endeavours. Yet, her timidity proved to be a barrier, as any endeavour beyond cuddling remained elusive.

To make matters worse, she frequently cited Bible scriptures emphasising the significance of *"fleeing from sexual immorality"* and reminded him that *"God would judge the sexually immoral and adulterous."* Nevertheless, despite this, Finlay had succeeded in stealing a kiss or two during those summer nights. Recently, Silvia had even permitted him to cup her breast in his hand. Finlay was convinced that she was on the verge of giving in; it seemed only a matter of time. Whether she wanted to or not.

Reaching the tree, Finlay settled onto the blanket of snow and gestured to the spot beside him. Silvia shivered as she took a seat next to him, promptly resting her head on his shoulder. This was the usual dance—they initiated contact and then pretended ignorance when the situation reached a point of no return. Finlay inhaled the crisp air, savouring the sweet scent of her hair. After a few quiet moments, he gently lifted her chin with his index finger, bringing her face closer to his, and leaned in for a kiss.

"What if someone sees us?" she murmured, pulling away.

"What about it? Besides, you heard what Aonghus said, let them do as young lovers do," Finlay replied, drawing Silvia closer. "You smell good."

"Do I?" Silvia giggled.

"Aye," he inhaled her scent. "Heavenly."

Before Silvia could respond, Finlay kissed her lips again.

"We said only ten minutes," Silvia mumbled between kisses.

"Mhm."

She moaned with pleasure as his tongue danced with hers, succumbing to his desires. He began unbuttoning her coat, dismissing her feeble protests and the chill in the air.

"We should head back," she suggested, pushing his hand away.

Silvia giggled, attempting to fasten her coat, but Finlay grasped her wrist, pulling her closer again. She was powerless in his arms, unable to resist. They always were. He slid his hand between her legs, rubbing them against her underwear.

"Stop," Silvia muttered.

He ignored her.

"Stop!" she insisted, pushing away from him.

"Am sorry, I got carried away," Finlay feigned remorse. "Just kisses, then?"

Finlay felt her submit as soon as he pulled her close and started kissing her neck. He placed his hands under her dress once more.

"Finlay, no..."

"Come on, you want it..."

"No-"

Finlay forced Silvia to the ground, her body pinned beneath his before she could even attempt to rise. He held her hands back, meeting her once innocent eyes, now clouded with fear. A surge of adrenaline washed over Finlay, reminiscent of the first time he had taken a life. In Silvia's eyes, he saw the same inevitability he had seen in the German soldier. She struggled, kicking and screaming until Finlay withdrew a switchblade from his pocket and pressed it against her neck. Silvia fell silent instantly. It was a familiar scene—the struggle, the resistance. But most eventually complied. Julia had. It was always easier that way.

"Finlay, stop! Please...no!"

"Shut up! You want it!" he replied. "I know you do. Why would you come out here with me if you didn't?"

He unbuckled his belt with a smile, which faded as he felt something smack the back of his head. The searing pain was followed by a thunderous kick to his shin.

"Shit!" he exclaimed and looked up to see Blanchette standing over him.

Silvia moved away from him, crawling on the ground, trembling, seemingly unable to stand due to the weakness induced by fear. She sat there, silently crying, uncertain about what to do next. There was no time to dwell on that now; he turned his attention to Blanchette.

"Ms. Clyde told me to look for you, seems you have been a naughty girl tonight," Finlay muttered and launched himself at the girl. She skillfully dodged him, and unfortunately slipped on the snow in the process, giving Finlay the advantage. He loomed over her, ready to pick her up, but just as he was about to do so, she swiftly wrapped her mouth around his shin and bit into it as hard as she could. Finlay howled in pain, forced to release his grip on the girl.

"Get help!" Blanchette yelled to Silvia.

Finlay watched Silvia scramble to her feet and run back towards the hotel. Realising that she was alone, Blanchette attempted to do the same, but Finlay grabbed her by her coat, trapping her.

"Where do you think you going?" he asked.

The girl turned and spat in his face, momentarily blinding him. He reached out with one hand, attempting to grab hold of her, but she was too swift, slipping out of her coat and evading his grasp. Finlay wiped the spit from his eyes, his vision clearing as he faced Blanchette. They both breathed heavily, tension crackling in the air, poised for action.

"You've heard what the Whites are up to behind closed doors? Do you think that's the story they'll tell? Have you seen what's in the basement? So many tales tonight, huh? Who'll believe you?"

Blanchette looked like she was about to explode, but then, perhaps thinking better of it, she turned and sprinted away. Anger surged through him in distorted waves, reminiscent of the central figure in Edvard Munch's painting. All he yearned for was to release his own scream to the world, as he had done in the past. Taking a deep breath, he attempted to calm himself. Maintaining levelheadedness was crucial if he was to navigate this predicament.

Considering his past, he knew his aunt would believe the girl, even if he was certain Silvia wouldn't dare speak against him. Her reputation and job were at stake, that alone would keep her quiet, just as it had Julia. Even if Ophelia believed the girl, there was nothing she could do to him. It was in her best interest to try and make the Blakesley girl appear troublesome.

He trembled with anger, realising he still clutched the girl's coat in his hand. Quickly, he dropped it to the floor, knowing that returning to the hotel with it would raise more questions than he was comfortable answering. He needed to pretend none of this happened. Clutching at his leg, he rubbed the area where Blanchette had dug her teeth in and wrestled with the implications of what had just occurred. He'd always been so careful, but now with the troublesome girl out there, who knew how things could escalate? Taking another deep breath, he ran his calloused hands through his hair, seeking to restore order to the tousled strands. The situation was a mess, and there was nothing he hated more than chaos. Yet, he might be forced to rectify it. Composing himself, Finlay began scanning the grounds for Blanchette.

URSULA

December 24th 1953, 10:46 AM

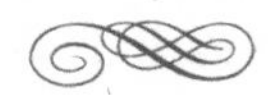

If death was an inescapable anguish, then the loss of a loved one was even more profound, and when that loved one was a child, it left an indelible mark on the soul—an unyielding weight of grief. When that child was your own, there was no well deep enough, no chasm wide enough to contain the sorrow a parent felt.

Since the loss of her daughter, Ursula's life had grown as challenging to navigate as a pool full of debris. The pain she experienced was so intense, so torturous that moving forward without carrying those scars felt impossible. At least she had her whiskey. Ursula wondered what Maude Blakesley would turn to.

Everyone turned to something.

Blanchette's body lay still, the light in her eyes extinguished as she gazed up at the old dilapidated ceiling of the small room her cadaver had been taken to. If not for the telltale blue hue of her lips and the pallor of her skin, one might have mistaken her for being awake. However, the sombre truth was that the girl would never wake, breathe, or smile again.

Ursula drew closer to Blanchette, scrutinising every visible inch of her skin. Bruises on the girl's face suggested she had been involved in a physical altercation, a conclusion supported by the state of her clothes. The dress bore stains of dirt and snow, with a ripped shoulder strap that hinted at forceful yanking—evident in the loose, jagged threads. Ursula also observed the absence of tights or socks, despite the fact that she was wearing shoes. It struck Ursula as extremely odd for someone to choose to forgo these items of clothing in the current weather conditions.

The constant murmuring behind her, momentarily caused her to look away from Blanchette and towards the pianist. Lyle sat there, eyes closed, engaged in a silent prayer. He had maintained that position, communing with God, since their return to the hotel. With head bowed and hands clasped together, he avoided eye contact with the lifeless body. Ursula wished she could have shared his unwavering faith in God, but her struggle to find meaning in Lucía's death kept her at a distance from her faith. Besides, Ursula didn't need God to explain what had happened; it was painfully evident. Blanchette had been murdered.

The room's door swung open, unveiling the Blakesleys, accompanied by James, Ophelia, and the groundskeeper. Maude Blakesley stood dead-still, her gaze locked on her daughter's bruised face. At that moment, Ursula saw a flash of something cross her eyes and disappear. Mr Blakesley placed a hand on her shoulder and attempted to guide

Maude towards Blanchette's lifeless form, but it was met with fearful resistance.

Everyone present remained silent, their heads bowed, almost apologetic for intruding in such a private moment. Maude Blakesley found her resolve and walked over to the body, extending a trembling hand as if to touch Blanchette's countenance. Yet, before making contact, she recoiled, turning away and burying her face in her husband's shoulder.

Ursula shifted her gaze from Maude and Theron Blakesley towards the window, where sheets of snow now whipped against the glass panes, distorting the world outside into a chaotic, white blur. She couldn't help but wonder whether the tumultuous dance of nature seemed to be mourning the death of a child.

"Perhaps, we should give Mr and Mrs Blakesley some time with her," Ursula suggested to the others, who silently agreed.

As soon as she closed the door behind her, Ursula turned her attention to the hotel manager. She observed a departure from the customary scowl that usually traced the woman's brow. In its place, there were lines of concern and even a hint of unease. Ophelia's trembling eyes and tightly clenched fists indicated some sort of inner turmoil that she seemed to be trying to hide from them.

"Is there anywhere else we could go?" Ursula asked.

The hotel manager nodded, slowly, her mind still distant. "The rest of the guests and staff have gathered in the library."

The library was situated on the ground floor, behind the stairs. It exuded an opulent charm, suffused with the rich tones of polished mahogany that adorned towering bookshelves and grand tables. Every piece of furniture seemed to breathe the heritage of time, carrying the weight of countless stories. The shelves, ornately carved and meticulously arranged, displayed rows of ancient books, leather-bound and gilded in gold leaf, preserving the wisdom of ages. The scent of burning incense wafted through the air, carrying an essence of solemnity, mingling with the faint fragrance of aged books and wood. Ursula could not help but feel a sense of tranquillity, which was a welcome respite from everything she had experienced.

The hushed conversations among the guests and staff were punctuated by the palpable weight of tragic news swiftly spreading. In a corner of the library, the kitchen maids and the awkward waiter sat, almost swallowed whole by the large high-backed leather chairs. The waiter remained so still as to appear paralyzed in time, but when he looked up, haunting eyes revealed the turmoil within. Meanwhile, Mr. and Mrs. White huddled with their friends, heads together as if holding a covenant. Across the room, Aonghus, the cook, stood with his back towards the group, his eyes firmly fixed on the snowstorm and wintry gales outside.

Ophelia cleared her throat, a sound that resonated through the library, signalling their entrance. All eyes were fixated on her, the air charged with anticipation as guests and staff alike awaited confirmation of the news, their breaths caught in a collective held suspense. Ursula's gaze swept across the room, realising that the revelation about to unfold would alter each person irrevocably. Blanchette's horrifying and untimely end would cast a shadow over every one of them, a burden carried in diverse and individual ways. The spectre of her tragic fate would linger, forever haunting not just this Christmas but all the future ones to come. Her name, once vibrant and alive, would gradually morph into nothing more than a story, shared in hushed tones, a sombre reminder of a Christmas stained by sorrow. A tragic narrative woven into the fabric of their collective memory.

"Unfortunately," Ophelia started, her voice severe. "Blanchette has passed away."

The room filled with audible gasps as Ophelia's confirmation sank in. Ariel and Ndeshi's faces reflected shared concern as they embraced, while beside them, Mr White and Hachem exchanged soft words that only they could hear. Hamish, no longer frozen with shock, broke down in tears, shaking inconsolably, a familiar sight to anyone who had experienced the loss of someone very dear to them. The kitchen maids, Silvia and Julia, surrounded him, and they were joined by Aonghus, the cook, who stood surprisingly composed as he consoled the young waiter. In the face of heart-wrenching news, he proved to be a pillar of strength.

"Does anyone know what happened?" Mr. White inquired.

"It's too early to say," Ophelia retorted.

"How terrible this must all be for the Blakesleys," Ariel White remarked, her eyes seeming lost in thought.

"Did you contact the police?" Ursula asked the hotel manager.

"Yes, they said it may be a day or two before they can get to us. The roads are completely blocked," she replied, then took a more hushed tone. "I gave them the list of names of everyone staying at the hotel. Since you checked in under the surname Doyle they asked if the Ursula Doyle had any relation to Robert Doyle, the detective."

Ursula's eyes scanned the room. Ophelia's attempt to keep this part of the conversation private had failed. Every gaze in the room was fixed upon them.

"Force of habit," she said and stopped to consider her words and the consequences they would have when she replied. Finally, she said it. "Yes, Robert Doyle was my husband,"

There was a long pause, broken by Oliver White.

"You're Ursula Doyle of Doyle and Doyle Detectives?" Mr. White asked, unable to mask his surprise.

"I use my maiden name now. Dankworth. But yes, that would be correct," Ursula responded meekly.

"That being the case," Ophelia interjected. "They have asked if you could lead the investigation until such time that they can get to us?"

Ursula allowed herself a moment of solemn reflection. As morbid as it might sound to anyone but her, or perhaps her ex-husband Robert, she had felt a small flame ignite within her during the search for Blanchette. That flame burned brighter as she examined the motionless body for potential clues. In essence, Ursula had already initiated the investigation, but agreeing to lead it presented an entirely different challenge. Firstly, she had never led one before; she had overseen aspects of some, always under Robert's careful supervision. Secondly, the last time she threw herself headfirst into an investigation, she failed resoundingly. The outcome was the murder of four more women, the names of whom weighed heavily on her conscience. She was not willing to add a fifth to that haunting list.

"I'm not sure I'm the right person for this," Ursula said finally.

"Very well," Ophelia replied with a slight bow of her head. "I'll let them know."

"Ms Dankworth," the singer said, turning to her, his tone serious. "There's no one better placed than you to help that girl find justice. Imagine that was your daughter. How would you feel if the only person able to help, refused?"

Ursula locked eyes with the singer, a glare met with his unwavering resolve. How could she convey to him that the desire to help find the culprit clashed with her paralysing fear of failure? How could she admit that, beyond that fear, the looming spectre of her struggle to distance herself from the numerous bottles of whiskey she had brought might hinder a successful investigation? A frustrated sigh escaped Ursula's lips.

"Wait," Ursula called after Ophelia. "Tell them, I'll do it."

"I'll call them now," Ophelia replied before leaving the room.

Something within Ursula stirred and shifted. Her back straightened, and her brain snapped into action as fragments of everything she had seen and heard that morning came flooded back. Nervousness coursed through her, causing her palms to sweat and her nostrils to clog up with the humid smell of fog. It felt as though she were in the alleyway again, her assailant hiding in the mist, waiting to strike. To dispel the eerie sensation, she closed her eyes, took a deep breath, and instantly felt the mist clear.

When she opened her eyes, the clarity revealed each guest and staff member more vividly than ever before. The two kitchen maids stood out — the young one, Silvia, rubbing nervously at her neck, and the other, Julia Majewski, staring daggers at the groundskeeper, Finlay Muir. Mr and Mrs White were in silent contemplation, their two friends with their own concerns — Ndeshi casting a doubtful glance at Ariel, and Hachem gripping a book so tightly that his knuckles had almost turned white.

The waiter, Hamish, remained broken, though now no longer wailing. The cook stood still, a bastion of calmness. Lyle, like a troubled ghost, remained quiet, as he had been since finding the body. And then there was James, the singer, whose words had spurred her to step forward. Could his charm be hiding something sinister? The air seemed to thicken with tension as Ursula scrutinised each individual, her determination tinged with a newfound awareness of the complexities surrounding her.

She could not, of course, overlook Mr and Mrs Blakesley. As sad as it was to contemplate when such murders occurred, the first course of action was to examine those closest to the victim. Ursula, however, would tread with utmost care. It was a delicate time for the family, and as a grieving mother herself, the last thing she wanted to do was inflict any more emotional harm upon another grieving mother.

"From this moment forward," Ursula said, addressing everyone in the room. "You are all considered suspects in the murder of Blanchette Darlow."

HACHEM

December 23rd 1953, 22:15

Hachem lay in bed, observing the rhythmic rise and fall of Oliver's chest as he slept. The faint smile on his face suggested to Hachem that he was at peace in a sea of dreams. Burdened as he was by the evening's events, sleep had become a distant hope for Hachem. For as long as he'd known Oliver, he had possessed the innate ability to leave his troubles behind and focus solely on the present. On the contrary, Hachem didn't believe in deferring contemplation of a problem when it presented itself. He preferred anticipation, fearing that unresolved issues would gnaw at his mind, creating inner turmoil that, unlike Oliver, he could not alleviate without resolution.

Hachem silently rose from the bed and approached the substantial sash window in his room, offering a view of the expansive hotel grounds. Outside, the winds rumbled like a hungry beast stalking the night. Shivering, he reached for his hotel robe, wrapping it around himself, feeling instant warmth. Plucking a chair from the writing desk, he turned it towards the window and settled into the seat, his gaze fixed on the darkness beyond as if he were engrossed in a captivating play. After a while, he shifted his gaze towards his lover's sleeping form. Hachem could have indulged in watching him for hours without growing weary; such was the depth of his passion for Oliver. Yet, it was that intense passion and the fear that something could threaten it that kept Hachem from immersing himself in the world of dreams alongside Oliver.

The only path to peace lay in finding the Blakesley girl and speaking with her. Hachem firmly believed that he could impress upon her the critical need to safeguard their secret. To her, it might be mere gossip, a naughty tale to share with her mother and friends, but for them, it constituted their entire existence. Homosexuality was a criminal offence in Britain, punishable by imprisonment and, worse, social exile. Hachem often wondered what Oliver would choose if his wealth and comfortable life were jeopardised. Would he choose love?

"I do love nothing in the world so well as you — is not that strange?" Hachem whispered, quoting a line from his favourite Shakespearean play, *Much Ado About Nothing*.

Oliver and Ariel had gone to great lengths to conceal the true nature of their relationship with Hachem and Ndeshi. At times, they posed as their servants, other times as business partners, and on this occasion, they portrayed themselves as friends visiting from Africa. Though this wasn't the life he had been promised, the act of sneaking around and living this falsehood seemed preferable to returning to Tangier. The firm rejection from his parents still echoed in his ears, his father's threat to end his life if he ever returned, remained chillingly clear. In hindsight, Hachem acknowledged that he had acted foolishly. Swept off his feet by Oliver's promises of eternal love and a better life, it had prompted him to come out to his family without considering the impact it would have on them. He thought about them often, especially his mother, with whom he'd been very close before his messy departure.

Determined to address the predicament they faced, Hachem strode purposefully towards the door. With a firm grip, he placed his hand on the doorknob, taking a moment to contemplate his decision before finally stepping outside. As he exited the room, he was startled to find Ariel standing directly opposite, outside the room she shared with Ndeshi. Her face bore a stern expression, her eyes devoid of the usual faux charisma she often displayed to those who didn't know her well.

"Hello," she said.

"Hi," Hachem replied.

Their relationship was undeniably turbulent. Ariel, accustomed to having her way, exhibited the characteristics of someone raised in the lap of luxury, where her desires were law. This dynamic extended into their home life, where everything had to align with her wishes, with consequences awaiting any deviation.

While Ariel shared Hachem's fear of their secret being exposed, her response was marked by an excessive caution that bordered on obsession. This meant that Hachem and Oliver had far less time alone than they had hoped for, constantly thwarted by Ariel's relentless vigilance. Even the idea of Hachem and Oliver travelling together was repeatedly dismissed, despite Ndeshi's attempts to intervene. Though their discord was never openly acknowledged, its presence was palpable. In the rare moments when they found themselves alone, the tension hung heavy in the air, impossible to ignore.

Hachem's opinion of Ariel crystallised last summer when the Metropolitan Police called to inquire about a tragic accident involving their gardener, Stanley. They relayed the unfortunate news that he had been run over a few streets away while heading home from work a couple of evenings prior. The driver of the car didn't stop to assist him, nor did they call for help. Initially, Hachem would have considered the incident a tragic accident. However, a few days before his accident, Stanley had unintentionally walked in on Ariel and Ndeshi in the kitchen, catching them off guard in what they believed was a private moment. Outraged by what she perceived as Stanley's disregard for privacy, Ariel promptly dismissed him from his duties. In retaliation, Stanley threatened to expose the scandal involving the Banking Tycoon's Wife and her Mistress to the newspapers.

"Odd," Hachem remarked to Oliver after the police had finished their questioning.

"What is?" Oliver replied, feigning detachment.

"The accident."

"Karma exists," Oliver said, before adding. "I'll make sure his wife and children are well taken care of."

They were later informed that Stanley had suffered a fractured spine and was unlikely to ever walk again. The suspicion that the accident had been more than a coincidence gnawed at Hachem, keeping him awake for nights on end. However, whenever he attempted to share his concerns with Ndeshi or Oliver, neither seemed willing to entertain his suspicions.

"The best thing you can do," Oliver advised, "is forget about it."

But Hachem couldn't forget. Every day, the memory lingered, and seeing the flash of anger in Ariel's eyes as she looked down at the Blakesley girl reminded him of Stanley and the heavy price he had paid for inadvertently stumbling across their secret entanglement.

"Can't sleep?" Ariel asked him.

"Unfortunately, not."

"You're a dreamer, that's the problem. Head always in the clouds or buried in your books."

"Must be," Hachem replied, forcing a smile.

"Goodnight," Ariel said, about to open her door.

"Do you ever get tired?" Hachem asked before she could disappear inside.

"Tired of what?"

"Pretending," Hachem said.

Ariel sighed, as if weary of the question. "We pretend because we must, not because we want to. There's nothing else I'd rather do than love Ndeshi openly."

"That is not the pretending I meant," Hachem said. "Do you ever get tired of pretending to be a good person?" he clarified. "Because I would find it draining."

Hachem walked away before she could respond, sensing Ariel's eyes drilling into the back of his head. He couldn't help but smile; there were few things he enjoyed more than unsettling her. Descending the spiral staircase to the first floor, he searched for the room number Blanchette had mentioned during their conversation that morning. After a few moments, he found it.

Now that he was standing there, doubt gripped him like a vice. It struck him as an extremely bad idea. What was he doing here? Was he really about to approach a young girl and beg her to keep their secret? A deep sense of uncertainty and embarrassment was embedded inside him. It felt like he was teetering on the edge of a decision with irreversible consequences. Hachem shook his head and decided to abandon this course of action, turning to leave, something towards the end of the corridor caught his eye. It was Blanchette, barefoot and visibly battered. The shock of it jolted him. *Stanley Redding*, he thought. He'd just bumped into Ariel. Coincidence?

"Are you alright? What happened?" he asked, his voice quivering with a mixture of concern and disbelief.

"I'm okay, thanks," Blanchette replied, her battered face holding a mischievous grin that sent chills down his spine. "What are you doing here?"

"I wanted to speak to you about what you saw," Hachem began, his words catching in his throat.

"What about it?" she replied evasively.

"I just wanted to help you understand—" Hachem continued.

"Understand that you're a homosexual?"

Hachem stood taken aback by her bluntness; perhaps this was not the right time—in fact, he was certain it wasn't. He observed her as she stood there, dirty and bruised. Something in her eyes and the way she carried herself transmitted an inner resolve, stubbornness even. At that very moment, Hachem realised that he would not be able to convince Blanchette, no matter what he said. After a few long, uncomfortable moments, Blanchette tried to walk past him. He stretched out a hand and grabbed her wrist. Slowly, she turned to look at him, her swollen eye twitching. Their eyes locked, and time seemed to stand still. Hachem felt a rush of conflicting emotions and thoughts, unsure of how to proceed. Eventually, he released her and moved out of her way, allowing Blanchette to enter her room.

NDESHI

December 24th 1953, 11:32 AM

A profound wave of homesickness washed over Ndeshi, as she looked out across the pale Scottish landscape. Despite having spent several years in Britain, she found herself grappling with an intense longing for her homeland. The sight of snow, so common in this part of the world, brought forth mixed emotions within her. While others reveled in its familiar embrace, reminiscing about past Christmases and cosy moments, Ndeshi couldn't help but feel burdened by its presence. The aftermath of the snowfall, the transition from pristine white to grimy slush and treacherous ice, only added to her sense of unease. Each snowflake seemed to carry with it a reminder of the sacrifices she had made for love—a love kept hidden, challenging to realise in both her native country and her new abode.

Ndeshi looked up at the stone-eyed fountain cherubs, envisioning how lively their display would be during the summer with water playfully sprouting from their mouths into the pool below. In her mind's eye, the hotel bloomed with laughter and vibrant, earthy colours that would have likely made her feel much more at home.

The soft crunch of footsteps in the snow drew Ndeshi's attention to Hachem, who navigated the frosty gardens with his customary companion: a book. His demeanour, as always, was sombre, his shoulders slouched and brows knitted in deep contemplation. Immersed in profound thoughts and the pages of literature, reading served as Hachem's escape from a life he had grown disillusioned with. Ndeshi often found him late at night, surrounded by a haze of cigarette smoke, absorbed in the works of Karl Marx or Friedrich Nietzsche. Even on warm summer evenings, he could be spotted in the garden, a half-empty bottle of Mahia by his side, engrossed in the pages of a Virginia Woolf novel or something similar. Hachem was undeniably intelligent and idealistic, driven by a passionate spirit and a profound love for life. However, like Ndeshi herself, he often followed the whims of his heart rather than the practicalities of the mind.

For a time, they stood side by side, enveloped in a cocoon of quietness, listening to the gentle murmurs of the wind. Ndeshi looked at the book in his hand, *Ulysses*.

"Good read?" she asked him.

"If only I could understand what was happening," Hachem replied with a thin smile before his expression became anguished.

"Did you do it?" she asked him after another moment's silence.

Hachem allowed the question to hang in the air, seemingly satisfied with the uncertainty it sparked within her. Gradually, he shifted his gaze towards Ndeshi, his eyes lost in contemplation. His next question cut even deeper, resonating with the unspoken doubts she had been wrestling with.

"Did *they* do it?"

"Do roosters crow at night?" Ndeshi retorted dismissively.

"If the lights are constantly on, then he may well crow at night!"

"How could you even think that?" Ndeshi glanced away from him, feigning disappointment.

"Do not pretend with me," Hachem said. "Remember Stanley?"

She moved away from him. Of course, she remembered; how could she forget? It had plagued her thoughts for months, but she dismissed it as mere happenstance. Ariel had vehemently denied any connection to Stanley's tragic accident, and Ndeshi saw no cause to doubt her. To entertain such suspicions would mean accepting the unthinkable: that the woman she loved had attempted murder. If true, then she may have attempted again, and maybe even succeeded this time.

"They wouldn't. She's a child," Ndeshi replied, pushing away any sentiment to the contrary.

"*Was* a child," Hachem corrected her and allowed for a pregnant pause before continuing. "You and I, Ndeshi...we are prisoners. The cell they have created for us is tender, but it is a cell. We are more than content to live in it...but make no mistake, they hold the keys to the gilded gates, that you and I have for so long mistaken for a palace when all it is, is a cell."

"The doors are open," Ndeshi replied. "What prison do you know with open doors?"

"The sort that understands the power it has over its prisoners. The kind that understands the power love holds."

Ndeshi's breath quickened with every word Hachem spoke; his words resonated deeply within her. Denying their truth seemed futile. While Ndeshi wasn't as disillusioned as Hachem, occasional "what if" thoughts were starting to surface, prompting her to nudge Ariel towards a decision. Living as they currently were, like undercover agents, was not something Ndeshi wanted to endure any longer. For the past two years, she had been relegated to the roles of friend and servant, rarely a lover. Ndeshi had become something to be enjoyed in secret, Ariel's forbidden fruit. She understood the need for caution, but could not help but feel disappointed by the situation.

The irony didn't escape Ndeshi – she'd left her home, with hopes and dreams that in this promised *white* land she'd be able to live as God made her, however, here, just as in Namibia, those of her sexual inclinations were met with just as much fear and disdain. She had abandoned everything she'd ever known for love, only to be in a foreign land, unable to be one with that love as freely as her soul desired.

"They did not do it," Ndeshi said firmly. "Besides, Ariel told me she saw you leaving your room late last night."

Hachem smirked.

"You think I am capable of such a thing?"

"You call that a denial?" Ndeshi retorted.

"I am offended you would even ask," Hachem said.

"I am offended you would speak such things about the people we love," she spat.

"I love what Oliver cannot give me," Hachem said, looking away into the distance. "We both know they stand to lose if the girl talks. If she doesn't talk, they do not lose."

"Talk to who, Hachem?" Ndeshi asked. "She is a child. Children say things."

"Have you met Mrs Blakesley, the whole of London will know quicker than we can utter the word *homosexual*," he quipped.

"I don't want to—"

"Hello?" came a voice.

Detective Ursula Dankworth interrupted their conversation as she strolled through the gardens towards them with a cigarette between her lips. Smoke danced and intertwined with the chilly air as she exhaled, creating delicate wisps.

"You know," she remarked, joining them, "It's always colder before it snows. Somehow, it's easier to endure right after. I suppose it doesn't snow much in Windhoek or Tangier."

Ndeshi raised an eyebrow, evidently Ms. Dankworth had already started her investigation into the murder.

"Snow in Tanger?" Hachem responded, turning his frown into a smile, almost seamlessly. "That sounds like the sort of book I'd enjoy."

Ndeshi envied the ease with which Hachem could turn his charm on. It was the one thing he and Ariel had in common, not that he would have ever admitted to it.

"I've never ventured beyond Europe, but I've always dreamed of visiting Africa," Detective Dankworth replied.

"If you visit Morocco you must try Mahia, it's a beautiful drink distilled from dates," Hachem replied, bringing his fingers to his lips and emitting a slight smacking sound.

"He drinks a bottle a night, whenever he gets the chance," Ndeshi added.

"I must make a note of it," Detective Dankworth said, taking a notebook from her pocket, before deciding it was best to get right to it. "What brings you to Britain? Business?"

"We're visiting our friends," Hachem said.

"Curious, both consulates have you registered residents since 1951, with a permanent residence in Mayfair. I cross-referenced the address with the guest book, and it matches the registry in the consulates. Strangely, it's the same address given by Mr. and Mrs. White."

Ndeshi rubbed her hands against her arms, seeking warmth amidst the biting chill of the detective's questioning.

"The last dead body," Ndeshi said without looking at Detective Dankworth. "That I saw was of my sister's. Magano. She was ten years older than me, beautiful and smart. One day we open our door to find her battered and bruised...and dead. We never knew what happened to her. Her real father was a wealthy coloniser by the name of Hans von Bismark. I suppose the wife became tired of hearing how much this local girl looked like her husband. But I don't know. We can only speculate. We never got any answers. I was only five years old when Magano was killed. She has appeared in my dreams ever since. But even though I know it's her, I cannot see her face. Can you believe I have forgotten what my sister looked like? I mean, maybe not forgotten, but it's a fading memory, a hair's breadth away, behind a curtain of mist that I cannot reach." Ndeshi turned to the detective woman. "Hearing about that poor girl...it made me see Magano's face clearly for the first time in a very long time, even if only for a moment."

"I am sorry to hear that Ms Nyambe," she replied earnestly. "Am I pronouncing that correctly?" when Ndeshi nodded, the detective continued. "I too lost a sibling. Rodrigo was my best friend. I don't think I've had one since he disappeared. I know what it feels like to lose someone and how the death of others can re-open wounds not fully healed. I have learned to deal with it in my own way. The one thing I have not learned to do is see others go through that pain. Particularly when there may be foul play involved."

"You're certain she was murdered?" Hachem asked, offering Ndeshi a glance.

"Do roosters crow at night?" she asked, with a twinkle in her eye. Only if the light is on. That is to say, I cannot be certain. But, it is my job to make sure I find out and that the crime, if indeed, it happened, does not go unpunished...as the one committed to your sister." Detective Dankworth said, looking at her. "Did you see Blanchette yesterday?"

"There are not many guests," Hachem interjected. "There is a chance we did."

Ms Dankworth turned the pages of her notebook until she found what she was looking for.

"There is an eyewitness that said they saw you leaving breakfast and talking to Blanchette," Ms. Dankworth said to Hachem. "Is this correct?"

"Yes, we exchanged a few words. She was asking me where I was from, that is it."

"In which case," Ms Dankworth retorted. "Mr. Benabid, the answer to my previous question is not that there is a chance you saw Blanchette. The answer is that you *did.* Otherwise, I may think, you are being purposely evasive. Is there a reason why you may be attempting to be evasive?"

"No, of course not," Hachem replied stiffly.

"When was the last time you saw her?"

"After breakfast," Hachem said.

"So you confirm you did not see Blanchette the night of her disappearance?"

"We can confirm this," Ndeshi said.

"Very well," Detective Dankworth scribbled into her notebook and closed it before turning back to them. "It is rather cold, I am going to head back in. If I have any other questions, I'll know where to find you."

She offered a smile and left. Hachem waited until the detective woman had entered the hotel before he spoke.

"We lied to her," Hachem said, rubbing the sides of his temples. "We lied in a police investigation."

"Calm down, imagine what she will think if she sees you like this," Ndeshi said. "Besides, we did not lie. We withheld *some* of the truth,".

"Lied," he repeated through gritted teeth. "Listen to yourself, you even sound like them!"

"So says you!" Ndeshi spat back. "If we told her what happened last night, it would implicate Ariel. I mean, she threatened the girl and a few hours later she's found dead? We cannot tell her what happened."

Hachem offered Ndeshi a wry smile.

"And still you do not see the prison you are in?" he patted her on the back and before leaving, added. "In love's tender cell, we willingly dwell..."

Ndeshi let out a sigh as his footsteps faded into the distance. She gazed at the untouched white expanse of the snow-covered highlands, feeling a knot tighten in her stomach. It wasn't homesickness this time; it was the unsettling doubt that crept in as the walls guarding her love for another began to crack.

URIAH

December 20th 1953, 17:44

Uriah had woken up to a horrifying sight: his mother hanging like fruit from a tree. Ever since that moment, he'd been plagued by the memory of her wide, grey eyes staring at him each morning, as if pleading for help. These haunting images embedded themselves deeply into his soul and persisted in his dreams. The fear of sleep gripped Uriah tightly. Each morning brought with it a sickening sensation in his stomach, an agony he couldn't escape. It became a ritual: waking abruptly, heart racing, stomach churning, followed by bouts of relentless vomiting. It seemed as though his body was trying to purge the profound sadness within him, but the sorrow clung to him like an unwavering companion. Uriah believed that by avoiding sleep, he could evade this distressing ordeal. Yet, occasionally, exhaustion overcame him, and he would reluctantly succumb to slumber, fearing that without dreams, the memory of his mother would slowly fade away.

The days following her death blurred into a painful haze, filled with condolences and fleeting faces offering little solace. Each word of sympathy only served to deepen Uriah's sense of loneliness and despair. He could not have known then, as he knew now, that what he was experiencing was the relentless ache of a heart tearing apart, bit by bit.

Weeks later, a man he knew to be his father, but had only seen in faded photographs, appeared. Uriah's mother had painted a picture of a loving and kind man, but when Uriah finally looked him in the eye, he saw only cold detachment and a sense that his very existence was an inconvenience. The hope he had clung to, that his father would come to save him, was shattered. Instead of bonding with him, his father made arrangements for Uriah to leave, sending him to live with his paternal grandparents in the quiet village of Nomansland in Wiltshire.

His grandparents, Ben and Lucy Blakesley, embraced Uriah warmly, showering him with kindness and generosity. For a time, their care provided a temporary respite from his sorrows. During those peaceful nights, Uriah found solace in dreamless sleep, free from the haunting memories of his mother. However, as time passed, the spectre of her wide eyes returned to haunt his dreams, shattering his peace and bringing back the shadow of fear he thought he'd left behind. Each night, he would awaken abruptly, his pyjamas soaked with sweat, his heart pounding with terror. Uriah would then sit in his bed, his eyes tightly shut, afraid that when he opened them, he'd encounter his mother's ghostly presence.

The void left by his mother's absence fuelled an uncontainable anger within Uriah. Initially recognized as fear, this emotion slowly morphed into something entirely different. This shift marked the genesis of his connection with Zeke, a companion who, like Uriah, sought nothing but acceptance. Though their bond might have seemed peculiar to outsiders, Uriah and Zeke shared an unspoken understanding. Only Zeke could comprehend the depth of his hatred. To everyone else, Uriah was perceived as a naughty, motherless child—a perception he despised. In reality, his hatred extended to everyone and everything in the world for the tragedies he had endured. He hated his father for his indifference, his grandparents for pretending to care, and above all, his mother for abandoning him.

In an attempt to externalise the turmoil within him and alleviate some of the anger and hatred consuming him, Uriah started acting out. Initially, his grandparents dismissed his behaviour as a typical reaction for a child undergoing significant upheaval. However, as Uriah's actions escalated into violence, their justifications began to falter.

"He'll change," his grandmother, Lucy Blakesley said one evening to her husband.

Eavesdropping became Uriah's favourite pastime. Grown-ups rarely spoke the truth around children, at least in his experience. Uriah thirsted for complete understanding. Eavesdropping offered him the knowledge that would have otherwise been denied.

"Change?" His grandad, Ben Blakesley, replied, his voice dripping with fury. "He cut the girl with a knife."

"Child's play gone too far," his grandmother replied.

"What about poor little Jessica? He said she fell down the stairs! But what if the boy did it?"

They had. But in his defence, she'd been making fun of him, calling him an orphan and singing songs about how his mother had killed herself. Things with Lauren, however, had been different. *They* wanted to hurt her.

"This behaviour won't change. It'll get worse, Lucy."

"What do you suggest we do? He's our grandson! Anyway, unless you're planning on kicking the boy out, our hands are tied. There's nothing to be done until Theron comes back," his grandmother said.

"*If* he comes back," Ben Blakesley muttered. "Knowing that son of ours, he probably knew the devil he spawned and left him here for us to deal with."

"Ben!" His wife admonished.

"If a man commits adultery with the wife of his neighbour, both the adulterer and the adulteress shall surely be put to death. Leviticus 20:10" Grandfather Ben said. "She went and hung herself with shame and if our boy doesn't come back from the war, we know why. God's Law."

"Theron is out there putting his life at risk to keep this country safe! How could you talk about him like that?"

"Oh Lucy, stop it! If he didn't make it all up as he is wont to do," his grandfather said. "Then the only reason he would be out there *'putting his life in danger'* is because it was either that or prison!"

Uriah peeked through the open door and saw his grandmother place a hand on her chest in shock. He had the distinct feeling, however, that this was not the first time his grandfather had spoken about his father in such terms.

"How could you even think that Ben?" she said sitting down.

"I love our boy, God knows I do. But he's a thief and a liar. You and I both know what he's been up to. Cares more for money than his own son!"

"I don't want to talk about it, Ben," his grandmother turned away from her husband.

"We have to talk about it someday, Luce. Our son was and is a charlatan and made a living out of swindling vulnerable women. He was bound to get in trouble at some point. God is always watching. And now that a child has been born out of sin, we expect him to be...normal? A child born out of sin is sinful by nature. Theron is my son and despite his ways I love him, Lucy, I do. I want him to come back safe and sound so we can give the boy back and I'll have naught to do with either of them. That is my wish."

That's how Uriah learned that the anger-come-hatred he felt in his heart wasn't wrong. He was born out of sin. He could no more control his behaviour than a ravaging wolf.

Months after the war, Theron, Uriah's father, returned as a decorated soldier, adorned with medals of bravery earned on the battlefield. Despite his accolades, his father remained unimpressed. Within weeks, Uriah's grandfather decided to have Theron leave, taking Uriah with him. Though his grandmother Lucy shed a few tears, there was a palpable sense of relief as she closed the door behind them. Uriah couldn't shake the feeling of being shuffled from one adult to another, unwanted and unclaimed.

For a period, they lived in a cramped bedsit in London, a place more wretched than Uriah had ever experienced. The scent of dampness and mould permeated the air, clinging to his lungs with every breath. Water from the tap ran a sickly brown hue, unfit for consumption. Crumbling, stained walls bore witness to years of neglect, adorned with mould and other signs of decay. In the quiet of the night, the scratching of mice against dilapidated surfaces filled the air, an eerie symphony of their destitution. Some mornings, bold mice would greet him on the table, their tiny eyes seemingly questioning their shared circumstances.

On one dreary evening, Uriah sat engaged in deep conversation with Zeke when the door to the bedsit creaked open, revealing his father. Theron Blakesley stood there, immaculately dressed in his army uniform, a smile spreading across his face as he approached Uriah. Since leaving London, Theron had spent most days ignoring Uriah, lost in self-pity and casting blame upon his son in various ways. Therefore, it unnerved Uriah to see his father beaming and walking with such unexpected effervescence.

"Uriah," his father looked at him with those blank loveless eyes of his. "I am trying to do right by you, and if my plan works, I am sure I'll be able to. But you need to promise me you'll behave, because if you don't. If this goes tits up because of your behaviour, I won't be able to keep you. Your mother is dead. Her family want nothing to do with you and neither do my parents. So, I need you to promise me you won't be strange or naughty or...angry."

Uriah nodded slowly, absorbing the implications of his father's words. It was evident that Theron was referring to his recent unsuccessful attempts to court newly widowed, wealthy socialites. In each of these failed courtships, the women had commented on Uriah's unconventional behaviour, particularly his attachment to Zeke.

One of the women, Mrs. Yates, had two young sons of a similar age to Uriah. They had skin the colour of alabaster and long, curly strawberry-blond hair that bounced when they walked. Uriah couldn't shake the feeling that Mrs. Yates treated them like her own personal porcelain dolls. One morning, the boys woke up to find their hair cut, with the scissors left by their pillow. Despite Uriah vehemently denying any involvement in the unfortunate incident, Mrs Yates was devastated and blamed him, thus ending her fleeting romance with his father.

Theron's anger was palpable, communicated through a prolonged period of icy silence. The absence of his father's voice had been so extended that when it finally resurfaced weeks later, Uriah almost didn't recognise it.

His father's new target was Maude Darlow, widow of Kenneth Darlow, a man whom his father had met during the war. They'd been in the same regiment, saved each other's lives on numerous occasions, and become something akin to brothers. Or at least, that was what his father had muttered constantly under his breath on their journey to Darlow Manor. Uriah did wonder, why, if this were true, he'd need to repeat it as if to not forget.

Disguised as messengers bearing a missive from the late Kenneth Darlow, they made their entrance. Uriah distinctly remembered the moment when he first laid eyes on Maude Darlow—tall, fair, and austere, clad in a flowing black dress. He couldn't help but notice the sternness in her eyes. However, that severity seemed to dissipate as his father, with his charismatic charm, engaged Maude and her daughter Blanchette.

"We saved each other's lives multiple times," his father said, handing over a handwritten letter from Kenneth Darlow to his widow. "He was like the brother I never had. We exchanged letters to give to our family should anything happen to either of us."

Uriah was certain he'd seen a fleeting look of surprise on Maude's face at the mention of the letter before she regained her composure and invited them to stay the night. Throughout the evening, his father entertained them with stories of Lieutenant Kenneth Darlow, some of which Uriah had heard several times before, with slight variations.

Time passed in the Darlow Manor as weeks turned into months and months into years. His father had wedged a new life for them, and Uriah, with the warning of abandonment still lingering in his mind, took great care not to draw attention to himself. Initially, Uriah found solace in this arrangement. Maude was pleasant enough, although he steered clear of her daughter, Blanchette. The girl was an insufferable know-it-all, revelling most when the spotlight was on her. She expected adoration and affection from all. Months transformed into a year, and then two, as their lives continued in this new family dynamic.

If there was ever a time of year when Uriah was most likely to disappoint his father, it was during the Christmas holidays. He couldn't deny his disdain for the season. Everything about it felt artificial and objectionable. Relatives they barely spoke to would show up, couples who seemed to constantly argue pretended to be madly in love, and Blanchette was at her most insufferable.

To compound matters, Maude had a tradition of spending a week in the Scottish Highlands at an old, dreary hotel. Uriah loathed every moment spent there, it was at Loch Linnhe where he had come closest to provoking his father's anger. The journey there was gruelling, and the holiday period felt endless, especially since Uriah had to share a room with his stepsister, Blanchette.

This marked their sixth year undertaking the long and tedious journey from King's Cross Station. Enduring several hours of travel, they finally arrived to a harsh, biting cold that swept through the highlands. Stepping off the train, they were met by Finlay, the surly groundskeeper, his weathered expression seeming to mirror the relentless winds. The gusts were so loud that they had to shout over their howling presence just to converse with each other.

"Mother, can I ride at the front?" Blanchette asked.

"If you must," came Maude's weary.

Uriah found himself wedged between his father and Maude, a heavy silence lingering in the air. It appeared that this year, the excitement of Christmas was confined to his step-sister alone. Holding Zeke tightly against his chest, he sighed as the Grand Loch Linnhe hotel loomed into view.

Upon arrival, Ophelia Clyde, the hotel manager, awaited them in the foyer. Petite and unassuming, Uriah always thought she resembled a smiling toad, albeit with less charm. She guided them to their designated rooms.

"I'm going to take a bath," Blanchette announced once they were settled in their room.

Uriah sighed in relief as the bathroom door closed behind him. This was his first moment of solitude since leaving London. Restlessness from the long journey propelled him downstairs to the dining room. Despite his reservations about Loch Linnhe, one aspect he enjoyed was the live band they hired for the holidays. He descended towards the foyer with mounting enthusiasm, the bands were always friendly, out-of-town sorts with as much passion for music as he had. Uriah inherited his love of music from his mother, who would have gladly spent entire days listening to Bing Crosby, Frank Sinatra, and Billie Holiday.

As Uriah reached the bottom of the stairs, he heard the first keys to *Suite Bergamasque* by Claude Debussy. He entered the dining room and spotted, a chubby, dark-skinned man behind the piano. His head swayed from left to right, captivated by his piano strokes. Noticing Uriah's arrival, he stopped.

"Hello," the piano player said, in a strong American accent. "You like the piano?"

Uriah nodded.

"Do you play?" He asked him.

Uriah nodded again.

"Come."

Uriah had only ever performed in front of his dad, Bernadette, Blanchette, or his piano teacher, Mr. Nikolaev. Mr Nikolaev often praised Uriah's natural talent and even suggested to Theron that he should consider sending Uriah to the prestigious Royal Academy of Music when he was of age.

"Don't be shy. There's no one here. I'll close my eyes," the piano player encouraged with a warm smile.

Double-checking the empty dining room with a quick scan, Uriah proceeded to the stage, gently placing his wolf companion atop the piano before taking his seat beside it. Without hesitation, he began to play Sonata No. 14.

"What's his name?" the pianist asked.

The question surprised Uriah. No one had ever taken the time to look at Zeke as anything other than a stuffed animal.

"Zeke," Uriah whispered with a hint of embarrassment.

"Cool name," he said with a smile. "Pretend, it's just you and Zeke," he placed a guiding hand on Uriah's. "Gentle touch, like a snowflake fallin' on another."

The subtle shift in pressure altered the notes, eliciting a smile from Uriah. Soon, the pianist joined in, playing a few harmonious notes. For a while, it felt as if only Uriah, Zeke, and the music existed... until the pianist unexpectedly rested his hand on Uriah's leg.

"Carry on," he encouraged. "That's beautiful."

Nervous and unsure how to handle the situation, Uriah pressed on, but the trance he'd been in was shattered. His leg twitched involuntarily as he kept his eyes fixed on Zeke, silently pleading for some form of assistance. The applause from the audience echoed through the dining room, abruptly ending the moment and prompting Uriah to leap out of his seat. He turned his gaze towards a tall, black man with honey-coloured eyes standing a few feet away from the stage. Though he wore a smile, his eyes betrayed a hint of something else.

"That was beautiful," the man said. "I'm James Wilson, I'm the singer," he walked closer to the stage. "Perhaps he should join us on the road? What do you think Lyle?"

Uriah descended from the stage, brushing past the singer without a word.

"You forgot something," the singer remarked, holding up Zeke.

Uriah, holding Zeke tightly against his chest, hurriedly exited the dining room, overcome by an unsettling feeling of contamination lingering from Lyle's touch. Climbing the stairs to the landing outside his room, he was consumed by a sense of powerlessness and fear. The sensation of grime clinging to him made him recoil; he despised feeling so vulnerable and tainted as if something unclean had seeped into his very being. Sitting on the floor, his breaths laboured and his mind racing, he struggled to regain his composure, finding solace in the familiar embrace of his stuffed wolf, Zeke. Amidst the tumult of emotions, voices began to clamour in his mind. Turning to look into Zeke's eyes...almost instantly, the voices quieted. All except Zeke's.

URSULA

December 24th 1953, 13:23

M*ary Lou Pearce. Kelly McDonald. Elizabeth Eddowes. Ann Stride. Jane Nichols. Catherine Chapman. Ada Millwood.* These names had become a haunting mantra in Ursula's mind since the lifeless body of Blanchette was discovered. Voices directed tortured screams at her within the dark confines of her mind, yelling the names of the victims whose murders had gone unsolved. *Mary Lou Pearce. Kelly McDonald. Elizabeth Eddowes. Ann Stride. Jane Nichols. Catherine Chapman. Ada Millwood.* The voices repeated *ad nauseam*, their syllables carving a conflicted path within her.

Ursula's hand reached for the glass of Chardonnay, seeking solace in its numbing elixir. Each gulp she took felt like a step towards the light, yet every stride echoed the relentless cadence of those names: *Mary Lou Pearce. Kelly McDonald. Elizabeth Eddowes. Ann Stride. Jane Nichols. Catherine Chapman. Ada Millwood.* They bore down on her conscience, a weighty reminder of the responsibility she willingly shouldered once again. Failure, as in the Anchor

Ripper case, was a burden she couldn't fathom bearing once more.

Her fingers trembled as she turned the pages of her notebook. Each one, meticulously filled with the names of the victims, narrated a tale of frustration and resilience. As her delicate finger traced the entry for Ann Stride, the subtle variations in her handwriting hinted at moments of exasperation. Yet, interspersed among them, neatly spaced letters betrayed glimpses of wavering hope in her relentless pursuit of solving the case.

Mary Lou Pearce. Kelly McDonald. Elizabeth Eddowes. Ann Stride. Jane Nichols. Catherine Chapman. Ada Millwood.

She glanced at the grilled salmon and vegetables, untouched on her plate, and decided to opt for the Chardonnay instead. It seemed she wasn't alone in her loss of appetite; the other guests, of which admittedly there were few, hadn't even made their way down for lunch. The Blakesley's absence was of course understandable, given that they were still in a state of shock and mourning. However, Mr and Mrs White and their two friends, Hachem Benabed and Ndeshi Nyambe, remained oddly absent, perhaps they were deliberately avoiding her. It was only fair to surmise that Ndeshi and Hachem had shared their encounter with Ursula. Surely they understood that their absence would only serve to raise her suspicions?

Ursula raised her hand, beckoning the despondent waiter. Hamish emerged, still bearing the weight of his sorrow from their earlier encounter in the library. His head hung between hunched shoulders as he made his way slowly towards her table.

"How can I help you, ma'am?" Hamish mumbled so deeply that his words were almost undecipherable.

"Could I have another glass of Chardonnay?" she asked.

"Of course, ma'am."

Ursula felt a profound sense of sorrow for the boy; he appeared as though happiness would elude him indefinitely. Her maternal instincts stirred, compelling her to reach out and offer comfort, to assure him that everything would be alright, that death, though seemingly insurmountable, could be used as a source of strength. She knew from experience that failure to do so could have long-lasting effects. As the boy walked away, a realisation dawned – only a broken heart could render a teenage boy so utterly disconsolate.

"Did you know Blanchette well?" Ursula asked.

Hamish hesitated, his eyes still fixated on the floor, as if looking for something.

"We, er, were friends," Hamish replied meekly.

"Close friends?" Ursula pressed.

"I thought so," the waiter said. "I'm not sure she did, though."

"Why'd you think that?"

"She said as much. Didn't seem to care," his tone was so severely drenched in sadness, it touched Ursula. "I loved her."

"When did you last see her?" Ursula asked.

"Last night after dinner, she was on her way to the second floor," Hamish replied.

"The second floor?" Ursula repeated.

"Aye."

"The Blakesley's rooms are on the first floor," she muttered, more to herself than the boy. "Why would she be going there?"

"I wouldn't be able to tell you," Hamish replied. "Are you still wanting the wine, ma'am?"

"Yes," Ursula replied distractedly, turning the information over in her mind. "Do you know if Mr and Mrs White have come down for lunch?"

"No ma'am," Hamish said before turning away.

The first tenet of sleuthing, as per Robert's teachings, was never to make assumptions. However, on this occasion, Ursula couldn't help but assume that Oliver and Ariel White were avoiding her, due to their conspicuous absence, which again, she assumed had been orchestrated by their acquaintances, whom she had previously interrogated. She'd also felt a very palpable sense of dishonesty lingering in the air when she had questioned Ndeshi and Hachem earlier that morning. The knowledge that Blanchette had been seen going to the second floor, solidified her suspicions. There were no other guests on that floor besides the Whites, Hachem, Ndeshi and herself.

"Hello," James said, sitting down opposite her.

Ursula turned to face the singer and smiled as Hamish returned with her third glass of Chardonnay and promptly left.

"So, you're kinda a big deal then, huh?" he said, returning the smile.

"I wouldn't say so."

"My dad, may he rest in peace, always said there was nothin' more dishonest than false humility," James quipped.

"Any plaudits thrown my way are my ex-husbands. Not mine."

"Well, suppose that were true," the singer replied. "The path to greatness can only be achieved with the help of an even greater partner."

"You're very kind," Ursula said, accepting the compliment.

"So, where do we start?"

"We?"

"Hell, yes! I'd love to help-"

"I'm not sure-" Ursula interrupted.

"Come on! Every great detective needs a sidekick. Holmes and Watson...errr, who else?" James said, struggling to think of another example.

"Nero Wolfe and Archie Goodwin?" Ursula remarked.

"Who?"

"Never read *Fer-de-Lance*?"

"I *'fer'* sure have not!" James joked, causing Ursula to laugh. "You know what I have read though, Batman and his trusted sidekick, Robin. A personal favourite of mine. I kinda think Dankworth and Wilson rings just as good."

Ursula chuckled, a delightful, fuzzy, warmth spreading through her as she found herself captivated by his soft, friendly eyes. Was he trying to chip away at her defences?

Mary Lou Pearce. Kelly McDonald. Elizabeth Eddowes. Ann Stride. Jane Nichols. Catherine Chapman. Ada Millwood.

The haunting names resurfaced, the nauseating cadence, echoing through the dark corridors of her mind once more, prompting Ursula to gracefully take a sip of the Chardonnay. She resisted the temptation to gulp it down, aware that indulging in such a manner might betray more than she was willing to acknowledge.

"Fine," she said, unable to deny herself the pleasure of his company.

"Hell yeah!" James exclaimed.

"But—"

"But...what?"

"Well, everyone is a suspect," Ursula said.

"I see. Well, then shoot!" James Wilson retorted. "Ask me where I was, what I was doin' or...whatever it is detectives ask."

Ursula had encountered a diverse array of suspects in her career, teaching her that the guilty party often lurked where least expected. Though she couldn't fathom James as a potential murderer, she recognised that her attraction to him clouded her judgement. Thus, she needed to conduct a thorough investigation, ensuring she eradicated any unconscious biases that might hinder her progress.

"What time do you usually set up for the evening's entertainment?" Ursula asked as she withdrew a fountain pen from between pages in her notebook.

"Lyle and I will usually rehearse, if you can call it that, just after lunch, so I'd say three o'clock and we'll do that for about an hour."

"That's what you usually do, but is that what you did yesterday?" Ursula inquired.

"Yes, we rehearsed until about four o'clock which gives Silvia and Julia time to reset for dinner. I went back to my room, relaxed, had a shower and then Lyle and I were back here at about six in the evening."

"Did you see Blanchette?"

"Yes, of course, there's not that many guests. Unless they don't come down for breakfast, lunch or dinner, we generally see everyone."

"When was the last time you remember seeing Blanchette?"

"Dinner, which would've been around seven o'clock. The couple with the two foreign friends, Mr and Mrs White, left first, the girl left soon after that and her brother followed not long after. I remember because moments before that Mrs Blakesley had caused a scene, demanding they be served the bottles of wine they brought from home."

"That's rather odd," Ursula commented.

"I guess, but that family is odd. I mean the kid talks to a toy. When I was thirteen I was tryna my darndest to get into places I had no business bein' in!"

"So, you've always been trouble?" Ursula quipped.

"Yes, ma'am! Mischief is my middle name!"

"Now, *that* does have a ring to it. Mischief Wilson," Ursula laughed. "What time did you leave the dining room?" Ursula continued.

"I'm not sure, I remember Hamish left in a hurry after clearing the tables, and that was already past seven o'clock."

"And after all the guests go back to their rooms, what do you do?"

"What I usually do is hang out with the guys. Finlay, Aonghus, Hamish and my cousin. We play cards. Last night was no different. Lyle stayed back a little bit longer. He enjoys playin' more popular music. You know Fats Domino, Ray Charles and the like. I took a shower and then met up with the guys around nine o'clock. We played cards til pretty late."

"Can you confirm who was at the card game?"

"Hamish, Lyle, Aonghus, Julia and of course myself. Finlay tends to join but he and Silvia slipped away for the night. Silvia showed up for like ten seconds and then Julia left with her, which was odd because when we saw the cards she had, it was a Royal flush. Who leaves knowing they have such a strong hand? She would have wiped us clean."

"Not a good poker player?" Ursula asked.

"No, I wear my emotions on my sleeve. Lyle wins enough for the both of us."

"What time did the card game finish?"

"When the bottles of wine were empty. My cousin can't handle more than a glass or two. He's pretty sensitive." James said. "But I would guess, we were all back in our rooms by eleven, maybe a little later. But to be honest, I'm not sure."

"Did you have any interactions with Blanchette? I hear she is quite the character."

"The girls have known her for a few years and they seem to think she's nice enough if a little bit obnoxious. But what teenager isn't, huh? Lyle and I have only been here since April, so this was the first time I met her and we didn't talk at all. I know you may not believe it, but I tend to stay away from guests."

"You're right. I don't believe it," Ursula smiled, making a few more notes and closing her notebook.

"So? Did I pass?"

"It wasn't a test, Mr Wilson."

"You know," he said, grabbing a green bean from her plate. "In your accent, my name even sounds like Watson."

Ursula smiled, unable to maintain a serious face around his energy.

"So," James said confidently. "When do I start?"

URIAH

December 23rd 1953, 19:26

Blanchette's off-key rendition of *'White Christmas'* by Bing Crosby grated on Uriah's ears like nails on a chalkboard. He clenched his teeth, enduring the assault on his musical sensibilities until, finally, Blanchette exited the room, leaving him in blissful silence. Uriah exhaled a sigh of relief, grateful for the respite. If he had to endure her musical shortcomings any longer, the temptation to fling himself out the window might have been too strong. Uriah couldn't help but wonder if his intense dislike of Blanchette fuelled his rejection of everything she did. Conversely, it also created a deep intrigue with regards to everything she did and her sudden departure, certainly did that.

He glanced at the clock on the wall. They had only just returned from dinner not too long ago, and with Blanchette's irksome friends not making the trip to Loch Linnhe this year, she didn't have anywhere to go this late in the evening. Blanchette did, of course, have a penchant for putting on a façade of maturity. At just fifteen, she often pretended to be much older, so Blanchette might have gone to the library to indulge in conversations ill-suited for girls her age.

Uriah turned to face Zeke, his steadfast companion, he too, was curious about where Blanchette might have gone.

"Do you think we should follow?" he asked Zeke.

Despite the torment they had faced, curiosity stifled their longing for a few more moments of peace and quiet. Deciding to act on his inquisitiveness, he swung his legs out of the bed and made his way out of the room, with Zeke in tow. In all honesty, Uriah found a peculiar satisfaction in disturbing Blanchette's peace. It wasn't driven by malice but a sense of retribution. Blanchette often projected an image of virtue, yet behind closed doors, she wielded threats against Uriah, threatening to tattle on him to Maude with lies. The friction between them had resulted in numerous confrontations, during which Uriah had lost his temper once and reacted rashly, playing right into Blanchette's hands. His father's warning came flooding back the moment he'd done it: *you need to promise me you'll behave, because if you don't, if this goes awry because of your behaviour, I won't be able to keep you.*

Uriah walked down the quiet hotel corridors, his gaze drawn to the portraits adorning the walls. The eyes in the frames seemed to follow him with an eerie intensity. Though their expressions remained frozen, their eyes conveyed a range of emotions, from accusatory to curious. These were not mere portraits; they were echoes of the hotel's past, capturing the spirits of former guests who had once traversed these very halls.

"How dare you?!"

He came to an abrupt halt, immediately recognising Maude's voice. Uriah retraced his steps to his parent's room and pressed his ear against the door. From within, he could hear his stepmother's voice, clear as if she were standing right beside him, her tone laced with a mixture of anger and disgust. Uriah had a knack for eavesdropping on conversations he wasn't supposed to hear, which had led him to stumble upon several of their arguments. Without these accidental discoveries, he might have continued to believe in their facade of a happy couple.

"Do what you need to do, but don't embarrass me," Maude thundered between breaths.

A loud bang reverberated against the door, startling Uriah and causing him to trip over his untied shoelaces, landing ungracefully on the floor. Frowning, he quickly tucked the wayward lace into his shoe. His father had often remarked about how pathetic it was that a boy his age didn't know how to tie his shoes, and given how often Uriah tended to trip over them, perhaps his father was right.

"Fuck!" he heard his dad exclaim.

"I'm sorry, I didn't mean to—" Maude began.

"Don't touch me!" his father interjected. Uriah got the impression, he'd been the one who'd collided against the door. "Ken told me all about this side of you... I always wondered whether his love of cock had made him so weak he couldn't defend himself against a woman, but you really are a nutter!"

"I'm sorry," Maude apologised again. "You know I haven't been feeling like myself lately."

"This isn't the first time, Maude. You know Kenneth hated you right?" his father replied. Uriah had been on the receiving end of his father's cruel words far too many times not to be able to recognise the venom in his tone now.

"Don't you dare mention my husband's name," Maude snapped.

"He rarely mentioned yours!" he retorted. "I mean, sometimes... he liked to call some of the boys in the barracks, Miss Maude, if you catch my drift."

"Even bent over he was more of a man than you will ever be!" Maude retorted. "He respected me enough to be discreet about his *abnormality!* But you'd rather embarrass me. I begged you not to make a scene. By all means, bed-hop as much as your cock desires, but do it discreetly...and yet here we are!"

"I have been discreet!" his father replied.

"You call impregnating my cousin discreet?"

The silence hung heavy in the air. Despite his father's constant threats and reminders about the importance of maintaining good behaviour, it was his father's own inability to behave that now jeopardised everything they had.

"Get rid of it," his father replied coldly after a brief pause. "I barely have enough love for the one child I have now. Quit your whining and tell her to get rid of it."

The door swung open, and Uriah, still sprawled on the floor, met his father's eyes. In that brief moment of eye contact, it was evident to his father that Uriah had caught every word of the heated argument. Instead of displaying any hint of remorse, his father maintained eye contact for a beat before turning on his heel and walking away.

"Where are you going?" Maude called after him.

She spotted Uriah on the floor, but more concerned with salvaging her marriage than tending to his feelings, Maude hurried after his father. Uriah felt a sharp pang in his stomach as the weight of his father's words sank in. He wasn't just a child conceived in sin, as his grandfather had asserted, but, bereft of his mother, Uriah was also an unloved one.

Uriah scooped up Zeke from the floor and drifted away in a haze of emotional turmoil. Oblivious to his surroundings, he continued to wander until he collided with an obstacle. Looking up, he found Hamish, the awkward waiter, leaning against the stairs, face buried in his hands, sniffling. When Hamish finally met Uriah's gaze, his eyes were red and puffy.

"Sorry, Mr Blakesley, I shouldn't be here," Hamish said, running down the stairs and out of sight.

He turned back towards his room, musing over the peculiarity of being addressed as *'Mr. Blakesley'* by those older than him. Once again, he came to an abrupt stop at the sound of thunderous footsteps making their way towards him. Pausing at the top of the staircase, he saw his stepsister hurrying down, cheeks flushed, tears streaking down her face. Uriah furrowed his brow—what could have provoked such a reaction from Blanchette? Had she witnessed the explosive argument between their parents, which might have continued elsewhere?

Straining his ears, he heard hushed voices arguing somewhere on the floor above. Intrigued, he made his way towards where Blanchette had emerged from and found Mr and Mrs White engaged in a heated conversation. Their foreign friends, the elegant black woman and the tall caramel-skinned man, were trying to hold them back from each other. Mrs. White, Uriah noticed, was draped in nothing but hotel bed sheets, being touched tenderly by the dark-skinned woman, clearly attempting to calm her. Eventually, she succeeded, and the two women disappeared into one of the rooms together. Mr. White then shifted his gaze towards the adjacent door, where his friend Hachem leaned against the frame, patiently waiting.

"What are we going to do?" Hachem asked Mr White.

"It'll be fine," Mr. White assured, planting a kiss on his lips.

Uriah gasped.

"Oliver," Hachem said, his tone serious. "That mother of hers is a nasty piece of work, I can tell. If the girl says anything, everyone in London will know quicker than we can say the word 'denial'. I have known you long enough to understand who stands to lose if the choice you have is me or your reputation."

"I'll speak to the girl."

"Tonight?"

"Tonight," Mr White confirmed. "Everything will be fine."

"It better be. I can't go back home. They will kill me. You know this, right?" Hachem pressed.

Mr. White surveyed his surroundings with a cautious air, as though a lurking suspicion hinted that someone might be watching. Uriah reacted swiftly, ducking out of sight just in time.

"Let's go inside," he said.

Uriah grappled with the scene he had just witnessed. Mr White had shared a kiss with another man. Could that be what had prompted Blanchette's tearful exit? Stunned, Uriah stood rooted to the spot, his mind racing from one thought to another. Shaking himself out of his daze with a deep, meaningful sigh, he resolved not to retreat to his room again. Instead, he decided to meander through the empty hotel corridors a little while longer.

Allowing his subconscious to lead the way, Uriah found himself drawn back into the recesses of his thoughts. The familiar strains of *Piano Sonata No. 9* drifted to him from the dining hall, prompting a silent exchange of glances with Zeke. The wolf's steady gaze seemed to urge him to follow the music.

Enthralled by the melody, Uriah descended the stairs towards the dining room. As he approached, the figure of the plump pianist came into view, causing his heart to jolt and his knees to tremble with fear. He glanced at Zeke, silently pleading for retreat, but the wolf remained steadfast, urging him forward.

The dining room was devoid of guests except for a solitary woman, whom Uriah had heard referred to as Ms. Dankworth earlier that afternoon. He observed her for a moment—she possessed a pretty face with silky, long brown hair and striking green eyes. Yet, there was a certain emptiness in her gaze, as if the light within had dimmed. Her head swayed on her shoulders, giving the impression of sleepiness, though Uriah suspected it was more likely drunkenness. He had witnessed many adults exhibit such behaviour after a night of drinking, but never had he seen a woman as attractive as her drinking alone. It was a lesson he had learned: adults consumed alcohol in proportion to their troubles.

As the song concluded, Uriah prepared to depart, but just as he turned to leave, the pianist called out to him. His fingers tightened around Zeke, the memory of the man's touch tracing down his thigh vivid in his mind, unfolding before him like a scene. Uriah instinctively recoiled, feeling his throat tighten and an unusual surplus of saliva accumulating in his mouth.

"I..." the man stammered, struggling with his words. "I'm sorry, I didn't mean to... it's just the music, and... I meant no harm."

The piano player extended his hand, offering a conciliatory gesture, and Uriah instinctively flinched.

"Are you going to tell anyone?" the man asked him.

Uriah remained silent, avoiding eye contact with the man and instead fixing his gaze on the intoxicated woman, tuning out whatever else the piano player said. Eventually, getting the gist, the man departed. Feeling tears welling up, Uriah quickly wiped them away before they could fall. Somehow sensing his discomfort, the woman stirred and rose from her chair.

"Are you alright?" she mumbled.

Uriah nodded in response. She offered him a smile and briefly touched his cheek before finishing her wine, grabbing her coat, and exiting the dining room. A surge of anger boiled within Uriah. He despised how the piano player had made him feel. Locking eyes with Zeke, they silently agreed to confront the man head-on. It was a reckless impulse, but Zeke always pushed him towards such actions. That's why he had pushed the girl down the stairs and cut Mrs. Yates' son's hair. Zeke was his only friend, and friends listened to each other, regardless of how foolhardy the advice might be.

Determined, he pushed through the staff-only door at the side of the dining hall, a path he knew led towards their rooms. A narrow, dimly lit corridor greeted him, its oil lamps flickering enough light to prevent him from stepping on scurrying rodents and cockroaches. He continued down the corridor, breathing in the pervasive smell of dampness and mildew that made him think of the bedsit he had shared with his father before they arrived at Darlow Manor.

The faint sounds of a record player, now louder, guided him towards the last room at the end of the corridor, where the walls were at their dampest. Despite his reservations, urged on by Zeke's counsel, Uriah pushed open the door and entered the modest room. It was windowless, with a simple metal-framed bed adorned with thin brown woollen sheets. As he surveyed the room, his eyes fell upon a picture placed on the bedside table. It depicted the pianist and the singer somewhere in the Alps. Beside it lay an envelope, with several images peeking out. Though hesitant, a sense of determination fuelled by Zeke's unwavering gaze encouraged him to investigate further. Uriah extended his hand and gasped as he pulled the images from the envelope.

The pictures revealed naked boys.

He dropped them as if he'd been electrocuted and turned to leave, only to bump into the pianist.

"It ain't what it looks like..." the pianist stammered, anxiety lacing his words.

Uriah attempted to step away, wanting to distance himself, but the pianist grabbed hold of him.

"Look, not a word, okay?" the singer implored with desperation in his eyes. "If James found out... he thinks... I told him I'm better..."

Uriah struggled to break free from the pianist's grasp, but the man tightened his hold around Uriah's waist. With a swift kick to the shin, Uriah attempted to free himself, making a desperate dash for the door. However, the pianist proved faster than expected, enveloping him in a suffocating embrace. Uriah could feel the man's heart pounding against his chest, the rhythmic thud echoing his own racing pulse. As the struggle ensued, Uriah grappled with a daunting choice—yield to this twisted situation or fight harder for his escape. Despite his fear and uncertainty, he turned his head towards Zeke, seeking solace in the steadfast presence of his loyal companion.

URSULA

December 24th 1953, 13:37

Ursula knocked on the door marked two hundred and twenty-one to the sound of James humming a cheerful melody in the background. The door swung open, revealing a grinning Hachem whose smile faded upon spotting them. Ursula's expression briefly flickered into a frown, momentarily surprised to find Hachem behind the door. Swiftly recovering, she masked it with a warm smile before Hachem could discern any hint of her initial confusion.

"Mr Benabid," Ursula said. "I'd like to speak to Mr and Mrs White, and was under the impression this was their room."

"It is," Hachem replied awkwardly. "Oliver, the detective is here. She wants to speak to you," Hachem announced, louder than necessary. Hachem stood looking past Ursula, towards the door opposite, evidently trying his best to avoid making eye contact. Faint nervous shuffling sounds emanated from within the room as they waited, heightening the sense of discomfort.

"Ulysses," Ursula said with a glance at the book in Hachem's hand. "A beautiful book. It was his attempt at retelling the Odyssey, did you know?"

"Yes," Hachem replied simply, his tone making it clear that he had no intention of indulging Ursula in smalltalk. "Oliver?"

Unfortunately, Ursula had been at the end of this behaviour on more than one occasion. It was common for suspects to react far more abruptly than they would otherwise have after being questioned. This was even truer if the line of questioning had touched upon a topic the suspect would have rather left unperturbed.

Mr White's appearance at the door forced Ursula away from her musings and back to the investigation at hand.

"Miss Dankworth," he said with a forced smile. "Sorry to keep you waiting—I had some business to sort out, but I am all yours now. Do come in."

"Thank you," Ursula acknowledged, entering the bedroom.

She glanced around the room and noticed that the bed was still undone—odd. The cleaning was typically done in the morning by the two girls, and there were only four rooms requiring attention due to cancellations. Continuing to survey the room, she observed the absence of personal belongings or any sign that Mrs. White had ever been there. According to the information provided by Ophelia, the Whites and their friends had checked in on the twentieth of December and were scheduled to depart on the second of January. A two-week stay at Loch Linnhe had been planned, making it improbable that Mrs White wouldn't have taken any of her belongings out of her luggage. Yet, Ursula did notice two pairs of male slippers neatly tucked under the writing desk.

"I assume you're here to talk to me about the Blakesley girl?" Mr White inquired.

Hachem walked over and sat at the writing table, his leg shaking nervously as he pretended to read the book.

"Assumptions are dangerous in my field of work but on this occasion, you would be correct," Ursula affirmed.

"And the singer?"

"James is assisting me," Ursula responded.

"Interesting," Oliver White remarked.

"What is?" Ursula questioned.

"A Negro singer turned detective."

The unnecessary remark lingered in the air, but James skillfully maintained his usual affable demeanour, deflecting the barb. The racial undertone of the comment took her by surprise, particularly considering the company he claimed as friends. Ursula's frown deepened, her eyes fleeting to Hachem, now biting his thumbnail, his gaze fixed on the open book without turning a page.

Mr. White's touch of mean-spiritedness stood in stark contrast to the glimpses Ursula had caught of him, exuding a brooding charm reminiscent of Hollywood's leading men, like Montgomery Clift. Redirecting her attention to Oliver, she surveyed the surroundings, noting the absence of female belongings once again.

"There are many things that are interesting, Mr White," Ursula replied, ensuring her eyes were locked with his.

Oliver White retrieved a packet of cigarettes and fidgeted in his pocket for a lighter, before struggling to light the cigarette he'd placed between his lips.

"Would you like some help with that?" James offered.

"No thanks," Oliver replied, finally lighting the cigarette and taking a deep inhale. As the smoke cleared, a somewhat calmer expression replaced the initial tension etched on his face.

Ursula opened her notebook and sifted through the pages, attempting to avoid the names that tended to ignite doubt within her. Unfortunately, she caught a glimpse of the name *Mary Lou Pearce*. She cleared her throat, feeling a moment of doubt creeping in. Another name echoed in her mind—*Kelly McDonald*. She looked up at Mr White's expectant face and felt her body tense.

"I need Mr Benabid to leave," Ursula pressed on.

Hachem stirred in his chair.

"Is it necessary?" Mr White countered, attempting to maintain a façade of composure.

"Is it necessary for him to be here? *Instead* of your wife?" Ursula replied, firm in her request.

Mr. White took another drag of the cigarette, and when he exhaled, it felt to Ursula as though he had directed the smoke towards her deliberately. It was a whimsical act of defiance, typical of a man accustomed to having everything go his way.

"James, could you escort Mr Benabid out of the room?"

The singer did as asked and escorted Hachem out of the room, leaving only the three of them inside. Afterwards, he strolled over to the writing desk and settled into the same chair Hachem had occupied moments before. Ursula kept her gaze fixed on her notebook, taking a few extra moments to survey her surroundings, allowing the silence to linger. It was a tactic she had learned from Robert; silence often heightened tension, serving as a valuable tool for the investigator.

"Mr. White," Ursula resumed, cutting through the mounting discomfort.

"Call me Oliver," he said, attempting a smile.

"Could you tell me where you were yesterday evening?"

"Sure," Mr White said. "I erm, came back to my room and stayed up late with my wife."

"What time would you say you went to sleep?" Ursula inquired.

"Eleven, maybe a tad later. I generally avoid staying up late so I can get up nice and early."

"Did you know Mr and Mrs Blakesley before this trip?" Ursula asked.

"No."

"You had dinner with them one evening," James interjected.

"Yes, we had dinner one evening. Given the lack of guests, we thought it would be a great idea to mingle."

"What did you talk about?" Ursula continued.

"I don't know, the usual when you're getting to know someone," Mr White replied. "Mrs Blakesley commented that she knew who my father was."

"Ms Clyde mentioned you've been coming to Loch Linnhe since you were a child. Is this correct?"

"Yes, although we rarely spent Christmas, it was mainly summer," Mr White replied.

"Do you perchance recall anything unusual about last night or the night you had dinner with Mr and Mrs Blakesley?" Ursula pressed.

"Not particularly," Mr White responded. "The girl was friendly, polite and didn't seem like trouble."

"Didn't seem like trouble? What do you mean by that?" Ursula made a note of his last sentence.

"W—What do you mean, what I mean?" Mr. White stumbled nervously.

"Why would you say the girl didn't look like trouble?" James repeated in her stead.

"It's a turn of phrase."

"Interesting turn of phrase, wouldn't you say?" Ursula remarked.

"What? No!"

"I could take that to mean that she *was* trouble, although she did not seem it," Ursula continued.

"All I mean is, whatever her behaviour might have been, she was just a child. She didn't deserve that end." Mr White trembled, unable to hide his agitation.

"Her *behaviour*?" Ursula arched an eyebrow and leaned into Oliver White. "What of it?"

"Nothing! Nothing of it! I don't mean a thing, alright?" Mr White sprung out of his chair and turned to face the window.

"I see," Ursula said plainly, exchanging glances with James. "I had a brief conversation with Ndeshi and Hachem earlier today, I am sure you are aware."

Mr White nodded.

"There are a couple of things I wanted to clarify. They said they were here visiting, but when I rang both the Moroccan and Namibian consulates, they had them registered as residents in the United Kingdom. The address on file matches the address both you and your wife gave to Ophelia upon checking in. Why would they be registered as residents if they are merely visiting?"

Mr White did not immediately respond.

"They visit often. It is easier for them to enter the country if they can prove they have permanent residence here."

"So if we were to request their passports, we would find regular stamps of entry into the UK? Or would the last stamp have been in 1951?"

Mr. White's face reddened, however, whether out of embarrassment or anger, Ursula knew not.

"What does this have to do with the dead girl?" Mr White asked.

"It has everything to do. If you are unable to provide an honest answer about something this simple, why should I accept that you are being honest about anything?"

"I didn't kill the girl!" he spat.

"I am not insinuating you did. I am insinuating that deception hangs loosely above your head and you are doing nothing to convince me otherwise," Ursula replied. "Do you know where your wife is now, Mr White?"

"I'm not sure...somewhere."

"And I assume, even if I did mention assumptions are not things we should do in my line of work, that wherever your wife is, there will Ndeshi be also."

Oliver turned back around to face her, his arms were crossed and his expression hardened.

"I think you know the answer to that already."

"Indeed." Ursula made a note. "When did you last see the Blakesley girl?"

"I'm not sure, I might have seen her at dinner yesterday,"

"You might have seen her? You don't remember?"

"No," Oliver replied simply.

"That's rather odd," James intervened. "Considerin' there were only four tables taken up by guests. You'd think you'd be able to remember who was in the room. I can confirm that she was there. I can also confirm that your table was the first to leave and that the girl left soon after."

"I don't have to answer you! Just who do you think you are? Did they keep you in the house back in the plantation? Is that why you're such an upstart?" Oliver spat.

"Mr White!" Ursula exclaimed, offended on James' behalf, who remained admirably muted despite this being Mr White's second obscene taunt.

"I might have seen her, I might have not," Mr White repeated stubbornly, turning his back to James.

"Very well. Thank you." Ursula stood up and closed her notebook. "If I have any further questions, I'll let you know."

Oliver White nodded silently, escorting them out and closing the door with a frustrated slam. They descended the stairs, moving towards the main foyer in relative silence until

James abruptly came to a halt. Ursula turned to him, awaiting an explanation.

"He's hidin' somethin'," James Wilson said.

"Protecting," Ursula corrected. "Whether that has anything to do with the girl or not, is a completely different question."

"I have a bad feelin' about that guy," James continued.

"I'm sorry about what he said," Ursula said.

"When you live next door to the Ku Klux Klan, a few light jabs from a wealthy Brit do nothing but scratch the surface. Don't you worry about me," James replied.

"In that case, it's a murder investigation. There are several more people to have a bad feeling about, Mr Wilson. Don't let personal opinion cloud your judgement. Now, come. I'd like to speak to Ophelia next."

Ursula adhered firmly to the principle of not rushing to conclusions prematurely. While Oliver White had shown flippancy and excessive nervousness, reactions under pressure differed from person to person. In her experience working alongside her ex-husband, she had encountered remorseless criminals who wept profusely, hiding their guilt behind a veil of innocence. Conversely, she had also interrogated individuals with impeccable alibis who exuded an air of culpability despite their innocence.

They found the hotel manager in her office, situated to the left of the foyer. Ursula tapped on the door, and Ophelia promptly opened it. With a curious glance exchanged between Ursula and James, Ophelia ushered them into her dimly lit office without hesitation. The room exuded a sense of lived experience, with weathered furniture and shelves cluttered with old books. Papers were scattered across a wooden desk, alongside an old picture depicting a younger Ophelia standing with a pram.

Ophelia walked to the seat behind her desk, her countenance stern, the solitary lamp flickering on and off every few seconds, adding to the forbidding atmosphere. Behind her hung a large portrait of an imposing man seated on a throne-like chair, identified by a small plaque as James Kimberley. Beyond the office was a door that led to the hotel manager's bedroom, modest in size with a cosy chintz chair beside a large window, left open despite the cold. It mirrored Ophelia's character: unassuming yet with concealed depths.

"How may I help you, Ms. Dankworth?"

"I was wondering if you'd be able to arrange a time when I can speak to the staff?"

"Of course," Ophelia responded.

"Brilliant! And perhaps, we can start with you now?" Ursula suggested.

"I did not imagine it any other way," Ophelia looked up as if noticing James for the first time. "Was there something you needed from me, Mr. Wilson?"

"He's assisting me," Ursula clarified.

"How so?" Ophelia replied startled.

"With the investigation," James said, standing tall with pride.

"I see," Ophelia acknowledged.

"Maybe I'll be able to sing a confession outta the killer," the singer quipped, attempting to lighten the mood. Unfortunately, the joke fell flat.

"How long have you been working here?" Ursula asked, taking out her notebook. She caught sight of the name *Ada Millwood* as she turned the pages.

"Forty-seven years," Ophelia replied.

"That is a long time," Ursula said. "You must really love it here."

"I've lived in worse places."

"You're not originally from Loch Linnhe?"

"No, from Orkney."

"What brought you here specifically, as opposed to Glasgow or Edinburgh or even London?" Ursula asked.

"I went to Edinburgh for a time. Left home when I was fourteen and was working in a pub, off Princess Street. I lived in a bedsit above the pub that I shared with another girl. You wouldn't imagine the kinds of people that frequented the place. After a year there I was approached about a job here and given the conditions I lived in, I thought I didn't have anything to lose," Ophelia explained.

"Who approached you about the job?"

"James Kimberley, the owner of the hotel."

Ursula's gaze shifted to the portrait behind Ophelia. The man depicted wore a thick moustache, sitting with a straight back, his eyes carrying a stern, judgemental look. Despite the sternness, there was an underlying charm and gentleness in his features that Ursula assumed made him appealing to women.

"That was a big decision, leaving a city like Edinburgh at such a young age."

"Life is full of decisions, some good. Some bad. All we can do is pray and hope the Lord listens to those prayers."

"Amen," James said with a smile that quickly faded when Ophelia turned to him sternly.

"Were you made manager straight away?"

"Oh no, I was a wee girl. I came over as a housekeeper. I didn't become the hotel manager until a year later, winter of 1907, if I am not mistaken. When I arrived I worked under Lisa Dudley, the hotel manager at the time. She and Mrs Kimberley were lovely to me," there was a slight tone of regret in her words.

"Do Mr and Mrs Kimberley visit often?" Ursula inquired.

"Mrs. Kimberley died in 1906. Pneumonia. She deteriorated quickly," Ophelia explained. "Mr Kimberley couldn't bear living here without his wife and moved to Edinburgh soon after her passing."

"What happened to the previous hotel manager?" James asked.

Ophelia frowned at the singer, affronted that he had dared ask a question.

"Lisa Dudley was getting on in age and without Mrs Kimberley, she soon retired and left. Mr Kimberley offered me the role which I humbly accepted."

"The other housemaids must have been pretty angry," James said.

"What do you mean?"

"Well, you'd only arrived a year earlier. Quite a thing to offer a young girl the job over more experienced people."

Ophelia shrugged. "I was the best person for the role, but I cannot pretend there wasn't a level of discontent."

"Have you informed Mr Kimberley of what's occurred?" Ursula asked.

"No, I didn't see a need," Ophelia shuffled awkwardly in her chair.

"A child has been murdered on his land, Ms Clyde," Ursula said with a frown. "If I were the owner, I would want to know. Especially if it could tarnish the reputation of my establishment."

"Mr Kimberley is an old man, I wouldn't want to worry him just yet. Once the case is solved, I will travel to Edinburgh and tell him personally."

Ursula made a note and turned to the hotel manager again, a persistent feeling that something was amiss lingering within her.

"Can you confirm if you saw Blanchette last night?"

"No," Ophelia responded. "However, Mr White came to my office just after eight in the evening to tell me that they had found Blanchette eavesdropping."

"Mr White? Are you sure?" Ursula pressed.

"Certain," Ophelia affirmed, rummaging through the paperwork strewn on her desk. She lifted a thick black leatherbound book. "Any complaints or comments made by guests about their stay are annotated here by me. I have been working this way for the last forty-seven years. And here, at three minutes past eight, I wrote about the complaint lodged by Mr White."

"He said he hadn't seen the girl," James chimed in.

"Do you know Mr and Mrs White well?" Ursula asked.

The hotel manager's countenance soured at the question.

"They were here this summer just gone," Ophelia retorted.

"Is it usual for guests to come back so soon?" Ursula asked. "Summer and then Christmas?"

"We have had several guests who do. Then there are those like the Blakesleys, who only visit during the Christmas peak. Mr and Mrs White generally keep to themselves, they spend their time with their two friends." Ophelia paused before adding, "I must say I am surprised he didn't mention it. He was quite cross about finding Blanchette listening behind their door."

"He might have overlooked it, I guess," Ursula replied.

"Quite a thing to overlook!" James exclaimed.

"Thank you, Ms Clyde," Ursula said, getting out of her chair and closing her notebook. "Please let me know when I can speak to the rest of the staff."

"Of course."

Ursula and James exited Ophelia's office and were almost blinded by the contrast in brightness that met them in the foyer.

"So...?" James asked expectantly. "I told you Mr White wasn't to be trusted."

Ursula nodded in agreement but remained silent. Instead, she turned to gaze out towards the gardens, still veiled in snow. James was right; Mr. Oliver wasn't someone they could trust, but neither was Ms. Clyde. There had been moments throughout the questioning where Ursula had felt as if a dark cloud hung over the hotel manager's head. So far, neither of the people she had questioned, James included, had any motive to wish the girl dead. Now, with the knowledge that Mr White had lodged a complaint and was, in the words of Ms Clyde, 'very cross,' Ursula had a reason to suspect Oliver White—but still no clear motive presented itself. Ursula sighed. The only way she was going to solve the case, she thought, was by uncovering the truths buried within the lies.

MAUDE

December 23rd 1953, 20:22

Maude stared at her reflection in the mirror, raising a hand towards her cheek with a wince. The lingering touch of Theron's cold, unloving hand left a painful reminder of how bitter their marriage had become. They used to be happy. The happiness hadn't lasted as long as she would have liked, but at least she'd been fortunate enough to finally experience the sentiment, however fleeting.

Happiness had remained elusive for Maude throughout her marriage to Kenneth. Despite her efforts to capture it, she quickly realised that he would never truly love her. His affections lay elsewhere, often with the handsome footmen he employed. Maude was familiar with men like Kenneth; she had even heard stories of her great uncle who had lived with a 'roommate' well into his sixties, following the death of his wife. Such tales were not uncommon in high society, filled with rumours and scandals of illicit affairs and clandestine activities. Yet, amidst these stories, one common thread prevailed: the effort to love one's spouse. However, Kenneth struggled to show Maude any appreciation, neither in public nor in private. As a result, she found herself adrift in a sea of loneliness and desperation, yearning for affection she knew she would never receive.

Meeting Theron felt like witnessing the sunrise after years of captivity. Despite her intuition warning her of his ulterior motives, she couldn't deny the overwhelming sense of being wanted, a feeling she had never experienced before. Theron had a knack for making her feel like the sole focus of his attention as if there were no other woman in the world he'd rather be with. It was because of this that the pain of his first infidelity pierced her like a sword to the gut, and the second felt like a twisted plunge. Yet, what choice did Maude have? Even if she did break free at her age, who would want her? It was better to stick with the familiar devil.

Her thoughts drifted to Mr. and Mrs. White, a stark contrast to herself and Theron. The Whites epitomised perfection—youthful, exuberant, beautiful, and unafraid to express their love openly. Maude couldn't help but watch, a quiet jealousy settling in as Oliver absentmindedly caressed his wife's hand or Ariel lovingly played with his hair. Their life appeared carefree, seemingly free from the burdens that often accompanied marriage.

Maude glanced at her wristwatch and sighed. Theron had yet to return after their argument. His disappearances were a familiar pattern, often leading him to seek comfort elsewhere. This time, however, there was no other distraction for him. With the lack of guests and the remote location of Loch Linnhe Hotel, Theron would have to return and confront the issues between them. Yet, Maude harboured doubts about how many more times they could talk things through. Fear of being alone gnawed at her, but the persistent troubles in their marriage were taking a toll on her well-being. If she had to choose between Theron or her sanity, the choice was clear. Otherwise, she might end up like her poor Aunt Grace.

The past couple of weeks, in particular, had taken a toll on Maude. If it weren't for her stubborn daughter, she might have considered cancelling the trip to Loch Linnhe this year. Each day, Maude woke up looking gaunt, and feeling tired, with occasional muscle cramping and a peculiar tingling sensation at the tips of her fingers. Concern heightened when abdominal pain set in, prompting thoughts of a possible pregnancy, but it turned out not to be the case. Her family doctor suggested that spending a few weeks in the Highlands, breathing in the clean air might help her feel better, suspecting that the issues could be stress-related.

Gazing out of the window, Maude took another deep breath, attempting to calm herself. She decided that waiting for Theron outside might be beneficial, allowing her to absorb the almost medicinal cold air of the Highlands in the process. Maude traversed the hushed corridors of the hotel, cinching her coat even tighter to shield herself from the chilly breeze that crept through an open window at the end of the hallway. This marked the first instance Maude had witnessed the hotel in such a lifeless state. In the thirty years of her visits, from childhood with her parents and siblings to her own family, it had never been so vacant.

At the foot of the steps, outside her office, stood Ophelia Clyde and Oliver White, engaged in a quiet conversation. As soon as he noticed Maude, Oliver turned and swiftly walked past her, ascending the stairs without so much as acknowledging her presence.

"Mrs Blakesley," Ophelia said, readying herself to tell her something, but paused, as her eyes found the bruise on her cheek. "Is everything alright?"

"I could ask the same thing. Mr White didn't seem like himself," Maude responded.

"Unfortunately not. He was very cross with your daughter, I'm afraid."

"My daughter?"

"Mr and Mrs White caught her listening in on them outside their room, whilst they were being—" the hotel manager blushed. "Whilst they were being intimate."

Maude's brow furrowed, her pulse quickening at the thought of her troublesome daughter. It seemed Blanchette couldn't resist the urge to embarrass her once again. The memory of last year's incident, when Blanchette was caught inappropriately interacting with the dishevelled waiter, still haunted Maude. The scandal had spread like wildfire throughout the hotel, causing Maude considerable distress. Upon their return to London, she had forced Blanchette to drink the tea that would ensure there were no unwelcome surprises.

"Please accept my apologies, Ms Clyde. I'll be sure to have words with her."

Maude stepped through the front doors, still seething. She stood atop the stone steps, gazing over the gardens and beyond the frozen fountain to the iron-wrought gates of the estate. A figure materialised in the distance, moving towards her with a hesitant gait, almost limping and battling to maintain an upright posture. With each step closer, the silhouette became more familiar until—

"Blanchette," she called out to her daughter.

Maude gasped as she descended the steps and caught sight of Blanchette. Her stepdaughter looked dishevelled, as though she'd been in a brawl. Maude's concern spiked. What trouble had Blanchette gotten herself into now, and why was she outside at this hour? As the heat rose in her despite the cold, Maude couldn't help but feel frustrated. Blanchette seemed not only petulant but also ignorant and stubborn.

"Mother," Blanchette trembled.

"Where have you been? What have I told you about being outside after dark?"

"I know...I went out for just a moment—"

Maude, unable to contain her anger, seized Blanchette with both hands, feeling the cold tremble of her daughter's arms as she pulled her close, the better to look at her.

"I've had Ms Clyde complaining about you," she told her. "What were you doing outside Mr and Mrs White's room?" Maude could sense herself getting angrier the more she spoke.

"I..." Blanchette started but found herself unable to defend her actions.

"I need you to apologise to them first thing tomorrow morning, do you understand?" Maude said.

"Yes."

"All you ever do is cause me embarrassment. I should have sent you away when I had the chance."

Maude turned to leave but was stopped in her tracks by her daughter's words.

"He doesn't love you, mother," Blanchette said.

Maude turned to face her daughter, noting a stark change in her demeanour. The bitterness in Blanchette's eyes was something she had not seen before. Despite the challenges in their relationship, Blanchette had always tried to be loving towards her. No matter how often Maude reprimanded, ignored, or humiliated her in public, Blanchette's love and desire for approval remained steadfast. However, at that moment, Maude observed none of that in her daughter's eyes. Instead, there was a cold, vacant expression devoid of any discernible emotion. Maude remained quiet, giving Blanchette time to reconsider her taunt. But the girl stood tall, and Maude knew instantly that her daughter had no intention of backing down, not now or ever again.

"He doesn't love you," Blanchette repeated.

"Be quiet!" Maude spat. "And go to your room!"

"No! I will not keep quiet any longer, Mother! I am not a child any more! I deserve to be heard! I fooled myself before tonight because...well, I wanted to have a family again. I wanted a dad again," Blanchette was shaking with anger. "Mr Blakesley was always so kind to me...kinder than you've ever been." Blanchette moved closer to her. "He doesn't love you. How could he? Why would he?"

"I'm warning you —"

"If he loved you, he wouldn't be out there with another woman."

"You are a despicable child! Do you know who never loved me? Your father. The man you seem to hold to such high esteem. Perhaps that is why you're as insufferable as you are. You are the product of a forced consummation of marriage. He disgusted me. His abnormality repulsed me! Yet I laid down for him as a wife should and bore him a child. I did my duty. What did he do for me? Except attempt to embarrass me and tarnish my reputation! You know when we received word of his passing, I rejoiced. I thanked God for answering my prayers, because, had the Nazis not killed him, I might have been forced to do so upon his return!"

"How dare you speak about my father like that?" Blanchette reprimanded, wiping away tears.

"I thought we were having a truthful conversation. There's your truth!" Maude replied without an ounce of remorse.

"It's no wonder Mr Blakesley rarely ever wanted to share your bed, mother. You are hateful. That's the true reason father preferred the attention of boys."

In a moment of fury personified, Maude seized Blanchette by the scruff of her dress and dragged her away from the hotel, unleashing a torrent of slaps. Each blow sent shockwaves through Maude, the sting of her hand burning with each strike. Blanchette's fragile frame, weakened from whatever she had been involved in, offered little resistance and succumbed to Maude's assault.

Stopping abruptly, short of breath, Maude's eyes bulged with anger. She glanced around as if seeing her surroundings for the first time, noticing Blanchette's motionless body. A horrified realisation struck Maude, and she took a step back, her hands trembling uncontrollably. Weakness swept over her knees, and panic surged within. Instead of behaving as any other mother might, Maude turned and left, abandoning Blanchette in the cold.

URSULA

December 24th 1953, 14:57

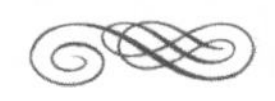

Ursula reached for the whiskey bottle perched on her dresser and, with a steady hand, lifted it to her lips. She took a long, soothing gulp, attempting to drown the tide of pain that threatened to engulf her. For the past hour, she had battled waves upon waves of dark thoughts assaulting her psyche like a battering ram. The echoes of the names of the women she had failed reverberated in a cacophony of diffidence. *Mary Lou Pearce. Kelly McDonald. Elizabeth Eddowes. Ann Stride. Jane Nichols. Catherine Chapman. Ada Millwood.* They continued to be a haunting chorus in her mind, a wraith from her past that looked down on her with unwavering disapproval. They were a relentless reminder that justice was yet to be served.

Fragments of the night she was attacked intertwined with their voices, calling out to Ursula like twisted nightmares. Through the mist, she could see the silhouette of a different woman. *Ada Millwood*, with her rosy cheeks and doe eyes. *Ann Stride*, her hair curly and demeanour merry. *Jane Nichols*, short in stature yet affable in spirit. As the memories flooded back, the menacing figure emerged once more from the shadows. Ursula gulped, feeling the weight of dread settle over her like a suffocating blanket.

She could feel the chill of fear as the hand tightened around her throat, hear the echoes of her own desperate cries piercing through the silence. The cold, daunting eyes bore into her soul, leaving her gasping for air, her breaths shallow and frantic. A tightness gripped her chest, suffocating her with memories she longed to forget. Ursula pressed a hand against her breast, hoping to quell the rising panic. Yet, a restless unease tingled through her limbs, signalling the onset of an overwhelming storm within. With each heartbeat, the images grew clearer, and more vivid. The menacing figure skulking towards her through the mist. The hand that grabbed her throat. The sound of her desperate cries...the cold, daunting eyes...The world around her blurred as a sense of impending doom loomed overhead, the names of the victims echoing like a mournful dirge she couldn't escape. *Mary Lou Pearce. Kelly McDonald. Elizabeth Eddowes. Ann Stride. Jane Nichols. Catherine Chapman. Ada Millwood.*

Ursula reached for the whiskey again, drinking until the elixir started to take effect, quieting the voices within and clearing the corridors of her mind. As her heartbeat seemed to return to normal, a knock on the door startled her, causing an unintentional jolt that sent the bottle tumbling, shattering on impact. She stood motionless, watching the amber cascade of liquid overtake her writing desk.

"Hello?" James knocked, again.

Ursula grabbed a towel, swiftly sweeping the glass shards from the table into it. With a quick twist, she balled up the towel and stashed it in the dresser before crossing the bedroom to swing the door open. As she stepped into the hallway, she couldn't shake the faint smell of whiskey lingering in the air. She turned the doorknob, mustering a forced smile, a slight sense of light-headedness accompanying her actions.

"Hope I'm not disturbin'," James said as soon as Ursula had opened the door. "Ms Clyde was looking for you, she wanted me to let you know that the staff are ready for questionin'."

"Ms Clyde knows where my room is," Ursula replied mockingly. "Did you use this as an excuse to try and get an invitation into my room?"

"Damn, was I that obvious?" James smirked, holding his hands up in mock defeat. "My bad. Detective Dankworth solves every mystery. I should have known."

Ursula's smile faded.

"If only that were true," she replied with a tinge of regret, before adding. "I was thinking that we could go see the Blakesleys first."

"Sounds like a plan!" James said enthusiastically.

"I'll grab my notebook and we can go."

Ursula and James walked in silence towards the shared room of the Blakesley children, where Ophelia had mentioned they had gone after keeping vigil over Blanchette's body. Ursula knocked on the door, and it swung open to reveal Theron Blakesley, his expression sombre. Without uttering a word, he gestured for them to enter and took a seat on a sofa chair near the large window overlooking the hotel's front gardens. Inside, Maude lay curled up on Blanchette's bed, absentmindedly caressing the bedsheets with a look of permanent shock replacing her usual composure. Meanwhile, Uriah sat on the other bed, his gaze fixed on the stuffed wolf toy clutched tightly in his hands as if it were the only thing in the room with him.

"Mrs Blakesley," Ursula began gently. "I can't begin to imagine how difficult this must be for you?"

Ursula could empathise with the situation more than she cared to admit. She had experienced that same heart-wrenching whirlpool of emotions herself, and in many ways, still found herself caught in its grip. Maude Blakesley shifted her eyes towards Ursula for a fleeting moment, silently conveying a shared understanding of pain, before returning her gaze to the emptiness before her. Sensing the depth of her suffering, Ursula turned her attention to Theron Blakesley.

"I know that it may not be the best time, but if possible, I would like to ask you and your son some questions to aid my investigation," Ursula continued.

"Of course," Mr Blakesley said, sitting up. "Uriah. Ms Dankworth is going to ask you some questions, okay?"

Uriah gave no sign that he had heard his father, but Mr Blakesley nodded, giving Ursula permission to proceed. She sat on the edge of the bed and cleared her throat.

"Hello Uriah," she started. "I know this is a difficult time but we're trying to find out what happened to your sister—"

Uriah stirred.

"Step-sister," he corrected.

"Yes, your step-sister. We're trying to find out what happened to her and I am going to need you to answer some questions if that's okay?" Ursula asked gently.

The boy did not respond, his eyes fixating once more on the toy.

"Uriah," his father intervened, crossing the room to reach his son's bed. "You need to listen to Ms Dankworth," he lifted Uriah, compelling him to sit up and pay attention. The two exchanged an intense stare. "Please, Ms Dankworth, go ahead."

"Thank you, Mr Blakesley," Ursula opened her notebook, removing the cap off her fountain pen, and offering a reassuring smile to Uriah. "Can you remember when you last saw Blanchette?"

The boy nodded, his gaze briefly flitting to the stuffed toy before returning to Ursula, as if seeking its counsel. Ursula had found his behaviour odd during breakfast that morning, though she reasoned that children often had imaginary friends, making it nothing particularly unusual in that sense. Yet, given his proximity to adulthood, such behaviour was undeniably peculiar. Her brother had been only a couple of years older than Uriah when he joined the Spanish Republican war effort at sixteen.

"She was humming non-stop," Uriah placed two fingers to his head, mimicking a shot to his temple to convey his frustration. "Then she left."

"Do you know what time that was?" Ursula inquired

"After dinner," Uriah replied.

"So, Blanchette came back to the room and then left?" Ursula pressed further, children were notoriously difficult to question.

Uriah looked at the toy again, before responding. "She was here and then she left."

Ursula looked down at her notes.

"So it would have been after seven in the evening," Ursula muttered.

"We were the last to leave the dining hall last night," Mr Blakesley offered, gesturing between him and his wife. "And that was a few minutes after seven."

"Was there anything different about her behaviour?" Ursula asked.

"No...she loves Christmas. She loves Loch Linnhe. Here is where I have seen her at her happiest. It reminds her of her father," Mr Blakesley replied.

"Did you know she and the young waiter were..." Ursula hesitated, glancing at Mrs Blakesley, before continuing. "Friends?"

"Um...I mean there was a bit of a brouhaha last year," Mr Blakesley explained. "Nothing but young teens, being teens, I expect."

"Hamish mentioned a run-in with Blanchette, did she mention anything about it?" Ursula asked.

"No," Mr Blakesley shook his head. "Do you think—"

"The kid is a little awkward, but he's not a killer," James said quickly.

"What would you know?" Mr Blakesley said dismissively.

"He's worked with him for quite a few months, so I would assume he knows more than we do," Ursula said protectively, glancing at Mrs Blakesley once more who remained muted.

"Do you remember when you last saw Blanchette, Mr Blakesley?"

"When she left for bed after supper," he confirmed.

"Ophelia mentioned she was seen roaming around later on in the evening, she definitely didn't go to see you or Mrs Blakesley in your room?"

"Certain."

"Do you come here every year?" Ursula continued.

"Uriah and I have been coming for the last six years, Blanchette and my wife have been regular guests basically all their lives."

"Would you say then, that your step-daughter was known to the staff?" Ursula probed. "Besides, young Hamish of course."

"Yes, I mean there's a couple of new faces, but all in all, yes. I would say that she is known to them." Mr Blakesley responded.

"Are there any staff members that are here this year that you'd not met before?"

"The singer," Mr Blakesley acknowledged, without looking at James. "The pianist too. But everyone else we've seen before. The groundskeeper is fairly new. He was here last Christmas."

"Uriah," she said, turning towards the boy. "Do you know if there was anyone she was friends with?"

Uriah looked up from his toy and held her gaze for a few moments before replying, "The monster."

Ursula furrowed her brow, taken aback by the boy's response.

"What do you mean, *the monster*?" she asked.

"Is she really dead?" Uriah asked, ignoring the question.

"Yes, I am afraid she is," Ursula allowed for a pause before continuing. "I am going to need you to tell me what you mean by the monster?"

"Do you think I could see her?"

Once again, the boy ignored her question. It was as if he weren't even present, but entirely consumed by his own thoughts.

"Uriah, please answer the question?" his father interjected, growing irritated.

"How about," Maude said, stirring for the first time in a while. "Instead of distracting yourself with talks of monsters that a child who speaks to stuffed animals tells you about, you continue trying to find the person who murdered my daughter? Maybe, I could help you?" She turned to her husband. "Theron, where were you on the night of Blanchette's disappearance? Oh yes, that's right. You were in bed with her!" she spat, pointing towards Ursula.

Maude's eyes bore into Ursula, the flush on her cheeks betraying her anger. It was evident that she was gearing up for a confrontation rather than a rational conversation. Ursula couldn't fault her; if she had known Robert spent the night with someone else, she might have been beside herself. However, had she discovered it on the day her daughter died, addressing the infidelity would have been the last thing on her mind.

Ursula took a step back, refusing to be drawn into a heated argument. Out of nowhere, the voices in her head materialised again...*Mary Lou Pearce. Kelly McDonald. Elizabeth Eddowes. Ann Stride*...as did the memories of her attack. The menacing figure skulking towards her through the mist. The hand that grabbed her throat. The sound of her desperate cries...the cold, daunting eyes.

Her throat felt dry. She longed for a drink. She needed the voices and the fragments gone...*Jane Nichols. Catherine Chapman. Ada Millwood.* The tightness in her chest and shortness of breath returned. She looked away towards James, their eyes locking and he, as if by a connection that had always existed, seemed to sense that something was the matter and stepped in.

"I guess," James said. "We can agree that your husband has an alibi for his whereabouts last night then, huh?"

Maude's eyes flickered with rage, but before she could respond with what would likely be a scathing retort, Ursula found the strength necessary to retort in James' stead.

"I appreciate this is a difficult time," Ursula said, trying to maintain her composure. "Unfortunately, if you want justice for your daughter, there is no other way but to ask questions, no matter how uncomfortable they may be."

Maude closed the distance between them until their noses were almost touching, an intense confrontation looming.

"You know, he likes vulnerable women," Maude sneered, sniffing the air. "I can *smell* the vulnerability."

Ursula shifted her eyes away from Ursula as her cheeks began to turn a shade warmer from her remark.

"Perhaps, it's best you leave," Theron said. "We're happy to resume the questioning a bit later or tomorrow, even."

"Of course, if there are any developments of note, I'll let you know," Ursula replied, turning to make her way out.

They were barely out of the room when she felt James place a gentle hand on her arm.

"Are you alright?" he asked, concern in his voice.

"Yes, but we should start making our way to the staff quarters—"

"I think perhaps, we could do that a little later," James said with a faux yawn. "This investigation business is quite intense."

"I can continue without you," Ursula said.

James grew uncomfortable, shifting his weight from one foot to the other. "I think it would help us both to, you know, lay down, think about everything we've learned so far, take a nap..."

"It's really best if we keep the momentum going," Ursula said, attempting to move away but he gently held her back.

"Ms Dankworth, remember when I said that every great detective needs a great partner?"

"Mhm."

"I wouldn't be a great partner if I didn't tell you that, it would be best if you went back to your room and slept it off."

Silence fell between them. Ursula's face burned with embarrassment. Mrs Blakesley's comment had not gone unnoticed by him either. Ursula's eyes remained somewhere just above his shoulder, looking intently at the paisley wallpaper. Could she continue with the investigation with her personal demons chasing her at every turn? What had she become?

"Perhaps you're right...I'll see you in an hour?" Ursula conceded.

"Sure, I'll be ready," James said with a smile.

BLANCHETTE

December 23rd 1953, 22:22

Blanchette's vision adjusted to the dancing flames in the hearth as she opened her eyes. The mingling scents of dampness and the delicious aroma of stew filled the air, making her more aware of her surroundings. Grunting in pain, she attempted to sit up, her body aching and her head heavy and foggy. The room revealed itself to her—a space marked by damp, mould-covered walls, yet with surprisingly high ceilings. A small window to the far side, allowed in a meagre amount of moonlight, illuminating the interior.

"Hullo," a voice grumbled.

Startled, Blanchette jumped and let out a sharp shriek. As she turned to face the source, her mouth fell open in surprise. Before her stood a giant of a man, towering well over six feet with a mass of matted black hair obscuring most of his face. She could glimpse only two twinkling eyes peering through the tangled strands. He moved closer, but sensing her discomfort, took a step back and settled into a chair that seemed fit for giants. Behind him stood a petite kitchen, the delightful smell she had perceived emanating from the stove. Her hungry stomach churned.

"Food?" he asked and Blanchette felt the deep resonance of his voice vibrating within her chest, with every utterance, "Food?" he repeated.

Blanchette nodded, each movement slow and reluctant, her eyes scanning the unfamiliar room. Where was she? Who was this man? How had she ended up here? The last fragments of memory clung to her—seeing Mr Blakesley with that woman and then the painful confrontation with her mother. A pang of heartache accompanied these recollections, coursing through her body with each nod. She looked up, observing the giant figure limping towards the stove, one leg noticeably shorter than the other. Steam billowed out as he opened the pot, swirling and mingling with the delightful aroma that filled the room. The man ladled a generous portion of stew into a wooden bowl, then approached Blanchette, handing it to her before retreating to his spot.

"Thank you," she said. "Smells lovely."

"Spoon?" he asked.

"Yes, please."

He returned with a wooden spoon and offered Blanchette the stew. It felt as though she hadn't eaten for days; her body craved the nourishment and comforting flavours. In relative silence, she savoured every bite, gradually inching closer to the crackling warmth of the fireplace. She focused all her thoughts on the dancing flames, afraid that contemplating anything else would drain her of the little energy she had left.

"Did you make this?" she asked.

"Mhm," he confirmed. "I made."

"It's very tasty. You should be a chef."

"Chef?" the man repeated, confused, cocking his head in thought.

"Yes. Maybe Aonghus can teach you. He makes the best Christmas Pudding and Apple crumble. I'm more of a Christmas Pudding sort of person, but mother is..." Blanchette paused, the word 'mother' sparking a sense of despondency within her. "Mother is more of an apple crumble."

She absentmindedly lifted her hand to her face, the memory of her mother's anger and disdain etched in her mind. Blanchette had never experienced the soothing warmth her mother associated with an apple crumble, a feeling she assumed a child should feel from a parent. Every hug Blanchette had ever received from her had felt stolen, and every smile forced.

"Your face.." The giant said, reaching out a thick hand towards her.

Blanchette frowned and gingerly touched her face, wincing at the soreness and swelling. The man rose once more and hobbled towards a drawer beside a large bed in the corner of the room. He retrieved a small hand mirror and handed it to Blanchette. Setting her stew down on the floor, she turned the mirror towards her face and gasped at the sight. Her right cheek displayed a nasty hue of black and purple, adorned with a small healing cut. Her upper lip was split, and her left eye had swollen. A tear trickled down her cheek.

Lost in her reflection, she hadn't noticed the giant move to sit on the floor directly in front of her. He gently took the mirror from her hand, revealing his own heavily weathered, lopsided face as he pushed aside the matted hair. His appearance shocked her; it was almost as if his face were melting. Yet, his eyes sat like two black jewels, twinkling so brightly that it was difficult to look beyond their kindness and warmth.

"See? No cry."

Blanchette smiled.

"Do you live alone?" she asked.

"Not alone," he grumbled.

He rose and walked over to a small cabinet where a solitary picture stood. A few moments later, he returned to sit in front of her and handed the picture frame to Blanchette. Her eyes fell upon the stern face of a woman she recognised, albeit several decades younger. Cradled in her arms was a small baby with the same lopsided features as the man now sitting before her.

"Oh," she said, looking around the room again. A thought came to mind. "Are we in the basement?"

"Basement?" he repeated, seemingly confused.

Blanchette stood up and pointed to the window. "Can you lift me so I can see?"

She gestured to mimic him lifting her, and the man understood. He lifted her from the floor as if she were a doll and took her towards the small window. As they approached, Blanchette confirmed her suspicion—it was indeed the basement of the hotel. Through the window, she could see the expanse of snow-covered grounds leading to the side entrance, near the staff area.

"Thank you, you can put me down," the man placed her back down. "You've been here all along, haven't you? Not a ghost after all!"

The man must have witnessed or overheard Blanchette's encounter with her mother from the window and brought her inside. Smiling, she reached out a hand towards his face. Initially puzzled, he gradually comprehended, lowering himself to his knees so Blanchette could touch his face.

"Thank you," she repeated earnestly. "I need to go now, but I promise to come visit okay? I'll whistle from the window, so you know it's me."

"No, don't go," the man said sadly.

"I need to..." Blanchette said with a twinkle in her eyes.

"No, don't go!" The man grabbed her by the arm.

She felt a momentary surge of panic.

"I need to but I'll be back, okay? We're friends."

He responded with another twisted smile at the mention of the word "friends," releasing her arm. From his pocket, he withdrew a weathered wooden spinning top, engraved with the letter 'T,' and offered it to her, his smile still contorted.

"Friends?" he repeated, holding out the spinner.

Blanchette accepted the wooden top spinner from him with a gentle grasp and returned a genuine smile before replying, "Friends."

JAMES

December 24th 1953, 17:16

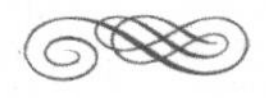

James stood at the foot of the main stairs, his gaze lost in the darkness enveloping the hotel, his mind drifting in its own labyrinth of thoughts. As he waited for Ursula's arrival, the delicate sound of footsteps echoed behind him, announcing the detective's approach. With hands firmly clasped behind his back, James turned to meet Ursula's gaze. He couldn't help but notice the lingering sorrow in her eyes, a sorrow that seemed to have deepened since her arrival at Loch Linnhe and intensified further after the discovery of the Blakesley girl's body. James couldn't shake the suspicion that seeing the dead body had stirred up Ursula's own trauma. One that lingered ever present, evidenced by her reliance on alcohol.

James greeted her with a reassuring smile, sensing a hesitancy in her every step towards him. Ursula's eyes remained fixed on the ground, a faint, trembling smile adorning her flawless heart-shaped face. He silently hoped she understood that judgement found no place in his understanding. James harboured no illusions of moral superiority; his moral compass had long shattered and lost its way.

"Hello," he said softly. His heart fluttered as they locked eyes. "Feeling refreshed?"

"Yes, much better. Thank you," she replied, with a widening smile.

"I was thinkin' you might like to go for a walk?" James said. "I want to show you something."

"Outside?" she enquired looking out into the frozen hotel gardens.

"Back home, goin' for a walk usually means goin' outside, yes," James replied with a smile. "Scared of the big, bad winter?"

Ursula laughed.

"Says the Alabama native who has only seen snow once in his life?"

"My, my...you are re-energised!"

"Yes and we have an investigation to take care of, did you forget?"

"I know...but...please?" James went on one knee, and placed both palms together, pleading.

"Put those dimples away," Ursula replied.

"Dimples? What dimples?" James pointed cheekily towards them with both index fingers. "You mean these two weapons of mass distraction?"

Ursula chuckled, slapped him gently on the chest and walked past him. "Well don't just stand there, let's go, we mustn't be too long."

James led Ursula through the front gardens, past the iron gates delineating the estate's limits, and towards the roadside where the local forest beckoned. The moonlit path stretched before them like a portal to a realm of mystery and enchantment. With each walk along this route, James found himself continually captivated by the tranquillity and serenity it offered. Life, it seemed, was gradually moulding him into somewhat of a country boy and he couldn't help but appreciate the perks of escaping the hustle and bustle of cosmopolitan living. Plus, the more secluded the location, the fewer interventions he'd have to make to keep his cousin out of trouble, a task he invariably found himself undertaking. Innocently at first, blinded by loyalty and familial bonds thereafter...but Zurich had marked a departure from that, there, he had been complicit. Admitting it hurt and disgusted him, but there was no other way to see it. His veil had fallen, yet he still protected Lyle.

"Where are we going?" Ursula asked, shivering.

"You'll see."

James' senses heightened the deeper they ventured, as every rustle of leaves seemed to echo through the night. Behind him, a branch snapped, and he turned towards Ursula instinctively, his heart skipping a beat as he saw her lose her footing. Before she could fall, James's hand reached out, catching her. The touch of her hand sent a strange sensation through him—a mix of surprise, comfort, and fluttering in his stomach. For a few moments, they stood there, their hands touching, and their eyes locked. The forest seemed to hold its breath, acknowledging the unspoken tension between them.

"Should we continue?" Ursula asked, breathless.

James nodded, silently leading her through the trees. He barely had to think twice about the direction they were going; he had made this journey so often it had become second nature to him. After a few minutes, a path appeared, and a clearing with two large oak trees, like sentinels in the night, revealed itself. James beamed as he saw Ursula's eyes widen in wonder at the sight before them. Underneath the branches of the trees were hundreds upon hundreds of ethereal fluorescent lights, creating a miniature, magical galaxy and offering a quasi-starry night illusion.

"Fireflies," James explained.

Ursula continued to gaze at the lights hovering above them, completely captivated by their beauty. A gentle smile graced her face as she twirled in a circle, entranced by the dance of fireflies. They flickered like little lanterns, casting a soft, warm glow that illuminated the darkness. The night was alive with their delicate hums, a soothing symphony that added to the enchantment. She looked so at ease in the environment; it was as if her troubles had abandoned her for this one moment in time, her demons forever lost.

James could have spent the entire night watching her; this was the true Ursula. Until now, he hadn't seen this side of her. She had allowed a moment of happiness, however fleeting, to take over. James had lost count of how many times he'd sat under those very trees, admiring those same fireflies, but sharing this moment with Ursula felt different. She had woven an unexpected magic into the night.

"You shoulda been here last summer...Lyle thought aliens had come to invade," he laughed.

"I've never seen fireflies before," Ursula said.

"Whenever...I'm havin' thoughts," James said, turning to her. "Missin' my family, my home...whenever I feel like I want out...I come here and I sit...and try not to think."

"What do you want 'out' from?" she asked him.

"Life," when he saw her alarm, he added. "Not in a, 'I wanna kill myself kinda way', but just, you know. Shitty situations."

"Do you ever think of going back?"

"All the time," the singer responded earnestly. "Every day. But I can't leave Lyle."

"He doesn't want to go back?"

"He can't go back. Unfortunately, Lyle is," he placed a hand on his chin as if thinking. "What's that fancy Latin term for not being wanted or welcome?"

"Persona non grata?"

"Persona. Non. Grata! That's exactly it."

"That's beautiful, your loyalty to your cousin. I don't know the details of why he can't go back home, but there's a lot to be said about not wanting to leave him alone. It's commendable."

"Is it? Or is it, plain stupidity," he replied with a hint of sadness. "Should we head back?"

"How so?" Ursula asked curiously.

"Well, suppose there's two of you. You and a friend," James explained. "Your friend has a gun, but you don't know that the gun exists, let alone that it's been fired. However, when the question of the gun arises and all signs indicate to your friend ownin' and havin' fired the gun, you hide it and move on."

Ursula took a moment to consider his words, trying to search his eyes for something she would not be able to find in the dark.

"I see," she said slowly. "Did I hide the gun certain of my friend's culpability?"

"Not the first time," James replied. "Thereafter, you had doubts, but you hid it again and again."

"James," Ursula started. "Does this have anything to do with Blanchette?"

"No!" he exclaimed. "Hell, no! Of course not. Just...life. Should we head back?"

"Yes, of course," Ursula replied, her tone contemplative. "And thank you," she added.

"The fireflies? I can't take credit for nature's wonders," he quipped.

"For bringing me here...for talking to me earlier today *and* for not judging me."

"Well...he who casts the first stone, right?"

They walked back through the forest in companionable silence, each lost in their thoughts. The magic of the fireflies seemed to stay with them, glowing like a memory in the darkness. Neither of them felt the need to fill the quiet with words. It was clear, unspoken, that they were content in each other's presence. James had always believed that the best people to be around were those with whom you could share silence and still feel a sense of comfort. Ursula seemed to epitomise this for him.

He stole a glance at the reluctant detective, her profile illuminated by the moonlight, her expression was serene and thoughtful. What James had planned as a means to distract

Ursula from her troubles had turned into something else, it was a shared experience. A connection forged amidst the wonders of the night.

"I've been thinking," James said, casting his mind away from the butterflies in his stomach and back towards the case. "Mrs Blakesley seemed a little off, don't you think?"

"How so?" Ursula asked as they reached the main road leading to the hotel.

"She barely reacted throughout the questioning, except to bring up your..." James paused, awkwardly.

Ursula smiled. "My tryst with her husband, you mean?"

"I was gonna say thingamajig, I just love that word! British people make everything sound so nice," he said with a grin, before continuing. "She seemed far more angry at that than the fact her daughter was dead."

"Signs of mourning manifest differently for different people," Ursula replied, taking a deep breath before continuing. "Some of us turn to drink to numb the pain, others to anger, or whatever helps them regain a semblance of themselves."

They stepped back into the hotel gardens, the night seemingly brighter, infused with the gentle glow of happiness they had created. Ursula halted, squinting into the night. Two fleeting shadows appeared to be running away from the hotel before coming to a sudden stop.

"Who's—" James began, but Ursula placed a gentle hand on James' arm as the two figures drew closer, speaking in hushed voices. He felt his heart quicken at her touch.

"No," one of the voices said. "What do you think is going to happen? How far do you think you will get?"

"I don't know," the second voice replied before breaking down.

Ursula and James approached the two figures slowly until they came into view. It was Julia Majewski, still in her uniform, teeth chattering as she spoke, and Silvia McPherson, wearing a thick grey woollen coat and carrying an overpacked duffel bag on her shoulders. The latter let out a small shriek, noticing James and Ursula.

"Going somewhere?" Ursula asked.

The question hung in the air, unanswered for what felt like minutes whilst the four of them exchanged glances, hearing nothing but the chirping of crickets.

"Silvia?" James finally said, breaking the silence. "What's goin' on?"

"I can't stay here," she replied, struggling to hold back fresh tears.

"Silvia, we're in the middle of a murder investigation, leaving right now is probably not the smartest thing to do," James continued.

"I told her," Julia said, "but she does not listen to me."

"I don't know anything about what happened to the girl!"

"Why do I get the feeling you do?" Ursula chimed in, locking eyes with the quivering girl. "Besides, all the roads are blocked by the snowstorm. There's nowhere you can go, not tonight. Why don't you come back to the hotel and tell me what you know?"

"Tell them, Silvia," Julia said, holding the younger woman's hand encouragingly.

"No, no... I can't!"

Ursula moved closer to Silvia and gently lifted her chin. The young kitchen maid trembled from a combination of cold and fear, but how her eyes trembled indicated to James that the latter sentiment had taken reign over the girl's emotions.

"If there's any information you think may be useful in helping us find out what happened to Blanchette, we need to know," Ursula paused for extra dramatic effect. "Her parents deserve to know."

Silvia hid her face behind her hands and immediately broke down in tears. James felt a wave of empathy wash over him as he saw the girl's quivering lips and the tears streaming down her face. What was she so afraid of that she was willing to risk looking like the culprit, James wondered.

"I told him no," Silvia said crying a little more furiously than before. "He's always been so patient with me, but what's a lad that's been in London going to expect?" Silvia wiped the tears from her face and looked away from them. Her cheeks turned red as she inhaled and exhaled in quick succession, clearly trying to gather enough courage to continue. "Last night, he wouldn't take no for an answer. He just kept on pushing and pushing..."

"Who?" Ursula asked, confused.

"Finlay, I was with him last night," she sniffled. "We've been friendly for a long time."

"He's not a nice man," Julia Majewski interjected. "Last summer, he erm..." She cleared her throat, she too looked away in what James read to be shame. "He was drunk. Could barely stand, let alone walk, so I helped him to his room, put him to bed...but erm...he, he would not let go of me, you know?"

"Oh god," James whispered, comprehension dawning. But it didn't make sense! Sure, Finlay was quiet and brooding and certainly quick to temper. James had seen flashes of it during their card games, but he wasn't the type to do what the girls were insinuating, surely? Had James been so blind as not to see the true nature of yet another person? What did that say about him?

"He wouldn't let go," Julia continued. "...and I erm...didn't want to cause a scene...he's Ms Clyde's nephew and I didn't want to cause trouble...so I lay there while he—"

"You don't need to continue," Ursula said softly.

"Oh, Julia!" Silvia said, throwing her arms around her friend, before turning back to Ursula. "She saved me."

"Who saved you?" Ursula asked.

"The girl. Blanchette. If she hadn't shown up...he would have — he would have —" Silvia broke down again, unable to complete her sentence.

"You saw her last night?" Ursula asked. "Where?"

"Finlay and me usually meet up by that tree a few minutes away from the gardens," Silvia replied.

"You said she saved you...how?" James queried.

"Sh-Sh-She kicked him, bit him on the leg I think...I ran away and left her there, what if he did something to her? What if it's my fault she is dead?"

Silvia threw herself onto the snowy terrain, burying her face between her arms and knees. James and Julia knelt beside her, offering comfort and support, trying to alleviate any blame the girl might place upon herself. After a while,

James looked up at Ursula, recognising the gravity of what the kitchen maid had just revealed. Could it have been the groundskeeper?

"Silvia," Ursula said, her voice gentle yet firm. "Thank you for your honesty. Go back inside now, get yourself a tea and rest."

Silvia looked up, tears still streaming down her face. "Are you going to tell him, I told you? You can't tell him! Please don't tell him!"

"No. Not if you don't want me to," Ursula assured her after a few moments.

The kitchen maid nodded and gingerly stood up, assisted by Julia. Both women made their way back to the hotel. A sense of urgency filled the air once they disappeared from view. Ursula paced nervously, the weight of responsibility obvious through the furrowing of her brow and the tightness around her lips. James felt a rush of adrenaline, understanding the significance of the truth they were unravelling.

"Those poor girls," James exhaled. "To think they have to see his face every day."

"It takes more strength than you will ever know," Ursula said, her words tinged with both empathy and sorrow.

"Are you gonna confront him?" James asked.

Ursula Dankworth sighed, deeply contemplating the question. The revelation that Blanchette had intervened to stop Finlay from assaulting Silvia and their altercation thereafter did offer a motive, but she seemed hesitant to jump straight to that conclusion.

"I don't think I can confront him about what he did to Silvia and Julia," she answered as they made their way back into the hotel. "It could put them at greater risk. But he has to be our next point of enquiry because right now, he is looking very much like our prime suspect."

FINLAY

December 23rd 1953, 21:07

Finlay Muir was embroiled in inner conflict. He was acutely aware that his altercation with the Blakesley girl would inevitably have repercussions. She would undoubtedly confide in her parents, who would then escalate the matter to Ophelia and she in turn, who was loyal to the hotel and its reputation above all, would have no choice but to act decisively. Family ties wouldn't protect him. Not this time. Not when his actions had affected such an esteemed guest. Maude's family had ties to the original owners of Loch Linnhe and still received a small amount of dividends from it every year.

He needed to determine his next steps quickly. Edinburgh was out of the question, especially after what had happened. He certainly had little desire to return to Orkney, where he'd be forced to confront the profound disappointment etched on his mother's face as he descended from the ship, back to the place he had vowed never to set foot on again. That look had hurt him more than the beatings he'd suffered at the hands of his father.

Finlay sat on his bed, head in his hands, feeling a slight sense of panic building as the walls seemed to close in around him. Seeking composure, he lifted his eyes towards the drawings on his wall, the gazes from the portraits seeming to bore into his soul. Standing up, he took two steps towards them, scanning every detail in the seven portraits. There was undeniable talent there, he thought, tracing the intricate lines with a gentle finger. The portraits were lifelike, almost tangible. An unfathomable idea took shape in his mind, tugging at the corners of his thoughts like a petulant child. What if he travelled to America? There was no better place to be, especially for someone attempting to leave his problems behind. He could chase his dream there, in New York. Could he dare to dream that one day his works would grace galleries alongside masterpieces by Rembrandt? The idea danced tantalisingly at the edge of his thoughts. Maybe, just maybe.

Finlay shook his head, feeling the weight of his internal struggle urging him to release his pent-up frustrations. It had been too long since he had let out the pain. In a swift motion, he retrieved a small key from his pocket and inserted it into the lock of his writing desk. With a gentle click, he opened a hidden compartment and retrieved the sketch he had been working on recently. His eyes focused on the half-finished face, marvelling at its lifelike quality. The portrayal of Silvia, with her distinctive round doe eyes, already displayed remarkable accuracy despite being only partially completed. After a moment of contemplation, he carefully placed it back in the drawer and locked it away.

Exhaling heavily, he recognized that the only path to resolve the situation was to try and have a conversation with the Blakesley girl. If that failed, he would have little choice but to leave. Finlay could not imagine Maude Blakesley would be the sort to accept it all as a misunderstanding. She was sure to demand the police be called, and dealing with the police was the last thing Finlay wanted to do.

Once things with Blanchette were smoothed over, he'd have to deal with Silvia. However, he didn't envision a world where that would be difficult. Even if Silvia told everyone about their encounter, she'd have a tough time convincing them that Finlay had done anything wrong. After all, she willingly joined him outside, knowing they would be alone. Silvia was old enough to have known what happened between two individuals with affection for each other. Finlay's actions should have come as no surprise; in fact, they should have been welcomed. Silvia should have been grateful he'd shown interest in what most would have deemed a bland, uneducated village girl. If the Blakesley girl hadn't intervened, he would have had his way with Silvia, and she would have been fine with it once it was over. They always were.

He exited his room and proceeded down the dimly illuminated staff corridor, coming to a stop outside Lyle's room. Another voice emanated from within—distinct from his cousin James or any of the staff. Perhaps it was the pretty black lass who had arrived with Mr and Mrs White.

"You promise?" he heard Lyle's voice.

"You son of a bitch," came a whisper from behind him.

Finlay's attention was diverted from whatever was happening inside the pianist's room to Julia who was standing behind him, her face the epitome of disgust.

"What now?" he asked, irritated.

Julia took a step closer to him. "You know exactly what! You just can't help yourself, can you?"

"Silvia couldn't keep her mouth shut, I take it? Pretending she didn't know what was going to happen, is he?" Finlay replied. "Unfortunately, we were interrupted, which confused things a wee bit. I am sure she would have loved it otherwise."

"Stay away from her!" Julia warned. "And stay away from me!"

"Bit difficult, we all work in the same place...but sure. I no longer have any use for you. I got what I wanted...Silvia...that's another matter."

Julia's face reddened with unrestrained anger, as she lunged at Finlay. However, he swiftly countered, grabbing her by the throat and slamming her against the wall. Their eyes locked. He could see the fear in her eyes. Finlay dug his fingers into her neck and watched the woman's fear turn to helplessness, the fight lost. He needed to repress his need to scream...

"What's going on here?"

Finlay turned to find Ophelia shrouded in darkness at the end of the corridor. He released Julia, who scrambled away as quickly as she could. Ophelia stood in silence until the sound of the lock clicking shut signalled that the kitchen maid had returned to her chambers for the night.

"We were talking," Finlay said dismissively.

His aunt's eyes searched something within his and she appeared to find it because her face soured as if in deep disgust.

"*Their end will be what their actions deserve*," Ophelia whispered. "Corinthians," she added before continuing. "No more trouble from the Blakesley girl, I take it?"

"None," he replied stiffly.

"The basement? Did you check it?"

"No, But if you warned her away, surely—"

"I've known her since she was a wee girl," Ophelia interjected. "She is a curious lass, warning her away won't keep her away. I need you to do as I said and keep an eye on her."

"Of course," Finlay replied.

Ophelia turned on her heels and walked away but as she reached the door, she said, "Oh and control yourself. We do not need any more undue attention."

Finlay held an intense disdain for his aunt, who paraded around with an air of self-righteousness. Yet, in truth, they were not so dissimilar. Allowing his anger to dissipate, he decided to head towards the basement, taking care to avoid being seen. No one else was aware of what lay down there, so he always had to be discreet when venturing in. Perhaps one day, he would intentionally let someone catch a glimpse of him. It would be amusing to witness his aunt scramble to answer their questions.

The dank odour lingering in the basement air stirred memories of the trenches he had endured during the war. Just like those war-torn spaces, the basement was infested with rats. Pausing, he noticed a sliver of light seeping from the slightly ajar door. Slowly, he approached and peeked through it, finding no one but Tytus lying on his bed, his gaze fixed on the intricately carved stone ceiling as if in a trance.

"Fin," Tytus grumbled, wearing his characteristic twisted smile.

Tytus rushed out of bed towards him and picked Finlay up, clearly elated by the visit. Finlay gently tapped his cousin's back, signalling for him to be put down, which he did after a moment. It was then that Finlay noticed two wooden bowls and a pair of white socks drying by the fireplace. Beside them, on the floor, lay a white cloth stained with blood.

"Tytus," Finlay said. "Was someone here?"

His cousin's face broke into another innocent smile as he nodded with excitement.

"Friend," he replied.

"What friend?"

"Pretty friend," Tytus said, then his face turned sad before he added. "Hurt."

"What friend?" Finlay asked, alarmed.

"Blanq," his cousin said.

"Bla—" Finlay started, confused but then looked at the white socks again. "Blanchette." Tytus grunted happily, confirming Finlay's suspicions. "I'm going to have to go now, okay? But I'll be back."

Finlay closed the door behind him, ensuring it was securely locked. Climbing the basement stairs, he made his way towards Ophelia's office, just adjacent to the main foyer. He knocked, and in moments, his aunt emerged. She was already in her nightgown, her usual tightly wound bun replaced by cascading black and white hair.

"Can I come in?" he asked.

"Is it urgent?" Ophelia inquired.

Finlay raised the bloodied cloth, watching as alarm flickered across his aunt's face. Ophelia seized his arm, pulling him in, and shut the door, plunging them into darkness. All was still until Ophelia lit a candle, illuminating the stained fabric.

"What is this?"

"Found it in the basement," Finlay replied, giving Ophelia enough time to process the information. "The girl was there."

"Is this—" Ophelia did not finish her sentence, too consumed with what it could all mean. There was only one conclusion to draw from finding a bloodied cloth. Ophelia sat at her desk, her eyes distant, the portrait of James Kimberley looming over them, a silent witness to the unfolding enigma.

"She's trouble that girl," Finlay added.

"How did she get in?" Ophelia asked.

Finlay shrugged earnestly. He had wondered the same thing.

"I checked in on him once the Blakesley girl had left," Ophelia said, suddenly, she remembered something. "Oh my, maybe...I forgot to lock it...?"

"Maybe. Either way, Tytus reckons she was in there, there's a pair of socks that look like they might belong to her and then there's this blood-stained cloth."

Ophelia leaned forward towards the candlelight and placed her palms together, deep in thought.

"There is no blood-stained cloth...and as you very well said yourself. The girl is trouble," his aunt replied coldly. "Was there anything else you needed?"

Finlay shook his head.

"Very well, goodnight," Ophelia said, leaning back in her chair and closing her eyes.

URSULA

December 24th 1953, 18:45

The last time Ursula had sat in a room with a lifeless body, it had been her daughter's. The unimaginable sorrow she had felt then seemed to echo at this moment as she held a vigil for yet another innocent child. Life, she mused, was an intricate tapestry of unforeseen events. It was like a Machiavellian puppet master manipulating the strings of fate. Each action, each revelation, felt like a calculated move in a grand chess game, where the stakes were immeasurable. The chessboard, though, was no ordinary one, which was why a trip intended to end her own life had now thrust her into the heart of a murder investigation.

A solitary oil lamp cast a solemn glow on Blanchette's bruised face. Ursula pulled her chair closer, leaning in to carefully analyse each bruise on the girl's alabaster countenance. A small cut on Blanchette's cheek hinted that the assailant might have been wearing jewellery, or that she had endured a forceful impact. However, the wound lacked the depth usually associated with a significant fall or collision. The bruises around her neck suggested strangulation—a method of murder often associated with cruelty and intimacy, sometimes indicating sexually sadistic motives. This raised the unsettling question of potential sexual assault.

Could Hamish be involved? Unrequited love, in her experience, often drove murders of passion, but Ursula did not think the young waiter was the culprit. The little she had spoken to Hamish led her to believe that he was not capable of such an act. He seemed too meek. If he were the culprit, it wouldn't be strangulation but a spontaneous burst of anger in the face of initial rejection. He would most likely have attempted to conceal the body to avoid detection. The fact that the perpetrator left the body in a location where it would be found suggested a different dynamic—perhaps remorse, or a desire to send a message.

Ursula startled at the sound of something hitting the floor. Her gaze darted around the dingy room until it landed on the red coat the groundskeeper had found earlier that morning, now sprawled on the ground. Curiosity piqued, she reached down to retrieve it, her fingers finding something nestled in the pocket. Pulling it out, she recognised it instantly—a Sheppard lighter. At that moment, realisation dawned, remembering exactly to whom it belonged.

Ursula hurried out of the room and descended the hotel stairs, her steps quickening with urgency. Skipping over a few steps, she nearly lost her balance in her haste. Soon, she reached the foyer, where the hotel manager was engaged in a quiet conversation with Mrs. White.

"Ms Dankworth," Mrs White said. "My husband informed me that you'd wish to speak to me?"

"Yes," Ursula replied. "Perhaps tonight after dinner?"

"Sure. I'll be in the library," Mrs White said with a smile.

"Perfect," Ursula said as Mrs White walked back up the stairs. Her mind racing, she turned to Ophelia. "Would it be possible to speak to Finlay?"

Ophelia did not hesitate nor ask why, it was as if she had almost expected it.

"Would you like me to gather the rest of the staff too?" Ophelia replied.

"Not right now. That reminds me," Ursula replied, placing her hand in her pocket and withdrawing the wooden top spinner she'd found earlier that morning. "Have you seen this before?'

Ophelia's eyes twitched as she looked at the top spinner.

"No," she said slowly, without looking at Ursula.

"Do you think Finlay would know? I found it near Blanchette's body...but with everything going on around me, I forgot. Look at this..." Ursula showed her the engraved letter 'T' on the top spinner. The hotel manager shook her head. "Would it be possible to give me your guestbook so I can reference all guests past and present whose names may start with the letter T?"

"Of course," Ophelia replied.

"Thank you," Ursula said with a smile.

"Please, come this way."

Ophelia and Ursula proceeded down the dim, narrow corridors of the staff area. The dampness in the air invaded her senses, triggering a tickle in her nose and a subtle tightness in her chest. Lost in her thoughts and discomfort, Ursula felt her heart race and her palms begin to sweat.

Mary Lou Pearce. Kelly McDonald. Elizabeth Eddowes. Ann Stride. Jane Nichols. Catherine Chapman. Ada Millwood. The haunting echoes of those names returned, but there was little time to recompose herself as Ophelia knocked sharply on Finlay's door. Following a few moments of silence, the groundskeeper appeared, his eyes scanning both women before offering a thin smile.

"May we come in?" Ophelia asked but did not allow him to reply.

Finlay stepped aside, allowing them to enter. A sweet musky scent greeted Ursula as she walked into the compact room, it was at once soothing after the dampness that lingered in the corridor, and nauseating. She tried to distract herself from the disconcerting mixture of sensations by casting a glance at the pleasant symphony of organisation in the room. Everything was in its designated place, perfectly arranged. The bed boasted impeccable hospital corners, and the wooden table held a tower of notebooks stacked with deliberate precision. It felt like stepping into a carefully composed painting, each detail arranged with apparent intention. Could someone so fastidious perpetrate the brutal assault on Blanchette?

On the wall above his writing desk hung seven portraits, rendered in exquisite detail. Ursula stood in awe of the groundskeeper's talent, marvelling at the lifelike quality and finesse in each stroke. Delicate and precise, the brushwork brought the portraits to life, captivating her with their vividness. In the corner of one frame, she noticed the words

'Replay Ache Mourn,' and another bore the signature *'Saint Nerd.'*

"These are beautiful," Ursula remarked, her finger tracing the contours of a portrait with gentle reverence. "Did you draw these?"

"Please be careful. They smudge easy," the groundskeeper advised, attempting a smile that didn't quite reach his eyes.

Ursula turned her attention to him, sensing a palpable agitation. She was unsure whether it was due to her intrusion in his room or the general presence of others in a space he held sacred. The man she had seen stropping around the hotel grounds did not seem to be the same person who sat in this room and created works of art. Then again, didn't everyone have demons?

"May I?" Ursula asked, pointing to the empty chair by his desk.

"Aye," Finlay replied as he took a seat on his bed.

The groundskeeper glanced over at Ophelia who remained rooted to the spot by the door. The expression on her face was dark and judging. Ursula cleared her throat and decided she would not ease into the questioning.

"Would you be able to recount your movements last night?" Ursula enquired.

"Last night?" Finlay repeated to buy himself some time. "The usual. I err, shovel away any snow from the entrances and exits. Do work around the grounds that needs doing. Then I have dinner and after that come to my room."

Ursula conjured a polite smile, removed her notebook from her bag and carefully flipped through its pages. Once again, she tried her best to avoid the haunting names etched on its pages, but the voices called out to her. *Ann Stride.* Ursula pushed the voices away and concentrated on the blank page before her.

"Right," she said. "Thank you for the general outline of your duties. Now, could you recount your movements from last night?"

Finlay Muir exchanged a fleeting glance with Ophelia, who appeared to be doing her best to avoid eye contact with him. The awkward exchange raised more questions in Ursula's mind. Was Ophelia aware of what had transpired between Finlay and Silvia McPherson?

"I did the usual," he replied. "I had dinner, then went outside for a smoke...I spoke to you for a little while."

"That's right," Ursula said. "You lit my cigarette."

"Aye," Finlay nodded, relaxing somewhat.

"You had a very unique lighter," Ursula said.

"Aye," the groundskeeper replied. "It's very useful when you're in the trenches or out at sea. No gas needed to spark a fire," he explained.

"How long were you —"

"The whole time," Finlay replied before she could finish the question.

"You must have seen some horrible things," Ursula continued. "One of my cousins was in Queen Alexandra's Imperial Military Nursing Services. She was part of the first women to arrive on the beaches of Normandy."

"It's war, horrible things are expected," Finlay replied blankly.

"Still, not everyone comes back the same," Ursula said.

"I heard a lot of soldiers talk about the 'after'. Making plans to go for a pint, double dates and such...Most of them didn't get to see the after."

"What did you plan to do after?" Ursula asked.

"I didn't think of it. I woke up every day thinking that it could be my last. Sometimes, wishing it was. Do you know what becomes of a man who knows he needs to wake up day after day, after day and do nothing but stay alive and kill? We kill so much that after a while, we don't even see them as men any more. Only a way out."

"You must have some attachment to that lighter then? If it's something you kept from the war...almost eight years ago," Ursula prodded.

"It's great in this sort of weather," Finlay replied.

Ursula looked away from him, towards Ophelia before rummaging in her pocket for the lighter. Slowly, she withdrew it and held it out to him.

"Would you agree that the likelihood of there being someone else in the hotel with this lighter is minute?" Ursula continued.

"I mean, I guess — but..."

"This *is* your lighter, is it not, Mr Muir?"

"Maybe, but I can't be—" the groundskeeper grumbled.

"This *is* your lighter, Mr Muir" Ursula asserted before he could finish his attempt at a denial. "Do you know where I found this lighter?"

"No," Finlay replied. "It must have dropped when—"

"When you attacked Blanchette?" Ursula interjected.

"What? No!" Finlay rose from his bed and retreated away from Ursula.

"I found this in her coat pocket, how do you think it could have ended up there?" she probed.

"I didn't do anything to that girl! She attacked *me!*"

Ophelia gasped. "What did you do? After everything I have done for you?"

"Shut up!" The groundskeeper bristled.

Finlay's sudden eruption of anger sent a shockwave through the room, prompting Ursula to inch her chair back, her heart racing in response to the sudden intensity. His expression hinted at an underlying capacity for uncontrolled aggression. Despite her fear, Ursula knew this was her only opportunity to unveil the truth. Summoning courage, she took a deep breath and prepared to press on.

"Can you explain how the lighter ended up in her coat pocket?" Ursula persisted, determined. "You said she attacked you. Why would she attack you?"

"I—"

"You were with Blanchette last night, weren't you? What did you do to that poor girl? Did you take advantage of her?" Ursula continued, unwavering.

"No—"

"But there *was* an altercation?" Ursula paused briefly to catch her breath, sensing that Finlay was on the back foot, she persisted. "How could you do that to a child?"

"I did not kill her."

"But you do find killing easy, do you not? *'Do you know what becomes of a man who knows he needs to wake up day after day, after day and do nothing but stay alive and kill? We kill so much that after a while, we don't even see them as men any more.'* Those are your words are they not?"

"Yes, but that's not what I meant—"

"What did you mean, Mr Muir?"

Finlay cast a pleading glance towards Ophelia, but the hotel manager remained hidden in the shadows, her posture stern and unmoved.

"Can you lift your trousers to the knees for me?" Ursula requested.

"What? Why?" Finlay retorted.

"I don't understand what this has to do with anything," he replied.

"Very well, Ophelia, can you call the police and let them know that I have concluded the investigation—"

"Wait, wait—"

Ursula turned back to Finlay, who reluctantly began to lift both trouser legs. On his right leg, a very obvious human bite mark was visible.

"How did you get that?"

She had him right where she wanted.

"The girl bit me," he replied softly.

"You sick bastard!" Ophelia exclaimed.

"Did you kill Blanchette Darlow?"

"No-"

"Oh, Finlay what have you done?!" Ophelia shrieked. "Do you know what this could do to the hotel's reputation?"

"You killed Blanchette, didn't you Mr Muir?"

"I did not kill her!" he repeated.

"You've ruined me!" Ophelia continued to shriek over her nephews' protests.

"I was with Silvia," Finlay said, drowning her out. "One thing led to another. The girl got the wrong impression of what was going on, and she attacked me. I hit her back, she bit me and ran off somewhere. That must be when I dropped my lighter. Ophelia, you know I couldn't have killed the girl... I spoke to you last night! You know where I was! You know what I told you!"

Ursula turned to the housekeeper.

"How can we believe anything you say?" Ophelia replied.

"Bollocks! *She* attacked *me.*"

"What about the girls in Edinburgh, did they attack you too?" Ophelia asked.

Girls in Edinburgh? Ursula thought, glancing at the pictures. His fascination with the female form was obvious. Silvia and Julia weren't the only victims.

"It was a misunderstanding!"

"Was Julia a misunderstanding too?" Ursula asked. "What about the women in the portraits? Are they real victims?"

"I did not kill the girl!" Finlay repeated. "After the altercation, I came back to the hotel, I went to the basement, I spoke to my aunt and I went back downstairs until he fell asleep, as I do every *fucking* night! And she knows it."

"Until who falls asleep?" Ursula asked, perplexed.

"Tell her, dear aunt."

"Ms Clyde, what is he talking about?"

"He is trying to distract you. You found his lighter..." Ophelia deflected.

Within two swift steps, Finlay was in his aunt's face. Their eyes met, charged with a palpable hostility that should not exist between family. It was evident that neither of them harboured any fondness for the other, even before this moment.

"I'm trying to distract? You have spent the last forty years distracting the world from your secret!" The groundskeeper spat. "You would rather see me arrested than open your eyes to reality."

"My eyes are far more open than you know. I see what your mother refuses to. Do you think I don't know about Silvia? You think I don't know about Dorrie before her...or Cath before her...Julia...you think I don't know what you are?"

A chilling, quiet fury flashed across Finlay's eyes, causing Ursula's hair to stand on end. At that moment, it was evident that neither Finlay nor Ophelia desired anything more than to destroy the other. Their feelings for one another were not fuelled by hatred; it was something far worse—it was disgust. Slowly, Finlay turned to face Ursula.

"It was Tytus," he said simply. "He told me the Blakesley girl was there. My aunt knows what he's like when he gets agitated."

"Who's Tytus?" Ursula asked, her gaze shifting between Finlay and Ophelia, her mind recalling the engraved letter 'T' on the spinning top Ophelia claimed to have never seen.

"Tell her!" Finlay screamed. "Tell her what I told you, about the blood. I was trying to protect him, but my dear aunt is so quick to throw me to the wolves..."

"Who were you trying to protect? Who is Tytus?"

Ursula, confused and anxious, looked towards the hotel manager, whose face had drained of all colour. Ophelia closed her eyes, almost as if this revelation was what she had feared all along.

"Who is Tytus?" Ursula asked again.

Ophelia Clyde took a deep breath, opened her eyes, and responded.

"My son."

OPHELIA

December 24th 1953

There was an alluring quality to monotony that Ophelia found comforting. Each morning, she would rise before the sun itself, close her eyes, and slowly roll her neck until she heard it click four times. Satisfied, she would open her eyes, gather her belongings, and take a cold shower, regardless of the season. The chilly water served to wake her up and prepare her for the day ahead. Returning to her room, Ophelia would sit by the dresser and meticulously comb her long hair until every strand was in place. She would then glance at a picture of her dearly beloved, James Kimberley, as she fashioned her hair into a tight bun, just as he had liked it. His compliments felt like a distant whisper from times long passed; she was now over forty years older than the last time she heard those words. Nevertheless, the memory lingered like a gentle murmur of days gone by.

After donning her uniform, Ophelia would draw her curtains and settle into the chintz chair facing the large window, patiently awaiting the sunrise. Ophelia revelled in the initial caresses of sunlight, each delicate stroke transforming the sky and filling her room with a comforting warmth. The winter sunrise, adorned with subdued hues of pink, orange, and gold, held a unique allure for her. Despite the softer colours, the air felt crisper, and the world seemed to exude a heightened clarity. With the room bathed in the gentle morning light, Ophelia would then turn her attention to the table, where her King James Bible awaited, ready to immerse herself in its passages.

That was how every day of her life had begun for the past forty-seven years. This morning, she chose a passage from Exodus 21:23-25.

"But if there is serious injury, you are to take life for life, eye for eye, tooth for tooth, hand for hand, foot for foot, burn for burn, wound for wound, bruise for bruise."

Ophelia pondered those words for a few moments, a daily ritual ingrained in her routine. After completing the holy trinity, she turned and stepped into her office, which was still enveloped in darkness, a deliberate choice and stark contrast to her sunlit bedroom. Excessive illumination did little to aid her concentration. Amidst the books, towering stacks of paperwork, and the comforting gaze of James Kimberley in the portrait, she felt a sense of tranquillity. Her eyes lingered on the captivating brown eyes of the portrait, a poignant reminder of a love unreturned despite the depth with which she had cherished him.

She jolted as the phone rang.

"Hello," Ophelia said, staring at a grandfather clock in the corner of the office. It was eighteen minutes past seven in the morning.

"Mrs Kimberley," said a gruff voice on the other side of the phone.

"Yes?"

"It's Mr Kentley from the bank," the voice continued. "I was wondering if we could speak to Mr. Kimberley. We've not yet received communication from him for an extended duration to the leasehold. It is imperative that we discuss this. There are only twelve months remaining before it reverts to the bank."

"Ah yes, of course. Unfortunately, my husband is unwell."

"We've been calling every month for the last two years, Mrs Kimberley —"

"He is a man of a certain age, I have requested a telephone appointment several times—" Ophelia responded.

"It is a matter which needs to be resolved in person, paperwork signed—"

"—I have offered to do it in his stead," Ophelia interjected.

"Unless you have power of attorney—"

"I do not," Ophelia said, annoyed.

"Then, as mentioned, he must make his way to Edinburgh, could you facilitate this?"

"I'll do my best," Ophelia said.

The man abruptly terminated the call, and Ophelia, consumed by anger, unintentionally slammed her phone harder than intended. For a fleeting moment, she feared it was damaged. She redirected her attention to the man in the portrait, realising that she was facing certain destitution.

Ophelia acknowledged the necessity of finding a solution to her current predicament, but without Mr Kimberley present, the forfeiture of the property was the inevitable conclusion. If the hotel were still generating the same income as a decade ago, it wouldn't have been a problem, Ophelia had learnt that money spoke louder than words.

While some families still frequented the hotel, a shift towards modern conveniences like air travel had impacted the business. A surge in cancellations, exacerbated by this year's snowstorm, had dealt a devastating blow. Ophelia faced the stark reality of having to sell. Of course, doing so without Mr. Kimberley would prove difficult, but she was determined to find a way, as she always did. Yet, as she grappled with the impending sale, a deeper question loomed: what would she do with Tytus?

If Tytus had been born normal, she might have been able to use him. He was, after all, James Kimberley's only child and therefore the rightful inheritor of the estate. Unfortunately, Mr. Kimberley had never acknowledged Tytus as such, and while it was something that pained Ophelia to this day, there were ways around that. Forging his signature onto Tytus' birth certificate was the easy part... but changing how Tytus was born was an impossibility. Ophelia had considered using Finlay instead, but the boy was volatile and certain to threaten to reveal her duplicity for as long as she lived. Her pride would not allow her to ask him for help; she would rather die in a workhouse.

An ear-piercing scream rang through the hotel, causing Ophelia to jump out of her seat. Alarmed, she rushed out of her office and bumped into James Wilson so hard she was almost sent crashing to the floor. The singer grabbed her firmly by the arm and smiled. He was sweating, wearing grey sweatpants and a matching jumper, with a thick wool black scarf and gloves.

"Sorry, I went out for a run and heard a scream as I walked back in," James explained, reading the question on her face.

"Yes, I am going to see to it now," Ophelia replied.

Ophelia hunkered up the stairs, breathing far harder than she used to, until she reached the second floor, where the commotion emanated from. Sat against the wall sat Maude Blakesley, completely distraught, with her husband kneeling beside her, attempting to provide comfort. Miss Ursula Dankworth and the other guests on that floor—Mr. and Mrs White, along with their friends Ndeshi and Hachem—were also gathered, observing the drama. Behind Ophelia, she heard the footsteps of Finlay, his pronounced limp catching her attention, which she hadn't noticed the night before.

"What's the matter, Mrs. Blakesley?" Ophelia asked.

"It's Blanchette, we don't know where she is," Mr Blakesley replied in her stead.

"Finlay, could you escort Mr. and Mrs. Blakesley to their room?"

"Aye," her nephew mumbled.

Mr Blakesley extended a hand to help his wife off the floor.

"My sincere apologies for the disruption," Ophelia said to the remaining guests.

"Do let us know if you locate the girl," Mr White said to her before going back into his room along with his wife and friends.

"Is there anything I can assist you with ma'am?" Ophelia asked Ms Dankworth who appeared lost in thought.

"No..." Ursula replied but stopped before entering her room. "Ms Clyde, do keep me informed."

"Of course, Ms. Dankworth. I'm sure we'll find her soon. Blanchette is a troublesome child, this would not be the first time she caused a ruckus."

Ophelia turned on her heels and walked back down the stairs, meeting Finlay along the way.

"Told you," he whispered in her ear.

Ophelia ignored him until they reached the bottom of the stairs.

"Come with me," Ophelia said, guiding him into her office. She closed the door behind him and turned on Finlay. "Burn this."

Ophelia opened her desk drawer and removed the bloodied cloth Finlay had given to her the night before.

"What if Tytus did something to her?" Finlay said.

"We don't know that he did —"

Finlay pointed to the cloth. "This and his admission that the Blakesley girl had been down there says otherwise."

"Neither you nor I need any attention brought upon us," Ophelia replied.

"Then you better hope your son didn't harm that girl. Because if he did, he won't be the only secret that gets out," Finlay offered Ophelia a malicious smile.

"You can be certain of that, Finlay. Now do as I asked and burn the damn thing," Ophelia replied through gritted teeth.

Finlay offered a mocking bow and turned to leave.

"Once all this is done, I'll need you to go to Edinburgh and take care of a few things for me," Ophelia added.

Her nephew didn't respond, but simply stared at her blankly before leaving Ophelia alone with her thoughts. At that moment, all she could think of was returning to her room, kneeling by the bedside table, and opening the Bible once more, choosing a passage from 1 Peter 5:8.

"Be sober, be vigilant; because your adversary the devil, as a roaring lion, walketh about, seeking whom he may devour."

URSULA

December 24th 1953, 19:11

Ursula had been steadfast in her belief in Finlay's guilt. Every piece of evidence seemed to point to him—the discovery of her coat by him earlier that morning, and within it, his rare Sheppard lighter, strongly indicating he was the last person to see Blanchette alive. Additionally, Silvia, the kitchen maid, had witnessed an altercation between Blanchette and Finlay, a detail the groundskeeper had conveniently omitted. Coupled with his history of violence towards women, Ursula was convinced of Finlay's guilt in the murder. However, with the revelation of the hidden guest and the discovery of the bloodied cloth still fresh in her mind, Ursula found herself wavering in her certainty.

In an effort to assert his innocence, Finlay reached for his desk, retrieving the cloth from within a drawer. The mixture of emotions—anger, betrayal, and disgust—displayed on Ophelia's face confirmed that, at least in this instance, Finlay was not lying. Such unexpected turns were what fuelled Ursula's passion for detective work. There was always a rush of adrenaline from the challenge of reevaluating every minute detail. However, haunted by past failures, Ursula hesitated. She feared that Blanchette Darlow would end up as yet another name on her list.

Ursula shifted her focus to the meticulously arranged drawings on the wall and the orderly organisation of the groundskeeper's room. Drawing from her investigative experience, Blanchette's murder didn't seem to align with the habits of a meticulous person. The lines on the drawings were etched to perfection as if they had always existed untouched by human hands—no smudges on any of the papers. If Finlay were the killer, one might expect the act to be executed with precision, showcasing his skill and pride in his work. However, Blanchette bore the signs of a brutal assault, with no apparent attempt to conceal the body.

Ursula couldn't reconcile this chaos with someone as evidently fastidious as Finlay. Frustration pierced her; she had hoped to find evidence implicating him, especially considering what he had done to Silvia and Julia. She couldn't shake the feeling that there were likely more women who had fallen victim to the groundskeeper's malevolence. She knew from experience that he would not stop if he continued to go unchallenged.

"Where is your son now, Ms Clyde?" Ursula asked.

"In his room," Ophelia replied quietly.

"See! She knows where I was. I go to him every night after dark, once all the guests have gone to rest for the night, I take him out for a walk. She knows this! I'm innocent!" Finlay added angrily.

"You may be innocent of *this* crime, Mr Muir, but you are not innocent," Ursula replied before, turning to Ophelia. "Is your son violent, Ms Clyde?"

"He can get a little restless at times, but —" Ophelia started.

"Could he have posed a danger to the Blanchette?"

"He can get a little restless at times," Ophelia repeated. "He isn't used to being around new people."

"Tell the truth," Finlay spat. "For once in your life, just tell the truth! You tell me to check on him because you're afraid of him."

"I'm not afraid...but —"

"But, what?"

"There have been instances where Tytus has gotten out of hand," Ophelia replied.

"Who looked after him before Finlay came to Loch Linnhe?" Ursula asked.

"I've had other groundskeepers. They all left."

"Did Tytus hurt them?"

"Sometimes, not often. As I said, he can get restless sometimes."

Finlay scoffed. "Don't forget about what he did to you."

"That was nothing," Ophelia said through gritted teeth.

"Care to elaborate?" Ursula asked, curious.

"There was an altercation days before the guests started arriving for Christmas," Ophelia explained. "Finlay was in Fort William for a few days, so in his absence, I took over his responsibilities. I spent a few nights with Tytus. It was nice. He was fine at first, but after a few days, he started asking me for Finlay. He's grown very accustomed to him. When I told him Finlay wasn't here, he became restless...he didn't mean to hit me...but—" Ophelia stopped. "He isn't violent."

Ursula turned to look at the bloodied cloth in her hand. "What about this?"

"How do we know Finlay didn't plant it?" Ophelia replied.

"You evil bitch!" Finlay shouted. "You told me to burn it!"

Shocked, Ursula turned to the hotel manager: "Is this true?"

"Look," Ophelia started defensively.

"Is it true?" Ursula repeated.

After a moment's hesitation, she got her answer. "I didn't think anything of it. Finlay expressed his concern that Blanchette may have found out about Tytus and he may have shown me the bloodied cloth, clearly our recollections differ, but that doesn't automatically mean Tytus had anything to do with Blanchette's murder."

"But you feared he might have, which is why you didn't mention it when I spoke to you earlier today."

"It might have slipped my mind—"

"I doubt anything slips your mind, Ms Clyde," Ursula interrupted. "How do I know you aren't both in on this together? You've known about your nephew's vile behaviour towards female members of staff. You clearly know something about his time in Edinburgh and it appears he has been keeping your secrets too. So tell me why I shouldn't think you're both involved in her murder."

"Because," Ophelia said slowly. "If I wanted rid of Blanchette, I would not have ordered such a brutal attack. If

I had wanted rid of Blanchette, she would have passed away peacefully in her sleep. If I had wanted rid of Blanchette, you would have never found her body."

Ursula's breath caught in her throat, her heart pounding with disbelief. The response hit her like a cold slap in the face, leaving her speechless. The chilling nonchalance with which Ophelia delivered her words made Ursula wonder, for a fleeting moment, whether the hotel manager herself could be capable of such a thing. Could someone so composed and collected on the surface conceal such dark secrets? Her earlier assertion that Mr. Kimberley had left her in sole charge of the hotel, after only a year of her employment there, hadn't sat well with Ursula. It added to the sense of foreboding that now enveloped her.

"I am innocent," Ophelia continued. "And I trust in my son's innocence, so I did not think mentioning him or anything Finlay had recounted was relevant."

"You didn't think telling me that you had information about Blanchette's movements on the night of her disappearance was relevant?"

Ophelia did not respond immediately, providing Ursula with a moment to grapple with the motivations driving the hotel manager's actions. In the intricate web of possibilities, the threads all wove into a single answer: love. Despite her choice to confine her son, Ophelia wouldn't have hidden his existence or shielded him from the investigation if not for love. This sentiment was difficult to discern through the hardness in her eyes and the bitterness etched on her face, but it existed—revealed through actions that spoke louder than words ever could.

"He isn't violent," Ophelia repeated. But, it sounded as if it was more to herself than Ursula.

"And yet, you didn't tell me about him, which makes me wonder if you actually believe that," Ursula replied. "I'll need you to take me to him."

"Yes, of course," Ophelia said thinly.

Ursula, Finlay and Ophelia exited the groundskeeper's room and made their way down the narrow hallway, just as James Wilson left his room.

"Hey!" the singer said. "I was gonna go looking for you. What did I miss?"

James frowned, sensing the mood.

"Would you be able to do me a favour?" Ursula asked him. "Could I ask you to track down Aoghan and Ariel White, ask them a few questions about last night, anything that may help us?"

James hesitated. Ursula could sense his nervousness.

"Are you sure?" he asked.

Ursula nodded and placed a reassuring hand on his arm before following Ophelia and Finlay down the stairs to the basement. The descent felt more like entering a mediaeval dungeon than a modern facility. The cold stone steps were steep, reminiscent of the rugged architecture of an old Scottish castle.

As Ursula reached the landing, she found herself in a corridor that seemed to whisper of a history predating the hotel's construction. Surprisingly wide, it hinted at its former life as part of a fortress, now seamlessly integrated into the modern structure. The walls, once adorned with mustard paisley-patterned wallpaper, had faded to a sombre black-brown hue, bearing singe marks in places—a testament to the passage of time and the stories they held.

Above, elegant chandeliers hung from the ceiling, remnants of the corridor's regal past. At the end loomed a tall, imposing metal door, secured by a weighty lock. Ophelia, her gaze flickering with uncertainty, proceeded to insert a large key into the lock, the heavy click echoing down the corridor.

The door creaked open, revealing a vast, cavernous chamber with walls of rough-hewn stone, evoking the oppressive atmosphere of a mediaeval dungeon, albeit with significantly more space. Ursula's gaze swept across the room, taking in its aura of dampness and dreariness. The only connection to the outside world was a narrow rectangular window, which offered a meagre view of the hotel grounds and allowed a trickle of fresh air and natural light into the otherwise sombre space. Her eyes settled on a large, weathered wooden table positioned at the room's centre. Upon its surface sat two bowls, their contents long since consumed, and a neatly folded pair of white socks rested atop a chair positioned beneath the table.

"Tytus," Ophelia called.

Ursula's gaze was drawn to the corner of the room, where a shape she initially mistook for a heap of clothes stirred and shifted. To her astonishment, it revealed itself to be a man of towering stature, nearing seven feet in height, if not more. As he turned to face them, Ursula struggled to conceal her shock, a gasp escaping her lips. She had never encountered anyone quite like him before—the man's face was severely lopsided, his features contorted in a way that seemed almost otherworldly. When he attempted to smile, it only served to accentuate the asymmetry. Nevertheless, there was an innocence in his eyes, as if he were untouched by the horrors of humanity. Tytus limped towards them, his movements slow and deliberate.

"Finney," he mumbled lovingly before embracing his cousin in a bear hug so deep that the groundskeeper was momentarily hidden from view.

"Alright, alright. Let me go," Finlay said, breaking away.

Ursula thought she detected a flicker of a smile on the groundskeeper's countenance. It struck her as odd; in all her days at the hotel, she couldn't recall seeing anything other than a furrowed brow adorning Finlay's face.

"Ma," Tytus then said a little less effusively as he placed a large hand on his mother's face before moving it away. "And this?"

Tytus turned to Ursula and widened his smile.

"This is Ms Dankworth," Ophelia explained. "She is here to ask you a few questions."

"Pleasure to meet you Tytus," Ursula returned the smile before turning her attention to the table again.

Her gaze shifted to Finlay, who had been observing her as if anticipating a sign of recognition. While the groundskeeper had been truthful about Tytus' existence, it didn't entirely absolve him from suspicion in Blanchette's murder. Due to Tytus' evident physical and mental challenges, Ursula struggled to believe that he would be capable of such a heinous act.

Ursula hesitated for a few moments before continuing. Her attention returned to the table and the two neatly placed bowls.

"Are you expecting company?" she inquired, pointing at the bowls.

Tytus's smile widened even more, exposing teeth so discoloured they could've been mistaken for wooden teeth.

"My friend," Tytus replied with glee.

"Finlay?" Ursula enquired.

Tytus shook his thick mane of hair. Stumped, Ursula thought of something else and removed the wooden spinning top from her pocket and presented it to Tytus. His face instantly beamed, recognising the toy. He grabbed it from her hand and spun it on his own.

"Blanq," Tytus said, spinning the top again.

"Who?" Ursula asked.

"My friend. Blanq."

"Blanche?"

"Blanq! My friend! Blanq! My friend!" he echoed innocently, and pointed at the spinning top.

Ursula heard Ophelia release a sigh filled with concern behind her and turned, her anger rising as she recalled Ophelia's denial of ever seeing the spinner. Now, it was unmistakably clear that it belonged to her son.

"T for Tytus," Ursula whispered, finally connecting the two. "Blanchette was here?" Ursula asked him and when Tytus assented with his head, she asked. "When?"

"Yest'day," Tytus replied. "Ma hurt her." Finlay and Ursula both turned to Ophelia and sensing the confusion

Tytus continued. "Not ma! Not ma! Ma hurt her. Blanq was sad, ma hurt her!"

Tytus walked over and stood in front of Ophelia protectively.

"I've known Blanchette since she was a wee girl," the hotel manager said as if this would confirm her innocence. Murder victims were often killed by those they knew well.

Unfortunately, Ophelia's secrecy only deepened Ursula's suspicions. A mother, driven by a fierce protectiveness, could go to great lengths to shield her child. What if Blanchette's presence had somehow unsettled Tytus, prompting him to lash out at the girl? It could explain the blood-stained cloth that Finlay had discovered, as well as the brutality of Blanchette's attack. Yet, when one considered that Tytus had set the table for two, seemingly expecting her return, such a theory became increasingly improbable. It seemed more likely that he had no awareness of Blanchette's demise.

Ursula sighed heavily, her mind a whirlwind of fragments. She shut her eyes tight, attempting to weave together the scattered pieces of information. But the more she grasped, the more the puzzle eluded her. Pacing the room, she scrutinised every detail, searching for a thread of truth within the lies. It seemed that everyone she had interrogated, from Hachem to Ophelia, harboured secrets they valued more than finding out what happened to Blanchette. Despite the fog of uncertainty, Ursula's focus honed in on Tytus, a central figure in this current enigma.

"Tytus...you said 'ma hurt her.' What did you mean?" Ursula inquired.

Tytus ambled towards a small window near the ceiling, offering a view of the front of the hotel.

"Blanq...Ma' hurt her," he said, mimicking a striking motion with his hand.

At that moment, Ursula finally understood.

JAMES

December 24th 1953, 19:15

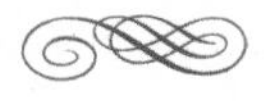

James found Aonghus in the kitchen, as anticipated. The cook sat tucked into a corner, a glass of scotch cradled in his hand, his eyes distant, lost in introspection. Despite his advancing years, Aonghus retained a tall and imposing stature, softened by his genial demeanour. His warmth and friendly nature had always fostered a sense of comfort, reminiscent of Father Christmas, welcoming and reassuring to all who crossed his path.

Next to him, Hamish sat, visibly lost in his own thoughts, his shoulders slumped and head bowed, a clear reflection of the waiter's ongoing despondency since learning of Blanchette's demise. It was obvious that Hamish had developed feelings for the Blakesley girl. The ache of young heartbreak was palpable in his expression. James couldn't help but recall his own first experience with heartbreak and the profound impact it had left. Sadly, as Hamish would no doubt discover, age didn't alleviate the pain of heartbreak; it merely offered more experience in navigating its depths. The moment of heartbreak was like being plunged to the bottom of the ocean and struggling for breath, feeling alone, and afraid you'd be forever lost to the murky waters. Eventually, he would break through and finding new love would feel like taking that first inhale of fresh air after emerging from the depths.

A sudden wave of hesitation washed over James as he approached. Here he was, about to interrogate a suspect in a murder investigation. He didn't really believe that Aonghus was capable, but as Ursula had emphasised, the first rule of detective work was never to make assumptions. That, and making sure to leave all preconceptions behind. Focusing on one detail could make him overlook a crucial clue. Detective stories had always fascinated James, but of course, the idea of becoming one back home was impossible. Luckily for him, he had music to turn to.

Fascination aside, James lacked experience in leading investigations. Ursula had always been the one spearheading the efforts, relegating him to little more than a spectator. Now, confronted with the daunting task of leading an interrogation, the weight of responsibility settled heavily on his shoulders, causing his knees to tremble. What questions should he ask? Would anyone take him seriously? James doubted his ability to conduct a thorough interrogation. Yet, Ursula had entrusted him with this role, implying that she saw potential in him. She believed he could rise to the occasion. She believed he could be her Watson.

James observed the two men from the shadows, summoning the courage to approach them. The idea of interrogating Aonghus felt wrong; he was the kindest person in the hotel, a trusted confidant for everyone, even Ms.

Clyde. The thought that such a gentle soul could be capable of such a deed seemed unfathomable to James. As a fluttering sensation stirred in his stomach and his palms grew moist, James reminded himself once more of the critical importance of keeping his perceptions and assumptions in check.

"Aonghus," James said. "I was wonderin' if I could ask you a few questions about last night?"

The cook turned to look at him with that ever-present twinkle in his eyes.

"Ah yes, you're helping Detective Dankworth," he replied warmly.

"Yes, I am."

"Grab a seat," Aonghus said, pointing to the empty chair in front of him. "Hamish, I'll check on you later alright?"

The young waiter nodded glumly and walked away, leaving Aonghus and James alone in the cold kitchen.

"God, how do you stand it here?" James asked, rubbing his hands together.

"The stove is rarely off, I spend more time sweating my balls off than I do cold. It's almost welcome, to be honest," Aonghus replied. "Do you want some tea?"

"No thanks," James said. "But I could do with a shot of whiskey."

"Drinking on the job, eh? Well, I'm not one to judge! We have a great single malt that I only open on Christmas day but given the circumstances..."

Aonghus hobbled to a cupboard, retrieved two glasses and a bottle of whiskey, and expertly poured the amber liquid into them. He then made his way back to the table and handed one glass to James. James took a sip, feeling the warmth of the whiskey spread through him, from his throat to his chest, instantly thawing the chill that had settled there.

"Thanks, I needed this."

"Ms Dankworth working you to the bone?" the cook quipped. "Would you like some apple crumble? Mr Blakesley asked me to make some for his wife, as a bit of a pick me up."

"I'm more of a pecan pie kinda guy. Can't beat my mama's pecan pie...well, actually her sweet potato pie was heavenly. Mama used to make the best sweet potato pie."

"I've never understood the idea of sweet potato as a dessert, but hey, to each their own."

"Look," James said, changing his tone. "I know where you were after dinner, you were playing cards with me. So I am sorta your alibi...but after the game finished, where did you go?"

"I always go outside for a smoke before bed," Aonghus replied." Well, a smoke and to clear the mind."

"How long were you outside for?"

"Twenty to thirty minutes."

"What do you mean by wantin' to clear your mind?"

"Once you get to my age, you have so many thoughts, memories, regrets...that sometimes you just need your brain to stop. The cold, the darkness outside, helps me to clear my mind. I sleep better for it."

"So kinda like meditation."

"Why, yes! I'd never thought of it like that, but yes, like meditation."

"Did you see anything out of the ordinary?" James probed.

"Have you been outside after dark, son? You can barely see anything. It's why I choose that time of day to decompress. Makes me feel like it's only me in the world, nothing else."

"You've worked here a long time—"

"Fourteen years," Aonghus chimed in.

"So you've known Blanchette for—."

"All her life. They holiday here every year. Her dad was a kind man. Loved his daughter to bits. Blanchette always had a bit of a rebellious nature about her, but her dad's passing changed her," Aonghus explained.

"How?"

"Well, he was her only source of love. Mrs Blakesley has always been a rather distant mother. Her and Kenneth had a troublesome relationship," noticing the look of askance on James' face, the cook continued. "We used to sit up to all hours every Christmas, just talking. He would come into the kitchen and talk to me just like you and me now. I don't think he quite liked his class of people, you know?"

"Who can blame him, eh?" James joked. "And how did Blanchette change?"

"Why, in the same way, anyone who loses the only love they have would. There was a need for constant attention. The only way to feel seen, to feel like her mother knew she existed, was by getting into trouble. Mrs Blakesley has quite a temper, mind."

"So you'd say her relationship with her mother was strained?" James asked.

"Strained is a nice way of putting it, yes."

"How about with Mr Blakesley, what was her relationship like with him?"

"Seemed fine. Cordial. He had her charmed...only—" Aonghus stopped to think for a moment, clearly there was something in his mind he was unsure of mentioning.

"Only?"

"Well, Blanchette once shared with me the story of how Mr Blakesley had met her mother," Aonghus remarked, savouring another sip of the scotch. "You see, he and Kenneth were in the same regiment. The tale goes that as Kenneth lay wounded on the battlefield, he remembered a letter he had penned in case of his demise. It was conveniently stuffed in his pocket. Given their deep friendship, so the story goes, there was no one Kenneth trusted more than Mr. Blakesley to deliver those final words to his wife."

"I could be wrong, but I detect a certain amount of scepticism," James asked.

"You detect well," Aonghus replied with a smile, although a scowl now framed his otherwise friendly face. "Kenneth *hated* his wife. The one thing he was not going to do was pen a letter to the person he hated most in this world. Now, if the letter had been written to Blanchette, why, that makes more sense."

"I mean, maybe their relationship got better with time?"

"They had no such relationship," Aonghus shook his head. "They were married, yes. But they didn't share a bed, and hardly spoke...there was no affection. Kenneth hated Maude. All those nights we stayed up talking until the wee hours of the morning...he told me. Everything. Mrs Blakesley would have been overjoyed at his death and I am telling you Kenneth would not have written a letter to her. Besides, Blanchette showed me the letter. It was the last memory of her dad, she carried it for several years as if it were gold. Not a drop of blood on it. Not a speck of dirt. Nothing."

"What are you exactly are you implyin'?" James asked.

Aonghus leaned in closer to James, the scent of smoked wood and vanilla in his breath hung between them.

"I am not implying, I am telling you that the letter Mr Blakesley says he got from a dying Kenneth Darlow to give to his wife, can't have been written by him."

James leaned back, allowing Aonghus' suspicions to sink in. He wasn't sure whether the whiskey was starting to affect the cook or whether he truly believed everything he'd just revealed.

"I see," James said softly, his mind abuzz with this new information. "Just a couple more questions, if you don't mind."

"Not at all."

"When was the last time you saw Blanchette?"

"Last night, before our card game. We had a little chat."

"What about?"

"She was upset about something, I'm not quite sure what, we didn't delve into the details."

"Thank you," James said standing up. "For talkin' to me and not bein' difficult."

"Why on earth would I want to be difficult?"

"You'd be surprised," James replied.

With a knowing gesture, he drew him into a hug, holding him firmly. James hesitated at first, then surrendered to the embrace, allowing the moment to envelop them. Suddenly, the tension that had gripped him throughout the interrogation melted away, as if it had never existed.

"Don't you ever let anyone question your worth as a human being. Not for a moment," he spoke with earnest conviction. The cook offered a smile, then turned and limped out of the kitchen, leaving James feeling both grateful for his comforting words.

URIAH

December 23rd 1953 23:34

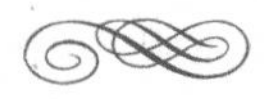

Uriah huddled in the corner of the bed, holding Zeke tightly as he observed the stocky, dark-skinned man. Lyle swayed back and forth, tugging at his cuffs, his eyes darting nervously from side to side. Occasionally, they landed on Uriah with a hint of concern before returning to his peculiar behaviour. While it was clear that Lyle didn't pose a direct threat, Uriah knew that caution was still necessary to navigate himself out of the unsettling situation.

"I'm sorry," Lyle muttered, averting his stare. "I promised my cousin I'd be better. If I let you go—"

"If?" Uriah interrupted. "Is there another option?"

Lyle seemed startled by the question, and stood stockstill for a few moments, as if frozen by time. When he next spoke, his voice was meek, even ashamed.

"Promise not to tell anyone?"

He nodded in silent agreement, though he knew there was little chance he would keep what happened to himself. There was no denying that Uriah had always struggled to differentiate right from wrong, but the images of children in Lyle's possession were undeniably wrong. His behaviour, the panic that had overtaken the man following Uriah's discovery, was evidence of that. The look in the eyes of the children depicted in the pictures was one he recognized; they held unmistakable traces of fear and sadness. He had been assailed by those sentiments far too often not to recognize them in others. At this very moment, he could see it in Lyle too, and a part of him felt conflicted. After all, he hadn't done anything to him; it had been Uriah who'd heeded Zeke and followed Lyle into his room. Perhaps it would be the right thing to keep his secret...

Perhaps we can use it, Zeke suggested.

"How can I trust you ain't gonna say anythin'?" Lyle persisted. "The last time I trusted someone..."

Lyle looked away, unable to continue, the unearthed memories too much for him to handle.

"What happened to the last person you trusted?" Uriah asked him.

"It was in Zurich," Lyle started, but stopped almost immediately, shaking his head profusely. "No, I don't wanna think about him."

"Did you hurt him?" Uriah probed.

"Oh, god no!" Lyle offered with affront. "How could you think that of me?"

"What about the children in the pictures?"

"I *never* harmed 'em...they are f-f-for...comfort," Lyle replied.

"Comfort?"

"You wouldn't understand—"

Adults always seemed to default to pointing out a child's supposed lack of understanding whenever they struggled to justify their actions or felt ashamed of them. Uriah's father had hurled that same phrase at him countless times. They didn't grasp that he wasn't like other children; he could understand, he craved understanding.

"I understand that if you are so scared of me telling someone about the pictures, then your comfort is wrong."

Lyle stopped rocking back and forth and looked at Uriah, clearly considering his words. After a few minutes of heavy silence, Uriah gradually shifted away from the corner of the bed and settled beside Lyle. He turned to face him, his gaze fixed on the troubled man.

"You want to touch me, don't you? Like you did back in the dining room?"

Zeke told him to say that.

Lyle turned towards Uriah, a hint of fear flickering in his eyes at the question posed.

"I don't like being touched," Uriah added. "Grandma Lucy hugged me all the time. Father doesn't. No one has, not properly, not since mother died. But you want to."

Lyle looked away from him again.

"I have bad thoughts sometimes too," Uriah said quietly. "They aren't my thoughts...someone else. Another voice. Is that what happens to you?"

Lyle turned his head slowly back to Uriah, and their gazes locked, a profound understanding passing between them.

"Yes," he replied. "I try to fight it but...it tells me it's alright. It tells me there's nothin' wrong with feelin' pleasure.

Tells me that I don't need to harm anyone, that I shouldn't, and I haven't...at least not purposely."

"Then it's a good voice," Uriah said darkly, not looking at Lyle but instead gazing into Zeke's unmoving eyes. "It's his voice I hear. I don't fight it any more...it's worse if I do. It huffs and it puffs...until I do what it wants. I pushed a girl down the stairs once. She didn't die, but I wished she would have," Uriah concluded, devoid of any emotion, before standing up. "There, you have my secret; I have yours. Will you take me back to my room?"

Lyle frowned, his struggle to mask his emotions evident to Uriah, who could discern the concern and fear beneath the facade. It was clear that the confession had unsettled him. Uriah had never before disclosed his secret to anyone. His grandparents had suspicions that he'd pushed the girl, but she had been too terrified to speak up. Uriah had made it clear that if she ever breathed a word of it, he would return to finish what he started. He felt a flicker of excitement at the prospect of sharing the knife incident with Lyle but quickly dismissed it. A secret for a secret.

As they turned to leave, a sudden knock echoed through the room. Lyle swiftly ushered Uriah out of view before cautiously cracking the door open.

"Hey!" It was the singer. "I was headin' to my room and saw your bedroom light was still on. I just wanted to tell you that you killed it tonight."

"Thanks," Lyle replied simply.

The singer hesitated for a moment, before continuing.

"But..listen....stay away from the kid," James' tone shifted. This was the true reason he'd knocked.

"James, I promise you—"

"No, Lyle. I saw what I saw and I won't pretend I don't know what you are any more," James interrupted angrily.

"What I am?" Lyle replied, feigning confusion.

"You know what I'm talkin' about, Lyle! Zurich...and all the accusations back home?"

"James, you know everythin' has been a big misunderstandin'," Lyle defended himself.

"Lyle, for the love of god! I saw you the other night! I ain't gonna allow myself to be blinded by you anymore! I love you, but I just can't..."

"I know," Lyle replied.

"I'm not sure you do. Goodnight, Lyle."

Lyle closed the door softly, his finger pressed to his lips in a gesture of silence. After a momentary pause, he cautiously opened the door once more, motioning for Uriah to follow. However, as they neared the entrance to the expansive dining hall, Lyle suddenly stopped in his tracks.

"We gotta be quick, someone might see us," he said.

It was clear that Lyle's conversation with James was weighing heavily on his mind. Uriah gave a quiet nod and watched as Lyle retreated through the dining hall and disappeared behind the staff doors, leaving Uriah alone. Moving swiftly, he was about to step into the foyer when he noticed the front door creaking open. To his surprise, there stood his father, with a fragile woman by his side. She seemed unsteady on her feet, relying on his father for support. He recognised her. It was the pretty woman he'd interacted with earlier that evening. They made their way towards the stairwell, but the woman stumbled and fell.

"Are you alright?"

The woman nodded as Uriah's father helped her to her feet. Unexpectedly, she leaned in and kissed his father, leaving Uriah taken aback. He stepped back in astonishment, watching from the shadows, expecting his father to push her away or reprimand her. However, to his surprise, his father embraced her even more tightly, savouring the moment. Was this a part of his father's new scheme? Did it mean they were leaving Darlow Manor?

Uriah had grown accustomed to his life as it was. Maude was slightly distant and Blanchette exasperatingly annoying, but it had become familiar territory to him. As his grandmother Lucy used to say, *'Better the devil you know.'* The sight of his father with another woman ignited a familiar anger within him. If Maude were to find out about yet another indiscretion, it could shatter their fragile family dynamic. Uriah seethed and wondered if his father was intentionally sabotaging their lives. Perhaps he wished for Maude to discover his infidelity, so he could fulfil his longstanding threat to send Uriah away. However, Uriah was determined not to be cast aside so easily.

MAUDE

December 24th 1953, 20:12

Maude found herself in a quiet sanctuary of solitude, feeling a fresh wave of tears welling up in her quivering lashes. She observed as they fell, each droplet tracing a delicate path down her cheeks before gently alighting on the white sheets below. They seemed to disappear, absorbed by the fabric as if they had never existed at all.

Her relationship with Blanchette had always been strained, hindered by Maude's inability to show affection due to her deep-rooted rancour. Blanchette was not only a product of multiple drunken attempts to consume her marriage, but also a result of an enforced, loveless union—a consequence of Kenneth's intrusion into Maude's room and forcing himself upon her. To add further insult to injury, Blanchette bore an unsettling resemblance to her father. Maude could not look at Blanchette without reliving the emotional torment inflicted upon her by Kenneth.

It was therefore bizarre and confusing that her heart would ache as much as it did. Each tear that fell on the bed echoed like the solemn pounding of a nail onto a coffin. Every protracted, laboured breath she drew felt akin to a dagger being gradually thrust into her ribs. Maude had never, in Blanchette's fifteen years of life, known that her love for her daughter reached such profound depths. Then again, the bittersweet truth remained that people only recognised a loved one's true worth in the absence of their embrace. For all Blanchette's shortcomings, she had always been affectionate. Unfortunately for her daughter, Maude's emotional wounds ran too deep to offer any semblance of love. Perhaps the pain she felt wasn't sorrow at all, but a mixture of fear, regret and guilt at what she had done.

A knock at the door shattered Maude's introspective reverie, pulling her back from the depths of remorse her mind was urging her to delve into. She glanced at Theron, who seemed to rouse from the lethargic state he'd been in all day. He made his way to the door and opened it.

"Hello," Theron said softly.

Detective Dankworth and the singer entered, their expressions sombre, mirroring the gravity of the situation.

"I hope I am of no disturbance," Detective Dankworth said. "I understand it's still quite a sensitive time, but it would be great to continue where we left off earlier today."

"Of course," Theron replied.

Maude sat up, sensing the weighty burden of turmoil stirring within her. Once again, she felt the lightheadedness that had plagued her for the last few months return. Along with it came the tingling of her extremities and a slight numbness, though thankfully, the symptoms did not persist.

"I do not mean to cause any additional distress with my line of questioning—," the detective continued.

"Get on with it, Ms Dankworth," Maude interjected impatiently.

Detective Dankworth gave a solemn nod before gracefully settling onto Uriah's unoccupied bed, withdrawing a small notebook from her pocket. A veil of sorrow seemed to envelop her, the anguish in her eyes unmistakable. Perhaps it was this suffering that drove her to seek solace in the numbing embrace of alcohol. Yet beneath it all, Maude detected a reservoir of self-worth waiting to be reclaimed.

"Where's Uriah?" the detective asked, looking around the room.

"He was a little restless, so I sent him downstairs. Playing the piano seems to relax him," Theron explained. "Do you need to speak to him again?"

"Later perhaps," Detective Dankworth replied, before turning to Maude. "Mrs Blakesley, could you confirm your whereabouts yesterday evening?"

The detective seemed to flinch ever so slightly as she turned the pages of her little red notebook on her lap, an action that struck Maude as rather odd. Glancing at the singer standing beside her, Maude noted his demeanour—like a love-struck puppy, ready to bark, jump, or roll at a moment's notice. It was both pathetic and beautiful. No one had ever looked at her the way the singer looked at Detective Dankworth.

"I had dinner," Maude started. "Then spent an hour or so with Mr and Mrs White."

"Are you certain? Mr White said he went straight to his room after dinner," countered Detective Dankworth.

"Ah, yes. I might be confusing the days. My apologies...as you can imagine—"

"Of course," Ms Dankworth said. "Take your time."

"We had dinner," Maude started again. "Then we went back to our room, it might have been around seven in the evening. Ophelia knocked to let me know there was a call for me, it was my mother. We were on the phone for five minutes, maybe a little longer. Then I went back to my room," Maude paused, casting a glance towards her husband. "Theron and I had a small disagreement. He left, and I followed after him. When I failed to locate where he'd gone, I went to bed and fell asleep waiting for him. Of course, now I know he was in your bed."

If the jab had pained her, Maude could not tell. Detective Dankworth merely smiled as she jotted down notes. There was, nonetheless, discomfort etched across Theron's face.

"What time would you say, you returned to your room?" Detective Dankworth probed.

"I didn't check the time—"

"But if you had to give a time?"

"I would assume I was back in my room by nine in the evening," Maude replied. "Maybe a little after."

The detective and the singer exchanged a look.

"We have an eyewitness account of an altercation between you and your daughter occurring after the time," the detective said.

Maude felt her heart sink to the pit of her stomach, and her breathing grew more intense with each word uttered by Detective Dankworth.

"An altercation?" Theron repeated, looking towards her.

"It is further alleged," Ms Dankworth pressed, ignoring Theron's question. "That there were bruises on your daughter's face. Bruises the eyewitness could not have known she had unless he'd seen her body—"

"Perhaps he saw her body," Theron offered, confused.

"We are certain that the last time our eyewitness saw your daughter, she was alive, and that it was immediately after the altercation."

"Have you thought," Maude countered, her tongue feeling distinctly heavier. "That perhaps it is this eyewitness who you should be focusing your attention on?"

"Yes, I have thought," Detective Dankworth replied pointedly. "And after careful thought, my thoughts and their eyewitness account have led me to the conclusion that I should ask you where you were between the hours of eight and ten in the evening?"

"Whilst you were fucking, my husband you mean?"

"Oh give it a rest, Maude! Answer the question!" Theron spat.

"You seem more heartbroken by the infidelity than your daughter's murder?" the singer said. "Ms. Dankworth is doin' a darn good job speakin' to you in British, perhaps you need somethin' a little more simple. So let me repeat it in American English. An eyewitness saw you *beat the shit* outta of your daughter the night before she turned up dead."

Maude, unable to move, nor open her mouth to respond, looked on silently. Her heart was thumping with such force she wondered whether it might succumb to the sudden strain.

"Ophelia mentioned on a couple of occasions," Detective Dankworth said taking the baton from the singer. "That Blanchette can be quite difficult. Is this correct?"

"Aonghus also mentioned that her behaviour changed after her father's death," the singer added.

"She's a dreamer," Theron replied. "Strong-willed and lacks a filter, but I wouldn't say she is difficult."

"Mrs Blakesley, can you tell us what made you go to Blanchette's room early this morning?" the detective probed. "Do you usually check in on the kids in the morning?"

Maude could feel a heat rise within her, flushing her ears and reaching her eyes, as if a hundred furnaces had suddenly been ignited. The urge to shed her dress and plunge into a cool pool was overwhelming. Her gaze fixed upon the three pairs of accusing eyes, their expectant stares weighing heavily upon her. Tears welled up once more as her heart raced with anxiety. The lightheadedness returned and the words became lodged in her throat.

"Maude?" Theron's voice reached her ears, but it felt distant as if muffled by a thick curtain. The thumping in her ears intensified, a crescendo of sound, drowning the world around her.

"Did you know she was dead when you raised the alarm this morning?" came the detective's voice.

The weight of her transgressions bore down on Maude, drowning her in a tide of horror and shame. How could she bring herself to admit it? Even by her own bleak standards, what she had done to Blanchette was nothing short of horrific. She looked around the room and could have sworn that the walls were closing in on her.

"She could be quite nasty sometimes," Maude said quietly.

"What?" she heard Theron whisper "No..."

"I am not sure why I'm so surprised. I can't say I'm any better," Maude ignored Theron and continued. "Blanchette had an innate ability to know how deep to twist the knife. Few people were privy to that side of her. Behind that smile, and amidst all her fairytale lay a vile and hateful girl."

"Maude, what are you saying?" Theron asked her.

"Oh, shut up will you," she snapped. "I didn't kill her." Maude's eyes lifted, fixing upon her husband's nauseating countenance. "At least, I don't think I did."

There it was, finally spoken aloud. The thought that had gnawed at her since the discovery of Blanchette's lifeless body. It left her teetering on the precipice of a bottomless pit of uncertainty. An uncertain truth perhaps, but one that had brought to light her inadequacies as a mother.

"Can you tell me what happened?" Detective Dankworth asked.

"After our argument," Maude explained. "I waited for Theron to come back. We've been making an effort to try and talk things through and not allow any animosity to filter onto the next day. When Ms Clyde approached me to tell me about Mr White's complaint, it angered me. She knows better than to be eavesdropping on the private lives of people. It is an act beneath her station," Maude felt silent tears stream down her cheeks. "I was cold and tired and angry and...there she was, walking towards me. We exchanged words, and it wasn't long until her spiteful side that so reminds me of her father showed itself. It took me to a place...a dark place, back to those cold nights as a young woman when I would have to *'welcome'* Kenneth into my bed. Do you know what it is like to sense hatred and disgust from the person who promised to protect you until death do you part? A veil fell over my eyes. I'm not sure I was conscious of what I was doing until after the fact. It was a blind fury. I hit her and hit her and hit her..."

Maude's panic surged uncontrollably, her movements frenetic until she abruptly halted, hands raised in front of her. Her gaze fixated on the dried blood stubbornly clinging to the chipped stone of her ring.

"I am not proud of what I did. I was beside myself with shame. That is why I went to check on her this morning. I wanted to try and talk to her. When I didn't find her in her room, I asked Uriah and he told me he'd seen her last night and she was badly hurt. He saw her go back out. I panicked. What if she'd been locked outside or fallen unconscious, or...I don't know...I panicked!"

Maude turned her gaze to the detective, thankful for the absence of judgement in her expression. Yet, the same couldn't be said for the singer and Theron. Their expressions mirrored the horror Maude felt, amplifying her shame to an unbearable degree. She wished for the ground to open up and swallow her, to escape this room and the weight of her actions

"Thank you for being honest, I know it can't have been easy," Detective Dankworth said, making a final note in her notebook. "We will have to corroborate part of your story with Uriah. He made no mention of Blanchette coming back to the room after she'd left the first time. It means her time of death may have been later than we originally suspected."

The detective closed her notebook and stood up, preparing to leave.

"Did I kill her?"

The question slipped out of her mouth, it was almost as if her subconscious was seeking validation. Yet, instead of easing her mind, Detective Dankworth's response only deepened the murky waters of doubt swirling within her, leaving Maude adrift in a sea of uncertainty.

"The injuries you inflicted may have been a contributing factor," she replied. "But the truth is...I don't know."

The detective looked genuinely apologetic about being unable to remove the feeling of guilt from Maude. With a brief smile, Detective Dankworth and the singer left the room. Theron retreated into the sofa, his silence erecting an emotional barrier between them. His eyes brimmed with unmistakable disdain, avoiding meeting Maude's gaze. She couldn't help but wonder if their marriage could weather this storm.

"You know," Maude said to her husband. "One of the last things Blanchette said to me was that I would die alone. I am not sure if she understood how prophetic those words were. I came here to save a dying marriage but instead, I have lost a daughter and a husband."

"Don't be melodramatic, Maude."

"Melodramatic?" she repeated, hardly able to believe he'd had the gall to utter those words. "We're finished, Theron. Finished. You don't love me and I certainly lost the last thread of love I had left."

Maude turned his back to him, seeking refuge in the tender embrace of her daughter's bed, returning to that hushed sanctuary of solitude. Through the night she lay there, a solitary figure illuminated by the moon's soft glow. Eventually, sleep overcame her, and Maude welcomed its arrival. In the sweet embrace of dreams, perhaps she would be able to look at her daughter's face one last time.

LYLE

December 23rd 1953, 19:37

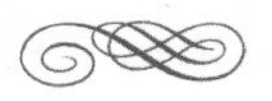

Lyle recalled the overwhelming sense of awe that swept over him the first time he laid eyes on the grand piano at the Grand Loch Linnhe Hotel. Its polished ebony surface shimmered gracefully under the gentle light streaming through the large dining room windows. In his mind's eye, he could still vividly feel the touch as he gently ran his hands across its sleek, expertly crafted contours. The level of craftsmanship and sophistication was unlike anything he had encountered before.

"Can I?" he asked the impatient looking hotel manager.

Before she could even respond, Lyle settled onto the bench and tenderly brushed his fingertips across the keytops, eliciting a subtle note. The keys responded with a delicate weight and exquisite responsiveness, conveying a sense of precision and craftsmanship. Each tone was imbued with richness, resonance, and nuance, confirming to Lyle that the instrument was of exceptional design. Never before had he encountered anything as breathtakingly beautiful and majestic as this piano.

Lyle closed his eyes, a surge of excitement coursing through his veins as he began to play the first few notes of *Claude Debussy's 'Clair de Lune.'* Instantly, he was transported to another realm, where each note became a soft whisper, reminding him of the profound beauty and transformative power of music.

Each morning brought Lyle a renewed sense of excitement and anticipation as he looked forward to another evening at the piano. The sheer joy of it all propelled him, often leading him to play for an extra hour past dinner, even if the room was empty. For Lyle, the music itself was company enough.

This particular night was different. A lone guest remained long after everyone else had departed. Entranced by the melody, her head swayed gently to the music, a serene smile gracing her face. Yet, her distant eyes betrayed an absence of mind, perhaps aided by the bottle of chardonnay resting on her table. Ms. Dankworth had arrived alone the previous day, a fact that seemed to intrigue his cousin, James.

One morning, as part of their routine, James embarked on his customary run, with Lyle lagging behind him, both immersing themselves in the wonders of the Scottish Highlands. Pausing by the frozen loch, they indulged in a ritual that had become integral to their lives since arriving at Loch Linnhe in April of that year. For Lyle, the transformation of vibrant summer greens into a warm kaleidoscope of autumn hues was a cherished sight, a testament to nature's artistic prowess. Amidst this tranquil interlude, James took the opportunity to share his thoughts about the enigmatic new guest, which elicited a cautionary response from Lyle.

"Stay away from that white girl."

"She's beautiful is all I'm sayin'," James replied.

"I thought you were doin' your thing with Julia?" Lyle asked.

"Julia is cool. We have fun but...you see that Ms Dankworth though?"

"I've seen how much she drinks, yeah! That lady drank for the whole of Scotland last night."

"Ah, it's Christmas!" James said with a smile.

The pattern of her drinking persisted into the second night, but who was Lyle to judge? Having someone listen to him beyond dinner, even in a drunken haze, brought him a sense of joy. Lyle played concerto after concerto as Ms. Dankworth ordered round after round, a service Hamish reluctantly provided. Perhaps the responsible thing would have been to summon Ophelia to escort the woman to her room, but he, too, needed this time to wallow in his own self-pity. Like a shot of whiskey, the piano's melody left a delightful and intoxicating burn within him, momentarily eclipsing his problems.

Lyle looked up from the piano keys, halting the melody, and noticed the awkward boy standing in the centre of the dining room, staring at him. Clutched firmly in the boy's grip was his ever-present stuffed animal. Lyle rose from the piano, attempting to engage the boy in conversation, but the child turned away, avoiding eye contact.

"I..." Lyle stammered, struggling with his words. "I'm sorry, I didn't mean to... it's just the music, and... I meant no harm."

Lyle descended from the stage, making his way towards the boy, and extended his hand in a gesture of goodwill. However, the child instinctively recoiled. A wave of shame washed over Lyle. The last thing he would have ever wanted was to make anyone afraid of him, especially a child. What did that say about him? He would never have wanted anyone, especially a child, to feel that way about him.

"Are you goin' to tell anyone?" Lyle asked him.

The boy remained silent, averting his gaze from him, instead focusing on the intoxicated woman.

"Look, it was a misunderstandin'. I didn't mean anythin' by it..."

Lyle stopped trying to explain himself. The Blakesley boy shuffled further away, his gaze fixed on his feet as if they held the answers he sought. He would have had better luck trying to hold a conversation with the stuffed toy. Exiting the dining room through the staff doors, Lyle walked towards his room, almost on autopilot. His mind buzzed with hypothetical scenarios of what might unfold if the Blakesley boy divulged their encounter.

The idea of leaving crossed his mind, but with the snowstorm raging outside, escape seemed unlikely. Even if he could flee, James wouldn't follow, not after the Zurich incident and their securing of the gig at Loch Linnhe. His cousin had made it abundantly clear: any repetition of such behaviour would result in Lyle's immediate report to the authorities.

Stepping into his room, he found himself engulfed in a whirlwind of negative thoughts. Longing for solace, he turned to the vintage vinyl player and selected *'I'll Be Seeing You'* by Billie Holiday. Leaning against the wall, he surrendered to the soulful resonance of Holiday's pain-ridden vocals, allowing the music to permeate his very being. Amidst the melancholic melody, his gaze was drawn to the briefcase discreetly concealed beneath the bed. He frowned, the weight of its secrets pulling at him. Stepping away, he tried to calm the clamour of voices in his head that sought to draw him closer to the contents of the suitcase. This was his daily battle.

Finally, he gave in and slid the briefcase from under the bed, withdrawing its contents. He carefully placed the images it contained on top of the bed, feeling his heart rate quicken with a mix of guilt and anticipation. He caressed the innocent faces in the images for a few moments before slowly starting to pleasure himself until he climaxed.

He turned to look at his reflection in the mirror and felt a deep wave of self-disgust wash over him. The weight of his actions bore heavily on his conscience, each deed etched into his soul like indelible scars. He longed to cleanse himself, to scrub away the stains of his misdeeds and rid himself of the perverse desires that consumed him. The guilt he felt was profound, a constant reminder of his own moral failure. He knew that these desires were an integral part of him, an unchangeable aspect that would forever taint his existence. It was a harsh realisation, an acceptance that despite his yearning for purification, he would forever carry the burden of his inner darkness. Lyle grabbed a towel and rushed out of his room towards the shared staff showers.

Stepping into the steaming cascade of water, he closed his eyes, hoping that the torrential flow would cleanse more than just his physical body. He tilted his head back, allowing the water to cascade over his face, imagining it as a torrent that could wash away his tormenting thoughts. Each droplet that kissed his skin felt like a tiny promise of relief, a brief respite from the haunting memories that plagued him. The water's gentle caress became a plea, a desperate plea for absolution, as he wished for a purification that could only exist in his wildest dreams. Yet, deep inside, he understood that no matter how vigorously he scrubbed or how fervently he yearned for redemption, his dark desires would remain, forever mingling with the purity he sought. The shower became both a sanctuary and a battlefield, where his longing for purity clashed with the relentless truth of his nature.

As Lyle returned from the shower he noticed that his bedroom door was ajar. Had he left it like that? He leaned in, placing his ear against the door and heard someone move inside it. When he entered he found the Blakesley boy, standing in the middle of his room, holding the images in his hand.

"It ain't what it looks like," Lyle said.

The boy tried to step away, but Lyle grabbed him.

"Look, not a word, okay?" Lyle implored with desperation in his eyes. "If James found out... he thinks... I told him I'm better..."

The boy wriggled, trying to break free from Lyle's grasp, but he tightened his grip around the Blakesley boy's waist.

Whilst he didn't mean the boy any harm, he also could not afford to let the boy go until he promised not to say anything. With a kick to Lyle's shin, the boy attempted to dash for the door, but Lyle was quicker, enfolding him in a protective embrace. Lyle's heart raced, fear and adrenaline coursing through his veins so intensely he thought he might faint.

"I don't want to hurt you," Lyle whispered. "I just need you to promise you won't tell anyone."

It had taken hours to convince the boy to keep quiet, and as Lyle lay down to rest that night with a heavy heart, he was certain that nothing would come of it. He trusted Uriah, though he couldn't deny feeling somewhat unsettled by the darkness the boy had revealed. There had been a flash of genuine malice in his eyes.

Just as sleep was beginning to take hold, he heard a light knock on the door.

"Hello?"

"Hi," Uriah replied softly. "I need your help."

Lyle shot up straight. "What do you mean you need my help?"

"It's important," Uriah said more firmly.

Lyle got out of his bed and approached the boy, closing the door behind him.

"I am going to need you to quieten down, okay? You shouldn't be here."

"But I need your help!"

"Okay, okay!"

Lyle took a deep breath before asking the question.

"What do you need me to do?"

URSULA

December 24th 1953, 20:45

Maude was undeniably guilty, but Ursula wasn't convinced that it was for her daughter's murder. She had committed an unforgivable act against her child, one far worse than physical violence. Maude had neglected her daughter, depriving her of a mother's true love. In Ursula's eyes, there was no act more violent than that.

There was always the possibility that Maude was withholding information, but the bruise around Blanchette's neck suggested that the cause of death had been strangulation. This was not typically a type of murder associated with women, at least not in Ursula's limited experience, where perpetrators of such brutal crimes had been female. While exceptions existed, they did little to change the pattern.

As they navigated the empty hallways of the hotel, Ursula elucidated the intricacies of the case to James. The singer listened intently, his brow furrowed in concentration, absorbing her words with thoughtful nods of agreement and visible expressions of disagreement where his thoughts diverged.

"The thing is, Mrs Blakesley ain't exactly honest," James said, leaning against the wall and crossing one leg over the other, engrossed in Ursula's ongoing analysis.

"Blanchette's body was found a mile away from the hotel," Ursula countered. "The footprints we found, we can both agree were too large to be hers. The smaller prints belong to Silvia and Blanchette. We have confirmation of that from both Finlay and Silvia. So if the larger footprints are Finlay's and the other two are Silvia's and Blanchette's...and the fourth footprint is too large to be Maude's, then she can't have killed Blanchette, unless you're insinuating that there's more than one person involved. And Remember those marks that looked as if they were caused by someone being dragged? Do you honestly think Maude would have been able to carry all that deadweight, for that long and in this weather?"

"Yeah...I get it...but what about Ophelia's secret son? Tytus?" James asked.

"The footprints aren't large enough," Ursula concluded.

"So suppose, she has nothing to do with her daughter's murder, why did she freak out as if she knew something had happened?" James asked. "Those screams this morning were of someone who knew exactly what we were all about to find out."

James raised a valid point, one Ursula had thoroughly considered. The peculiar and potentially incriminating behaviour certainly warranted scrutiny. However, Blanchette's case differed significantly. Not only had the girl stumbled upon Mr. and Mrs. White's clandestine activities earlier that night, but she had also uncovered Ophelia's hidden guest—a revelation the hotel manager clearly intended to keep under wraps. Additionally, Blanchette had been a witness to Finlay's assault on Silvia, adding another layer of complexity to the situation. While Finlay's troubled past might make him wary of police involvement, would he resort to murder, knowing it would invite the scrutiny he sought to avoid? It seemed unlikely. Then there was Blanchette's rejection of Hamish, the lovestruck waiter. Strangulation was far more likely to come from an ex-lover than an immediate family member.

"She admitted to attacking Blanchette," Ursula said slowly. "Perhaps what drove her to go check on Blanchette was remorse and what drove her to panic was...mother's intuition," Blanchette paused and changed the subject. "What about Aonghus?"

"His story checks out. Woke up, prepared breakfast, then started workin' on lunch, then dinner, then went out for a smoke, he did say he saw and spoke to Blanchette—"

"What about?" Ursula asked.

"Her dad. I guess he was checkin' in on her. He doesn't seem to like Mr Blakesley very much, seems to doubt a lot of what he says. He insinuated that his meetin' Mrs Blakesley was planned, but I dunno, I think he just doesn't like the guy. He was very fond of Blanchette's dad. Maybe that makes him suspicious of Mr Blakesley. The more I think about it, the more I start to think that Hamish and the jilted lover scenario could be the way to go."

"We've all been that age before. When a heartbreak happens, life has no meaning. He is heartbroken. And while heartbreak can sometimes break someone's character, all I see in that boy is dejection," Ursula smiled. "Anyway, thank you for being a gentleman and walking me to my room. You didn't have to."

"Oh, but it would have been such a long and treacherous road otherwise. I'm just tryna be gallant, Prince Charmin' or whatever it is you gals fall for this side of the pond," James replied.

"Well, the first thing to note is that," Ursula retorted with a smile, before mimicking his accent. "Us gals aren't looking for a Prince Charming...although a little bit of charm is nice."

Their eyes locked, tracing each other's features as if in a dance of hesitation and longing. Ursula could feel her heart racing, her pulse echoing in her ears. James took a step closer, closing the distance between them. Her cheeks tinged with a faint blush, she lowered her eyes feeling a hint of vulnerability. James reached out a hand, lifting her chin to meet her eyes. Ursula's breath caught in her throat as she searched his eyes, seeing the sincerity in them. The hallway seemed to shrink, as they focused their attention only on each other. In that charged moment, they leaned in, the world around them fading into the background. Their lips met, tentative at first, exploring this newfound territory. The tension melted into a sweet surrender. Their connection that had been evident, and now finally acknowledged.

"You know this doesn't mean you get to come into my room, right?" Ursula said once their lips had parted.

"Yes, of course," the singer responded earnestly.

"You were great tonight. You're a natural," Ursula said. "I'll see you tomorrow?"

"Only if you want to," James smiled broadly and walked down the corridor, leaving Ursula to look after him.

Ursula closed the door behind her, the soft click marking a moment of solace. She let out a long, contemplative breath, feeling the weight of happiness tingle through her body. But beneath it, there was also some apprehension. She felt somewhat guilty for allowing herself to be swept away by the allure of James while still navigating the tempestuous waters of the case.

She settled on the bed's edge, her mind conflicted. Ursula had encountered charming men before—those whose words wove golden promises only to shatter later. Yet, James seemed different. There was a genuineness about him, a vulnerability that lurked beneath his charming demeanour. Despite this, caution remained her steadfast companion. After all, Robert too had been kind, genuine, and charming, yet he had ultimately acted as coldblooded towards Ursula as any of the killers they'd helped put behind bars. He had dismantled their relationship and departed as if she had never meant a thing to him. Whether friend or foe, men often turned out to be unpredictable. Ursula believed in happy endings, but she had yet to experience one. It was therefore crucial for her to tread carefully.

Ursula strolled towards the window, her gaze fixed on the velvety darkness enveloping the estate, recalling the previous night and her intricate dance with Lady Death by the cliff's edge. It seemed surreal to think she had teetered on the brink of answering her final call, and now, just a day later, she stood with the embers of life rekindled. Contemplating her presence here, Ursula questioned whether it was an unspoken desire to escape, to dissolve into the unknown, or if the hand of fate guided her, orchestrating the stars to place her precisely where she needed to be at precisely the right time. Had she not stood there, on the precipice, intimately close to Death's icy whispers, Ursula would have been adrift in the bustling streets of London, seeking solace in the depths of a glass of whiskey. Instead, the call of Death had propelled her into this moment, thrusting her into an investigation that breathed fresh life into her weary spirit. James had played a part. He was one of the melodies in this orchestral narrative, but he wasn't its sole protagonist.

Ursula began to undress, her movements fraught with an undercurrent of agitation. Her fingers fumbled with the buttons, inadvertently mirroring her struggle to untangle the knotted mysteries before her. Each twist and turn in the investigation seemed to ensnare her further in a web of confusion. A deep sigh escaped her lips, heavy with the burden of a puzzle unwilling to surrender its secrets. She chewed on her tongue, a nervous tic betraying her vexation, while a furrow creased her brow as she wracked her brain for a breakthrough. It felt like chasing shadows, and she longed for the clarity of daylight to pierce the darkness veiling the answers she sought.

Except for Tytus, everyone she had interviewed had a motive. The maelstrom of possibilities and uncertainties swirled within her, leaving Ursula on the edge of both anticipation and exasperation. She decided that her first point of call in the morning would be Hamish, she wanted to explore his relationship with Blanchette further before tracking down Mrs White whom she hadn't yet spoken to. Ursula closed her eyes, took in a deep breath and attempted to clear her mind of all thought before finally turning off the light, making herself comfortable and allowing herself to drift off to sleep...

In the realm of dreams, she found herself in a world where her daughter Lucía was alive and well, her joyful laughter echoing in the air. The sun beamed down, casting a warm and comforting light, and the scent of blooming flowers filled the atmosphere. Lucía and her father, Robert, ran in circles around Ursula, singing a haunting nursery rhyme that sent shivers down her spine. The words carried an eerie tune, one that seemed out of place in the idyllic scene.

Suddenly, Lucía and Robert ran towards a clear pond, standing on its surface as if defying the laws of nature. Ursula frowned, a sense of unease settling in. How was this possible? The dream seemed to blur at the edges, a disconcerting feeling seeping into the otherwise perfect tableau.

Ursula felt her feet moving towards them, her heart worried that they would both fall into the depths of the pond. As she reached the edge, the dream shifted, and she found herself back in a dark London street, squinting through the fog. There, she saw the menacing figure skulking towards her. Fear gripped her, and she prepared to flee, but a hand grabbed her throat, silencing her. The sound of her desperate cries filled the night, and then she saw them clearly for the first time since the attack—the cold, daunting *blue eyes*.

She jolted awake in a sweat, her heart racing, expecting to see her assailant, only to realise she was in her room. Ursula took a deep breath and sat at the edge of the bed, attempting to calm herself. She noticed the shiny whiskey bottle in the moonlight. She wanted to resist but knew drinking was the only solution for her nightmares.

URSULA

December 25th 1953, 06:07 am

Mary Lou Pearce. Kelly McDonald. Elizabeth Eddowes. Ann Stride. Jane Nichols. Catherine Chapman. Ada Millwood.

Ursula whispered the names repeatedly throughout the night, their syllables forming a hypnotic cadence that transported her into a trance-like state. The repetitive ritual resembled a form of meditation, akin to that of a Buddhist monk deep in contemplation. Each uttered name carried the weight of her past failures, compelling Ursula to absentmindedly reach for the dwindling bottle of whiskey, taking a swig after every invocation. Thankfully, with the numbing elixir nearly depleted, Ursula stopped her drinking a few hours before sunrise. Left with little else to occupy her restless mind, she sought solace in a bath, hoping its warm embrace would cleanse her of emotional turmoil.

Lost in her ruminations, the passage of time slipped through Ursula's fingers until a knock on the door abruptly jolted her back to reality. It was then that she realised how long she had been submerged in the water—her fingers were pruned, and the once-inviting bath had turned cold. Ursula hastily wrapped herself in a bathrobe, wondering who could be knocking so early. Glancing at her wristwatch, she went to open the door and found a concerned Ophelia waiting outside her room.

"Ms. Dankworth," she began, visibly agitated and struggling to articulate her thoughts, before simply urging, "Come."

Perplexed by the uncharacteristic unease in the usually composed figure, Ursula followed the hotel manager down the stairs at a brisk pace. Taking a right on the first floor, they approached Mr. and Mrs. Blakesley's room. Without hesitation, Ophelia entered, revealing a distraught Theron Blakesley on the bed, his head buried in his hands. Slowly raising his gaze, Theron's bloodshot, puffy eyes spoke volumes of his distress.

Meanwhile, Ophelia continued towards the bathroom, leaving the door ajar. A fleeting glance revealed a lifeless hand dangling over the edge of the bath. A sharp pain stabbed through Ursula's stomach as the scene unfolded, evoking haunting memories of Lucía. There, Mrs Blakesley lay submerged in the bath, her distant eyes and tilted head signalling her demise. Beside her, on the bathtub's edge, an open vial and scattered pills painted a grim tableau. A broken glass of wine lay shattered, its contents splattered across the bathroom floor. Feeling a slight sense of nausea at the sight as well as the memories it was reviving within her, Ursula walked out of the bathroom.

"What — err..." she tried to compose herself. "What happened?"

Wiping away tears and sniffing, Theron looked back up towards her, shrugging. "I — she...was fine...I mean not fine...but she was fine when we went to bed — I mean...she was upset but fine. She just couldn't live with herself— what she err done...she was wasn't herself...I went to sleep...I guess she took a bunch of her sleeping pills...and..."

Theron's sentence remained unfinished as he choked up, tears streaming down his face, drenching the collar of his pyjamas. Ursula, closing her eyes, couldn't shake the memory of Maude's desolation when she failed to confirm that her actions had no bearing on Blanchette's death.

Maude Blakesley.

A new addition to the list of failures. Another name etched into the tapestry of her regrets. There was no room for dwelling now; what good would it do? Mental lashings could wait; for the moment, thinking on her feet took precedence.

"Ophelia, could you prepare a room for Theron and Uriah? I think it would do them good to be elsewhere," Ursula said, turning to the hotel manager. "If you could also be so kind as to ask someone to...move Ms Blakesley."

"Of course," the hotel manager replied, leaving the room immediately.

"You should gather yours and Uriah's things, ready to move into your new room," Ursula suggested as soon as Ophelia had left.

"Uriah didn't go back to his room last night," Theron replied, wiping away tears with the palm of his hand. "I asked Ophelia to check on him...she said he wasn't there."

"Oh," Ursula said, surprised. "When was the last time you saw him?"

"Last night, before we spoke to you," Theron replied.

"Ah, yes, you mentioned he went to play the piano?"

Theron nodded in confirmation.

"He might still be downstairs," Ursula said, but understanding almost immediately, that it wouldn't quite make sense for that to be the case. "I can't imagine there's anyone else awake. How about I try to go find him and bring him back to you once I do?"

Theron nodded slowly, but absently, his eyes distant. Still in her bathrobe, Ursula walked out of the room and made her way towards the main foyer. She walked briskly, shivering as she did from the cold that permeated the corridors. She should have gone back to her room first, she rued with a tut. Realisation dawned on Ursula as she descended the grand staircase: today was Christmas day. It sent a shiver through her, for it marked the second year in a row that she found herself engulfed in a sombre atmosphere. Ursula couldn't remember the last time she had felt happy at Christmas, and neither did she want to. It would only serve to generate memories of her daughter that were simply too painful.

Ursula had lost everyone she once cherished. Her brother had vanished in the unforgiving whirlwind of the Spanish Civil War. Her ex-husband remained a distant figure, estranged and devoid of any familial connection and her parents, pillars of her early life, had long since departed this world. And then there was her daughter—her precious Lucía—forever gone, leaving a void that seemed impossible to fill. The cheer and warmth that others seemed to revel in at this time of year felt foreign to her, like a language she could no longer comprehend. The holiday season now served as a cruel reminder of her profound loneliness, emphasising the void left by the ones she had loved and lost.

Ursula stepped into the dining room, sensing an even colder atmosphere. Her progress halted abruptly as she noticed Lyle Wilson. He, too, came to a stop, cradling a steaming cup in his hands, wisps of warmth spiralling upward in thick white tendrils. The air appeared to shimmer with the ascending heat. Their eyes met briefly, but Ursula saw a flicker of something—perhaps a glimpse of vulnerability, a hint of anxiety—crossing Lyle's face before he turned away. It was a fleeting moment, gone almost as soon as it had come. She couldn't ignore the unspoken weight in the air, the hidden stories that seemed to dance in his eyes.

"Lyle," she said. "As fate would have it, you might be able to help me."

"Me?" Lyle replied awkwardly.

"Yes. Mr Blakesley said he hasn't seen his son since last night," Ursula explained. "Uriah came downstairs to play the piano. Did you see him by any chance?"

"No," Lyle replied a little too quickly.

"I see," Ursula said, suddenly remembering. "Well, now that we're here—" Lyle had already turned to leave, but stopped, Ursula continued. "I've not had the chance to speak to you about the night of Blanchette's disappearance if you could spare a few minutes of your time? Can you confirm where you were?"

"Yes. Here," Lyle began hesitantly. "We play until the last guest is gone. You were the last guest that night, coulda been eight o'clock. Played cards with Hamish, James and Julia, until like eleven maybe a little later than that. After the game, I went to sleep."

"And had you ever had any direct contact with the Blakesleys or Blanchette before?" Ursula asked.

"Whattaya mean direct contact?" Lyle replied, placing the cup on a table. Ursula looked at the contents of the cup and noticed it looked like hot chocolate. The aroma of cocoa wafted towards her, a comforting scent on this cold Christmas morning.

"Did you ever have any conversations with Blanchette or any of the Blakesleys?" she clarified.

"Not that I can recall, no," Lyle replied, but Ursula detected a subtle shift in his demeanour.

Ursula's brows knitted together in a frown. "My memory of that night is a little murky, but you mentioning that I was the last person in here sort of triggered something," Ursula said carefully. "Uriah was in here that night...I saw you talking to him."

Lyle seemed to hesitate. Ursula noticed his eyes darting back and forth as if he was anticipating an attack. The unease in his response only fuelled her growing suspicion.

"I'm not sure," Lyle responded slowly.

"Oh, but I am," Ursula said pointedly. "You said you hadn't spoken to any of the Blakesleys—"

"I've been here since April, I've spoken to so many guests—"

"Is the hot chocolate for you?" Ursula asked, her tone pointed, probing for the truth that seemed to be hiding just below the surface. There were growing signs of nervousness.

"It's a hot chocolate kinda of mornin', don't you think?"

"I prefer the bitter taste of coffee," Ursula replied. "Although the smell of it reminds me of when I was a little girl. My mother liked to add a dash of cinnamon to it. Have you ever tried that?"

Lyle shook his head slowly, his eyes looking towards the exit.

"I should really get back to bed, get an extra couple of hours of sleep-"

"James mentioned that you were allergic to chocolate. A throwaway comment for the most part, but considering you're carrying the cup of the very thing you're allergic to... "

Ursula gazed into his small, untrusting eyes, her mind racing with possibilities. A solitary thought, bubbling beneath the surface until that moment, started to buzz like a persistent fly, and unable to swat it away, Ursula asked the question to try to alleviate the intense feeling of discomfort starting to overwhelm her.

"Do you know where Uriah Blakesley is?"

Lyle's expression twisted into a mask of mock indignation, his attempt to deflect Ursula's probing question clear. Yet, amidst his façade of offence, Ursula couldn't help but notice the subtle clench of his jaw, a giveaway that betrayed his underlying nervousness.

"Why would I know—" he started, attempting to maintain an air of innocence.

"That isn't a denial, Lyle," Ursula interjected, her tone assertive.

Every ounce of her training told her she was on the right track. She had faced situations like this before, where the truth danced on the precipice of exposure. The accused often denied their misdeeds until the truth became inescapable. But she knew to tread carefully, for if they felt cornered, their actions could turn desperate, even violent. The room was charged with unspoken tension, a palpable force urging Ursula to press further, to unravel the truth hidden beneath layers of deceit. And then, like a flash of lightning, the memory of Lyle slipping over the footprint struck her, and her heart sank. The puzzle pieces were starting to fall into place, and the truth was inching closer to the surface.

A new harrowing question dawned in her mind.

"Do you know what happened to Blanchette?"

The accusation hung in the air like heavy fog, shrouding the room in an uneasy silence. Ursula watched Lyle, who seemed momentarily paralyzed, his face a contortion of rage and animosity.

"How dare you? I would never! I could never! How dare you?!" Lyle's voice lashed out, dripping with aggression and fury, causing Ursula to instinctively step back.

Ursula understood the danger of provoking someone on edge, yet she couldn't ignore her suspicions. With a reassuring smile, she tried to defuse the tension, intending to discuss her concerns with James later. However, Lyle intercepted her path, his face contorted with simmering anger, sending a jolt of alarm through her.

"Perhaps we should have this conversation later when you've calmed down," Ursula said, attempting to defuse the escalating tension.

Ursula was unsettled by a troubling thought: had James been privy to everything from the start? Had he pieced together the puzzle before her? Was that why he vehemently opposed Maude Blakesley's innocence? Ursula had long suspected that only something grave could have compelled him and Lyle to Loch Linnhe, a location far removed from their usual haunts.

As Ursula turned to leave, a sudden, sharp cracking sensation rocked the top of her head, sending waves of pain radiating through her skull. She staggered, instinctively reaching for her head, her fingers coming away wet and sticky. The room spun around her, disorienting her, and she struggled to maintain her balance. Summoning her last reserves of energy, she attempted to rise, but the world seemed to swirl into a dark abyss.

Desperately trying to focus, Ursula fixated on the chandeliers above, their lights now mere specks in her blurred vision. A deafening crash reverberated through the room as she collapsed, her injured head striking the unforgiving marble floor. Through the haze, she glimpsed the distant chandeliers before darkness extinguished her consciousness.

URSULA

December 25th 1952

Ursula never wanted to be a mother, and, perhaps if she hadn't succumbed to the societal pressures that labelled her as unnatural for feeling that way, she never would have. Now, standing amidst the suffocating tendrils of grief, she succumbed to the sort of anguish reserved for mothers who had endured the injustice of burying their children.

Her love for Lucía surged like a tempest, a storm raging beyond the confines of her being. It was a love unforeseen, unasked for, yet it consumed her in relentless waves of unimaginable agony. Ursula had heard of such love before, but it wasn't until Lucía that she truly comprehended it. The joy of witnessing her first smile, the pride in her first steps—these moments etched in her memory. Ursula marvelled at the shaping of her daughter's unique personality, a journey filled with wonder and awe.

The loss of Lucía, so sudden and final, defied expression. It felt as if someone had cleaved away a piece of her, leaving behind an agonising void. Ursula, who had denied and resisted this love for so long, now cradled the weight of its absence, forced to reckon with the profound sorrow that surged through her.

Ursula raised her eyes from what may have been her third or fourth glass of wine and locked eyes with the indifferent stare of the man who had once been her husband. His face was stoic, his receding hairline and weary, darkened eyes revealing the toll Lucía's passing had taken on him. This was not the self-assured man she had adored and held close to her heart. Correction: *still* held close. Her love for him persisted, intense and unwavering. It was precisely that love, coupled with his rejection of it, that had driven Ursula to the depths of depression.

Their lives had become a series of fragmented memories, remnants of what once constituted a beautiful mosaic of love. Ursula reminisced about the nights they would sit by the fireplace, exchanging sweet nothings and laughing until their sides ached. Yet, the warmth and camaraderie of those bygone days now felt like a distant echo. They found themselves adrift in a sea of grief, grasping at shards of the past, attempting in vain to bridge the ever-widening chasm that had emerged between them.

"I'm sorry for your loss," she heard, uttered in varied tones of sadness. The auteurs of those words were friends and acquaintances, their faces vaguely familiar to Ursula, however, through the haze of sorrow, she struggled to recognise them. They were mere floating visages, detached from any meaning.

The surge of resentment flooded her, rendering the offered condolences hollow and inadequate. Ursula's fists clenched, nails biting into her palms as if to tether herself to reality amidst the swirling emotions. The room, once spacious, now felt suffocating, the weight of grief pressing down on her chest, constricting her breath. Every fibre of her being screamed for release, a primal urge to unleash the pent-up pain and anger. But societal expectations held her in check. With a tight-lipped smile masking her turmoil, she muttered her thanks—a façade demanded of women. They were expected to embody unwavering strength, to endure trials with the resilience of a hundred men, yet to bend to their every whim. To withstand blows, both physical and emotional, all while maintaining an unyielding façade. Feelings were to be suppressed, buried beneath layers of composure, whether in the company of others or solitude. These were the expectations, imposed like chains, binding her to an unrelenting standard.

Lucía.

The name echoed in her thoughts, conjuring a vivid image of her daughter's beautiful heart-shaped face, adorned with large mahogany eyes and accompanied by captivating dimples that could melt Ursula's resolve in an instant.

Lucía.

Ursula whispered the name to herself, a solitary tear tracing its path down her cheek. Lucía—the name she had chosen with reverence and longing, a tribute to her grandmother's legacy of strength, passion, and boundless love. Though she had never met her grandmother, the stories passed down by her mother painted a vivid picture of a woman whose presence transcended time. The letters from Córdoba, tenderly translated by her mother, bore witness to a love so profound it left an indelible mark on Ursula's heart. Through her daughter, Ursula cherished the memory of two generations of remarkable women who had shaped her into the person she had become.

"Ursula dear," she heard a gentle voice say.

She looked up and stared at the blurry face until it came into focus. It was her friend Leah. Ursula smiled. The warmth in Leah's eyes and the gentleness of her touch reminded Ursula that amidst the sea of condolences, there were genuine connections.

"Would you like me to get you anything?" Leah asked.

"Can you get me out of here?" Ursula replied loudly.

Leah spun around, her fingers nervously twirling strands of her hair as her eyes darted around the room, a subtle tension evident in her shoulders, betraying her discomfort at her response. Ursula could almost hear her friend's thoughts echoing through the silent space. Leah, ever mindful of appearances, would likely disapprove of Ursula leaving her own daughter's wake, seeing it as a breach of decorum. For Leah, the optics of social perception held far greater significance than they did for Ursula. Behind Leah's meticulously maintained pretence of a loving marriage lay the harsh reality of profound unhappiness and the overwhelming strain of raising four boys. The truth was that Leah consumed alcohol with as much fervour, if not more, than Ursula. And perhaps, had she faced the loss of one of her own children, Leah would have cared just as little about the optics as Ursula did.

"Perhaps a tea or a coffee?"

"What for? To pretend I'm holding it together? I don't want to pretend anymore," Ursula said solemnly.

"Ursula, I—"

Ursula held up a hand, interrupting her friend. She felt everyone's eyes on her.

"I don't want to pretend. And I don't want your tea! Let me deal with my sorrows the best way I know how!" Ursula stumbled out of her chair and had it not been for Leah, she would have fallen over. Her eyes scanned the faces that filled the room. "I need you all to get out of my house. GET THE FUCK OUT OF MY HOUSE!"

The room fell into a thick, charged silence after Ursula's outburst, her raw anguish palpable in the air. Leah appeared stunned, while other guests exchanged uncomfortable glances. Gradually, attendees rose from their seats, their voices subdued to hushed whispers, as Robert repeatedly apologised on Ursula's behalf. Leah and her husband remained, the last to leave, leaving Ursula and Robert alone in the house.

Robert cleared the sitting room, gathering the empty glasses left by departing guests, and took them into the kitchen. Upon his return, he sank into a seat, his gaze fixed on the floor, lost in thought.

Ursula, drained from the emotional upheaval, perched on the edge of the sofa, head bowed in her hands. The weight of the day's events—the funeral, the loss, and the confrontation—pressed down on her, leaving her utterly exhausted.

"Later, once you've composed yourself, I want you to call my mother and apologise," Robert said after a while.

"For giving birth to a heartless son?" Ursula spat. "I don't even recognise you anymore. Who are you?"

"Who am I?" Robert seethed. "Who are you? Do you even understand what's happened?"

"More than you will ever know!"

"I doubt that very much! You never wanted her; I should have taken Lucía with me the moment I walked out of this house! I should have known something would happen under your drunken watch! I should have known the very moment you rejected our daughter that you weren't fit to be a mother!"

"I loved Lucía!" Ursula's voice cracked, her eyes filling with fresh tears. "You can't possibly think I didn't love her?"

"YOU WERE FORCED TO LOVE HER! THAT IS WHY I COULDN'T BEAR TO BE WITH YOU. IT IS WHY YOU DISGUST ME! WHAT KIND OF WOMAN WOULD REJECT HER DUTY TO GOD AND HUSBAND FOR THE SAKE OF TRYING TO BETTER HIM? YOU DARE ASK WHO I AM? WHO ARE YOU? YOU HAVE BEEN NOTHING BUT A DISAPPOINTMENT...YOU SHOULD HAVE BEEN THE ONE WHO DROWNED! NOT OUR POOR GIRL! IT SHOULD HAVE BEEN YOU!"

For a split second, Ursula found herself unable to breathe. Panic gripped her body as the realisation hit that the man she once adored, loved with every fibre of her being, could deliver such a devastating verbal blow. It was as if a lightning bolt had struck her, piercing straight through her core. Didn't he understand that she already carried the weight of guilt for Lucía's passing? Couldn't he grasp her longing for an escape from her own existence, a reprieve from the overwhelming pain? The last thing she needed was to be pushed closer to the precipice of despair. Ursula closed her eyes, absorbing the immense hurt inflicted upon her. She felt shattered, each word from Robert like a shard of glass piercing her soul. But she refused to break in front of him, fighting back the tears, denying him the satisfaction.

"I think you should leave, and it would be great if the very last things you still have in the flat were collected by the end of the week," Ursula said, her voice steady despite the storm raging within her.

Robert stood motionless, waiting for a further response, but eventually gathered his jacket and hat, departing without a backward glance. Ursula sighed in relief, but with the painful realisation, her life was forever altered. Turning, she reached for a bottle of scotch. Time seemed to blur as she drank, the pain momentarily subdued, resurfacing only in fleeting waves of despair whenever her daughter's name crossed her mind. With each resurgence, she took another sip, attempting to drown not only her sorrows but also the haunting echoes of Lucía's memory.

"Mama," Lucía's soft voice danced in the air.

Ursula turned abruptly, a mixture of disbelief and hope in her eyes.

"Lucía?"

The voice resonated, carried by a wind that seemed to swell with joy, and Ursula's heart soared. Tears began to fill her eyes as she extended her arms to embrace her daughter. But just as they were about to connect, Lucía began to fade, dissipating into wispy smoke, leaving Ursula bewildered and heartbroken.

"Mama?" Lucía's voice called again, now tinged with distress. Panic seized Ursula, her heart racing as she swiftly followed her daughter's desperate cries, the dread growing with each step, like an invisible hand tightening around her throat.

The sound of rushing water greeted her as she entered the bathroom, the atmosphere heavy with foreboding. Ursula's eyes darted around, searching for the source of the sound. In horror, she realised the bath was overflowing, water cascading over the edges like a river unleashed.

"No, no, no..." Ursula whispered, her steps heavy with dread, her mind racing. She felt like she was moving through a thick fog, her senses dulled by the dread that had taken hold.

With trepidation, she approached the overflowing bath, water splashing onto the floor, a chilling precursor to the truth that awaited her. Her breath caught in her throat, her heart clenching in unbearable pain.

There, in the overflowing bath, lay Lucía's lifeless body, her skin pallid and her eyes devoid of the sparkle that once held the promise of a beautiful life.

"LUCÍA!"

Ursula's scream tore through the air, laden with the anguish of a mother beholding her child's lifeless form. The walls of the room seemed to converge upon her, suffocating her in the stark reality of loss. Her legs buckled beneath her, unable to bear the weight of despair any longer, and she collapsed to the floor, consumed by the overwhelming agony of grief.

JAMES

December 25th 1953, 7:33

The frozen expanse of the loch began to reveal itself as a warm smile tugged at the corners of James's lips.Thoughts of Ursula and the kiss they had shared occupied his mind incessantly. Her soft lips lingered in his memory, and the sweet scent of her perfume seemed to drift through his senses, igniting a fervent desire within him.

James continued his run through the serene, snow-kissed fields of the estate, a daily ritual he upheld without fail. Each morning, he sought solace by the loch, finding refuge in its tranquil embrace. Since the incident in Zurich, he had felt a subtle erosion of his inner peace, but amidst the wintry landscape, he endeavoured to reclaim it. While his summer runs had been effortless, even in the face of occasional rain showers, the biting cold of winter posed a more formidable challenge.

His thoughts wandered back to the unsettling events in Zurich, a chapter he had yet to share with Ursula. Doubt gnawed at him; were those details pertinent to the current investigation? After all, Lyle's interactions had solely been with Uriah Blakesley, not Blanchette. However, James could not dismiss the lingering concern that his cousin might pose a threat to children. He furrowed his brow in consternation, hesitant to blindly assume Lyle's innocence. Not this time.

James wrestled with the urge to confront Lyle about the night of Blanchette's disappearance, hoping to dispel his nagging doubts. Yet, the memory of Lyle's early return to his room after the card game restrained him. Despite this, uncertainty persisted like a shadow, whispering unsettling questions: What if Lyle had roamed elsewhere? What if he crossed paths with Blanchette? What if she glimpsed his darker inclinations and threatened to expose him? The timeline of events remained nebulous, fostering doubt and dismissing Lyle's involvement seemed premature. After all, there were too many troubling incidents tied to his cousin: from the unsettling episode with little Armand in Zurich to accusations in Portugal surrounding Tiago. James grappled with his complicity, having blindly supported Lyle through each ordeal. It was part of the reason why he had been so keen to help Ursula, he wanted to feel he had helped seek justice, and he wanted to be on the right side of things for once.

He wondered how Ursula would react when he eventually told her. Her presence had been a comforting anchor. James had found an inner peace whenever he looked into her eyes that he had not known existed. It was as if everything and everyone around him vanished and the only being that mattered was Ursula. The last time he'd experienced such profound happiness was far removed in his past, back in the sun-drenched days of Alabama. James wanted nothing more than to prolong what they had but understood that being forthcoming with the whole truth, was crucial to helping Ursula resolve the investigation.

James paused at the point where the snow met the frozen loch, pivoting slowly to fully embrace the wintry scene. As he stood there, he took a deliberate breath, savouring the crispness of the cold air that filled his lungs. The sensation was invigorating, making his breath almost feel anew. The refreshing chill provided him with a surge of energy, awakening his senses. For a brief moment, he closed his eyes, letting the cold air envelop him, and allowing his heightened senses to absorb the serene world around him. In that quiet interlude, the biting cold became a rejuvenating force, revitalising both his body and spirit.

When he reopened his eyes, his focus shifted to the snow beneath him. There, he noticed a stark contrast—a crimson stain against the pristine white canvas. Turning around, he saw a set of footprints, identical to those they'd discovered the previous morning. He turned, his eyes following the footprints and at the end of the tracks, James saw an unsettling sight—a motionless body floating in a cracked section of the frozen loch. Adrenaline coursed through his veins, quickening his pace as he hurried forward. Each step he took sent spiderweb cracks racing through the ice. James reached the motionless figure, and with an unmistakable sense of dread, he recognised it...

"Ursula!"

James called out desperately, plunging into the icy water, his voice echoing through the desolate landscape as he shook her lifeless form. She remained unresponsive as he cradled her closer, his heart pounding in his chest as he began swimming with her to the bank. His teeth chattered uncontrollably as the cold seeped into his bones. James felt weak, his muscles protesting with every stroke. The thick ice was blocking their path and in a desperate bid to try and get to safety, he raised one trembling arm and delivered a series of punches to the ice, breaking through it with a loud, echoing crack. Each punch sent shockwaves of pain through his arm, but the vision of Ursula's limp form drove him forward. With renewed determination, he fought his way through the opening, all the while struggling to keep himself and Ursula afloat. Every second felt like an eternity, but he couldn't afford to falter. He needed to get her to safety.

Reaching the safety of the bank, James lay there for a brief moment, his eyes drifting up to the overcast sky as he tried to summon warmth from within his chilled body. Slowly, he turned his attention towards Ursula and leaned over her motionless form, his fingers finding their way to her jawline, tilting her head back gently. He pinched her nose shut and covered her mouth with his own, delivering steady breaths into her lungs. Time seemed to stretch into eternity as James pressed on, his breath mingling with the icy air in futile attempts to revive her. His heart pounded in his chest, a drumbeat of desperation urging him on. Yet, Ursula remained still, but James refused to yield.

His hands moved to her chest, fingers interlocking as he applied firm pressure, willing her heart to respond. And then, a flicker—a barely perceptible flutter beneath his touch. Hope surged within him, a fragile ember amidst the icy despair. He sensed a pulse, faint but undeniable, coursing beneath her skin, a beacon of life amidst the darkness. With a deep breath, pushed himself to his feet. Summoning one last surge of determination, he lifted her limp body onto his shoulders and embarked on the journey back to the hotel. James felt his legs shake, the burden feeling increasingly heavy, and the biting cold gnawing at his core. He fell to his knees, grunting in pain, his breathing far more laboured now, but he would not let her die. Not on his watch.

URSULA

December 25th 1953, 15:17

"Lucía!"

Ursula's scream clawed through the stillness, a raw symphony of terror. Her heart galloped in her chest, a wild creature desperate to escape. In her haste, she stumbled, the world tilting, and she crashed to the floor. Pain, a merciless hammer, reverberated through her head, each throb threatening to fracture bone. As if an unseen force wielded a relentless drumbeat against her skull, shockwaves of agony pulsed from her temples to the back of her eyes. Slowly, she cracked open her eyelids. A cruel assault of light stabbed through her pupils, unleashing another surge of torment. Her disoriented gaze darted around, the surroundings unfamiliar, and panic surged, compounding the unbearable distress. Had she, in some twisted trick of fate, been transported back to the gloomy streets of London? The unknown gripped her, a vise tightening around her chest, intensifying the waves of panic that already threatened to drown her.

"Ursula," she heard a soft voice whisper.

Ursula looked up to find James Wilson standing over her, his tall frame silhouetted against the dim light of the room. A thick blanket draped over his shoulders, despite this, he was still shivering uncontrollably. Ursula noticed a bandage encircling his hand, which, coupled with the despondent expression on his face made Ursula wonder what had happened. Had someone else been killed? Had she failed yet another person? The absence of the usual spark in his eyes sent a shiver down her spine.

Without a word, he extended his unbandaged hand, a silent offering of assistance. With a gentle grasp, he helped Ursula to her feet, his touch conveying a warmth that belied the somberness of the moment. Wordlessly, he guided her back to the bed, his movements slow and deliberate. The room seemed to echo with a heavy silence, broken only by the faint rustle of fabric.

"My...daughter...she..." Ursula attempted to rush towards the bathroom, but the singer stopped her, gently pushing her back down.

"Your daughter isn't here," he said.

The weight of those words rekindled the haunting memory of the day she lost Lucía, enveloping her in a profound numbness she was unable to shake. The pain it unleashed ran so deep that it rendered her speechless. Her silence enveloped the room, a dense fog of unspoken grief that suffocated all sound. Slowly, she turned to meet James's gaze, her eyes locking onto his with a steady intensity. In the depths of his eyes, she sensed a complex tapestry of emotions—concern mingled with a shadow of guilt.

Ursula cast her gaze around the room again, her initial confusion giving way to recognition. She was back in her hotel room. The throbbing pain in her head seemed relentless, and her parched throat further heightened her discomfort. In a raspy voice, she managed to croak out a request for water.

James, ever the attentive presence, rose from his seat and made his way to the bathroom. Moments later he reappeared bearing a crystal-clear glass filled with chilled water. The cool liquid slipped down her throat like a soothing balm, easing the dryness that had plagued her for hours. Each sip was a small reprieve, a moment of respite from the turmoil of her thoughts. Setting the glass down on the bedside table with a gentle clink, Ursula turned her attention back to James.

"How are you feeling?" James asked concern etched across his face.

"James," Ursula began, her voice quivering as she attempted to sit up on the bed. Pain shot through her head, causing her to wince. "This morning—"

"I heard. Ms Clyde told me," he interrupted. "As if one family could handle any more tragedy."

Confused for a few moments, Ursula soon realised that James was referring to Mrs Blakesley. "Yes, but...something doesn't quite fit...however, what I meant to say was that this morning, after talking to Mr Blakesley, I went to look for Uriah. He'd been missing since before we interrogated Mrs Blakesley...and I...bumped into Lyle. I thought to question him...I'm not sure why..." Ursula explained, her memory of those morning's events coming to her thick and fast. "I think...no. I am pretty sure he attacked me."

A weighted silence filled the room. James sat, unmoving, as Ursula's accusation hung heavy in the air, thick with tension. The stillness was punctuated only by the soft exhale of breath. Slowly, almost imperceptibly, James's shoulders sagged, the weight of Ursula's words bearing down on him like an anchor. With a heavy sigh, he leaned back in his chair, the wooden legs creaking softly in protest. His once-confident posture now seemed entirely deflated.

"Are you sure?"

"Certain," Ursula replied. "He didn't seem himself. Particularly when I asked him if he'd seen Uriah. He denied ever having spoken to him and that reminded me that I had seen him speak to Uriah the night of Blanchette's disappearance. It got me wondering, why would he lie about that? Why would anyone lie, unless they didn't want to be tied to the Blakesleys whatsoever..."

Ursula's eyes remained fixed on James, her heart pounding as she awaited his response. Yet, to her growing dismay, he sat there, unmoving, his eyes locked onto a singular spot on the floor. Silence hung in the room like an oppressive shroud that heightened her anxiety. What was James hiding? What did he know that he wasn't sharing? Ursula felt her breathing begin to quicken and her eyes clouded with tears as she waited for James to say something. She *needed* him to refute the growing notion that everything she had started to feel for him might have been manipulated. Her mind spun with disbelief, torn between the memory of their shared moments and the possibility that they had been part of an elaborate ruse.

"Ursula..." James paused. "Lyle is...he..."

The singer, whose entire persona had been built upon his amiable and gregarious nature, suddenly found himself incapable of stringing a sentence together.

"Lyle is prone to...behaviours..." James explained. "Every single time...he said, it had been a misunderstandin'... that's why we had to get away from Zurich...he was caught tryna—" James did not finish his sentence.

"What is it you're saying, James?"

James breathed in and closed his eyes.

"I am sayin' that Lyle has been known to place himself in situations with underage boys that are very easy to be accurately misconstrued," he replied without looking at Ursula.

Ursula's breath caught in her throat, her mind reeling in disbelief. For a moment, the weight of James's words held her in a stunned silence. Slowly, like a ship navigating treacherous waters, she began to regain her composure and with a determined breath, Ursula gingerly swung her legs over the edge of the bed, her muscles protesting the movement. Each step felt like a delicate dance, a balancing act between pain and resolve. With trembling hands, she reached for the bedside table, using it as a steady anchor to pull herself upright.

"What are you doin'?" James asked.

"I asked him if he knew what'd happened to Blanchette, just before he attacked me! What if he—"

"What? No! He wouldn't...look, he needs help and I have been tryna to fix him—"

"Fix him?!" Ursula thundered. "You think you can fix him?"

"Look, he isn't a murderer!"

"How the hell would you know?" Ursula said, pushing James away. "Do you know?"

"What? No! I've been helpin' you this whole time," James replied, stung at the insinuation.

"To what end?"

"I know my Lyle has issues, but he wouldn't do somethin' like that. It can't have been him. We played cards, and I spoke to him after that. I stopped by his room."

"What about the footprint, yesterday morning? The one he *conveniently* slipped on and smudged? What if it was his footprint?"

James frowned at this suggestion as if connecting the dots.

"Lyle isn't dangerous," he whispered, but his defence of his cousin did not sound as resolute this time.

Ursula turned around to James, anger now seeping through her every fibre.

"Not dangerous? Even after what you just admitted, you still think he's not dangerous?" Ursula allowed the question to simmer. "Have you known? Have you known all along?"

His expression twisted with unmistakable disgust at her question. At that moment, her concerns ebbed away. His eyes, like pools of sincerity sparkled and a part of her was happy to see that the unwavering sincerity that had drawn her to him from the very first moment, still shone brightly. But she could not let him know. There had still been deception, however, she was starting to think the ruse had been self-inflicted.

"How could you think that?"

"How could I not?" Ursula replied. "You should have told me as soon as Blanchette went missing!"

"I didn't think to—"

"Let me guess, you didn't think that it was relevant to tell me you've been harbouring a child molester?"

"That's not what I've been doin'!" James screamed angrily. "I was gonna tell you. But I didn't know how. I know I fucked up. I may not have pulled the trigger but I sure as heck drove the car."

James appeared visibly dejected, his downtrodden demeanour speaking volumes to Ursula. In that moment of clarity, she realised that James' sole transgression had been his unwavering love and faith in his cousin and failing to recognise that Lyle's struggles couldn't simply vanish by evading them. Ursula approached him gently, placing her hand against his cheek, offering a tender gesture of comfort. As James lifted his eyes, tears streamed down his beautiful complexion, encapsulating the profound sorrow etched on his face.

"Why would he do this to you? If I hadn't found you..." he said quietly.

Ursula wiped the tears from his cheeks.

"Do you know who the most dangerous animals are? Those who feel trapped and without escape. Do you know what they do in the most vulnerable of situations?"

"They attack," James responded.

Recognising the urgency of the situation, Ursula hastily draped a jacket over the nightie she still wore, and with James closely following, she left her room. Though she wished she could manage on her own, her body ached with every step she took, and she soon had to ask for James's assistance when descending the spiral staircase. Ursula clung tightly to his wrist for support, occasionally glancing at him, but neither of them broke the heavy silence that hung between them. As they reached the bottom of the stairs, she couldn't help but wonder if her initial judgement of James had been too harsh. However, she decided that such questions could wait for another time.

"Ms. Dankworth, what are you doing out of bed?" the hotel manager said as they reached the foyer.

Ursula winced, still feeling pain coursing through her body. "Could you call the police and tell them I was temporarily incapacitated but I am now back on the case. It would be great to get an update from them regarding when they believe the roads will be cleared. I want them here today if possible."

"So you figured it out?"

"Ms Clyde, as a matter of urgency, please call the police and get back to me as soon as you have information," Ursula interjected firmly.

"Of course," Ophelia agreed before retreating into her office to make the necessary calls.

As Ursula and James entered the dining hall, their eyes fell upon Theron and Uriah Blakesley seated at a table near the window. Despite the weight of recent loss, Uriah sat with quiet dignity, his shoulders squared and his gaze steady. Ursula couldn't help but marvel at the resilience of children in the face of tragedy. Unlike adults, who often struggled to come to terms with death, children, perhaps because of their inability to fully understand the permanence of loss, were far better equipped to move on. That being said, having already lost his mother at a very young age, perhaps, Uriah had come to terms with the inevitable passing of loved ones. Perhaps that stuffed toy he so cherished was his way of keeping in touch with them - with his mother, in the afterlife.

"Ms Dankworth," Mr Oliver White said, approaching her. "We're glad to see you've recovered."

"Thank you," she replied, walking past him.

Ursula moved towards the table with the Blakesleys, settling into her seat without a single word.

"He showed up this morning," Theron explained with a tone of relief.

James leaned into Ursula, "I am going to find Lyle," he said before leaving.

Ursula offered Uriah a warm smile, but her expression shifted as he began speaking. Uriah's directness caught her off guard.

"What happened to you?" he asked with a tone devoid of the typical childlike curiosity.

Ursula sighed softly, her voice gentle, "Someone tried to hurt me, just like they did Blanchette."

Uriah pondered this for a moment, his eyes fixed on his stuffed animal. His response was stoic, "But you're not dead. Not like she is. Not like Maude."

"No, I'm not."

"Are they really dead?"

Ursula found Uriah's question peculiar. There was a noticeable absence of emotion in his inquiry, which struck her as odd and left her intrigued. It seemed as though he was detached from the tragedy of his stepmother and sister's deaths.

"I'm afraid so, Uriah," she said. "The last time I spoke to Maude, she mentioned going up to your room on the night of your sister's disappearance—"

"Step-sister," Uriah corrected her.

"Yes," Ursula said slightly thrown by the interruption. "Your step-sister. She told me you'd said Blanchette had gone for a walk, is this true?"

He shrugged, his demeanour almost unsettling in its calmness. Then, a whispered exchange with his stuffed animal as Theron shifted uncomfortably.

"Can you tell me where you went last night?" Ursula pressed on, becoming acutely aware that the other guests were now standing around them.

"I was with the piano player," Uriah offered. "He took me," the boy added to audible gasps.

"Took you?" Theron repeated. "Did he hurt you?"

"No, he doesn't hurt boys...not in the way you think," came Uriah's chilling response.

Ursula's gaze remained fixed on the boy, her mind racing with thoughts and questions. Suddenly, the dining room doors burst open, and James strode in, his voice tinged with urgency.

"He's gone!" His words hung heavily in the air, causing a ripple of concern to sweep through the room.

"Who's gone?" asked Ariel White.

"Lyle," James replied between breaths.

Theron bolted up from his chair.

"Gone? What do you mean, he's gone? What's he done to my son?"

"He can't have gotten very far, not in this weather," Oliver White chimed in. "We should go after him! The boy and his sister deserve justice..."

"And who's to say what he may have done to poor Maude," Ariel added.

"Justice?" Ursula responded with a hint of scepticism.

"Yes! The man has run away," Hachem, whose presence Ursula had barely noticed said. "You heard what the boy said about him?"

"Does he have anything to do with what happened to Blanchette?" Ndeshi asked, her tone far less judgemental than the rest of her companions.

"I couldn't say for certain, not until I speak with him," Ursula replied cautiously.

"So he *is* a suspect?" Theron pressed.

"Right now, everyone is a suspect, Mr. Blakesley," Ursula stated firmly.

"I overheard you ask Ms Clyde to call the police," Ariel White said. "It sounded like you'd come to a conclusion. He was the one who attacked, wasn't he? You confronted him and he must have attacked you...left you out there to die."

"Is this true?" Ophelia Clyde asked, having walked back into the room. Her face was white with fury. "Staff attacking our guests?"

"Why are you protecting him? Why are you protecting them?" Theron spat angrily.

"It's what she gets for associating with such characters," Oliver sneered.

"I beg your pardon?" Ndeshi said turning to him. "What kind of characters?"

"Oh, Ndeshi," Ariel interjected. "Ignore him, he didn't mean a thing by it."

Ndeshi ignored her lover.

"What kind of characters?" she repeated.

"You know—"

Oliver's cheeks reddened.

"I don't. Enlighten me."

"Their sort of character," Oliver said pointing at James.

"Males? Singers? Americans...*Negroes?*" Ndeshi made sure to utter every syllable of the last word.

"The man who kidnapped my son and might have killed Blanchette is missing!!!" Theron screamed. "We need to go after him now!"

"I agree!" Oliver White said, walking away from Ndeshi with a sigh of relief that the conversation had veered away from him.

"*We* will not," Ursula replied sternly.

She was unwilling to let a mob mentality prevail, particularly when the accused hadn't had the chance to defend himself. Despite the possibility that he was responsible for the attack on her and the unsettling secrets James had disclosed, she believed he deserved the chance to present his side of the story. Ursula turned to Ophelia, the hotel manager standing beside her, and gave her a clear directive.

"Can you ask Finlay to prepare the car so we can search the grounds for Lyle?"

"Of course," Ophelia replied, promptly leaving the dining room.

"I'll grab my coat," Theron said.

"You will not," she stated firmly and then turned to Oliver White and Hachem who seemed to be preparing to do the same. "Neither will you. Finlay and James will be enough."

URIAH

23rd December 1953, 23:55

Uriah Blakesley was deeply unsettled, concern clung to him like an unwelcome, persistent shadow. It lingered, stubborn and persistent, trailing him to his room. His father's abrupt disappearance into the woman's room troubled him deeply, reminding him, as it often did, of the fragility of their relationship with Maude. For Uriah, such missteps could have dire consequences. He'd be sent away were things to end. He would end up somewhere that would remind him just how unwanted he was.

He had waited in the hallway, desperately hoping his father would emerge armed with a reasonable explanation for his actions. As minutes dragged on, Uriah's hope began to wane, replaced by a growing certainty that his father was entangled in something dubious. The air in the hallway seemed charged with tension as Uriah grappled with the foreboding notion that he was about to confront a truth he'd rather not uncover.

He lingered, gazing at the door as if it could impart wisdom or shield him from the impending confrontation awaiting inside. Uriah hesitated, reluctant to reenter the space shared with his quarrelsome step-sister. Finally, he pushed the door open and stepped inside.

Blanchette lay on her bed, still fully clothed, her bare feet hung just above the carpeted floor, they were caked with dirt as if she had been traipsing through muddied terrain. Sensing his presence, she slowly sat up, and his gasp escaped before he could stifle it. Her face bore the marks of a brutal assault—severe bruising, a cut on her cheek, and another on her lip. Bruises marred her arms and legs, telling a tale of a fierce altercation. But with whom? Could it have been the waiter boy? Uriah knew they'd had a secret relationship the previous Christmas. This year, however, enamoured by the exotic friend of Mr and Mrs White, she had completely ignored him. Could that have driven the waiter to violence?

"What happened?" Uriah asked, his voice tinged with concern.

Blanchette took a moment to reply, her eyes distant. "What hasn't," she said, her voice laden with a heavy weariness. "I started my day looking for a prince and ended it enjoying the presence of a gentle soul some would consider a monster."

Uriah remained still, unsure of what she meant.

"I see," he responded cautiously.

"Where have *you* been?" Blanchette inquired.

"Just about," Uriah replied nonchalantly, avoiding any details.

Blanchette studied him for a few moments as if taking his measure and after a prolonged pause, she walked closer to him, her eyes searching his.

"You know, I always wondered if your disagreeable nature was due to not having a mother," she said. "But then I remembered, that unlike me, you have had a mother's love. Perhaps, that's why I've always been cruel to you. Envy. Your mother may be dead but at least while she was alive, she gave you her love. I've never had that."

A familiar sense of unease stirred within Uriah. He had heard this tone in Blanchette's voice on numerous occasions. It was the prelude to one of her grand finales, designed to goad him, perhaps even provoke him into actions that could turn the situation against him.

"Maude has never loved me. To her, I am nothing but an offspring of a loveless marriage. Do you think that if a child is conceived in hatred, they too carry that hate in their heart?"

Uriah took a cautious step back, acutely aware that something had shifted in Blanchette tonight. The familiar malice still simmered within her, but there was an additional element he couldn't quite put his finger on, something he hadn't experienced from her before.

"I'm tired," Uriah said, attempting to shift the conversation. He tried to walk past her, but she seized his arm, pulling him back towards her.

"What are you doing?" Uriah questioned with a mixture of confusion and apprehension.

"I want you to know that even though I do not like you, it is not because of that that I will make it my aim to ruin my mother's marriage to your dad. I want to see her alone. I want to see her die alone and without any love. I want her to be deprived of love just as she did with me. That may, of course, mean that you and your dad go back to the hovel you came from."

Uriah cast a glance at Zeke, the crescendo of his voice amplifying within Uriah's head. Despite his best efforts to repel those emotions, the surging anger proved challenging to contain. Clouds of frustration shrouded his mind, his eyes welling up with tears. He locked eyes with his step-sister, witnessing the cold, hateful eyes.

In that intense moment, Uriah confronted a truth within himself: there was no one he loathed more than her, and he doubted there would ever be anyone else he could despise to the same extent. The simmering rage reached a boiling point, and as he visualised an imaginary set of stairs behind her, he grappled with the unsettling acknowledgement that given the chance, he would have pushed her down them.

"You can't do that," Uriah said breathlessly.

"And who's going to stop me?"

Beneath his boiling anger, a growing fear crept in. His father's warning from the past resurfaced in his mind again. If his relationship with Maude did not work out, Uriah would be abandoned. All the progress he had made with his recent good behaviour, ignoring Blanchette's taunts and her irritating singing, and keeping her secret meetings with the waiter boy under wraps, couldn't be in vain.

"He'll send me away! Who will I have then?"

Blanchette smiled maliciously and planted a kiss on his cheek.

"Goodnight," she said quietly before returning to her bed.

Uriah stood there, immobile, his gaze locked on her dirty, bare feet, swinging gently just above the floor. Her eyes remained closed, but the eerie smile on her face persisted, a twisted expression of joy. Uriah released the chains within his mind, finally allowing Zeke's voice to be heard loud and clear.

URSULA

December 25th 1953, 17:43

The jeep's engine let out a roar, although its sound was more akin to the anguished cry of a wounded creature than the confident beast it outwardly resembled. In the passenger seat, Ursula sat with narrowed eyes, scanning the surroundings for any trace of Lyle. The tense silence within the car distorted the passage of time. Seconds stretched into minutes, and minutes seemed to extend into an apparent eternity. The first hour of the search felt interminable. The treacherous Scottish highland roads, cloaked in darkness and blanketed by a thick layer of snow, posed a formidable challenge. Yet, Finlay navigated through this perilous terrain with remarkable skill and ease. Despite occasionally veering off course, he recovered without a word of complaint. In this daunting environment, Ursula unexpectedly found a sense of safety by his side.

As the car sliced through the frigid air, Ursula's mind swirled with thoughts about everything that had led them to this crucial moment. The footprint they had discovered in the snow on the morning of the girl's disappearance had been Lyle's, she was sure of it now. She hadn't immediately recognised its significance, but in hindsight, there had been a hint of hesitation before Lyle placed his foot over the top of the print, clumsily smudging it. It had seemed genuine at the time, but now she saw the subtle manipulation that had taken place. Her thoughts raced as she pondered the puzzle before her. Everything, except the motive, seemed to align with the possibility that Lyle was the culprit.

Ursula felt a mix of confusion and determination gnawing at her, urging her to uncover the truth. The journey through the snowy highlands mirrored the inner turmoil of her mind, each turn in the road a reflection of the twists and turns in their investigation.

The shadows cast by the snowy landscape were metaphorical extensions of the shadows that surrounded Lyle, their meaning veiled in obscurity, the darkness outside mirroring the darkness of the case. The car's tires continued to crunch against the icy ground, each noise a reminder of the path they had embarked upon, one that could lead to the resolution they desperately sought. With Finlay steadfastly navigating the snowy roads, Ursula's mind remained consumed by the enigma of Lyle's involvement. The doubts that once plagued her now seemed like mere distractions, faint echoes in the vast landscape of her determination. The swirling snow and the uncertainty of the night could not deter her from the path she had chosen. The truth, she knew, waited patiently, hidden among the shadows, and Ursula was determined to uncover it.

"There!" James said, pointing to his right.

Ursula didn't see it at first but then her eyes caught a flicker of movement in the distance. Finlay steered the car towards Lyle, who seemed to have been so consumed in his attempt to survive in the cold that he had not noticed the car's lights until it was too late. Lyle made a meek attempt at an escape but ultimately fell to his knees and remained thus until they reached him. When Ursula and James stepped out of the car, they found him with his head tilted upward, his mouth moving in silent prayer. His trembling figure made no acknowledgement of their presence as he battled the elements, clad only in a t-shirt and a cloak of vulnerability.

"Did you hurt her?" James spat at his cousin. The anger and aggression in his voice shocked Ursula. He'd been incredibly reserved the entire journey.

"James—" Ursula tried to interject, but he cut her off.

"NO!" the singer screamed at her before turning his fury back towards Lyle and leaning in so close their noses were almost touching. "Did. You. Hurt. Her." James demanded but was met with Lyle's silence once more. Without warning, James slapped him with such force that Lyle fell backwards like a puppet without its strings.

There was no reaction from Lyle. He merely lay in the snow until Ursula and Finlay slowly lifted him back up and guided him into the warmth of the car. Ursula turned back around to James who stood alone in the enveloping darkness, lit only by the car's spotlight. She placed a hand on his face but he was unable to look her in the eye and walked back into the car without saying another word.

Returning to the hotel, they guided Lyle discreetly through the staff entrance, sidestepping any potential encounters with Theron Blakesley and other guests, recognising the urgency of obtaining answers before any public character condemnation unfolded.

Finlay Muir led them down the narrow staff corridor to a small, forgotten room at the very end. The cramped space had been used for storage of kerosene and oil lamps, no longer needed since the dawn of electricity. James guided Lyle to a solitary table against a damp, mouldy wall, directly opposite a cabinet filled with kerosene containers. After lighting an old oil lamp, Finlay left, leaving James, Lyle, and Ursula to confront the unsettling silence. The dim light of the oil lamp cast flickering shadows on the peeling walls, enhancing the sense of confinement and unease. Despite the absence of a window, an icy chill permeated the room, blending with Lyle's anxious energy to create an atmosphere thick with tension. Ursula perched on the table, while James leaned against the door, forming an unspoken barrier in case Lyle attempted to escape. However, there was no fight left in him.

"Lyle," Ursula started. "I want to help you, believe me, I do."

There was a long pause before Lyle replied.

"Even after what I did to you?"

"I don't think you meant me any harm," Ursula said. "Just as I am sure that you meant Uriah no harm. I think you panicked."

"Uriah said he was with you last night? He said you *took* him? What was the Blakesley boy doin' in your room?" James chimed in.

"Why do you care?" Lyle said looking at his cousin for the first time. "I disgust you. I can feel it. You can't even look at me."

"Yes, Lyle," James responded through gritted teeth. "You do disgust me and I can't wait to get away from you, but you're the only family I got. Why didn't you come talk to me if you were havin' thoughts? I coulda helped you. I tried to help you—"

"You can't help me, James! No one can!" screamed Lyle, beside himself.

Ursula listened intently at their exchange, the stage was beginning to be set for the truth to unravel.

"Why did you take Uriah? Does it have anything to do with what happened to Blanchette?" Ursula asked softly, trying to lower the tension in the room.

"We're friends," Lyle responded. "I wouldn't take him against his will."

"You can't be friends with a child, Lyle!" James said with frustration.

"Why not?"

"Jesus! Are you listenin' to yourself? What happened to you? When did you become *this!*"

"You've always known, deep down...admit it..."

James advanced, his intention to strike Lyle evident in his clenched fists, but Ursula intercepted him, her arms outstretched, blocking his path. Locking eyes with James, she held her ground until his fury began to subside. With gritted teeth, James took a step back, turning away from Lyle, his anger palpable in the tense set of his jaw.

"Did something happen between you and Uriah? Did Blanchette find out? Is that what happened?"

"No! We're friends! He was upset and I helped him," Lyle replied.

"Help him, how?" Ursula asked.

Lyle withdrew into a wall of silence, his lips trembling. Confidence was never his strong suit, but now, any sense of self-worth lay shattered. He looked like an empty shell. Ursula turned to James for support, knowing he might be the one to draw a confession from him.

"Listen, Lyle," James said, understanding the gravity of the moment. "We know you have your... struggles, but you... you wouldn't harm a child, right? I mean, not intentionally?"

James approached his cousin, each question feeling like a heavy burden on his heart. Ursula noticed a tear escaping from his eye, realising that the pursuit of truth might lead to him losing the last family member he had, his final connection to home.

"Did you kill her?" James pressed him. "Did you kill the girl? Is that why you had the boy with you? To keep him quiet? Is that why you attacked Ursula? Because she figured it out?"

"I just wanted to make you proud...I was tired of lettin' you down...and...I don't know, I — I didn't know what I was doin'"

Ursula leaned in as Lyle began speaking, anticipating what she believed would be his confession to the murder. However, before he could proceed, a cacophony of voices erupted from the corridor. Amidst the chaotic sounds, signs of consternation flashed across Lyle's face, hinting at the internal struggle he grappled with, concealing the truth he harboured.

"Sick bastard!" came the yells which Ursula recognised as belonging to Theron Blakesley. "Where is he?"

The voice heralded Mr Blakesley's imminent arrival, accompanied by a chorus of other guests and staff. Lyle visibly recoiled, retreating towards the far corner of the room, his arms wrapped tightly around his legs, forming a protective shell. Only his wide, fearful eyes remained visible, growing more apprehensive with each approaching footstep and escalating voice outside. Ursula couldn't suppress a twinge of concern for Lyle's safety, her worry mirrored in James's defensive posture, which grew more pronounced as the commotion outside intensified. Two loud thuds against the door echoed through the room, signalling the frenzied mob's proximity, and the tension inside escalated in tandem.

"Mr Blakesley, we mustn't inter—" Ophelia was saying, trying to calm him down.

"How dare you stand in our way?!" came Mr White's voice.

"Didn't you hear what the boy said?" added Ariel White. "The man needs to be hanged!"

"Let me in, I demand you let me in immediately!" shouted Mr Blakesley.

"I think it's best we go outside and appease them," Ursula said to James.

"Are you sure?"

"They're not going to go away, James."

The singer took a deep breath and opened the door slightly. Immediately, he felt pressure against it as Theron Blakesley tried to get in, but James managed to keep him at bay, pushing him against the corridor wall. It was then that Ursula noticed that Theron was holding a handful of pictures in his hand.

"Do you know what he is?" he spat, his face red with fury, he threw the pictures at her and James.

Ursula and James gathered the scattered images, her gaze sweeping the faces in the corridor before landing on the pictures. Everyone seemed to be present – Aonghus, Hamish, Mr. and Mrs. White, Ophelia, and even Julia and Silvia. Finlay stood aside, his eyes averted from the unfolding scene. Ursula redirected her attention to the pictures, only to be confronted with scenes of indescribable horror. A soft *"Oh, God!"* escaped James as he recoiled, dropping the pictures back to their original place as if they were scalding to the touch, stepping away as if singed by their disturbing contents.

As a mother herself, her heart ached with a profound empathy for the victims in the images. She couldn't fathom the depths of darkness that must have consumed someone to create or possess such disturbing images but the weight of the discovery burdened her as a human being, not just as a mother. It was a reminder of the potential for evil that lurked in the world, and it shook her to the core. The images seared into her mind, and she knew they would haunt her thoughts for a long time to come. Perhaps, forever.

Ursula rolled the pictures and tucked them inside her coat, it would be crucial information for the police when they finally arrived. Her eyes locked with the guests and staff. Their gazes carried such pain, disgust and hopelessness at the assumption they now held of what may have happened to Blanchette that Ursula knew it would be impossible to say anything that would alleviate their concerns. She turned her attention to Theron, completely lost to the momentary madness that had taken hold of him and then to Ophelia who stood rooted to the spot, hand over mouth.

"Where did you get these images from?" Ursula asked Theron Blakesley.

But before Theron could respond she felt James shift beside her.

"Lyle..." James' voice broke with a mixture of disappointment, anger and disgust but when he managed to speak again, the tone had changed to panic. "L-Lyle?"

Alarmed by his change in tone, Ursula turned towards the room and was met with the sight of Lyle's trembling hand releasing a container of kerosene oil, its contents cascading to the floor and drenching him from head to toe. The pungent odour assaulted her senses, filling the room with its acrid scent. In his other hand, Lyle clutched a wicker rope, its end ablaze with flickering flames. He stood there, a shattered figure, seeking some form of redemption amidst the chaos.

With tear-filled eyes, he mouthed apologies to his cousin, his words a desperate plea for forgiveness, before pressing the flaming wicker against his body. As soon as the fire made contact, a scene of unimaginable agony unfolded before the horrified onlookers. Lyle's screams pierced the air, carrying with them a raw intensity of suffering beyond comprehension. It was as if all the pain he had caused and endured throughout his life had converged into this single moment. Everyone stood frozen in shock and disbelief as they bore witness to Lyle's torment. The anguished cries of the burning man held them captive, rooted to the spot, their expressions mirroring the unfolding horror before them.

Just as despair threatened to consume everyone present, a figure emerged from the shadows – Finlay. Thinking quickly on his feet, he entered the room opposite, grabbed a wool blanket and rushed forward, trying to wrap Lyle with it and managing to extinguish the flames just as Lyle's voice was starting to break. However, the damage was already done. Lyle's injuries were devastating, with large patches of his skin charred beyond recognition. The stench of burnt flesh permeated the air, a horrifying reminder of the irreversible consequences of his desperate act.

As Lyle lay there, gasping for breath, his life force seemed to flicker like a dying candle. His body trembled with pain, and his eyes, filled with regret and sorrow, searched for James, who knelt beside his cousin. In those last moments, time seemed to slow down, and silence enveloped the room as everyone stood in stunned silence. Hearts weighed heavy with horror and powerlessness. Lyle's last breaths were feeble and laboured as if he were trying to hold on to life for a little longer, to make amends or find some semblance of peace. But fate had taken its course, and there was no turning back the hands of time.

URIAH

December 23rd 1953, 23:37

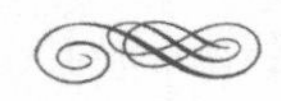

Uriah stood immobile. His eyes fixed on Blanchette as her grubby, bare feet dangled just above the floor. Despite her closed eyes, a twisted smile adorned her face, exuding a peculiar form of happiness that churned Uriah's stomach with anger. Zeke's voice continued its familiar whispers, initially ignored by Uriah. However, the murmurs grew louder, compelling him to confront the suggestions it had been screaming at him for the last few moments.

He crept into the bathroom, clutching Zeke tightly as he shut the door behind him with a soft click. In the dim light, he gazed at his reflection in the mirror, a small grin tugging at the corners of his lips. It was almost as if his reflection smiled back at him, casting an eerie yet oddly comforting aura in the small space. Taking care not to disturb Blanchette, who lay fast asleep in the room, Uriah slipped out silently, making his way downstairs.

The tranquillity of the night usually brought him solace, offering a peaceful refuge where he could delve into his thoughts undisturbed. But tonight felt different. The hushed atmosphere in the hotel was palpable, laden with an anticipation that sent a shiver down Uriah's spine. It was as if the stillness itself held a premonition of what was to come.

Each step seemed to amplify the haunting silence as he descended the stairs and Uriah found himself unable to shake off the eerie sensation, even as he tried to focus on his thoughts elsewhere. The memories of the hotel's vibrant past mingled with the shadows, making the night feel strangely alive. Uriah entered the dining room and proceeded through to the staff area until he reached Lyle's room. He knocked lightly on the door.

"Hello?" Lyle called from behind the locked door.

"Hi," Uriah replied softly. "I need your help."

There was a momentary silence as the portly man gazed at Uriah, his expression one of confusion akin to a deer caught in headlights by the unexpected announcement. Uriah couldn't help but draw a comparison to pandas he'd read about—large and endearing creatures, yet often depicted as less intelligent, displaying a limited grasp of self-preservation.

"Whattaya mean you need my help?" Lyle replied without opening the door.

"It's important," Uriah said more firmly.

Lyle cautiously glanced out of his room, ensuring that Uriah was alone before beckoning him inside and firmly shutting the door behind them.

"You shouldn't be here."

"But I need your help!" Uriah said a little louder.

"Okay, okay!" Lyle replied, his voice trembling. He walked away from Uriah, turning around to take a deep breath and recompose himself before asking the question.

"Whattaya need me to do?"

Uriah took a deliberate pause, savouring the tense silence that permeated the room. This intentional break also provided Zeke with an opportunity to voice his thoughts. Positioned on the bed, Uriah faced Lyle, who nervously bounced back and forth on the balls of his feet.

"Whatever I ask you to do, you have to do it, okay?" Uriah's voice was serious, as he tried to assert control.

Lyle hesitated, "Well, it depends on what you're asking for..."

With a cold, expressionless face, Uriah dropped the bombshell, "I took your pictures." Lyle's reaction was immediate – his breathing quickened, and panic painted his features. "The ones I found – I took them all," Uriah stated flatly, feeling a mix of satisfaction and defiance.

Lyle frantically darted under the bed like a startled badger, retrieving a small briefcase filled with envelopes. Horror washed over his face as he discovered the missing photographs. Desperation tightened its grip on him, and he lunged at Uriah, seizing him by the neck in a futile attempt to intimidate him.

However, Uriah remained impassive, staring defiantly into Lyle's small, black eyes. The fear flickering in them only fuelled Uriah's sense of power, evoking memories of the terror he had witnessed in the girl's eyes before he had pushed her down the stairs. It sent a chilling thrill coursing through him.

"You promised!" Lyle said through gritted teeth, wiping a disgusting amount of spit from his mouth. "*You promised*!"

"I can give them back, but I need you to do something for me."

"No," Lyle said, letting go of him. "I want them back now."

"I can't do that, not until you help me."

"But you *promised*!" he repeated pathetically.

Uriah stared at Lyle for a moment, struck by the brattish and childish behaviour emanating from him. With measured movements, Uriah rose from the bed, intending to make his way to the door, but Lyle positioned himself in his path, blocking his exit. The man's breath came in ragged gasps, his eyes bulging with intensity. If Uriah had ever pondered the appearance of a frenzied badger, he would have found the answer embodied in the figure blocking his way.

"What are you going to do, hold me hostage?" Uriah asked.

It was a rhetorical question; Uriah knew Lyle would cave and comply with his demands. Of course, there was always a small chance the plan could backfire, but Uriah trusted in Zeke. The risk of Lyle holding him hostage or worse, was akin to handing the incriminating images over to the authorities. The game had reached its conclusion, and Uriah was confident that Lyle wouldn't risk holding him against his will—it would only cause more harm than good. Lyle's feeble attempt at a standoff ended with his submission.

"Whattaya need?"

Uriah paused once more, his ears attuned to the instructions Zeke was relaying to him. With precision, he transmitted the nefarious plan to Lyle.

"I need you to kill my sister."

Lyle furrowed his brow as if confused by the instruction.

"I'm sorry, what?"

"I need you to kill my sister," Uriah repeated.

"You can't be serious?"

"As serious as the police are going to be when they find out the kinds of things you like to do with children...the kinds of things you did to me."

"I didn't do anything to you!" Lyle shrieked pathetically.

"Who do you think they will believe?" Uriah said. "The pictures speak for themselves."

"I would *never* harm a child!".

"Good luck explaining that," Uriah said, walking towards the door and turning the knob just as Lyle called after him.

"Wait!"

He turned and watched as the man paced up and down the room, thinking of what to do, He turned and observed as the man paced back and forth across the room, his mind racing to find an escape from the labyrinthine maze of malevolence that Uriah had constructed. Lyle's chest rose and fell in a steady rhythm, a testament to the inner turmoil raging within him, torn between his instinct to resist and his need for self-preservation. Gradually, Lyle pivoted towards him and nodded, and Uriah couldn't help but smile at the apparent simplicity of it all, like pieces moving on a chessboard, two lives intertwined in a single move.

LYLE

December 24th 1953, 00:12

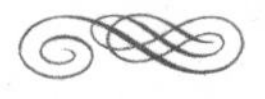

Lyle lingered in the shadows, his eyes fixed on the sleeping girl while Uriah and his ever-present stuffed toy observed from a short distance, his eyes wide with anticipation. In the eerie silence of the room, his heart pounded so loudly that he feared it might wake her. He tried to focus on the rhythmic beats, hoping to calm the turmoil in his mind, but the haunting echoes of uncertainty persisted, leaving him paralyzed with fear, doubt and the certainty that his life would never be the same.

Carefully, he settled on the edge of her bed, his gaze fixed on her serene countenance. Bathed in the soft glow of the moonlight, her porcelain-like complexion and cascading strawberry-blonde curls lent her an ethereal beauty, reminiscent of a delicate porcelain doll. Drawing nearer, he noticed the bruises marring her otherwise flawless skin, stark evidence of someone's callousness. Was it Uriah responsible for this brutality? Had that been the reason he tasked Lyle with this deed? No, Uriah wouldn't be so reckless; whoever had inflicted those wounds would inevitably be implicated in her demise. The thought lingered heavily in Lyle's mind, stirring a disquieting mix of apprehension and uncertainty about his own fate and Uriah's ability to uphold his promise.

Blanchette stirred beside him, her breath brushing against his face, a stark reminder of the life he was on the brink of extinguishing. A fleeting glance passed between Lyle and Uriah, laden with consternation and doubt, as uncertainty clouded Lyle's thoughts. What if he chose to face the consequences of his actions rather than commit the ultimate crime? Admitting to everything would undoubtedly cost him James, consigning him to a life of violent retribution in prison once his deeds were laid bare. Yet, Lyle couldn't shake the belief that he didn't deserve such a fate. After all, they were just pictures, and his interactions with little Armand and Tiago had been innocent gestures of affection.

A surge of indignation briefly welled within him, but it swiftly dissipated under the weight of his task. Lyle grappled with conflicting emotions, torn between the desire to shield James from his true nature and the unbearable weight of his impending deed.

His inner struggle reached a breaking point as Lyle's yearning for self-preservation overpowered whatever moral compass he had left. Without a second thought, he leaned forward, his hands wrapping around Blanchette's fragile neck. Her eyes snapped open in terror as she fought against Lyle's grip, slapping at his arms in a desperate attempt to break free. Her gaze darted around the room, landing on Uriah. Blanchette reached out to him, pleading for help, but the boy merely sat on the floor, cross-legged, placing Zeke in between his knees and continuing to watch the scene unfold with a curious detachment. Lyle felt Uriah inching closer as if he were watching the most captivating performance he'd ever seen.

Unaware of his tears, Lyle felt the wetness on his cheeks as one drop fell onto Blanchette's pale, blue face. He was suddenly struck by the harsh reality of the situation, realising the magnitude of his actions. Yet, he couldn't stop himself. His grip tightened, and Blanchette's resistance slowly faded until her body went limp. Lyle's heart sank as he knew, with grim certainty, that she was gone, her life stolen by his hands. It was a sight he'd seen too many times before in Alabama, often as a consequence of a lynch mob fulfilling their thirst for innocent black lives — lifeless bodies, void of any spark of vitality.

"You should hide the body," Uriah said calmly, without taking his eyes away from his dead sister.

The chilling timbre of Uriah's words penetrating to his core. How could someone so young exude such malevolence? There was no hint of remorse or empathy in Uriah's demeanour, his features an enigmatic mask, devoid of emotion or perhaps even humanity itself.

Initially drawn to Uriah's mystique, his solitude, and what appeared to be a vulnerability, Lyle now saw him for what he truly was: a predator disguised in the guise of innocence. Uriah was a wolf in sheep's clothing, a perilous entity that must be contained before its malevolence unleashed further harm upon the world. With a heavy heart, Lyle rose to his feet and gathered the lifeless body in his arms, the weight of guilt and dread settling upon his shoulders like a suffocating burden.

His voice trembling and cracked, Lyle dared to ask, "You promise?"

"I promise."

Lyle slipped out of the room, moving with cautious steps through the deserted corridors of the hotel, the silence pressing in around him like a tangible presence. Despite the emptiness, he couldn't shake the feeling of unseen eyes watching his every move, silently passing judgement on the unforgivable deed he had committed. Aware of the urgency of his situation, Lyle opted to exit the building via the staff area, enveloping himself in the cloak of darkness that draped the night.

Outside, the world seemed to hold its breath, the stillness of the night broken only by the muffled sound of his footsteps on the frost-covered ground. Each step weighed heavily on his conscience, the burden of guilt and regret growing with every passing moment. In the darkness, the boundaries between right and wrong blurred, leaving Lyle ensnared in a web of moral ambiguity from which there appeared to be no escape. His connection to Uriah and the sinister events of the evening would forever tarnish his conscience.

Shivering in the cold night air, Lyle squinted into the darkness, periodically glancing back to ensure the faint glow of the hotel lights still pierced the night sky, guiding his way like a distant beacon. His destination remained uncertain, the weight of his decision hanging heavy on his shoulders. As he traversed the desolate landscape, the night became his cloak, offering a veil of anonymity as he sought out a secluded spot to lay the girl to rest.

URSULA

December 26th 1953, 12:12

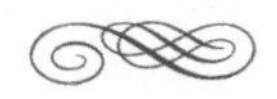

Death had become her unwelcome Christmas companion, Ursula mused, her gaze fixed on her reflection in the mirror, as she carefully pinned her hair into a bun and applied a deep crimson hue to her lips. Tonight wasn't meant for anything but mourning the loss of innocent lives, yet Theron's proposal to gather and remember Blanchette and Maude over food and drink felt strangely appropriate. Loch Linnhe had been their happy place, it made sense that they were remembered here.

Despite the solemn occasion, Ursula's thoughts kept returning to Lyle. While far from innocent, the haunting mixture of sorrow, regret, and helplessness she had glimpsed in his eyes before he set himself ablaze lingered in her mind, refusing to fade. His agonised cries echoed alongside the names of the Anchor Ripper's victims as if he too were counted among them.

A faint knock on her door broke her reverie, and Ursula moved across her suite to open it. There stood Theron Blakesley, his attempt at a smile faltering, unable to mask the trauma he had witnessed. She was certain that the harrowing events of this Christmas would weigh heavily on every one of them for years to come.

"Hi," he said. "May I come in?"

"Certainly," Ursula replied.

Theron Blakesley entered the room, a momentary silence enveloping him as he awkwardly surveyed his surroundings. Seemingly grappling with how to initiate the conversation, he shifted his attention to the expansive view outside Ursula's large windows. The relentless rain, pounding against the hotel, provided a cathartic release, washing away the snow that had confined them for days. Theron seemed to find solace in the gradual transformation of snow into rivulets of dirty mush, his eyes wide as if entranced by the snow's reluctant surrender to the relentless rain.

"You have a beautiful view," Theron said. "I can't remember the last time it rained. All I can remember is cold...nothing but, never-ending, bone-chilling cold...and darkness. May I sit?"

Ursula nodded quietly, gesturing towards the chair next to the writing desk. She settled onto her four-poster bed, suppressing a wince, her muscles still throbbing from her ordeal.

"I want to thank you for everything you did to help Maude and me," he said. "Even though she isn't here, I am sure she's looking down on us with a smile. Justice has been done."

"You do not need to thank me, Mr Blakesley —"

"But I do. I know what demons you're fighting and still, you pushed through to make sure we could have closure."

"I'm sorry if..." Ursula faltered. "If I had any part in Mrs Blakesley's...death."

"What do you mean?" Mr Blaksley asked.

"When she asked me if her actions had killed Blanchette...I wasn't able to tell her otherwise. But had I known...I would have told her. Perhaps I should have told her. I knew that's what she wanted to hear. It might've kept her alive."

"You know, Detective, people are fragile, who knows why they do the things they do? A handful of pills, a bottle of wine - it's amazing how people can choose to escape it all. They say the best poison is one that leaves no trace..." Theron's tone shifted. "And well, Maude was a poison...the way she treated Blanchette...what she did to the girl...I guess, eventually, she just couldn't live with herself. There's nothing you could have done or said. If I knew Blanchette, she would have thought, better dead than alive and have to live with the shame of what she did."

Ursula was taken aback by Theron's sudden shift, unable to shake the feeling that this was not the same man she had encountered on her first night. The charm that once defined him seemed to have been replaced by a more ominous demeanour. Nevertheless, she maintained her professionalism.

"Be that as it may, I am genuinely sorry for your loss," Ursula replied, starting to feel something gnawing at her conscience and intensifying with each passing moment. "Would I be able to speak with Uriah again?"

Theron Blakesley did not respond immediately, instead, he kept his gaze firmly fixed on the intensifying rain.

"No, I do not think that's a great idea," he responded simply. "He's been through enough."

"I completely understand, but it would help with my investigation—-"

"Ms Dankworth," Theron said sternly. "I think given that Lyle was someone of questionable morals, you should overlook anything you aren't quite sure about and conclude your investigation," and then with a dismissive smile, he changed the subject. "Will I be seeing you at dinner tonight?"

"Yes," Ursula replied disconcerted.

"See you shortly," Theron replied.

The conversation left Ursula with a growing sense of unease and it was only once she was alone in her room once more that she realised that she was shaking, whether in anger or distress at Mr Blakesley's reaction to her request to speak with Uriah, she wasn't altogether sure.

Ursula found Ophelia in her office, her head buried in her hands, utterly devoid of the composure she typically maintained in front of guests.

"I'm sorry," Ursula apologised.

"No need," Ophelia replied. "I was just gathering my thoughts. Would you like a drink?"

Ophelia reached for a whiskey decanter and two intricately hand-cut glasses before Ursula could decline. Pouring liquid into both, she handed one to Ursula, who accepted it politely, placing it on the table away from her line of sight. However, Ursula's mouth began to salivate.

"I fear this is the end of the hotel," Ophelia continued. "Things haven't been the same since air travel became a thing. Why come to Loch Linnhe when you can fly to Cape Town? And now *this*? Three deaths in the space of a couple of days. Maude's family were our biggest investors. Mr Blakesley has already told me he won't be continuing. Even if he did, the damage to our reputation..."

Ursula subtly pushed the glass of whiskey further away from her with the tip of her fingers.

"If there is something I have learnt the last few months, is that nothing is ever as bad as we think," Ursula said, trying to offer words of comfort. "Things have a funny way of sorting themselves out. Quite curious that Mr Blakesley is already discussing family business."

"Only the poor mourn the dead. How do you think they stay rich?"

Ursula paused for a few moments, observing the old hotel manager drink her worries away. She couldn't help but wonder if that could be her in a few years if she wasn't careful—alone and afraid. Pushing that thought aside, she leaned in closer to Ophelia.

"I wanted to ask if you could let me into Mr and Mrs Blakesley's room?"

"Sure, but whatever for?"

"Detectives," Ursula shrugged. "We have to make sure we've crossed our t's and dotted our i's."

Ursula had long sensed that death left an indelible mark upon a room. The exact nature of this weight eluded her, but whenever she stepped into a space that had witnessed death, the atmosphere seemed to thicken. Her breath became more laboured, and at times, she questioned whether the lingering spirits of the departed were attempting to convey vital messages from beyond. Entering Mr. and Mrs. Blakesley's room was no exception. Even Ophelia, standing behind Ursula, hesitated before mustering the courage to follow her inside. The palpable presence of the departed lingered, and the air itself carried an unspoken weight that heightened Ursula's awareness of the profound events that had transpired within those walls.

"Everything is as we found it," the hotel manager said breathlessly. "Just like you asked."

Ursula nodded and surveyed the room. She opened the wardrobe. All of Mrs. Blakesley's clothes remained untouched. She continued to examine the surroundings, something beneath one of the pillows grabbed her attention. The edge of an envelope peeked out, and Ursula reached for it, holding it in her hands. She cast a questioning glance at Ophelia, silently seeking her thoughts on the discovery. Ursula opened the envelope and withdrew the letter. Her fingers shook as she unfolded it delicately and read its contents.

Dearest Mother,

I am penning this letter to you with the gravest of tidings, news that no esteemed grandparent should ever find themselves confronting. It is with a heavy heart that I inform you of the heinous fate that has befallen your beloved granddaughter, Blanchette, whom, I must confess, I failed to cherish as befitting a mother of my standing. I am haunted by the uncertainty of whether I played a role in this atrocious act.

As luck would have it, a diligent detective is spending Christmas here, at the Grand Loch Linnhe Hotel. She is evidently troubled but seems to have unwavering resolve in her pursuit of the truth. It may sound unnatural, but years spent looking at her through the lens of her father's image, whom I harboured disdain for, blinded me to the maternal love I ought to have bestowed upon her. I can no longer subject myself to such feelings. This sorrowful revelation has brought to light two undeniable truths. Firstly, your discernment regarding Theron has proven accurate; our relationship is akin to water and oil, incompatible and irreconcilable. Secondly, I find myself unable to perpetuate this charade any longer. I have resolved to return to London, where I shall mourn my dearest daughter and initiate the process of legal se—

The letter, evidently penned by Maude to her mother, remained incomplete, lacking both a date and signature. The final sentence was also left unfinished, suggesting an abrupt ending. Upon closer examination, Ursula noted a disparity in the handwriting, indicating the possibility of a sudden interruption. In the letter, Maude made mention of returning to London to mourn for her daughter. The question lingered: why would she, mere hours—perhaps even minutes—later, choose to end her own life?

Ursula carefully placed the unfinished letter back into its envelope and turned her attention to the bathroom. Entering the dimly lit space, she found the scene mirroring the one she had encountered earlier that morning. The vial of pills scattered on the floor, the bathwater now slightly depleted without Maude's presence, and the remnants of a shattered wine glass and the lingering stain—a sombre tableau illustrating the unfolding tragedy. Ursula knelt beside the scattered pills and the vial, proceeding with caution to avoid injury from the shards of broken glass. Methodically, she gathered all the pills, placing them back into the vial with meticulous care. Upon completing the task, she observed that the vial was nearly filled to the brim as if none of the pills had been consumed whatsoever.

"Mr Blakesley said she'd taken a bunch of her pills, did he not?" Ursula turned to Ophelia, whose sombre expression revealed she had understood exactly what was going through Ursula's mind.

The hotel manager nodded slowly, almost afraid to confirm her suspicions.

"Then why, doesn't it appear that way?"

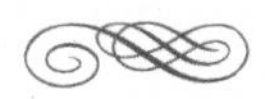

"B*etter dead than alive.*"

Theron's words reverberated persistently in Ursula's mind as she prepared for dinner that evening. Reluctantly, she decided to attend, driven by the need to maintain a façade of normalcy despite harbouring the unsettling truth close to her heart. Deep down, Ursula was convinced that Maude's death was not a suicide, but murder. The vial of pills remained seemingly untouched; Ursula had even counted them, finding that the number inside matched the label—sixty pills remained. Coupled with the tone with which Theron had spoken to Ursula, there was little doubt in her mind that he was the main suspect.

Confronting him with this accusation, however, seemed futile. She could foresee the predictable course of events: he would vehemently deny any wrongdoing, citing his anguish over the deaths of his wife and stepdaughter. Eventually, he would paint Ursula as a troubled alcoholic, claiming he had saved her from self-destruction. The ensuing narrative would be contested, but in the eyes of the police, would they trust the word of James, a black man whose cousin was accused of Blanchette Blakesley's murder? Would they believe Ursula, a woman who would struggle to deny her troubled relationship with alcohol and would confirm that Theron had indeed intervened to prevent her from committing suicide? The answer, though terrifying, was simple: no.

The police would likely find a way to tie Maude's death to Lyle. After all, he had killed Blanchette. They would not delve into the inconsistencies of their theory. Ursula may have been tasked with leading the investigation, but the harsh truth was that she was a woman navigating a man's world, and James, was a black man in a white man's world. In this unforgiving environment, logic and truth held little sway. Ursula would, of course, inform the police of her suspicions. However, for now, all she could do was note down Maude Blakesley in her notebook. She would seek justice for her, as with every other name on that list. If it was the last thing she did.

"The truth is in the eye of the beholder," Ursula whispered as she left her room and made her way towards the dining room.

Before she had even set foot on the first step, Ursula was met with the sounds of strained anger echoing from below. Hurrying down the staircase, she found James engaged in a heated argument with Ophelia. The singer stood at the bottom of the steps, clad in his travelling jacket, with his suitcase resting by his feet.

"Ms Dankworth," Ophelia said awkwardly.

"Ms Clyde," Ursula replied looking from the hotel manager to the singer and then to the suitcase on the floor.

"She wouldn't let me see you," James said quickly. "I just wanted to say goodbye."

"Why?" Ursula asked, turning to Ophelia.

"The guests are uncomfortable with his presence and have requested we ask him to leave—"

"I just wanted to say goodbye!" he repeated frustratedly.

"Staff should not be going up to guest areas," Ophelia offered.

"If you are forcing him out, it would mean that his employment here is terminated, which means that he is no longer a member of staff," Ursula said with a twinkle in her eye. "I must say, Ophelia, considering how god-fearing a woman you are, I am quite shocked and disappointed to see you behave in such a manner. Seems rather unkind to force a man out during this most sacred of holidays."

"It is because I am a god-fearing woman that I do this. The sins of the father shall be visited upon the children," the hotel manager said narrowing her eyes and holding herself up as straight as possible.

"Is that so? Is the sin of not returning your love the reason why you keep Mr Kimberley's son locked in a basement?"

Ophelia was unable to hide the shock and affront.

"As I said, the other guests are uncomfortable—"

"Is he to walk to the station in the pouring rain? You wouldn't even offer him a ride to the station?"

"Why should that be my concern—"

"When I found out you locked your son in a dungeon," Ursula interjected. "I thought, god, she's a cruel bitch. But then, I wondered whether you were trying to protect him from the cruelty of this world. That being the case, there would have been an ounce of kindness in the act...but perhaps you are just a cruel bitch."

Ophelia stood rooted to the spot, taken aback by the vehemence of Ursula's words. She moved to stand next to James and held his hand firmly, he pressed hers with thanks.

"James is a guest at this hotel. You will take his suitcase to my room and offer him a key. Have I made myself understood or will I have to write to James Kimberley? He still owns this hotel, am I right? Do you have an address for the elusive Mr Kimberley...or would I also be able to find him in the dungeon?"

There was a long pause, where both women seized each other before the hotel manager replied.

"I'll see Mr Wilson upstairs."

"Perfect," Ursula said. "If the other guests have an issue with it, please tell them to speak to me."

The smell of burning flesh permeated the corridors of the staff area, a haunting reminder of the horrific events that had transpired. It was no surprise that James had chosen to leave. Who would want to wake up every morning and be reminded of their cousin's atrocities with their very first breath of the day? As Ursula made her way down the corridor, she paused outside the room where the tragedy had unfolded, the scene still fresh in her mind, surreal and unsettling. Gathering her resolve, Ursula moved on and knocked on Finlay's door. After a brief moment, he answered, clad only in a towel, a testament to the rawness and vulnerability that lingered in the aftermath of the ordeal.

"I'm sorry, I just left the shower," he responded.

"I can come back later."

"No, please come in."

Ursula stepped into the pristine room, admiring the impeccable orderliness of Finlay's space. As he busied himself in the wardrobe, she couldn't help but be drawn once again to the collection of drawings adorning the walls. Her gaze lingered on each one, noting the intricate details and the subtle nuances captured in each stroke. Among the images, her attention was caught by the distinct signatures in the corners. One bore the whimsical moniker 'Saint Nerd,' while another was signed simply 'Candy Medlock.' Ursula couldn't suppress a smile at the playful creativity reflected in these names, adding an intriguing layer of mystery to the artwork.

"Are these your pen names?"

"You can call it that."

"What do they mean?"

Finlay shrugged. "Whatever you want them to mean."

Ursula offered a smile, recognising the allure of Finlay's enigmatic demeanour that seemed to draw women to him like moths to a flame. Yet, beneath his dark mystique, there lingered a sense of detachment that gave Ursula pause, an unsettling quality that hinted at depths she couldn't quite fathom.

"Have you always drawn?"

"Aye. Ever since I can remember. I used to draw in the sand when I was a wee lad and just sit and watch as the waves washed it away."

"I wanted to thank you," Ursula said.

"What for? Not being the killer?" Finlay asked with a smile as he put on his trousers under the towel that preserved his decency.

"For what you did for Lyle."

"I saw many a man burn in the war, I acted as any soldier would have."

Her eyes returned to the hand drawings on his wall again. "You should pursue this. You are very talented. Maybe one day, I'll have you paint a portrait of me."

"I should be so lucky," Finlay smiled.

They were both enveloped by silence as Finlay placed his boots on and Ursula traced her fingers on his neatly stacked notebooks.

"Was there anything else I could help you with?" Finlay asked.

A musky, nausea-inducing scent of vanilla hung in the air, assaulting her senses. Ursula turned abruptly and let out a tiny scream. Finlay had crept up right behind her, silent as a thief in the night.

"No," she said.

Leaving the groundskeeper's room, Ursula couldn't shake the overbearing feeling that lingered within her. Finlay had always struck her as surly, even somewhat creepy, but now, a deeper unease lurked beneath the surface. Recalling the incidents she had heard about only intensified her discomfort. The attempted sexual assault on the kitchen maid and the admission of a physical altercation with Blanchette revealed disturbing aspects of the groundskeeper's character. It wasn't just one incident that troubled Ursula; the disturbing pattern of his behaviour sent shivers down her spine. As she walked away from his room, Ursula took a deep sigh, trying to distance herself from the unsettling thoughts. She knew that dwelling on it at this moment wouldn't change anything. She resolved to let her thoughts rest and focus on getting through the day as best as possible.

URSULA

26th December 1953, 18:07

Rain cascaded from the heavens, wrapping the castle in a curtain of water so thick that the surroundings of the Grand Loch Linnhe Hotel were obscured from view. Ursula felt a light throb on the back of her head as she bent down to put on her shoes.

"Everything alright?" James asked, sensing her discomfort.

"Yes," she lied. "Just tired. I can't remember the last time I was this excited to go to bed."

Ursula stood up, and sensed a slight soreness in her rib area, prompting a wince, albeit not so noticeable that James might discern. She turned her attention to the singer, who'd resumed the same position he'd been in for the last couple of hours, slouched in the chair by the window, completely motionless.

Each glance at him stirred an overwhelming mix of sorrow and disappointment within Ursula. His omission of crucial facts surrounding his cousin had left a harrowing scar, one that hadn't yet healed since the end of her marriage. She wasn't sure if they'd ever be able to rekindle their connection. Although Ursula was convinced of James's innocence, she couldn't help but assign a fraction of culpability to him. Ursula knew she was being harsh; ultimately, love, whether familial or otherwise, possessed the power to blind people to things they might have otherwise seen.

"Are you ready?" she asked him.

"I'm not gonna go," he replied without turning to her.

"It might help distract you," Ursula said.

"You think their silent accusations will help distract me? Besides, I am not hungry."

Ursula approached him, the click-clacking of her heels blending with the rhythmic patter of rain outside, creating a hypnotic harmony. Sighing, she knelt beside him, placing a gentle hand on his.

"I've spent the last year blaming myself for my daughter's death. The truth is, my sorrow had a part to play in it. I'd been careful not to drink around her...to ignore the trauma...the flashbacks of..."

Ursula shut her eyes and was immediately confronted by the lurking figure in the alley, shrouded in fog. His broad shoulders and muscular physique emerged with a clarity that had eluded her memory since that fateful night. Hastily, she snapped her eyes open, forcefully pushing the haunting image away.

"...then my friend Leah called me to tell me Robert had met someone new. He'd moved on, and there I was still holding onto the ghosts of our relationship, hoping and praying that he'd come back. I spiralled. I became the very thing I mocked: a woman pulled at the heartstrings by the whims of a man. We are human; we are allowed to feel. Sometimes our troubles get the best of us. I drank. My daughter drowned. That momentary lapse did have a part to play in her death. There is no escaping that. But I no more killed my little girl than you committed the atrocious acts of your cousin. Do we have a level of culpability? Yes, undeniably, but we cannot let that dictate who we are. I need you to put on your best smile and come with me downstairs."

She smiled, feeling a sense of kinship with James as his eyes burned into hers. For a time, she sat beside him in comforting silence, absorbed by the comforting sound of rain assaulting the hotel. It seemed to echo the emotions churning inside them – grief, guilt, and the yearning for connection and understanding. James' stomach emitted a loud groan of hunger.

"What are we doin'?" James asked. This was a simple, yet complex question that Ursula was unsure she would be able to answer, not while she still felt so many conflicting emotions.

"Right now, we are going to eat—"

"That's not what I meant. You know what I mean."

"Yes, I do," she replied earnestly. Could she ever allow a man into her heart again? "I think that is a conversation for when we're back in London," Ursula replied.

James broke into a smile. "Sure."

"Let's go disrupt Christmas," Ursula said mischievously.

Despite Ophelia's protests, Ursula and James strode into the dining hall, welcomed by a stifling hush from the other guests. Tension hung in the air, palpable as they made their way through the dining room. Theron Blakesley, a portrait of seething resentment, chewed on his tongue, his eyes shooting angry daggers at James and Ursula. On the adjacent table, Mr and Mrs White, accompanied by their friends Hachem and Ndeshi, maintained an awkward silence. Ursula, attempting to diffuse the tension, flashed a warm smile at the Whites and their companions as she and James settled into the seat nearest the stage. Only then did she register the presence of young Uriah at the piano, his stuffed toy perched with care upon it. It became evident that the boy had been the source of entertainment prior to their arrival.

"Maybe I am not so hungry after all," James whispered.

"Nonsense," Ursula replied as she beckoned Hamish. "Could we have the best sauvignon blanc you have and the menu?"

Hamish nodded tersely, his eyes lingering on James before abruptly pivoting on his heels, a visage of desolation etched across his face. At that moment, Oliver White approached, a faux smile adorning his face.

"Can I sit?" he asked.

"I don't know, can you? Who knows what you may have been up to," Ursula quipped.

The taunt achieved its intended impact; Oliver White's face reddened with embarrassment, his initial smile dissipating and morphing into a profound scowl.

"I don't mean to be rude—" he started.

"If you gotta start a sentence with those words, you most certainly intend to be rude," James said.

Oliver ignored him, keeping his attention on Ursula.

"I appreciate that the two of you have...a—" Oliver paused. "Well, a - whatever this is. But I think it is a bit insensitive to have him here, considering what his cousin did."

"You want to punish him for something someone else did?" Ursula asked.

"The chances he didn't know what his cousin was..." Oliver paused and offered James a glance filled with contempt. "Who knows if he doesn't indulge in that himself—"

"How dare you?" James said, getting up from his seat.

Oliver took a step back. Ursula saw Hachem stand at the same time ready to take action, should it be necessary.

"You people are exceedingly aggressive! All, I am trying to say," he continued, with his hands held up in a faux sign of peace. "Is that I do not think this is altogether appropriate."

Ursula nodded with measured slowness, observing in silence as Hamish reappeared with the bottle of wine. He methodically poured it into Ursula's glass, followed by James, before retreating from the scene. Ursula swirled the sauvignon, savouring its aroma, and then turned to dignify Oliver White with a response.

"Would you say your father, the most prestigious banking tycoon, knows who you are?" Ursula asked, taking a sip of wine, feeling it soothe her insides as it made its way down her throat. "Would you say that, despite what is evident to anyone with eyes, your father knows who Hachem is to his beloved son? And if he does, do you think he may not be saying anything because he too indulges in that kind of thing himself?"

Oliver White's cheeks turned a bright shade of red, his embarrassment plain for all to see, Ursula continued.

"Do you know what I don't think is altogether appropriate? That you and your wife gallivant around the world with those two poor souls, making them think that they will ever be anything other than a pastime. What I also find inappropriate is the deception you decided to partake in. Where is the morality in perverting the course of justice during the investigation into a child's murder, just to protect your nighttime activities?"

"I—I..." stuttered Oliver White.

"You—You better get back to your seat," James smirked, drinking his wine in a single gulp and smacking his lips in satisfaction.

"Was there anything else you wished to discuss, Mr White?" Ursula added.

"No."

"Merry Christmas," James Wilson said with a smile.

As Oliver retraced his steps to his seat, Uriah, seemingly prompted by some unseen cue, began playing sombre notes on the piano, capturing everyone's attention. The melody unfolded with darkness, punctuated by dissonant chords and chilling progressions that seemed to slither up their spines. Each note hung in the air, reluctant to dissipate, intensifying the already unsettling atmosphere.

Uriah's fingers danced across the keys, his smile widening, almost taking on a maniacal quality as if he revelled in the eerie sounds he conjured. His eyes gleamed with twisted delight, a sinister joy evident as they locked onto the expressionless gaze of his stuffed toy. A growing unease gripped Ursula, who had believed the atmosphere couldn't become more eerie. Then, the boy began to sing, his voice sweet and note-perfect, akin to an angel's—if that angel happened to be Gabriel guiding you through hell.

For want of a nail, the shoe was lost
For want of a shoe, the horse was lost
For want of a horse, the rider was lost
For want of a rider, the battle was lost
For want of a battle the kingdom was lost
And all for the want of a nail....

As the song reached its conclusion, a realisation struck her with chilling clarity: behind Uriah's façade of innocence lurked something far more sinister. The boy met her gaze, almost tauntingly and she saw a knowing glint in his eyes, a silent acknowledgement of the dark truth hidden within the lyrics of the song. It was his confession, laid bare for anyone astute enough to decipher its meaning.

What if Lyle had never 'taken' Uriah against his will? What if it had been the boy who'd discovered the images and asked Lyle to do his bidding? Could Theron's steadfast refusal to allow Ursula to question Uriah once more be a veiled confirmation that the boy had played a role in

Blanchette's murder? Ursula couldn't help but wonder if it all came down to the smallest of details, the proverbial nail that had set everything in motion. For want of a nail, a kingdom could be lost — or, in this case, a life taken.

URSULA

27th December 1953, 11:12

Officer Kevin McKinley, a stout man with a handsome face, possessed brown eyes that bore the weight of hopes and dreams dulled by life's experiences. Each sigh and roll of the eyes unveiled a cynicism crafted not by genuine disbelief, but rather by the circumstances life had dealt him. Pausing for a moment, the man straightened his back, squared his shoulders, and puffed out his chest. He carried himself with a level of self-importance he seemed oblivious to. His pen hovered above the surface of his notebook as he absorbed Ursula's accusation.

"So," he said, his voice carrying a heavy tone of apprehension. "Lyle Blakesley—"

"Lyle Wilson," Ursula corrected.

Officer McKinley looked down at his notes to confirm and nodded, scratching out the incorrect name and writing the right one just above it.

"That's right, Lyle Wilson," the officer said. "Him. You said he killed the girl, Blake Blakesley, was it?"

Ursula frowned. "Blanchette."

"Yes, yes, of course. So, he killed her and did you find out why? He just a creep, I take it?" he asked.

Ursula gritted her teeth. They had gone through it three or four times already. What irked her even more was Officer McKinley's deliberate decision to leave her for last. It was foolish. He ought to have sat down with Ursula first to delve into everything she had uncovered before engaging with the suspects. Instead, he entered the interrogations with minimal information, making himself more susceptible to influence. Who would believe the truth when the lie made far more sense?

"There is a possibility that Blanchette found the images Lyle had in his possession," Ursula replied. "But, I can't confirm that without being able to interrogate her or him."

"So your *theory* is—"

Ursula felt her blood boil. However, she couldn't dispute it. It was a theory, but in her mind, Theron and Uriah Blakesley were unreliable.

"I do not believe Lyle had any reason to want to kill Blanchette. I think Uriah found the images and blackmailed Lyle with them."

"You think the little boy convinced a grown man to kill his sister?"

"I know it sounds far-fetched—"

"Maybe because it is. Suppose I believe you, what motive would the boy have?"

"I don't know, but he didn't seem to have a good relationship with Blanchette."

"Brothers and sisters fight all the time. We don't go around ordering them strangled," Officer McKinley laughed and shook his head as if Ursula was completely mad. Besides, you agree the fella, Lyke Williams, killed her?"

"Lyle Wilson. And yes, I do." Ursula replied simply.

"So, there must have been a reason, unless you're insinuating he was off his head? In which case, I'd be careful with that James Wilson, ain't he the cousin?"

"He is."

"And you're certain he wasn't involved? We know what his sort are like. Violent."

"Is that so?"

"Yeah, dangerous sort."

"Ah yes, and the history of the British Empire certainly confirms that theory, doesn't it, Officer?" Ursula said tartly. "Are we done?"

"Look," Officer McKinley said leaning forward, reminding Ursula of the kind of man that was designed to make women feel stupid and inadequate. "I hear what you said about Mr Blakesley and his boy. But considering that Lyke Williamson tried to do things to the boy...what makes sense is this," he continued in a tone that became far more condescending with every syllable. "Poor Uriah confided in his sister about what happened with Liam—-"

"Lyle," Ursula corrected.

"Sure," Officer McKinley said pressing on. "Blanchette probably tried to confront him, threatening to tell everyone about the pictures. He took the boy and bullied the lad into letting him into the room and killed Blanchette there and then. For good measure, he decided to do Maude Blakesley in."

"Why?"

"What do you mean, why? Blanchette probably told her mother and Lyke was shit scared they'd tell the police."

"Is that what makes sense, Officer?" she asked, offering him a steely glance.

"It is," he replied.

"Then we should do what makes sense and ignore the truth."

"I know you think yourself a big shot from London. But word on the street is you and your husband are the reason the Anchor Ripper got away, so I wouldn't be looking at me that way like you're something better. I just dismantled your theory in the fraction of the time you were investigating this. You're pretty. If you smiled a little bit more and drank a little bit less, you might even be good at this. I certainly see potential."

"Do you have any further questions, Officer?"

"No more questions, but we do want to extend our thanks," Officer Mcknley stretched a sweaty palm, which Ursula rejected, leaving him in stunned silence.

The hearse vans arrived shortly after lunch, carrying the bodies of Blanchette and Maude, covered in white sheets, along with what remained of Lyle Wilson. The Blakesleys departed in the police vehicle, with Officer McKinley, who would be escorting them to the mortuary for the necessary preparations to transport the bodies back to London. Soon after, Oliver and Ariel White, as well as Ndeshi and Hachem, left in the car they had arrived in, leaving Ursula and James alone. The two sat in relative silence, awaiting Finlay to transport them to the station. Although they were leaving together, the uncertainty of their future lingered, with nothing conclusively ruled out for the time being.

The jeep's horn signalled Finlay's arrival, prompting Ursula and James to seize their suitcases. Standing outside, shielding herself from the rain, was the hotel manager, Ophelia Clyde. She wrapped a shawl around her shoulders for warmth and wore a far more light-hearted expression than Ursula was accustomed to seeing.

"I like to see off every guest. I've done so for the last forty years," Ophelia said with a thin smile.

"May you do so for forty years more," Ursula replied. "I'm sure it'll all work out."

"And if it doesn't...well, I've lived, which is far more than we can say for poor Blanchette. Good luck Ms Dankworth," Ophelia turned to the singer and offered a light bow of the head. "Mr Wilson."

"Ma'am," James bowed in return, watching the hotel manager walk back inside.

Ursula cast a final glance at the hotel, reflecting on the whirlwind of events that had unfolded in such a brief span. There was a sense that being there had, in some way, saved her life.

"Ms. Dankworth! You're going to miss your train!" Finlay exclaimed, stepping out of the car and immediately being engulfed by the rain. He sprinted towards them, grabbed their bags, dashed back to the jeep, and threw them into the trunk.

James and Ursula hurried down the stairs, getting drenched within seconds. They climbed into the car, exchanging looks with faces dripping with water, and burst into laughter. Soon, Finlay started the engine and began to drive away. Ursula stole one last glance at the hotel, its shape blurred by the incessant downpour. James remained resolute, refusing to look back, his memories of the place forever tainted by tragedy. Ursula squeezed his hand tightly, silently pledging to help him overcome his grief.

As they left the hotel far behind, a magical transformation unfolded. The rain, which had relentlessly thundered for the past two days, began to relent its heavy downpour, yielding to the emergence of bright sunlight. It was as if rays of hope pierced through the clouds, casting an optimistic glow over the landscape. Ursula and James exchanged glances, marvelling at the sudden change in weather. The car continued forward, each mile carrying them closer to a new chapter in their lives. Upon reaching the train station, Ursula and James stepped out of the car and bid farewell to the groundskeeper.

"Stay out of trouble," Ursula said to Finlay, who smiled meekly before driving away into the distance.

Hand in hand, they boarded the train to London, weaving through several carriages until they found their seats. A finely dressed older gentleman with snowy white hair and beard occupied the seat in front of them. As they settled, he abandoned the newspaper he'd been reading, his eyes shifting from Ursula to James, his furrowed brow steeped in disapproval.

"They really didn't believe that Uriah Blakesley was behind it all?" James asked, oblivious to the stare of the man in front of them.

Ursula shook her head. "Unsurprising. It is far easier to believe that Lyle is the sole perpetrator. Besides, a creepy song isn't reason enough. I just don't have anything to connect him to it."

"What about Maude's murder? Did you tell them about the pills?"

Ursula nodded. "Yes and I showed them the letter...but they're pointing fingers at Lyle...to them, it's what makes sense. I've still got some friends in Scotland Yard, I'll reach out and tell them everything."

"Why? What's the point?"

"The point is," Ursula said, turning to him. "I am certain Uriah pushed Lyle to it. I'm also certain that Maude wanted to end things with Theron. It would have left him penniless."

"I mean, it's obvious to me, surely the police will understand if you explain it to them again?"

"I did...but Lyle's crimes were heinous enough that they're happy to attribute it all to him. Getting away with this will only make them both bolder," she rued.

Ursula extracted her red notebook from her handbag, feeling her heartbeat quicken as she recalled the contents within its pages. Confronting her failures was inevitable. Taking a deep breath, she slowly flipped through the pages bearing the names— *Mary Lou Pearce. Kelly McDonald. Elizabeth Eddowes. Ann Stride. Jane Nichols. Catherine Chapman. Ada Millwood.* For the first time in a long while, Ursula didn't feel the weight of shame when looking down at the names; instead, she sensed her resolve intensifying. It was time to set aside her differences with Robert and reach out to him once she returned to London. Ursula was determined to solve the Anchor Ripper case.

For the present, all she could do was sit and watch the scenic Scottish Highland views blur past them, attempting to quell her mounting frustration. As had become habitual in James, he sensed her current state of unease and turned to offer her a smile, his calm eyes immediately soothing her and providing a sense of tranquillity in the chaos of her thoughts.

"Ursula, you'll get him," James said softly.

"I know," Ursula replied, her attention turning back to the scenery. She understood that the concluding chapter of this gripping mystery remained unwritten.

Ursula Doyle stepped onto the bustling streets of London once again, a sense of purpose coursing through her veins. With determination in her heart and a steely resolve in her eyes, she marched forward, ready to unravel the remaining mysteries that lay ahead. For in the heart of London, amidst its winding streets and whispered secrets, Ursula knew that justice awaited, and she was prepared to chase it down until the very end.

VICTOR DE ALMEIDA

THE LOCH LINNHE MURDERS